THE ALIGNED

KRISTY BERRIDGE

Shadow Ink Press

P.O Box 352n, Cairns North, Queensland 4870 Australia

Email: shadowinkpress@hotmail.com

First published in Australia 2015

This edition published 2015

Copyright © Kristy Berridge 2015

Cover design, typesetting: Working Type Studio

The right of Kristy Berridge to be identified as the Author of the Work has been asserted in accordance with the Copyright, Designs and Patents Act 1988.

This book is a work of fiction. Any similarities to that of people living or dead are purely coincidental.

Berridge, Kristy

The Aligned

ISBN: 9780987524768

pp432

Born in Perth, Western Australia in 1982, Kristy Berridge was ushered into the world in a decade of bad hair, parachute pants, and blue eye shadow. Fortunately, she managed to avoid all three by immersing herself in the business of growing up, and hitched a ride with her fun-loving, and adventure-filled parents to the sunny state of Queensland. Here she completed most of her education.

Besides learning that boys *don't* have cooties, and that algebra *wouldn't* kill her, she pointedly set the path of her high school career towards success in Art and English-based subjects, and won numerous awards for her efforts.

After high school she went on to study Graphic Design and Illustration at James Cook University, furthered her studies at the local TAFE college with an Interior Design course, and then undertook a three-year Design course at Rhodec International in London.

Clearly the girl just can't sit still. Kristy now pens fanciful fiction novels in her spare time finding creative new ways to scare herself and others in the dead of night, promote girl-power with gritty action sequences and, of course, highlight teenage idiosyncrasies with hard-hitting hormonal moments of lust.

She currently resides in Cairns, procrastinates constantly, now studies nutrition and tries desperately to avoid the delicious temptation that is the peanut butter aisle at the supermarket.

*For Kacey Elsdon-Bell, a beautiful girl,
determined and inspiring in so many different ways...*

PREFACE

Araqiel's fist slammed upon the gilded table before him. Groaning in protest, the surface quaked beneath the power of his divine touch. Determined to remain intact, the marbled centrepiece divided him from both aggressor and ally, serving in judgment's realm for many millennia. The angel's fist was not the first to make acquaintance with its beautiful, veined surface, nor would it be the last.

'I am not interfering,' Araqiel repeated, voice quiet and controlled. Rage was fleeting, focused entirely within the centre of his tightly clenched palm. Angels did not succumb to extreme sentiment. Angels were divine, spiritual — agreeable.

Weak, he thought quietly to himself.

'Araqiel, you come before us with a request we cannot grant.'

With narrowed eyes, Araqiel studied the demon across the vast marble table. A gnarly-horned creature with the body of a man and the head of a goat sat pregnant with barely contained satisfaction. Chocolate-brown skin glistened with the heat of the underworld and his eyes were the colour of fresh blood. Samael was one of four council members who sat in judgment in Purgatory. His counterpart Mammon, minions of Lucifer and advocates of all that is evil and unjust, were opposed on principle to anything Araqiel requested.

Nakir and Munkar, the remaining council members, sat pretty and seemingly indifferent amongst the sanctimonious, sulphur-belching miscreants at the marble table.

Araqiel noted Samael shift gleaming, ruby-coloured eyes over the angel, perhaps conscious of recent, unsolicited activities. Was the demon aware that Araqiel had provided Elena with divine intervention, propositioned a Vampire named William to protect her? Interference was against angelic and demonic policy, perhaps why Samael gloated; rubbing his calloused palms together.

Araqiel had skirted the rules and now there were consequences. William had fallen in love with Elena, outside the scope of Araqiel's plan, but at least she'd remained unharmed because of that love … until now.

Continued protection was paramount. Elena was the key to the past and the Archangel Michael's salvation, Araqiel's own chance of re-entry back into heaven merely the icing upon the cake.

'All I'm asking,' Araqiel continued, 'is a chance to help free Elena from the Werewolves. She is still a child, an innocent and—'

'The blood of Vampire *and* Werewolf run through her veins, Araqiel,' Munkar said. 'She is not entirely innocent.'

'She is the result of a terribly unfortunate situation,' Araqiel reasoned. 'How is she accountable for her birth?'

Samael shook his head. 'She is a half-breed, spawned from the seed of the damned. Some of her abilities are clearly a result of darkness. She has fed from an Alpha wolf and knowingly consumed the blood of a Vampire named …' Samael shuffled through the papers in front of him. 'William?'

Araqiel bit his tongue and suppressed the sigh nestled at the back of his suddenly dry throat. This plan involved considering the variables of Elena's impulsive and unpredictable nature. But the sexual interest in William was unexpected, the ardent exploration of each other's lips and subsequent blood exchange even more so.

Definitely not part of the plan.

'She did not know what she was doing.'

'I do not believe that,' Samael argued, whiskered nose creased to echo his haughty expression. 'She knew that taking the Vampire's blood would change her.'

'She was caught in the moment.'

Nakir's snowflake complexion melted as he blushed. Mammon laughed, perhaps amused by the angel's discomfort. 'Yes, we have all seen this moment you speak of. It's inconsequential whether her amorous activities are a result of her human hormones or damned blood.'

Araqiel pursed his lips, heated gaze flitting across the crimson skin of the sweat-slicked demon. 'All I ask is to lead someone — anyone — to her aid, be it Vampire or angel. Elena is the daughter of the master Vampire and her blood is suffused with Vânător, but she is still human, therefore worthy of my help.'

Mammon rested his hefty weight across his elbows, leaning menacingly across the marble table. 'What is it about this half-breed girl that fascinates you, Araqiel? This is the third time you have petitioned the council for permission to interfere.'

Furtive looks shifted between the angelic brethren. The demons could not know that Elena had the power to wipe clean the eternal bloodlines of both Vampire and Vânător, and to free Michael from an eternity in Purgatory.

'Elena is a curiosity,' Araqiel answered with a cavalier flick of his wrist and bored expression. 'She is the sun in which all darkness appears to revolve around — a highly entertaining development.'

'Mere curiosity?' Mammon goaded. 'I do not believe your petition is valid based on this seemingly superfluous motivation. Unless, of course, you have more to reveal, Araqiel?'

Araqiel was uncertain whether he could maintain this depth of deception. 'I cannot stand back and watch her needlessly suffer.'

That admission of weakness seemed to please Samael and Mammon. 'We vote no,' Samael concluded. 'The girl has already been gifted visions of her father and ...' Samael frowned again, shuffling first through his own papers, and then through Mammon's. 'Who is Sebastian?'

Araqiel chanced a glance at the other two angels; their metallic eyes glowed with caution. But before he could respond, Mammon growled, his long, rubbery tail rising behind him like a serpent rearing to strike. He stabbed a greasy finger against the stack of papers before him. 'Wait, it says here that she has been dreaming about "Sebastian" for years. Why would you feed her these thoughts, Araqiel?'

'I did not feed her thoughts of the Vampire,' Araqiel answered honestly. 'Her dreams are her own.'

'Yet you showed her two guiding visions: one of her father, Lucius, and then one of this Vampire Sebastian?' Mammon pressed.

'I petitioned for this because Elena was in danger. Lucius offers safety, and Sebastian is a trusted member of his coven with unparalleled tracking skills.'

It appeared that Mammon and Samael remained unconvinced. 'Yet you say her dreams are her own?'

'Yes.' Araqiel eased himself into one of the stiff-backed

chairs, waiting with barely contained trepidation for the council's final decision.

'Why would she dream of a Vampire she has never met?' Samael asked.

Araqiel concealed his grimace. He had not travelled the Ley-Lines to Purgatory to unfold the many layers of deceit he'd been hiding. He came to protect Elena. It was only by sheer luck that she'd so far avoided rape or death from the Alpha Vânător known as Roshan. There wasn't much time.

'Araqiel?'

'Yes, Samael?'

The goat-headed demon bristled, an irritated grunt escaping his whiskered mouth. 'You heard me, Angel. Why dream of an unknown Vampire?'

'I thought you were speculating aloud.'

Mammon touched Samael's shoulder and whispered in his twitching ear. Finally, they both turned back to the angel with unsettling hostility. 'We'll be looking into this.'

'How?'

'The usual channels.'

Araqiel's trepidation melted as an idea bloomed, the whisper of a smile forming. He cleared his throat, feigning ignorance as he said, 'Does that mean Samael will start following me around again?'

Nakir's head snapped up, nostrils flaring. Munkar shoved an accusatory finger against Samael's chest. 'You left Purgatory?'

Samael paled, fur-tipped ears folding flat against his head, but his eyes flashed fiery crimson defiance at Araqiel. 'Only once.'

'You are never to leave Purgatory! It is not the place of the council to choose sides!' Munkar scolded. 'We have others to do research on such matters.'

Samael grunted, flashing yellowed teeth. 'We do what we must to maintain balance.'

'As do I,' Araqiel reminded them. 'And thus, I ask only to protect Elena. The balance in which I must maintain as darkness surrounds her. So in lieu of Samael's clear violation, do I have the council's permission to help her?'

'No,' Samael rasped.

Mammon took a steadying breath, a sulphuric emission filled with resignation. He squeezed Samael's shoulder, calming his brutish counterpart. 'You cannot use the Vampire William again,' Mammon finally murmured. He shifted his gaze, levelling demonic eyes upon Araqiel. 'You have forced him to help the girl twice now and we do not like that these encounters have weakened his darkness, encouraging sentimentality.'

'Agreed,' Araqiel responded, knowing that William's growing attachment was problematic. 'I propose using Elena, giving *her* the power to communicate with Sebastian.'

Suspicion rode the demon's features like a wild horse bucking at the gates of truth. 'Why him, yet another Vampire?'

Araqiel squared his shoulders, giving nothing away. 'Sebastian is the most capable of finding her before the Alpha wolf compromises her innocence.'

'She is not so innocent,' Nakir whispered.

'Her attraction to the Alpha is based on the blood that runs through her veins. Her soul does not wish to be with him in any capacity.'

'And you claim to know the desires of her soul?' Mammon asked.

Araqiel bowed his head, studying the curled fingers in his lap. 'I may be one of the fallen, but I know the difference between right and wrong, good and evil.' He looked up again, shifting dazzling sapphire eyes over all before him. 'I can still feel a soul's true desire. I am not completely without the grace of God.'

Mammon and Samael snickered.

'Do I have permission, or not?'

Mammon sniffed, rubbing a sweaty palm over his face, erasing lingering delight. He gazed at Nakir and Munkar, then back at a snarling Samael. He sighed, shoulders slumping. 'In light of the forbidden travel, we will vote in your favour.'

'No!' Samael roared.

Nakir and Munkar nodded. 'As will we.'

Araqiel bowed his head once more, hiding a smile that begged claim over the corners of his supple lips. He rose, hesitant to shatter the fragility of this small victory by lingering. Who would have thought that the surreptitious behaviour of both angel and demon would broker the most favourable result?

Turning to face the wind, Araqiel stretched his wings out behind him, the light from the three moons above filtering through the feathery surface in tiny shards of brilliance. Weightlessness claimed his limbs as the beat of his wings lifted his feet from the crispness of the stone pavers.

'Araqiel?' Mammon shouted, raspy voice calling the angel back. The whistling winds of Purgatory ceased blowing a gale through the nest of pert white feathers at his back. Had his deception been more clearly analysed?

Araqiel faced Mammon. His pitchfork tail sashayed behind him with deliberate, hypnotic persuasion. 'Yes?'

'I wish to ask you another question.'

Araqiel met with solid ground once more, curious despite the hint of anxiety knotting his shoulders. 'Pray tell.'

More papers were shuffled by greasy fingers. Eye contact

was never broken, intimidation undoubtedly the goal. 'Do you know where the Archangel Michael is?'

'I ... what?'

'It's been two thousand years since he graced us with his presence,' Mammon continued. 'Nakir and Munkar cannot lie to us. They would have confirmed if he was back in Heaven.'

'And?'

'And he is not. Do you know where he is?'

Araqiel had been taught impartiality and encouraged to disregard emotion. Discussing Michael tampered with his neutrality. He may have been bound by the truth, but knowledge of Michael's whereabouts was not Araqiel's to impart.

'I'm waiting, Araqiel.' Mammon's grubby fingers beat a steady rhythm upon the marble.

'Yes. I know where Michael is.'

'Tell us.'

Araqiel shook his head. Lying was impossible, but he could dance around the truth. 'I have answered your question.'

'Then where is he?' Samael shouted, slamming his fist on the table.

'At this precise moment, I do not know.'

Samael seethed, ears flapping back and forth. Both demons understood the rules and how to bend them, but their anger marred intelligent thought. They loitered on the precipice of revenge, determined to find Michael and punish him for imprisoning Lucifer in Hell. Asking the right questions would yield better results.

'You would be rewarded for your answer, Araqiel,' Samael continued, simmering down as he tried his hand at bribery. 'As you served in Heaven, so you shall rule in Hell.'

Araqiel shuddered at the thought of fiery pits of tortured souls and slippery demons belching terminal disease and riotous blasphemy. 'There is nothing you can offer me.'

Samael and Mammon conferred. Nakir and Munkar looked on vexingly. 'Are you so sure about that?' An evil glint appeared in Samael's blood red eyes as the crooked slant of his tufted eyebrow reaped provocation.

'Yes.'

Samael *tsk tsked* him, waggling a stiffened finger. 'What if I offered you the Time Contract?'

Rigidity claimed Munkar and Nakir, surprise robbing words of protest free of their open mouths.

'The Time Contract?' Araqiel repeated in awe.

'You cannot!' Nakir finally gasped.

'No, but my master *Lucifer* can.'

Araqiel's stomach tightened. Only the two great masters of existence had the authority to present the Time Contract — God or Lucifer. Its power was known to reverse certain historical events or all that had come to pass, a fresh canvas, total annihilation. Knowing that the present could be reshaped by the choices of one chosen entity? Entirely too tempting.

'Araqiel? What is your answer?' Samael pressed.

Araqiel closed his eyes, praying for absolution. The temptation of power hastened his prayers as he begged for the goodness still nurturing his soul to charter his plans to their end, to follow the right path where he would inevitably choose wrong.

'I will give you Michael.'

'Araqiel!' Nakir and Munkar shouted in unison. 'He is your brother!'

Araqiel silenced the urge to lay the stirring sickness inside at his feet. Catching the congratulatory handshake the demons shared only served to exacerbate the twisting muscle and bile within. 'Wait.'

'What is it?' Mammon snapped. 'You cannot change your mind now.'

'I said I will give you Michael, but it will be at my choosing.'

The self-righteous smiles faded.

'Have the contract ready. No tricks, no ulterior motives. When the time is right I will make sure Michael returns to Purgatory for final judgment. In the meantime, I beg you all to protect Elena from harm.' Araqiel ruffled his feathers, ready for flight. He needed distraction from his sweaty palms and mounting sickness. 'I bid you all farewell.'

'I want Michael dead within three months,' Samael persisted. 'He has been hiding on the earth plane for far too long.'

Araqiel acknowledged the request with a quick tip of his head, bent his knees and kicked off the pavement. His wings stretched behind him, a feathered shield, strong and sleek. They flapped with purpose, taking him higher and higher until the air grew cold, just like his heart.

As Araqiel kissed the frigid atmosphere to meet with the soft glow of the three moons and intersecting Ley-Lines, he bowed his head. Once more he prayed for understanding, trust and the gratification of answered litanies. There was only one problem. God had not answered him in a very long time.

CHAPTER ONE

Captivity

Through the confines of the concrete prison surrounding me, thunderous bursts of firepower erupted with vigour. The dawning New Year was an unwelcome celebration, yet another reminder of my current plight and that the world was moving forward without me.

I imagined families and friends gathering to celebrate the occasion, toasting to prosperity, health, and exchanging stories of the past year. Meanwhile, as countless strangers jovially discussed intentions of change, I sat alone in the darkness.

Why was I bitter about de-corked champagne and New Year's resolutions? And how did I wind up alone in the dark, suffocating because of the cement box that held me prisoner?

It's a long story but, basically, it's because I'm an idiot.

My name is Elena Manory, daughter of Lucius Valerius — master Vampire. I have selective hearing and a problem with authority. I am my own worst enemy and, in this instance, pissed that I hadn't listened to Lucius when he'd ordered me to stay home and out of trouble. Easier said than done when entertaining grandiose ideas of saving the world. Perhaps I aim too high because I always get caught.

Confusing? Let me get back to basics.

I am destined to become a Vampire, or something a little hairier. An accident at birth left me with Werewolf — or Vânător — DNA. Currently I'm human, albeit with a few God-given and self-inflicted modifications, but still mortal.

Yes, my constant obstinacy has led to fangs, bloodlust, strength, and telekinetic abilities. I can also self-heal, but that's not exactly new for me. I may sound handier than a Swiss Army Knife, but lately I'm beginning to think I'm just a giant pain in the ass.

Case in point, I'm trapped in yet another basement cell under the constant surveillance of lecherous Vânători — this being the second incident in the last six months. My actions are repetitive, this time ... definitely my fault, but who's counting?

I sighed, pulled my knees to my chest and wrapped goose-pimpled arms around chilled and dirty limbs. My mind wandered, strolled through the memories of the past, remembering those that keep the embers of my spirit well-stoked and warm. Sebastian was at the forefront as he constantly tried to save me from myself. I should have heeded his warning about returning to Bucharest.

I pondered Lucius's reaction once he'd learned I'd been taken by Roshan's pack. Sebastian was blameless. I had chosen this fate to protect others from certain death. I'd become a commodity, the catalyst for a serum that could change the fate of all Vampires, and a Vânător plaything — agenda: possible rape and mutilation. Lucius would be beside himself; Sebastian would be laden with self-appropriated guilt.

At last touch of freedom, Vampires were hunted in Paris, probably by Julius, a rogue Vampire hell-bent on personal revenge. Our allies, The Protectors, a group of human magic-wielders, had disappeared, taking the mysteries of a serum they'd manufactured from my blood with them. There was also the acute absence of my maybe boyfriend slash pain-in-the-ass-Vampire, William Granville.

Then there was Roshan, my captor. I strongly suspected a 'struggle snuggle' looming on the horizon, but I'd yet been violated — strange to be sure. Had he realised how to use my blood in a way to enable self-healing? Or did he truly keep me here out of some other twisted, nefarious intent?

I almost jumped out of my skin as one last thunderous crack signalled the end of the fireworks. I strained, listening for barks and howls in the silence that followed. With each passing second of solitude, relief trickled through me. This den housed sixty bloodthirsty, dangerously aroused Werewolves. For the moment I was safe, so I sent up an extra prayer for my adopted brother, Lucas.

Lucas is a Protector, but nothing like the Bucharest division of scientists who recently incited my captivity and experimentation. He is honourable, kind and fiercely loyal, if not just a little bit of a pussy. Lucas is the son of George and Susan Manory, the two Protectors controlling the Cairns faction of the Institute of Magical Intervention, the two people who raised me as their own and then handed me over for dissection.

Enough said.

If there were sides, Lucas would be 'team Vampire'. George and Susan had destroyed his ideals, hiding evidence that the IMI had planned to strap me to a gurney and drain me dry.

Been there, done that, got the damn t-shirt. Thankfully Sebastian had helped me escape. If only the happily ever after had started there for all of us.

I released my cramped legs and crawled across the chilled, concrete floor. Tufts of fur met with my grasping fingers, fragments of discarded bones and musty blankets gathered under my knees.

I found the thick-hemmed edging of the sweat-stained mattress Roshan reserved at dawn. I sank into its plump surface, closing my eyes as dust plumes rose around me in greeting, the dank smell of mould and urine an afterthought. Any minute Roshan would return from his midnight feed. He would demand my subservience, the power of his Alpha timbre a force I could not resist.

My eyes snapped open, darting warily to the steel door across the basement, the seals aglow from the backlight of the room beyond. The locks disengaged painfully slow. I held my breath and listened as the door savagely scraped the dusty floor. Silence ensued, ending all too soon as that door slammed home, reverberating inside my head.

The silhouette melted into the renewed darkness , but footfalls drew near. There were no prizes for guessing who it was. I didn't even bother rolling over to greet him.

'Elena,' Roshan whispered. 'I've missed you.'

His rumbling voice and heated breath on my shoulder bred familiarity. I needn't look upon his tawny skin or the long veil of jet-black hair for recognition. I would sense Roshan in any camouflage, despite knowing that Vânători could shape-shift into any human form they had tasted the blood or flesh of.

Creepy but true.

The mattress dipped as Roshan's weight sank like a sack of sand into the softness at my back. His fingers skimmed the length of my arm, stopping at my hip. He pressed his lips against my neck, legs now entangled with my own.

As I attempted to wriggle free, Roshan growled, cinched my waist and dragged me possessively against his firm body. 'Don't even think about it.'

'My thoughts are the one thing you can't control,' I snapped.

Roshan's muffled retort was lost to the eager nuzzling his lips sought against my salty skin. 'You smell good today.'

I grunted, straining to avoid his probing tongue and the slow eruption of fangs. With my irresistible blood, it was only a matter of time.

Roshan paused, picking at the tatty sweater that barely clung to my chilled shoulders. 'I have a present for you.'

Unless it was letting me go, I really didn't give a shit.

'Elena, turn around and face me.'

'And if I said no?'

'I will make you.'

The Alpha scent more than just a looming threat, I promptly rolled over, trying to ignore the fact that he was naked, yet again. Darkness would never hide his eagerness, but would throwing on a pair of pants really kill him?

'There now, I can see your beautiful face. Do you want to see what I brought you?'

'The only thing I want is to get outta here.'

He frowned, amber eyes glowing in the darkness. 'You know I can't do that.'

'Then why do you keep me here?'

In one swift movement, Roshan rolled until he was above me, his dark hair falling like a velveteen curtain around my face, lips only inches from my own. 'Because I want you.'

I took a deep, shuddering breath, trying not to squirm, trying not to notice how close we now were, how warm, hard, and disturbingly compelling his lustful gaze was. 'I–I don't want you,' I stuttered, annoyed that my response sounded doubtful.

His hot breath, sweet like the blood of his victims, fanned my pallid skin with promise. 'You won't always feel this way,'

Roshan said, grasping one of my thighs and grinding himself intimately against me. I gasped, only to be rewarded with a satisfied grunt. 'I can smell your need, Elena. Pretending that there's nothing between us is a game you are quickly losing.'

I placed my trembling hands against his chest, nails cutting deep as I attempted to push him away. 'You're an Alpha. I have no choice but to do what you say.' I snapped my teeth for effect. 'Do you really think I want you touching me? You're an overgrown dog posing as a human being.'

Tufts of fur sprouted in indiscriminate patches across his chin and around his rapidly shifting mouth. Saliva-slicked fangs continued to protrude, lengthening their menace. As he rolled into a crouch, his amber eyes shifted, now ablaze with obsidian fire. 'I know you want me,' Roshan lisped. 'You resist because you think that I am wrong for you, but you are half Vânător, and therefore, rightfully my mate!'

'I was born a Vampire!' I sprung into an opposing crouch, unsteady on the mattress beneath me. I inched backwards, finding stability on the cold, concrete floor.

'Denying the truth does not alter your DNA.'

'I'm not one of you, Roshan, and I never will be.'

'As long as our blood runs through your veins, you will do as I say.'

'Congratulations, Mr Puppeteer, but you can kiss my ass.'

Roshan barked and snapped his elongated jaw. 'You will soon shout your submission.' He rushed forward, only the mattress separating us. His knuckles sunk within the cotton layers, bringing him another inch closer. His powerful legs flexed, ready for attack despite the spongy surface. 'I will have you, Elena. I will take your blood and your body, and make it mine if it's the last thing I do!'

Clarity settled upon my anger-ridden shoulders. I could

sense my Vampiric soul rising for want of blood. I balanced the bulk of my weight on the balls of my feet, positioned my hands for stability and levelled a contemptuous glare upon Roshan. Our noses now just inches apart, his sudden, derisive laughter stirred the stale air between us. His brutish fingers snapped out, groping for whatever exposed flesh he could compromise.

I was forced to retreat, lunging out of his immediate grasp.

He caught my wrist; fingers tight as sharp nails bit into delicate flesh. 'Are you going to attack me, Elena?' Roshan whispered, his predatory grace hypnotising as he bobbed like the snake that he was.

'I'm seriously considering it.'

His gaze narrowed and biting grip tightened. 'You don't want to do that. I'm executing a lot of restraint. It would be wise for you to remember who you're challenging.'

'Likewise, or did you conveniently forget that I helped kill thirty-seven members of your pack when you apprehended me in Bucharest?'

Mock laughter escaped his wolfish lips. 'I have a healthy respect for your telekinetic abilities, Elena, but you seem to forget that I own you now.'

I hissed, tempted to spit in his face. 'Nobody owns me.'

Roshan chortled, yanking me close enough to release a heated breath of Alpha compulsion. Avoiding inhalation? Impossible.

I shivered as the overwhelming desire to obey claimed my limbs and stirred the beast within to madness. If only I could, if only I could …

'No matter how much you protest, I own you, Elena. Now put your fangs away like a good little hybrid and kiss me like you mean it.'

No. No. No. No. No.

Cursing wildly, my canines obediently retracted, my body slumping. My knees hit the mattress, followed by hands that pulled me across the dirty cotton and on to trace Roshan's well-defined chest. I traded anger for lust, disgusted as my creeping fingers wormed their way to the back of his neck, pulling him to me.

Our torsos now aligned, I pursued fervent kisses, dusting the warm flesh of his neck with my lips. Roshan responded with another bout of Alpha sway, cementing imminent victory.

Inside I was screaming. I wanted his blood in my mouth, the feel of irreparable arteries gurgling precious life upon the flesh I covered with stolen kisses. I wanted to paint his body wet with crimson, and watch the light fade from his eyes as I swallowed the last of his immortality. But I couldn't gain control. I was lost to his call, helpless to resist baser instinct.

Roshan's arms encircled me like steel, trapping, lifting, and then throwing me back against the mattress with enough force to steal breath. In seconds he was pressed against me, clumsily knocking his teeth against mine, his swiftly shifting mouth taking greedy possession of my lips.

Disgust and satisfaction rose in equal measure as the feverish kisses trailed across my flesh and the urgency of his tongue proved pleasurable and sickening. Try as I may to ignore the Vânător within, it did little to alter facts — my body longed for his touch, but my mind prayed for his death.

'I want you, Elena,' Roshan breathed urgently against my mouth. Patches of fur that gathered around his slightly mangled jaw tickled my skin. 'I want all of you, body and soul.'

No!

Roshan's demanding claim of my lips continued. He ripped the hem of my dirtied shirt, calloused fingers focused on cupping and kneading the swell of my breasts. Terror twisted my insides and stirred the sickening fear of possession. I tried turning away, wriggling until I wrenched free to claim fresh, untainted air. I didn't want this. I didn't want any part of him inside me — ever!

Roshan's probing fingers fell from my chest. 'You're fighting me.'

Tears welled in the corners of my eyes. I felt powerless, so ashamed. 'You know I don't want this.'

Roshan didn't immediately answer. Instead, he pressed his nose against the hollow in my throat, inhaled, and then slid slowly down the length of my body, stopping at the button fly on my jeans. He tugged on the stiffened fabric, amber eyes filled with gluttonous satisfaction. 'I can smell your need, Elena. It clings to your skin like cheap perfume.' He sighed dramatically, further burying his nose against the buttons. 'Do you know what this scent does to me?'

'I just want to go home,' I whispered, swiping at a stray tear.

'You are home. Sooner or later you'll realise that.'

I shook my head. 'I won't.'

Like a slimy insect, Roshan crawled back up the length of my body, feathering any exposed flesh with wet, insistent kisses. 'I believe that on your eighteenth birthday when your Vânător side emerges, you will feel more at home here in a den amongst your own kind.'

'You can't know that. You have no idea what I'll think or feel.'

'I know what it's like to be a wolf, Elena, and I know you *will* eventually long for the pack.'

'I will never long to be with you.'

A wicked smile curved Roshan's lips as he surveyed my stiff body beneath him. 'That may be true now, but you will change your mind, especially as each passing night teaches me more about how to make you howl my name.'

My tears evaporated. Fear was a lingering discomfort I refused to show. I forced myself to harness aggression and hopefully dispel his essence. And as rage lessened the tether of Roshan's Alpha scent, I found I was moving, rolling until my knee connected with damaging accuracy between his parted legs.

Bravado now trickling through my veins, I scooted backwards, following the manoeuvre with a second kick to his torso. Roshan belched pain with a howl, landing clear across the room. Mortar crumbled and rained upon his huddled body, his hands concentrating on nothing more than cupping his surely battered and bruised ... ego.

He looked at me then, incensed, eyes glowing within the darkness. An eruption of anger escaped his lips, his entire body rippling and shaking with barely contained ire.

My breathing hitched as certainty of retribution reminded me of earlier fears. Roshan's limbs lengthened and cracked, punishing muscle and sinew before re-shaping into clawed paws and powerful legs. Ribs snapped like chicken wishbones and his diaphragm expanded like a well-played accordion. The bronzed kiss of his smooth skin mottled grey, tearing open like Christmas paper as the beast within emerged.

I was back on my feet, fangs exposed and eyes focused on the enormous wolf across the room. Roshan stalked forward, his thick nails tapping ominously against the concrete floor. *Tap, tap, tap* — menacing, a dripping faucet of promised revenge.

We began a circular dance, only the mattress once again

dividing us. As he moved to the right, I ducked to the left. Growling accompanied every movement, an exposure of pink, drool-covered gums and blood-tinged breath instilling the thrill of the hunt.

I cracked my neck and rolled my rotator cuffs, loosening up. What was he waiting for? 'Come and get me.'

Roshan lunged, his body a deadly streak that hit me like a ton of bricks. Our combined weight took us to the floor, a mess of tangled limbs, rolling and tumbling until the immovable steel door met our backs.

I scrambled to disentangle myself, ignoring pain to grab him by the throat. I squeezed precious air from his oesophagus and followed through with a right jab to the side of his snapping jaws.

I let him go, having sliced my knuckles on the sharp points of his teeth. I barely had time to think before he came at me again, eyes swirling with vicious, black fury.

I met him halfway, ducking under the jaw-cracking assault of a determined predator. I skidded across the gritty floor, rolled, and then flipped back to my feet, but Roshan pounced from behind, forcing me back down. I hit hard, gasping for breath, sucking greedily at stale air. His nails tortured the flesh of my shoulder, piercing the filmy sweater, drawing blood.

I wheezed, inhaling unknown fibres through a nose forcibly pressed against the concrete floor. I tried regaining control, but Roshan buried his nails deeper, his full weight upon me. Pain was immediate and intense, a torrent of fresh blood now seeping from the wound and down my neck.

Roshan had never spilt my blood before now, nor had he been present when others had. His restraint beckoned curiosity, his intentions frankly terrifying.

Roshan's stiff posture and snout against the back of my

neck suggested it called to him, just as it did for all blood drinkers. Could he continue to resist? For that matter, why or how had he resisted so long?

Locks disengaged and the scrape of metal on concrete screeched protest as the steel door opened. I should have realised that the howl of the Alpha would attract the pack, though not usually an issue when my veins were intact.

Just great.

I rammed my elbow into the side of Roshan's sniffing muzzle. His head snapped to the right and we were rolling again, his claws still embedded in my flesh. Sinew tore and blood flowed anew. He wasn't giving up and neither was I.

The nastiest expletive exploded from my mouth as his claws tore through my back in my attempt to flee. While he lunged, I scrambled, praying that the right hook that clipped him underneath the jaw would keep him down. Roshan collapsed in the centre of his advancing pack, taking them out like pins at a bowling alley.

Strike.

Before any regained ground, I dashed to the furthermost corner of the room. Too many wolves barred exit through the door, so I used the only arsenal I had left — telekinesis. Thanks to lessons with Lucius, I now found it easier to manipulate air particles to form impenetrable, inescapable nets.

The wolves tested my defences, attacking the barrier I'd created around me in both human and wolf form, to no avail. I was safe for now, but couldn't maintain telekinesis for long — half an hour at the most. My mind would eventually unravel; the threat of aneurisms going off like popping candy, enough to make me stop. I just had to hold out long enough for Roshan to regain consciousness. I was in a room with unrestrained Vânătors, covered in blood.

Stupid.

Untold minutes passed. A dull throbbing already festered in the back of my head. I concentrated on reducing the size of the barrier, drawing it closer to avoid over expenditure of energy.

A renewed frenzy with the wolves began.

I watched an unconscious Roshan, willing his twitching limbs and flickering eyelids to move. Knocking him out was a rookie mistake. I'd only hoped to distract him from my blood.

Roshan, like all Vânǎtors, is fast and strong. He is immortal but not invulnerable. Transformed via the bite and mutual exchange of blood from a *born* Vampire, his species cannot self-heal, hence he is vulnerable.

Thralls are the only exception to that rule.

By order of the devil himself, upon Lucius's turning, he was instructed to create nineteen other men with his tainted blood. Fast, strong, agile and only a minor affliction to sunlight, these suckers are hard to kill. Born Vampires are the result of Thralls mating with human women, ergo my existence.

Lucius is impervious to death. He believes he is cursed to walk the earth for eternity, his soul the binder of a contract brokered with Satan, traded for vengeance after the murder of Lucius's wife and son.

But what did any of that matter now when I was surrounded, and clearly outnumbered?

Roshan bucked, his jaw snapping. His paws twitched; the guttural growl from his throat suggested he was finally coming to.

Several of the wolves abandoned guard, slinking towards their Alpha, sniffing at his extremities and tentatively licking his muzzle.

Roshan rolled slowly onto his side, opening those dark, desolate eyes. His brow furrowed, branding his expression with a sense of menace.

He pulled himself up onto forepaws, hind legs unsteady. My nut-cracking skills saw him limping; his powerful jaw clenched as he stalked me.

The wolves fronting my barrier backed away, abasing themselves at Roshan's paws. The remainder watched and waited, hanging their heads and pressing bodies close to the floor.

I sat transfixed as Roshan's fur began to dissolve, his greyish pallor washed away by the cloth of metamorphosis, the tawny hue of his human complexion gleaming. Strong, powerful limbs transformed; paws became hands, talons became fingernails. His head lolled and snout reshaped; jet black hair cascaded down his back like a thick veil of silk, covering re-shaping muscles.

Roshan straightened, cracked his neck and knuckles for relief and then levelled the recognisable amber gaze upon me. He smiled — surprising given our earlier conflict. Perhaps he was mistaking my curiosity for shape-shifting as romantic interest.

He staggered forward several more steps, pressing his palms against the shield separating us. 'I won't hurt you, Elena. You know that.'

I fingered the drying blood on my neck and offered it for inspection. 'Your clawing of my back says otherwise.'

'I did not intend to harm you that way.'

'What do you intend?'

'To protect what's mine.'

I seriously considered blowing a raspberry at him. I would never be his, but at present I was in no position to argue. My head was pounding and the wolves within the room seemed to keep multiplying.

I braced for attack as I ceased telekinesis, wrapping my arms around my head in meagre protection. I waited, counting the seconds before my flesh was shredded. There were just too many to fight on my own.

Bittersweet relief coursed through me as Roshan lifted me into his arms. The Vânătors snivelled and yelped, but his Alpha sway descended, his dismissive words final as they scattered from the room like frightened puppies.

'Are you all right?' Roshan murmured, lips grazing my forehead in concern.

I looked up at him, noting the bruises forming under his chin, around his nose and left eye where I'd first let loose. 'Better than you, I expect.'

He brushed tender fingers through my knotted hair, dragging it from my face. I continued staring, confused by his concern.

'Why are you being so nice to me? I just beat the crap out of you.'

Roshan bared his teeth, attentiveness evaporating under the weight of a wounded ego. 'And I just stopped you from being raped and mauled by sixteen members of my pack. Show some gratitude.'

'Put me down.'

'Are you going to run?'

'I'm always going to try.'

'Then you stay where you are.'

'No.' I aimed for the sweet spot, my knuckles connecting with badly bruising flesh. I was so gonna get it.

Roshan roared, abandoning his steely grip on me. I chased freedom by running for that partially-opened door. I just had to make it through a den of wolves. I just needed to get outside …

As I reached the threshold, I was yanked back by my

flowing mane of hair. Kicking and screaming, I was dragged to the mattress and tossed like a rag doll into its centre.

'I've had enough!' Roshan shouted, claiming a thick patch of my hair as he wrenched his hand free.

I cradled my bleeding scalp and sniffed back tears. Roshan stormed over to the steel door, slammed it home and locked it. He soon faced me, lips shaping a vicious sneer.

'I've tried to be patient with you, Elena, but no more. It's high time you realise that no one is coming. No one will ever find you here, and becoming my pack mate is an inevitability you can no longer avoid.'

'No,' I moaned, pitifully.

'Oh, yes.'

'I'll never stop fighting you.'

Roshan laughed, quickly covering me with his bulk while slapping away pointless attacks. He grabbed my flailing legs and yanked me across the mattress, slamming me against his powerful thighs. He cinched my ankles, spreading my legs wide to accept his weight.

I bucked and screamed, my fists aiming for glory, but Roshan deflected every blow, landing one of his own against my ribs.

'Stop moving,' he grunted.

'Never,' I gasped. He knew where to hit so it counted.

'Then so be it.'

'No!'

Frustration and a healthy dose of fear descended upon me. His Alpha sway filled every pore, clogged every vestige of sanity and urged obedience.

'Elena, you will do everything I say from this moment forward,' Roshan said, grinding his weight against my submissive body. 'You will pleasure me until I say so. You will not fight, attempt escape, or try to kill me, but endure all

I have planned.' He paused, an evil smile spreading across his face. 'Let's start with this …'

A violent scream tore through me as fangs punctured my neck's tender flesh. Tears stained my cheeks, a manifestation of the insufferable futility of my unresponsive body. Against his compulsion, my abilities were useless, my hands inoperable weapons by my side.

I screamed like someone might hear my pleas. I even prayed, uncertain of the outcome given my lineage to Satan. Believing that the angels I'd read about in Lucius's library might watch over me was help I shouldn't hope for. Was it too much to ask to not be shit on for one day? Wasn't being eternally damned enough?

Happy freaking New Year, I thought drowsily. Blood trickled down my shoulder like a creeping spider, soaking my sweater with fading warmth.

Great. While the rest of the world celebrated the New Year, I lingered between the ravenous jaws of life and death. Maybe I'd get lucky and death would find me quick. Or maybe I'd fade away slowly, wake up later and find this whole night had just been a terrible nightmare.

Likely?

I'd never been that lucky.

CHAPTER TWO

Accord

Roshan's gaze flitted anxiously over Elena. Unconscious, she lay deathly still beneath him, her neck a mangled mess of blood, torn flesh and exposed bone, and though he was fascinated by her quick healing, he was angry for relenting to thirst and causing pain.

Blood trickled across her ravaged skin as muscle and sinew fused together like old lovers rekindling an affair. Roshan marvelled at the healing brutality he'd caused; couldn't deny the satisfaction gained from sampling her essence.

John, his deceased Alpha brother, had bragged of her blood and body. His words offered no comparison in experiencing the taste of Elena across his tongue — thick, pungent, sweet and thoroughly addictive.

Elena's pulse was faint now, a clear indication he'd taken too much. The last thing Roshan wanted was her death. She was far too important, the pleasures of her flesh yet to be realised.

Roshan rolled onto his back, stared at the ceiling, rubbing his distended stomach, content. Elena's blood satisfied all urges, an oddity to be sure.

As he cupped the bruised and strangely gratified flesh between his legs, he recounted their first interaction — a meeting of eyes at an Australian airport terminal. He'd imagined their bodies writhing in untold pleasure then, but now he couldn't recount the reasons for his urgency.

Sharing with the other Alphas was not an option. Elena's vampiric nature made her desirable to taste, but also strikingly beautiful. She was an addiction impossible to overcome and Roshan was already hooked.

She could not be allowed to leave the den.

A muffled howl from beyond the basement startled Roshan. Now alert, he sprang for the door, cracked it open and scanned the outside passage. 'What?' he barked. A young pup whimpered by his feet. Sighing, he scooped the pup into his arms, stroking the fur between its eyes. 'What's wrong, my child?'

The newborn nuzzled closer, licking Roshan's nose.

'Oh, I see,' Roshan murmured, exiting the room and locking the steel door behind him. He carried the pup down the deserted passage and trudged up the stairs into the secondary basement. 'You're upset because you got left behind.'

The pup nipped playfully at Roshan's fingers.

'In a few more days, you'll be fully grown, able to run with the rest of the pack.' Roshan continued stroking its soft fur, thinking. 'I do have something to keep you occupied until the others return.' He put the pup back down and snapped his fingers, beckoning it to follow.

The tiny furball trotted obediently beside him, nostrils flaring and tail wagging as they approached the ripe, decaying body callously strewn across the floor, seemingly forgotten in lieu of fresher hunts.

Barely reminiscent of the curvaceous blonde Roshan had taken six days previous, the pup responded with visceral tenacity, chewing enthusiastically on marrow and lingering tissue.

Guilt or remorse concerning this woman's untimely demise did not affect Roshan. This well-picked corpse had satiated blood lust, fulfilled sexual urges, and ultimately birthed him the ravenous newborn. It was the circle of life.

Roshan left the pup to feed, heading upstairs, his bones cracking and body shifting as he moved, the wolf within emerging rapidly. Beyond the basement was an abandoned steel factory, eerily silent without his pack scouring the grounds.

Roshan's paws swept him across the dusty factory floor and out into the night. The urge to hunt was a distant thought, Elena's blood satisfying on many levels, but to stretch, run and feel the wind in his pelt was an urge undeniable.

He faltered, the distant howl of a distressed wolf slowed his pace. Ears twitching, Roshan strained to hear more. His lean muscles bunched and tightened; his powerful hind legs trembled. And with a secondary call punctuating the silence, Roshan was off, the ground nothing more than a blur beneath his paws.

Deserted back alleys and darkened side streets were Roshan's preference. Within minutes he'd crossed half the city, closing the distance on the choked, intermittent yips of barely repressed panic.

Through a cluster of unpruned hedges, Roshan locked eyes with the reckless Vampire previously pressing for an accord. Julius sat prone on a low hanging branch of a withering conifer, disinterested as the alarmed wolf circled below.

Why had Julius returned to Paris? Did he know that Elena was in his possession?

Roshan and Julius's deal was simple: hunt and kill Vampires from the Italian coven ruled by Lucius Valerius and, in exchange, Julius would reveal Elena's location. But Roshan had made alternative arrangements with The Protectors. He no longer needed Julius; killing him was a probable and appetising solution.

A procession of thunderous cracks and tearing sinew harmonised Roshan's shift back to human form. With a final roll of knotted shoulders, he brushed the browning leaves of the dense foliage aside, stepping into the untamed yard beyond.

Julius sat pretty, back against the tree-trunk, one leg perched on the branch in which he sat, and the other teased the riled wolf below. 'You came,' he said, launching from the creaking limb. He landed soundlessly upon the whispering grass below. 'I was hoping the little wolf would send word.'

Roshan kept his distance, cautious of the Vampire's devious and callous nature. 'What do you want?' Roshan growled. 'I'm not accustomed to being summoned.' The other wolf snarled in solidarity, racing to flank his Alpha.

Julius stopped near enough that Roshan could see the fleck of blue in his eyes, glowing like the centre of a simpering flame. 'It's time for you to uphold your end of the bargain.'

Roshan tore his gaze from the hypnotic play of light and colour within the Vampire's eyes. He stifled an amused outburst and flexed his muscles in an unintentional display of physical prowess as he folded his arms across his chest. 'Why do you pursue the master Vampire? You've already said he cannot be killed.'

'Revenge. He murdered my wife for her bloodlust. Now I wish to take away what is precious to him.'

'And that would be?'

Julius lowered his eyes, perhaps studying divots in the grass or the dried leaves caressing their feet. 'Did you know that Lucius hunts me as we speak?'

'Why would I care?'

'Because the coven are currently together, making it easier to bring them down.'

'If it's so easy, why haven't you killed them yourself?'

'Lucius can sense me; my blood is his blood.'

Roshan scoffed, annoyed that Julius was yet to spill his endgame, and quick to avoid the heavy lifting. 'You're a Vampire. If you can't bring them down, then what hope do the rest of us have?'

'Your strength is in your numbers,' Julius explained. 'You may not be as fast or as strong as we are, but you are many, and you are united. Vampires are crippled by the lingering, human emotions and thus we make mistakes.'

Roshan pinched his agitated brow between forefinger and thumb. 'As fascinating as this little lesson has been, you did not answer my question. If Lucius can't be killed, what do you gain from killing the rest of the coven?'

'No need to trouble yourself with the details, little wolf.'

Roshan snarled and wrapped a thick hand around the Vampire's throat. He didn't like to play games. Despite the death grip, Julius's smile was mocking and a further irritant to Roshan.

'I will not cry out "mercy", little wolf, if that is what you are waiting for. I do not value breath the same as you.'

Roshan tightened steely fingers around the Vampire's oesophagus.

'I'll heal,' Julius reminded him. 'Might I suggest putting me down before I retaliate?'

Like a piece of discarded waste, Roshan threw Julius against the gnarled conifer in which he'd previously resided. Wood splintered and spewed kindling and pine needles, covering the grass in a decoupage of destruction. The tree's roots begged release, groaning as the trunk ripped free of the grassy mound at its base and rolled into one of the neighbouring yards.

Julius took only seconds to rise, enraged as he plucked dried leaves from his hair and wiped dirt from his overly starched pants. 'Do you feel better now?' Malice oozed from every pore.

'I'd feel better if you were dead.'

'Come now,' Julius flicked an insect from his shoulder, 'is that any way to treat a business partner?'

'Do not treat me like a fool, Vampire.'

A single eyebrow arched, as he waited for elaboration.

'I want to know your endgame, and do not spew words of revenge as explanation.'

'I want Lucius's coven dead — satisfaction my reward. How is this not clear?'

Roshan massaged the stubble staining his jaw. 'The vendetta is pointless. You will still be hunted and my packs will be endlessly pursued for retribution.'

'Perhaps.' Julius shrugged.

Roshan shook his head at the delusional Vampire. 'War will change nothing.'

Another shrug ensued.

The thought of devouring vampiric blood made Roshan's mouth water, but the variables were many. Revenge was a swift motivator, but there had to be more to Julius's plan, something he was missing.

'I'll have to rethink this.'

Julius's nostrils flared, his feet shifting to flee or fight. 'But you already agreed …'

Roshan sniffed, every bit as dismissive as Julius earlier shrug. What did the Vampire really have to offer him any more?

Julius reached into his pocket, extracted a thick, white

envelope and slapped it angrily against Roshan's chest. 'You will uphold your end of the arrangement, wolf.'

Roshan chose to ignore the thinly-veiled threat and focus on the bulky stationary. 'What's this?'

'I don't want you sinking your imprudent jaws into like-minded members of my race. So, for Satan's sake, study these photos carefully.'

Roshan considered reprisal; having his intelligence insulted was enough to urge him to violence, but he pried open the sticky tab on the envelope instead. The photos bore unending similarity — pale skin, attractive features and exemplary dental care.

He committed each face to memory, peering closely at one in particular. 'I know this one.'

Julius's dark curls tickled Roshan's face as the Vampire leaned close. 'That's Sebastian Marcellus,' he murmured, stumbling as Roshan shoved him back.

Sebastian.

Roshan remembered him clearly. Shoulder-length sable hair, piercing emerald eyes streaked with grey, and physically imposing. The Vampire had twice impinged his efforts in taking Elena. Roshan wasn't a fan.

Julius plucked the photo from his grasp. 'Be careful of this one,' he said, fanning it in front of him. 'Sebastian's—'

'Dead?'

'I was going to say, an enigma.'

Roshan's raised eyebrow pressed for further explanation.

'He's extremely resourceful and an excellent tracker. No one can hide from him for long. It is why I'm constantly on the move.'

Roshan snorted, unafraid. 'What is it about him that puzzles you?'

'His origins. I distinctly remember Sebastian being human and then one day, he simply wasn't.'

'So, he was turned?'

Julius shook his head. 'It's complicated, but know that he's not a normal Vampire. He is too powerful, too charismatic, too—'

'Pretty?'

'Make jokes, little wolf, but even I tread carefully where Sebastian is concerned.'

'Are you suggesting he's like Elena?'

Julius looked as if he was considering the possibility then just as quickly dismissed it with a wave of his hand. 'No, he's just … other.'

Roshan tucked Sebastian's photograph back into the envelope. 'Who are the rest?' Curiosity had gotten the better of him.

Julius went through them one by one, giving detailed descriptions and pointing out vulnerabilities. The master Vampire's unique abilities snagged Roshan's attention.

'Say that again,' he demanded, ambiguity fading and conclusions drawn as dark hair, spotted hazel eyes and other memorable features swam into focus.

Julius frowned. 'Which part?'

'Lucius's abilities.'

'Telekinesis. Yes, that could be a problem. He can manipulate any object he chooses. In some cases, I've even seen him create shields, somehow manipulating particles in the air to form barriers between him and his opponents.'

It couldn't be a coincidence.

'Lucius is Elena's father, isn't he? Same eyes, same face shape.'

Julius seemed taken aback. 'How did you—?'

'Her abilities, his abilities. She killed thirty-seven

members of my pack not more than a week ago with this same power.'

Julius's surprise melted into suspicion. 'So, you've seen Elena more recently than our last conversation?'

'I see her often,' Roshan said smugly.

'So, you know where she is, then?'

'I've known where she is for quite some time now.'

Julius's eyes became darkened slits, swimming with distrust. 'Why are you here? Why did you agree to this deal if you already knew where to find her? Tell me *your* intentions, Vânător!'

Roshan shook his head, poised to return earlier ridicule. 'Don't bother yourself with the details, little Vampire.'

Julius hissed as fangs were unveiled and veins throbbed with need, his skin now disturbingly transparent. 'I'll kill you.'

'No you won't,' Roshan said, gambling with fate and turning his back on the Vampire. No one noticed the slight trembling in his hands. He buried one in the soft pelt of the wolf beside him, and the other he clutched to his chest, the envelope firmly encased.

Julius filled his vision, looming large and disturbingly close.

Roshan continued to pet the wolf, thinking of ways to defuse the unhinged Vampire on the precipice of spilling blood. 'Be calm, Vampire.'

'Be calm?' Julius rasped, fangs dripping venom. He inched closer.

Roshan silenced the wolf who growled in his defence. 'I don't comprehend your endgame, Vampire, and that makes me nervous, but I will continue forward.' His fingers tightened around the crumpled white envelope. 'I now have my own reasons to pursue some of these coven members.'

Julius remained uncomfortably close, nostrils flaring. 'Go on …'

'Using Elena as your bargaining chip is no longer an option.'

'Then what is it that you want?'

'Keep the location of my den a secret and lead the Vampires away from this area. Your presence draws unwanted attention and if I am to keep Elena safe, I need Lucius to leave Paris.'

Julius begun to pace, hands knotted behind his back. 'He will find her regardless.'

'Perhaps.'

'But I cannot leave Paris just yet.'

The wolf scampered off to explore exposed tree roots and overturned earth. Roshan barely noticed, his eyes on the photo of Sebastian peeking from beneath the envelope's fold. 'Your presence could expose my den and Elena.'

'I am aware.'

Roshan closed the distance between them, pressing the envelope against Julius's chest. 'Then you should know this. If you don't leave soon, my wolves will hunt and kill you. If you drive the Vampires away, I'll give you immunity amongst the Vânǎtors — all Vânǎtors. If you don't …'

Julius re-pocketed the envelope, sneering. 'You leave me with little choice.'

'My pack is my first priority.'

'And Elena?'

'No longer your concern.' It was time to leave.

Roshan and the wolf retreated to the unpruned hedges, glancing at a lone photograph half buried in trodden earth. He knew the face well — another bothersome vampire who'd claimed Elena as his own.

Roshan scooped the photograph up, holding it out for

Julius to see. He was surprised the Vampire still lingered. 'Who is this?'

Julius snatched the photo from Roshan, adding it to the others inside his pocket. 'This is William Granville, once a member of the Roman Guard and avid hunter of all things Vânător. How do you know him?'

Roshan's fists involuntarily clenched. 'He killed my Alpha brother and kept Elena and I apart. I want you to find him and bring him to me.'

Julius pursed his lips. 'So, you want me to do your job for you?'

'If you know where he is, yes.'

Julius did all but stamp his foot. 'Fine. But if I find William and bring him to you, I want to see Elena.'

Roshan was taken aback. Why the sudden interest in Elena? 'Explain yourself.'

Julius shrugged. 'My reasons are my own.'

'Not good enough, Vampire. I will not share her with anyone and, frankly, your interest makes me uneasy.'

'Then I want everyone dead yesterday!' Julius spat, angry. The wolf at Roshan's side bared teeth and growled, hackles raised and shoulders squared.

Julius spun on his heels, taking leave like a shadow weakened by the noontime sun. The cloying scent of his blood still lingered, but the cold breath of his barbed retorts were nothing but a memory.

The growls turned to chuffs and whines, the wolf's anxiety slowly easing. Roshan was equally relieved to be rid of the Vampire, a sigh of relief escaping his parted lips. 'Go and find the others,' Roshan told the wolf. 'Tell them to return to the den. I have new orders.'

Julius had given Roshan plenty to think about: blood

connections between Elena and Lucius, head tracker Sebastian, and famed Vânător hunter, William.

Roshan's den was not all that was at risk. He knew this situation carried more weight than he could handle alone, the possible merging of territories with one of his other Alpha brothers a likely act of self-preservation.

His gnarly world of deception encouraged war, exactly what The Protectors wanted in exchange for the serum. The weight of all his self-serving deals was a crushing responsibility.

Preparing his pack for what was to come was priority. Deciding on a just punishment for William Granville for the death of his Alpha brother? Rewarding. Simply killing him wouldn't satisfy, he needed to suffer.

An idea flourished.

Elena and the Vampire would be reunited. Perhaps then she would see the similarities between herself and the pack she refused to join. Her humanity would dissolve and her true nature take claim. Her thirst would bring pain, and ultimately, the destruction of his enemies.

All he had to do now was wait.

CHAPTER THREE
Resolutions

'appy New Year!' everyone shouted. Glasses collided clumsily, bubbly liquid erupting over the edges and dribbling down hands.

Happy New Year, indeed, Lucas thought to himself, making an effort to smile and shake hands with The Protectors, their presence suffocating.

What was there to be happy about? Elena was still captive, his parents were traitorous liars and his body was playing havoc with his abilities and mind. A happy new year seemed unlikely with so much uncertainty in the air.

At least this mystery magic coursing through him exacerbated his already proficient skillset. It was the physical changes he was undergoing that worried him. Lucas was somehow taller, brawnier and chiselled in a way that begged drug tests for logical explanation.

How long would the IMI would play him for a fool? They'd targeted Elena with their experiments in the past; was it safe to assume their treachery extended to him now?

'So, what's your resolution?' Vincent slurred, dropping like a lead weight onto an old, rickety bench.

Lucas sipped at the orange juice he'd been given, bitter.

Apparently he wasn't old enough to drink alcohol despite his looming eighteenth birthday. 'I don't have one.'

'Aw, everyone has to have a New Year's resolution. It's tradition.'

A zealous swig of beer saw foam dribble down Vincent's chin and roll across the sweat-slicked skin of the drunken lawyer's neck. Lucas refrained from pointing out the benefits of a bib.

'My New Year's resolution is to sell my share of the law firm to Kim.'

Lucas was so startled that he couldn't answer. Vincent and Kim had met at law school and signed a partnership arrangement after a few years of crossing 'T's' and dotting 'I's' in other firms. They'd been in business together for fifteen years now, lawyers by day and Protectors by night.

'Kim doesn't agree with Bucharest's recent ideas of advancement. Besides, it's time for a change.' He laughed, burped, and then elbowed Lucas in jest. 'You can't be the only one.'

'Wait … what?' Lucas moved closer despite the acrid smell of Vincent's breath. He needed to know more.

Vincent tapped his nose. 'Attorney client privileges and all that.'

'Really? You're pulling the lawyer card after such a teasing proclamation?'

Vincent alternated between laughter and throwing his head back to suck down another alcoholic dose of false security. 'I keep forgetting you don't know yet. Shhh.' He placed a shaky finger against his wet lips. 'Pretend I didn't say anything.'

Vincent leapt to his feet, his meaty hand clamping Lucas's shoulder for support. The drunkard stumbled, let go, and then sailed face first into Sarah's rather plump rear end. She shrieked, lurched sideways and fell into Malcolm's arms. They were all on the ground in no time.

Beer bottles and wide-rimmed wine goblets spewed foamy tidal waves of alcohol in every direction. Glass smashed and Vincent surrendered his dignity, passing out on the soft, fire engine red carpet.

'Lucas!' Susan yelled from across the room. 'Come and give your mum a New Year's kiss!'

'I'm coming,' Lucas grumbled, stepping around the Protectors still scrambling around on the floor. Pathetic.

Susan planted a sloppy kiss on Lucas's cheek and slung a slender arm around his waist. 'Happy New Year, darling.'

Lucas nodded, having nothing else to offer.

'Any New Year's resolutions?' Peter asked.

'No,' Lucas murmured, taking a sip of his drink. 'But apparently Vincent does. He said something about selling his share of the firm to Kim based on advancements being implemented by the Bucharest division of the IMI — whatever that means.'

Panic? Surely that wasn't the expression Lucas saw pass between Peter and his mother? Up until now he'd taken Vincent for a rambling drunk. Now he wasn't so sure.

'Vincent's had a little too much to drink,' Peter remarked, nervously scratching at the scar that marred his left brow and cheek.

Lucas glanced at the horizontal lawyer. His face was smothered by the thick, crimson pile and a puddle of drool that seeped in gelatinous abundance past his lips. Miraculously, he still held his beer. 'That's an understatement.'

Susan broke into a beaming smile. 'Maybe we should just tell him?'

'Tell him what?' George said. His father's sudden appearance raised the hairs on the back of Lucas's neck. He pushed between Lucas and his mother, planting a chaste kiss on Susan's lips.

'You know …' Susan murmured, seeking a secondary kiss. 'School is finished and Lucas's pledge to The Protectors' cause has been received and approved by headquarters. He might be as excited as we are to learn of our upcoming schedule. Besides, Vincent is drunk and, well … talking.'

George didn't look happy about being put on the spot, especially by his own wife. 'Susan, orders have only just been issued. While the alcohol is flowing, I don't think we should talk about this. People are already saying more than they should.' He pointed at Vincent who was now awake and attempting to stand.

'Case in point,' Peter concurred. 'Vincent is flat-out drunk.'

'So what he's saying is relevant?' Lucas pressed. 'What are the orders from Bucharest, Dad?'

'George …' Peter cautioned.

'Put your clothes back on!'

Everyone turned, eyes locking on Vincent who was attempting to straddle a chair and ambush Sarah with a sleazy striptease. Malcolm was a good sport, helping redress the drunken stripper despite his tenacity to prolong the floor show.

Susan, George and Peter rushed to help Malcolm. Sarah clutched a chubby hand to her ample cleavage, cursing the inebriated behaviour. Vincent remained undeterred.

'Do you ever wonder how Sarah became a Protector?'

Lucas, startled by the rush of hot breath at his ear, glared at Karina over his shoulder. 'Not really.'

'Oh, come on …'

'It's no mystery, Karina. Magic is inherent, not learnt, remember?'

'That's not what I meant,' she said. Her slender arm brushed his own, a whisper like caress across his skin. 'I was referring to the fact that someone actually had to spend time training such a sanctimonious, self-righteous ...'

Karina's voice faded in Lucas's ears. Long, raven coloured hair floated around her shoulders, smelling like grapes and all things sweet. The silken strands teased him, filling him with thoughts of it wrapped around his fingers as he pulled her close. The figure-hugging red dress she wore emphasised the swell of her breasts and encouraged foreign, perverted thoughts.

Bloody hell.

'Well,' Lucas said, coughing to clear his gravelly, hormone-riddled throat, 'as a Protector, Sarah can condemn, maim and kill creatures of the damned. It's the perfect job for a bigot.' He scratched his throat, annoyed that the warble in his speech remained. Giving Karina's cleavage another once over didn't help either.

Perhaps concerned by the extraneous throat clearing, Karina patted Lucas's back sympathetically. 'I suppose you're right. I never really liked her, though.'

'I don't think anyone does.'

'Kim does,' Karina argued.

'I don't like Kim, either.'

Karina's rosebud lips curled into a devilish smile which she tried, unsuccessfully, to hide behind the rim of her glass. She sipped gingerly, eyes locked on the adults attempting to shove steaming coffee down poor Vincent's throat. Sarah was still harping on about his lack of underpants.

Lucas shook his head, nudging Karina's shoulder. 'Hey, do you know what's going on?'

'You mean besides Vincent's date with the porcelain bus in the morning?'

Lucas snorted. 'Yeah, besides that.'

She shrugged. 'You're telling the story. What's up?'

'Vincent mentioned some things about the IMI and then, well, Mum and Dad acted like there's this big secret I'm missing …'

'Hmm,' Karina murmured, tapping a finger to her chin, 'the IMI and big secrets. Now there's a shockingly unexpected sentence if ever I've heard one.'

'Seriously, Karina, something's going on. Has your dad mentioned anything to you about the IMI's future plans for this faction or even its members?'

'Define *anything*.'

'I really don't know,' Lucas grumbled, staring at his half-empty glass of orange juice. 'I guess I was hoping that Malcolm might have mentioned … I don't know. Don't listen to me.'

Karina toyed with the rim of her own glass. She gathered pith from the surface of her juice, meticulously scooped it up and flicked it onto the floor. After several seconds engrossed, she looked up, her face twisted in a grimace. 'All I know,' she began, voice barely above a whisper, 'is that things are about to change.'

'Tell me.'

She plucked at invisible lint upon her dress. Was she nervous? 'If you don't already know then there's probably a very good reason for that.'

'But Mum was about to tell me everything before Vincent's lap dance.'

Karina giggled, reflexively covering her mouth. In no time at all, she was back to separating the pith from her juice. 'Dad said that he got a promotion — linguistics or something like that.'

'So?'

'So he said we'll be moving soon — some ridiculous top secret destination. You know how it is with the IMI. Not even we know the details yet.' She lifted her gaze; earnest yet intoxicatingly beautiful, her eyes were green like the waxy leaves of rainforest trees. 'You're moving, too, Lucas.'

Lucas gaped. 'Hey? That can't be right. Mum and Dad would have said something by now.'

'Maybe they don't want you to know. I know I'm probably in deep shit just for talking to you about it.' She sighed. 'I just can't keep up with the secrets, you know?'

Lucas knew alright. He smoothed his palm across the stubble of his recently shaved head, creasing his brow and then pulling it taut with each frustrated pass. 'I just don't understand any of this.'

'Headquarters was breached by some rogue Vampires. They had to evacuate. I'd say that's what started all this.'

'Yeah, but what does that breach have to do with us? And what exactly has been started?' There were too many questions and not enough answers.

'Your guess is as good as mine.'

Lucas gave up trying to massage sense into his head. He already knew about the evacuation. Elena and her vampiric friends had stormed the proverbial castle, revealing the desertion and finding nothing but a brand new trap for capture. Elena was now with the Vânătors and Lucas was … well, he had no idea anymore.

'*You* must know something,' Karina urged, dragging him from his reverie. 'I mean, look at you.'

'What are you talking about?' Lucas was still trying to understand his parents' deception and why it would involve leaving Cairns. Karina now watched him like he'd just swallowed a small child. He was missing far too many clues.

'Really?' Karina prompted, poking him in the arm. 'Have you looked in the mirror lately? Are you on steroids?'.

'Of course not!'

She pursed her delicate lips. 'It's not just your body, Lucas. Your powers have increased.' She shook her head. 'You do know that's not possible, right? As Protectors we have a very small repertoire, one that you seem to have surpassed.'

Lucas failed to respond. What could he really say? He was just as baffled as she.

Karina appeared to contemplate his silence for a minute more before sipping the remnants of her juice. Lucas had barely touched the warm and unpalatable liquid in his own glass, his stomach churning.

'Look, Karina …' Lucas began, needing to clarify his 'freak' status by some way of explanation.

'I've heard the adults talking,' Karina said, the words firing from her lips like gunpowder backed their exit. She blushed, covering her mouth with her hand. 'Sorry.'

'No, it's fine. What were you going to say?'

She rocked on her heels, glancing nervously over her shoulder. 'The adults … sometimes they talk about you and Elena when they think no one is listening.'

Intriguing. 'What do they say, Karina?'

'Just … stuff.'

'You can tell me. I won't say anything.'

'But if you were meant to know, Lucas, then Susan and George would have told you.'

Lucas shot her a filthy look. 'What a crock of shit. You just said you've been eavesdropping!'

Karina slapped her manicured hand against his shoulder and squeezed tight. 'I want to tell you, but I don't want to get into trouble, either.'

Lucas winced, surprised that her touch troubled the

old scar he'd acquired during childhood. It was long since healed, but lately, throbbed with fresh pain.

'What's wrong?' Karina probed, tugging at the corner of his collar to get a better look. Lucas helped by inching closer, turning his head to give her greater access.

'How's it look today?'

'What is that?' Karina guided gentle fingers over the raised flesh.

'It's an old scar that I've somehow aggravated. It got itchy about a month back, but now it just hurts.'

'What happened?'

Lucas shrugged. 'I don't really remember it all that well.'

A closer inspection crumpled Karina's previously smooth brow. 'It looks fresh, though. It's red and angry looking.'

Lucas released the collar of his shirt. 'I guess I knocked it around in training, or something.'

Karina's dubious look said it all. 'Looks like a bite mark.'

'Well, that's because it is.'

By the time the alcohol stopped flowing and wishes of merriment subsided, it was almost three o'clock in the morning. Lucas could barely keep his eyes open, let alone question his parents further. He'd landed face-first on his pillow, stirring only when a putrid smell roused him.

Stumbling down the stairs, Lucas spotted a casserole bubbling away on the stove — Susan's attempt at edible food. His nose wrinkled; the smell was indescribable. He swallowed down a rising mouthful of bile. Breakfast suddenly seemed like a terrible idea.

Lucas headed for the living room. His parents sat sandwiched between a jungle of boxes and squeaky packing material. 'So we *are* leaving?' he groaned, annoyed that Karina's admission had been accurate. 'When was someone going to tell me?'

Susan focused on wrapping a DVD in a tight, bubble-wrap coffin. 'Who told you?'

'Vincent's babbling and you shoving shit into packing boxes kind of gives it away.'

'I notice you're not protesting,' George said, eyeing him optimistically.

Lucas slumped into his favourite armchair. He swung his legs over the arm and curled up against the soft cushioning. 'Why would I protest? I'm not going with you.'

'I beg your pardon?' George countered, voice raised just a touch as he came to his knees.

Shrinking back into the cushioning, Lucas replied, 'I'm eighteen in less than a month. I figure, why bother moving when I was planning on backpacking through Europe for a while, anyway?'

By 'backpacking', Lucas really meant hauling ass to Rome to help Sebastian and the other Vampires find Elena and bring her home safely.

'Oh, were you now?' Susan drawled. 'You've never mentioned anything to us.'

'I guess that makes us even.'

Susan threw a DVD with a little more force than necessary into an overflowing packaging crate. It bounced off the surface and hit the ground. Lucas suspected she cared little for its fate.

'You can't go to Europe,' George grumbled, squeezing a handful of bubble wrap between clenched fingers. The plastic whined and popped — perhaps the sound of his aneurism in the very near future.

'Why not?'

'There are factors to consider.'

'Such as?'

George stopped assaulting the packaging material, fists now propped upon his narrow hips like a pissed off teapot. 'As you might know, the alliance between Vampire and Protector is crumbling and Headquarters was recently infiltrated because of this. Retaliation requires sacrifice on our part.'

Lucas, usually one to shy from conflict, sat ramrod straight in his chair, looking his father dead in the eyes. 'Retaliation? You can't be serious? You know as well as I do why Vampires "infiltrated" the Bucharest division.'

'There is neither rhyme nor reason for their bloodlust.'

Lucas couldn't hide his cynicism, his features twisting in revolt. 'Bloodlust? That seems like a convenient copout for an underlying issue.'

'Do you know something I don't, Lucas?' George asked, voice saturated with disdain.

'Dad, I've read a lot of your IMI documentation. At least try not to treat me like an idiot. You know that the Vampire's unscheduled visits have everything to do with Elena's imprisonment and nothing to do with the alliance's collapse.'

A heady flow of crimson flushed George's face and neck.

'Seriously, Dad, whatever's going on, just give it up. Why are you really being ordered to leave Cairns?'

'The location and reasoning is restricted information!'

'Restricted information?' Lucas mocked. 'Do you all have super-secret code names, too? And if so, can I please, from this day forth, be known as Obi-Wan?'

'This isn't a joke, Lucas!' Susan snapped, slapping the side of his leg. 'You're a Protector and your presence is required by the IMI. End of story.'

'Don't dismiss me like my opinion doesn't matter. I have the right to know what's going on here.' Lucas refrained from rubbing the sting blooming like a poisonous flower on the exposed flesh of his calf. He hadn't been smacked with such gusto since he was a child.

'I thought upholding the code used to mean something to you?' George continued, fists still anchored firmly to his hips.

'That was before you started lying and sent Elena away, knowing that she would be defenceless against experimentation.'

'Do you know where she is, Lucas?'

'Do you?' he taunted.

'I've had enough!' George roared. 'This isn't open for discussion, anymore. Go upstairs and start packing.'

Lucas counted to ten, certain that punishment would be swift when he answered. He forced the bundle of gyrating nerves in his stomach to settle by taking a deep breath. 'No.'

'Lucas …'

'Dad, I'm so sorry it's come to this, but I'm not going with you.' There, he'd said it, despite the urge to throw up.

George's scowl was matched only by the displeasure marking his mother's face. An unspoken conversation passed between them and George rose to his feet. His forehead beaded with perspiration and his fingers twitched by his …

Oh shit!

Red light caressed George's knuckles, magic that coated the skin and touched the mind, erasing memories and truth. It usually didn't work on Protectors, but when the magic was combined and the power strengthened with united resolve, there was no escape.

Lucas bolted from that armchair quicker than lightning,

but Susan was like a tightly coiled snake waiting to strike. She grabbed his ankle with venomous accuracy, forcing him to his knees.

'It's for your own good!' she shouted, further tackling him to the ground. Her pulsing red fingertips were all over him, spreading magic over his skin like unwanted sickness.

George settled his weight across Lucas's back, placing his throbbing hands on any exposed flesh.

'No!' Lucas screamed, struggling against their hold. 'Please, you can't do this!'

'We should have erased your mind the moment you found the documents, but your mother was insistent that you would come around to our way of thinking. Clearly that was a mistake.'

Susan pinned Lucas's flailing legs, harrumphing at George's jibe.

Lucas tried in vain to appeal to his mother's softer nature. 'Please, Mum, don't let him make me forget!'

'It's better this way,' she murmured, though her voice held a note of hesitancy. 'You'll be *our* Lucas again.'

'No, wait—'

'*Defenacus*,' they both whispered. There was a split second of comforting warmth and then gelatinous darkness, pouring like thickened cream into every crevice of his mind, artfully collecting thoughts to be obliterated by those seeking oppression.

Colours faded, humiliation passed and anger ebbed. The emptiness consumed and then there was nothing at all but the fleeting emotion of loss.

Lucas peeled open sleep-laden eyes. The world was blurry and Sam Sparro's *Black and Gold* beckoned attention from somewhere under his bed. There had to be a logical explanation as to why the mattress was singing.

Lucas tried to ignore it and go back to sleep but it was persistent. He finally gave up, groaned and tossed back the doona to peer under the bed. Floorboards stared back at him with a hidden agenda.

Lucas slipped onto the floor, reaching until he found the knotted edge of a loose board. Inside the hidden compartment was last month's *Penthouse* and a mobile phone. How odd.

Shrugging, Lucas pressed the phone to his ear. 'Blondie?'

'You know I hate it when you call me that,' Marianne hissed.

Lucas smiled at the Vampire's snappish attitude. She was always on the defensive, having been ignored by her twin brother Thomas and long-lasting, pointless crush, William Granville. 'What's up?'

'What's up? This isn't a social call, Lucas.'

'Don't be so grumpy. I was just asking why you called.'

'Are you serious?'

'Sometimes.' He crawled out from under the bed and clambered back up onto the mattress.

'You sound *peppy*,' she said, suspicion marring her tone. 'Have you received word?'

'Word about what?'

There was a slight pause. 'Is someone listening to your call?'

Lucas studied his closed bedroom door. 'I don't think so. Why? Are we going to have phone sex?'

'Lucas, seriously, what the hell is wrong with you? You're acting like more of an idiot than usual.'

Lucas smiled, stretching his legs out and flexing his toes. 'Everything is going to be all right, Marianne. So … what are you wearing?'

Marianne cursed. 'What's going on? Have you heard something about Elena, or not?'

'Everything's perfect. She's safe.'

'Has she been found? You called me a week ago and told me she'd been abducted by Roshan.'

Lucas slapped his cheeks, certain he'd just heard wrong. 'Say that again?'

'You said she went back to the IMI to get info on the serum and Roshan took her.'

Lucas picked at an insect bite on his leg, distracted. 'Nah, that doesn't sound right. Elena's safe. She's with the IMI at the new headquarters. I'm going to visit her soon.'

'Lucas, are you high?'

'I don't think so. I would know if I was, right?'

'What have they done to you, Lucas?'

'Who?'

'The Protectors, you idiot!'

'Why would they do something to me? I *am* a Protector. Dad said I'm going to be the best Protector there is.' The little scab on his leg was bleeding now. He wondered if Marianne could smell it through the phone. Wait. That didn't make sense at all.

'Hey, how are William and Thomas? Did William end up going to visit Elena? Is Thomas there?'

For the longest time, muttered profanities were all Lucas could hear.

'Hey there, Lucas,' Thomas said, apparently commandeering the phone. 'How's it going?'

'Hey man, I'm great. How's London? Have you seen William lately?'

'William has cut contact, Lucas. You know that. He went to Bucharest to be with Elena, but things didn't go as planned.'

'Did they break up?' Lucas asked, genuinely concerned. How did he not know about this?

'You don't remember?'

'Should I?'

Thomas went quiet. 'I'm sorry, Lucas — sorry that your own family has used magic against you.'

'What are you talking about? Everything is great. We're moving soon. We're going to visit Elena at the new headquarters.'

'Where is the new headquarters?'

'It's a secret, Thomas. You know how the IMI work. Ooh, but I can tell you that my new code name is going to be Obi-Wan.'

It was Thomas's turn to curse, though Lucas was uncertain why his two Vamp buddies were so upset with him. 'Will you promise me something, Lucas?'

'Sure.'

'Take a good look at the people around you. You've been brainwashed by magic, Lucas, and I'm uncertain what they've stolen from your mind. It could be information to help Elena, or information on the serum, so please think long and hard when you encounter blank spots.'

Lucas scoffed. 'Yeah, okay, Thomas. Elena is fine.'

'Seriously, Lucas. Elena is in trouble.'

Lucas frowned, waiting for the punch line.

'Just think about it, Lucas. If anyone has the power to get their memories back, it would be you. Marianne speaks fondly of your progress.'

'Hey!' Marianne shouted in the background. She cussed

out her brother. 'Lucas, quit fooling around. You need to shake the idiot right out of you and come back to yourself.'

'I don't know what either of you are talking about, but I'm starting to get worried.'

'Good. You should be, because we wouldn't lie to you about this.'

Thoroughly confused about the status of this practical joke, Lucas answered, 'I will.'

'Good. We should go now.'

'Make sure you take good care of my future wife,' Lucas added with a grin.

'I'll *never* marry a dementia-ridden blood bag,' Marianne spat down the line.

'I love you, too, Blondie.'

'Don't call me that!' she wailed.

Lucas disconnected, tossing the phone back into the hidey-hole under the bed. Confusion still rumpled his brows despite the amusement teasing Marianne usually bestowed. Was Thomas right? Had he really lost his memory? Were The Protectors he loved and trusted really stealing his thoughts to cover some heinous crime?

Nah. Not possible.

CHAPTER FOUR
Under

Darkness was an oppressive wave of emptiness that surged around me, pressing upon my consciousness, beckoning surrender. It was almost too easy to give in, deflect responsibility and place choice in the hands of an unknown entity. Fighting was getting me nowhere.

I searched the obsidian shadows, blind and deaf, my senses mute, my soul lost.

Time passed. It could have been seconds, minutes, hours, days. I had no real concept of time. Why was I trapped here? Was I dead? Was this Hell?

A flash of blinding light startled me. It seemed to reflect off tunnelled walls, perhaps the imaginings of my own distorted vision. But I could now see the outline of my body — a pair of jeans, scuffed sneakers, torn sweater stained with blood. What happened?

I traced a path from breast to neck, fingers searching for damaged flesh. I was drawing conclusions, connecting my shabby appearance to unclear memories filled with blood and panic. The light helped gain clarity.

Wolves? Teeth? Roshan?

I gasped.

How could I forget?

I plucked at my bloodstained clothes, panicked. Roshan's assault had been brutal, exacting. What if I hadn't self-healed? What if I'd been drained dry, my heart never to beat again? Should I avoid the light? Would there even be a light if I was truly damned?

See his face, a voice whispered through my mind.

'What?' I said to no one in particular.

Follow the light, imagine his features.

Great. I was totally talking to myself in creepy baritone again. I thought I'd stopped hearing strange voices back in Bucharest.

You're not crazy, Elena.

'Sure I am,' I mumbled.

Follow the light, see his face.

'Whose face? What are you talking about?'

Smooth. Now I was having a conversation with my subconscious. Where was a padded cell and straitjacket when I needed one?

Think about Sebastian …

Sebastian? I thought to myself. Why would I think about him at a time like this? Would he have a torch?

Sebastian's face swam before my eyes — prominent jaw, high cheekbones and mesmerising, grey-green eyes. Waves of shoulder length, dark hair, inquisitive brows and supple lips made for … never mind.

The light brightened, seemingly responsive to the invocation of Sebastian's memory. Its brilliance was momentarily blinding, causing pain that covering my eyes couldn't ease. But soon it was gone and I was peeking through the slits of my fingers, a lavishly decorated hotel room now before me.

What the …?

I circled the sumptuous space, stopping outside a partially closed door. I assumed a bathroom lay beyond. Wisps of steam escaped through the crack in the door, the smell of soap and leather stirring the air with familiarity.

Sebastian?

I reached for the handle, eager to see him before the vision faded. I'd had these unexplainable projections before, but was still clueless as to how or why they occurred.

Wait ...

I stopped, fingers poised on the handle, my lower lip now victim to my gnawing teeth. It was time to check my conscience. Bathrooms meant showers and hot showers meant steam, which of course could only mean one thing. Sebastian was probably in said shower ... naked.

Dilemma.

Did I want to see him naked?

Hell yes.

But did I want to see him naked right this minute?

Um ... yeah.

I mentally slapped myself and paced, watching the steam slowly rescind, the air grow clear and Sebastian's scent envelope. Focus. That's what I needed, not new material for night-time fantasies. He'd surely be out soon. Hopefully dressed ... or not.

What if he does come out naked?

What if he doesn't come out at all?

What if he comes out naked and decides not to put clothes on ... ever?

Jesus.

I staggered; the door flew open and Sebastian swaggered out. My hands eclipsed my eyes like I had front row seats to a horror film.

This was no horror film.

Dripping from head to toe, Sebastian embodied a wet dream I didn't want to wake up from. My chest pounded and nervous sweat ran in rivulets down my back. Peeking through my fingers proved he wasn't buck naked, but wrapped in a towel — convenient yet disappointing.

I lowered my hands. Who was I kidding, anyway?

Sebastian remained oblivious to my presence. He flung open the closet and sifted through the clothes inside until he found his black leather pants and a plain white T-shirt. He threw them onto the bed behind him, hunting blades and handcrafted sheathes soon joining them.

Closing the door, Sebastian tugged at the towel wrapped loosely around his narrow hips. I gasped as it fell away, spinning on my heels and glancing straight up at the ceiling. I'd like to say it was to give him privacy, but in all honesty, it was to protect my sanity.

Counting to twenty, I turned back around, half relieved and half disappointed to see him covered.

It was time to act. Who knew how much longer I had? I approached him, praying I could somehow transmit my presence. 'Sebastian, can you hear me?' I asked, testing the possibilities of this … vision.

He stopped and turned briefly in my direction, eyes searching. Finding nothing, his attention evaporated and he resumed dressing. I started to shout his name again and again. I even jumped up and down, waved my arms like a windmill and cursed when touching him proved pointless.

Eyes unfocused, he looked right *through* me. He raised his hand, immobile in front us, fingers twitching in an invitation I eagerly accepted.

At first nothing happened. He was solid and I was … I didn't know. But as I began to despair, I felt a tingling sensation and the press of his flesh against mine.

I grinned in relief, our fingers now entwined like old

lovers reunited and our eyes locked. Everything would be okay. Sebastian would find me.

I had my arms around his waist in no time, my face pressed against his chest and my fingers locked behind his back. I could not let my freedom go. I inhaled his fresh scent, comforted by the solidarity of his embrace and the smell of home.

When I looked up again, Sebastian's mouth moved as if speaking, but his lips were blurred and absent of sound. What hope did I have of understanding? I shook my head to reflect my struggle.

He was suddenly free of my embrace like he was once again intangible. I stared at my empty arms as Sebastian headed across the room. I began to question if he'd felt me as I had him, but when I turned, he was already coming back towards me, furiously writing on hotel stationary.

Where are you? his note said.

I shrugged. Could he see me shrug? I didn't know where I was. How could I convey anything when I was essentially a ghost? It was miracle we'd progressed this far.

Sebastian was already writing again.

We think you're in Paris. Lucius has felt the echoes of your telekinetic energy, but not enough to locate the source of your power. Can you tell me anything about your location?

'I'm in a concrete basement,' I said, knowing my short-comings, but also aware that the two-thousand-year-old Vampire across from me was a major smart-ass who could definitely read *my* lips.

Sebastian nodded and began writing again.

More detail? Can you hear anything? Smell anything of interest?

'Tonight I heard fireworks. They were close but not right above me, either. The den smells like wolves, sweat, blood and damp. There's also a faint whiff of … oil? Anyway, there are at least two levels to the basement and I'm right at the bottom. I think it could be an old factory or something industrial, but that's all I've got.'

Sebastian lowered the notepad, his eyes drawn to the ripped remains of my bloodied sweater. The swirling orbs, always in perpetual motion, now bled to the darkest of grey. Like a storm breaking over the coast during the winter, I knew that anger coiled in the pit of his stomach, spilling into his eyes.

He bowed his head and concentrated on the paper in front of him. His fingers shook as he wrote, the pen suffocated and in serious danger of haemorrhaging ink. His teeth were clenched tightly, the muscles in his jaw setting off spasms of outrage.

How badly are you hurt?

I refused to answer. What would poring over the details accomplish besides more anguish? I'd been trained by the IMI to deal with a lot of bad situations and I would get over this attack, too.

A shiver broke out across my spine as an ugly thought waged war with the denial inside me. What if Roshan had raped me? What if I woke up, brutally violated and impregnated with Vânător spawn? I would sooner see myself dead than become Roshan's newest incubator.

Oh, God …

The full gravity of the situation suddenly pressed upon me and I couldn't breathe. Years of training was rendered useless under the assault of my own fear. 'H–help me, Sebastian,' I stuttered, 'You have to find me!'

Sebastian dropped the notepad and reached for me, his face a myriad of conflicting emotions — pain, guilt, inadequacy. I saw them all as tears marked my cheeks and the darkness slowly rolled in.

I blinked, trying to find focus through the wet onslaught of emotion, but Sebastian was fading and I was drifting back to the reality of a dirty mattress, a gluttonous werewolf and flesh painted with dry, flaking blood.

I took a much needed breath, shaky and wracked by sobs as I tested opening my eyes. It was sweet relief to find the mattress beside me empty.

I sat up sluggishly and began the dreaded inspection — no tell-tale sign of violation but definitely a presence of pain. Blood loss ensured the onset of severe stomach cramps, like clawed fingers ripping apart my insides and twisting them into knots.

I was thirsty.

No.

I was starving! But at least I was still whole.

I was momentarily distracted by the offering beside the mattress: a tetra pack of blood teased me with the promise of satiation. I wasted no time forcing the bendable straw into the pack and placing it between my lips. I didn't care if it was poisoned or came at a price. My stomach congratulated the rash decision as the lukewarm liquid coated my insides and eased the building fire gaining momentum in my throat.

'You're finally awake,' Roshan said.

Startled, I scuttled into a corner like a frightened animal, holding the tetra pack close, sucking greedily at its contents. How did I not hear him enter?

'I thought you'd never come around. You've been out cold for three days.'

Three days? Wow. He'd really put me through the wringer.

Roshan was hesitant in his approach, placing one foot painfully deliberate in front of the other. 'Are you all right, Elena?'

Trick question, surely?

'No.' I shook the empty tetra pack, making certain it was drained before throwing it at him. 'I need more.'

'That's all I have.'

'One pack of blood after all you took isn't enough.'

Roshan was so close now I could smell the salty sweat of his skin. He reached out, presumably to wipe the excess blood from my lips, but I was gone, darting around the basement like the caged tiger I was starting to become.

'Don't touch me.'

The patient farce Roshan pushed ebbed quickly as my dismissal renewed anger replete with a suffocating wave of Alpha timbre. 'Elena, come to me,' he beckoned.

I clenched my teeth and fought back tears as I stumbled into Roshan's embrace. Fighting was useless; craving freedom was a luxury I could no longer afford.

'I'm sorry I took so much blood. I didn't know you were going to taste that good. Next time I promise I will pace myself.'

I struggled in his grasp. 'Next time? I'm not a chew toy, you bastard!'

A warning growl vibrated within Roshan's chest. 'I *have* to taste you again, Elena.'

'I'm not on the menu.'

Roshan lowered his face to mine and whispered Alpha scent straight between my parted lips. 'It's either drink your blood, or take your body.' He rubbed himself against me to make his point. 'The choice is ultimately yours.'

Hatred filled my eyes to the point of overflowing. 'I don't want *any* part of you touching me.'

'Blood or body, Elena. What's it to be?'

Nostrils flaring in revulsion, I said, 'So if I let you feed from me, you won't try to …' I couldn't finish. The mere thought of him inside me made me want to blow chunks.

His low, menacing chuckle tortured my already frayed nerves. 'Believe me. I want to feel my body ravaging yours, Elena, but this is my compromise. For now.'

It was hardly a compromise. Either way I was still being violated. 'How often?'

'Nightly.'

'I can't … the blood … my thirst—'

Wait. Am I seriously considering this?

Roshan mocked my fears with an eruption of provocative laughter. This situation was not funny at all. 'Don't worry, I can get you blood, Elena. Do we have a deal?'

A deep breath did little to settle my churning stomach. 'I don't really have a choice. You'll make me do whatever you want, anyway.'

'That's true.'

'Then why are we even having this conversation?'

'Then it's settled,' Roshan said, patting my backside condescendingly. 'Now, let's get you cleaned up. We don't want you looking all battered and bloodied when our guest arrives.'

'What guest?'

Roshan took my hand, grip bruising and unshakeable. He continued to ignore my question as he walked us to the steel door. His scent was ever present and I was captive — a passenger in my own body as we left the basement and headed for the upper levels.

Wolves lounged on the floor by our feet. They roused as we passed, sniffing the wake of my passing, black eyes locked on the patches of dried blood decorating my savaged sweater.

The smell of death and decay was everywhere. Plugging my nose did little to dispel the putrid stench and I was even more repulsed by the sight of human remains resting in the corner like discarded waste. A skull was propped against the wall, flesh and rotting sinew hanging by meaty threads. A nearby Vânător chewed on the leftovers, digging out the marrow with an eager tongue.

Throwing up seemed like a good idea.

Roshan shoved me into the next room, slamming yet another door behind us. In this derelict space was a shower, rusted but serviceable, a steady, muddy-coloured drip indicating functionality. I almost salivated at the thought of being semi-clean.

Roshan kicked a small pile of clothes on the floor towards me; a ridiculously short skirt and filmy sweater. 'These should fit. I chose the woman based on your height and build.'

I held up a hand, not wanting further detail. I'd seen enough outside. 'Can you turn around, please?'

'You know the answer to that.'

'Fine.' I ignored the offering and stepped into the cubicle fully clothed.

Roshan growled, slamming his fist against the door jamb. 'No games, Elena.'

Tears threatened to fill my eyes and my lower lip quivered. If it was his plan to debase me, prove his Alpha status and cement the notion I was merely just another pack mate too weak to resist his urges, then he was onto something.

I closed my eyes, took a deep breath and sailed to a foreign destination in my mind. I was now absent from reality, stripped to my barest while pretending to wander a deserted beach in the middle of the Caribbean, alone and free.

The violent icy spray that pounded my filthy flesh soon shattered all illusion. I was back to standing immobile, immersed under cold water, cursing my rapid heartbeat and the fading image of sand squelching between my toes.

'Hurry up,' Roshan barked.

I jumped, quickly turned off the faucet and fought the urge to dislocate his kneecaps. I reached for my tatty, discarded jeans on the floor instead.

'No,' Roshan said, kicking them out of reach. 'I want you to wear *these* clothes.'

I eyed the dead girl's black miniskirt and sweater. 'They won't keep me warm.'

'I'll keep you warm.'

The bastard had an answer for everything.

Once again arguing seemed pointless, I was naked and Roshan was staring, so I slipped on the clothes and stamped down the rising bile in my stomach. A part of me wondered why he'd bothered letting me redress in the first place. Perhaps he liked to unwrap his presents and savour the final debasing.

He continued to leer, licking his lips as he reached for me. 'Much better.'

I was suddenly dragged through the basement again, Roshan's fingers slipping on my wet skin. My only focus was avoiding the snapping jaws of passing Vânǎtors and tripping over my own feet.

Bite free and back behind the steel door, Roshan threw me down onto the bloodied mattress. His body covered mine before I'd even had time to ponder defence. I didn't like where this was heading at all. The miniskirt was a terrible idea.

I bucked underneath him, furious. 'You promised!'

Roshan pinned my hands above my head and sort solace with my trembling lips. 'I promised not to mate with you; everything else is open to interpretation.'

The burning heat of his possessive touch set a determined course down the soft flesh of my neck. I stiffened, unable to resolve the war raging within. On one hand I imagined ploughing my fist through his chest cavity and removing his beating heart. On the other, I was receptive to his essence, my head turning to allow him greater access to the blood throbbing in my veins.

Stupid. Stupid. Stupid.

Get up! Run! Fight! Do something, anything!

'Don't fight me, Elena. Stay perfectly still. Enjoy the experience.'

As if I could.

But the heat of his breath was like a warm blanket against my chilled, moist flesh. The touch of his lips — hot pillows of promise hiding pointed daggers that grazed my jugular. I was soon captured between hungry jaws, his eager tongue lapping up every drop of blood that oozed from my throat.

Fight, damn it!

The room faded and earlier cramping reared its ugly head. Breathing proved laborious and protest pointless. He'd taken too much blood and I was furious with myself for not acting, not doing something to prevent this subjugation of my will.

'Stop,' I whispered, my voice coarse, pleading.

Perhaps sensing my urgency, Roshan detached his fangs, suckling the slow healing wounds instead. But I knew it was too late.

I was already gone.

When I next attempted to open my eyes they felt heavy, as if bags of sand had been poured in the corners and weights rested across the lids. The real question was should I even bother? Circumstances remained unchanged. I was still in the basement. I was still with Roshan. Better to remain comatose.

Roshan obviously felt different. 'How are you feeling?' he asked, stroking my cheek.

Words were lost on me. My throat felt as if I'd swallowed razorblades and my insides burned as if coated in molten lava. My lips attempted speech, but in the end, it was my erect middle finger that did the talking for me.

'Hmm, I see you're still angry with me.'

You think?

'You should feed,' Roshan said, holding out a new tetra pack of B positive.

I snatched the foiled lifeboat from Roshan, tore it open and sucked down the contents without pause. When it was empty I was greeted with another blood pack, uncertain of the play or why he'd lied about his possession of them. I was too hungry to care.

'You've drunk all the blood I have,' Roshan said, slapping a half-eaten sandwich into my upturned palm. 'Here, eat this instead.'

The sandwich was stale and probably out of a garbage can, but I was in no position to knock sustenance and thus I greedily shoved it into my mouth and swallowed it down. Unfortunately my supernatural side argued the nutritional value, my stomach still a riot of uncomfortable cramps that only blood could alleviate.

'I need more blood,' I croaked. 'You took too much again.'

'And you shall have some, tonight, when our guest arrives.'

I wiped the crumbs from my mouth, frowning. 'What's going on?'

'You'll see soon enough.'

'Don't play games with me.'

'You're in no position to dictate, Elena.'

I shook my head, bewildered. 'I just don't understand …'

'Understand what?'

'Everything. I've been here for weeks and you've never questioned me about my genetics. I know John told you what I could do and I know you've decided I can somehow benefit your pack. What I don't understand is why you haven't moved forward with any plans you might have for me.'

A small smile touched Roshan's lips. 'What makes you think I haven't?'

'Then talk to me.'

'Subordinates do not require explanation.'

I bristled. 'I'm not your bitch, Roshan.'

'You're wrong about that,' he jeered.

I slapped his face … hard.

'Careful,' he cautioned, nostrils flaring, 'I keep you because I want you, not because I need you. I'm far more resourceful then you give me credit for.'

'Are you?'

'Let's just say that there are other like-minded individuals out there brimming with ideas and eager to collaborate.'

My eyes went wide as a million dark thoughts raced through my mind, all of them drawing inconceivable conclusions. 'What exactly are you saying?'

Roshan sneered, fingering the angry red welt on his cheek. 'Do I look stupid to you? I'm not revealing my secrets. But I think it prudent you remember that your place in this pack is only certain as long as I desire you.'

He didn't need my blood, he *wanted* it. That was a startling and confusing truth. I didn't believe for a second he'd given up on curing his races' weakness, so I could only assume …

'Wait,' I groaned, clutching my stomach as a fresh onslaught of cramping began. 'How did you figure it out?'

'Figure what out?' he chuckled.

'Don't play dumb. I know what I am and my blood's worth to you.'

'That's something I'll keep close to my chest unless you finally agree to become my pack mate.'

'That's never going to happen.'

'Then I guess you'll never know,' he taunted, pleased with himself.

His smarmy grin and my predatory crawl towards retribution were cut short by a procession of thunderous howls beyond the steel door.

'That's my cue,' Roshan said, jumping to his feet. 'I won't be long.'

'What's going on?'

'Dessert.'

'Roshan?'

He slammed and locked the door behind him, his laughter a mocking ode to the basement's choir of excited barks and howls. I was left alone with my thoughts, possibly more dangerous than the fanged creatures that kept me captive — especially as I had a really bad feeling I wasn't going to like dessert.

CHAPTER FIVE

Truth

Lucas surveyed his empty bedroom, larger now that his possessions were gone. The furniture had been collected yesterday by burly men with hairy chests and sweaty armpits. His parent's mentioned something about his favourite desk chair heading for a thrift shop. What remained of his clothes were piled into a suitcase, everything else considered expendable.

'Lucas! It's time to go!' Susan shouted from downstairs.

'I'll be there in a second.'

Lucas dropped to the floor, and hunted for his secret hidey-hole. He caught the edge of a board and pulled it up to reveal the secret stash of porn magazines and the darkened space beneath. He deposited the mystery mobile back into its prison, not sure why, but certain at some point he'd had his reasons for its secrecy.

Marianne and Thomas argued that the *Defenacus* spell had been used against him. Since he couldn't recall the truth, he figured the best place for the phone was where he'd originally stashed it. He just wished he could remember why.

With footsteps pounding on the stairs, Lucas slid the floorboard back into place and stamped it down, ensuring the seal was not visible.

'Lucas?' George pushed the flimsy timber door aside and

barged right on in. Apparently knocking didn't apply to him. 'We're waiting for you.'

Lucas nodded, eyeballing the bedroom a final time. 'I just needed a minute to say goodbye.'

'We need to go now. The taxi's waiting.'

'Okay.' Lucas refrained from glancing back at the floorboard and followed his father downstairs, uncertain and unsettled.

'Are you ready?' Susan asked as Lucas entered the living room.

'Do I have a choice?' The words were out before he truly understood the bitterness behind them. Leaving suddenly felt wrong — so wrong.

'Lucas, that was rude,' Susan chided. 'I want you to apologise.'

Momentarily bewildered by the spit-fire response, Lucas shook his head. 'Sorry, Mum. I don't know what came over me.'

The taxi ride to the airport was crowded and uncomfortable. What luggage didn't fit into the cramped confines of the boot was stacked between Lucas and his mother. The suffocation continued with overextended lines at the terminal gates and an economy class ticket sandwiching him between both parents for three solid hours.

'So, what are we doing in Melbourne?' Lucas asked for the umpteenth time as he and Susan waited by the baggage carousel.

'We aren't staying in Melbourne so it's hardly relevant,' she answered, yanking George's suitcase from in between a *Hello Kitty* trolley and a badly damaged surfboard.

'Where are we going then?'

'Susan?'

Lucas sighed at the interruption. A short, slightly rotund,

middle-aged woman with chocolate brown hair and amber eyes grinned at his mother.

'Annabel?' Susan dropped George's belongings, the greedy momentum of the conveyer belt once again reclaiming them. 'Oh my, Annabel! Fancy seeing you here! Have you been reassigned, too?'

They were suddenly embracing.

Lucas turned back to grab his own suitcase as it hurried towards him, barely recognisable amid the sea of travel paraphernalia.

'Is this our little Lucas?' Annabel asked, reaching out to pinch his cheeks.

'It is.'

'He's grown so big! The last time I saw him he was, well, about this big.' She indicated as much by holding her hand about four feet away from the ground.

Lucas smiled politely, having nothing to add that wasn't laced with sarcasm. It must have been a real eye-opener discovering that he was a big boy now and not a garden gnome. What a shocker.

'So how many members of the Melbourne contingent are flying out today?' Susan asked, finally releasing Lucas from her iron-clad grip. It was back to business.

Annabel smiled, her attention once again fixed on Susan. 'About six. I was just waiting on Justin's group coming in from Sydney. They haven't been to the Melbourne Airport before.'

'Everyone's flying in today?' Susan asked, surprised.

'Not quite. Adelaide, Perth, Broome, Alice Springs and Darwin came and went yesterday. The other minority groups went the day before, ensuring they were on time to catch the boat with yesterday's people.'

'Boat?' Lucas said, lifting an eyebrow.

'Oh, yes,' Annabel murmured. 'We need to make—'

'Annabel,' Susan said, her long, slim fingers grazing Annabel's forearm, 'we haven't told Lucas the location yet.'

Annabel nodded. 'I suppose that's for the best when dealing with the younger ones.' She leaned close to Susan, supposedly whispering, 'Given that Elena is still missing and information continues to be leaked to the Vampires, we have to keep a tight lid on everything.'

'Elena's missing?' Lucas gasped, trying to make sense of this new information. 'You told me she was waiting for us at the new headquarters!'

Could Thomas and Marianne have been right about everything?

Annabel looked on apologetically while Susan forced a reluctant smile. 'She's fine, Lucas. Everything is fine.'

'Fine?' Lucas had the sudden, violent urge to high five his mother in the face with a luggage cart. *Fine?* The dark feelings of doubt that slithered across his trembling limbs proved that he, and this topic of conversation, was anything but fine. Why was he so angry? How did he know that lies bloomed in Annabel's whispered words?

'Elena *is* at headquarters, Lucas,' Annabel confirmed, squeezing Susan's hand. 'I got my wires crossed. I'm sorry. I didn't mean to alarm you.'

'But you just said that she was missing.'

'From the training tournament we held yesterday. Again, my mistake. We eventually found her in the mess hall.'

The frown on Lucas's face spoke volumes. He didn't like being lied to.

'When are you expecting Justin?' Susan asked Annabel.

'Any minute. Their plane landed a little before yours, but apparently there was some delay in offloading passengers.'

She patted Susan's arm. 'Speaking of delays, where's George? I haven't seen him.'

'He went to the Men's room.'

A knowing look passed between them, followed by a fit of giggles. Lucas, mood still lingering on the dark side, decided it was the secret language of women and set about hunting down rogue suitcases instead.

'Isn't this exciting?'

Lucas jumped, but it was only Karina, squeezing between him and another passenger to claim her pink, floral suitcase.

Lucas, ever chivalrous, helped her lift it off the conveyor belt and onto solid ground. He passed Karina the extension handle, unsure he felt anything besides confusion and a slight case of dehydration.

'We're going to see snow!' she smiled brightly.

That piqued Lucas's curiosity. 'How do you know that? Where are we going?'

'Dad told me it's a surprise.'

'But he told you about snow?'

'Why do you think I have this with me?' She unfolded the bundle draped over her left arm and held up a fluffy pink jacket, entirely ineffectual against subzero temperatures. Honestly, he'd thought it was a stuffed toy or some crazy pillow when he'd first seen her with it on the plane. 'Where's your jacket?'

Lucas didn't own a jacket, let alone one crafted from pink polar bear. 'Maybe Malcolm told you about the snow to throw you off the true scent, our *real* destination.'

Karina frowned. 'Why would my father lie to me?'

'Because he can.'

'Well, that's just—'

Everything got loud then. The Sydney branch flooded the terminal with their bleached-blonde hair and wide toothy smiles. Raucous laughter, hugging, clasping of hands and zealous back-patting were suddenly in abundance.

Lucas felt like a fish out of water, but he'd learned a few things: One, Karina looked smoking hot in a pair of skinny jeans. Two, Annabel's father established the Melbourne branch during the forties. He was older than dirt and his breath smelt like mothballs, but he also farted every five minutes without care, amusing Lucas's juvenile side. And three, the blow-ins from Sydney were *all* family — an incestuous bunch intent on keeping the bloodline pure, the magic true.

Spew.

Lucas glanced at the monitor above the check-in counter, now flashing the imminent destination. He did a double take. The word 'Hobart' was plastered across the screen in bold.

Hobart? What the hell is in Hobart? I thought we were catching a boat?

Some questions were answered a few hours later when they departed the Hobart Airport and headed for the docks via free shuttle buses and numerous taxis.

'Can you believe this?' Vincent said, lowering his suitcase. He studied the looming vessel in awe, rocking back on his heels and craning his neck to appreciate the sheer size of it. 'We're finally ready to start the real journey.'

Lucas gaped, momentarily speechless as he surveyed the rusted barge with its flaking paint and inescapable portholes. 'Please tell me we're not getting on that ancient piece of crap.'

Vincent laughed and slapped Lucas's back in jest. 'Show some respect. The *Ice Queen* has been doing trips between Hobart and Antarctica for years.'

'Antarctica?' Cue total and utter jaw-dropping surprise.

'Be serious.' Cruising in a twisted pile of metal was one thing. Setting course for the ass end of the planet was quite another.

'Think of all the icy outdoor fun we'll have.'

Fun? Lucas's eyes trolled every inch of the rust bucket, certain even a minor collision with an infant penguin would consign him to a watery grave. 'Have the IMI gone crazy?'

'This reassignment is important, Lucas. Isolation ensures the continued success of our top secret projects and training.'

'What top secret projects?'

Vincent rubbed his hands together. 'You'll just have to see.'

'What about Elena? She is at this new headquarters, right?'

Vincent smiled extra wide, all teeth. 'Of course she is.'

Liar.

There it was again, that steady stream of uncertainty clogging his thoughts.

Damn. Why can't I think clearly? Why can't I remember anything Thomas told me?

Vincent heartily slapped Lucas's back again, laughing as he grabbed his suitcase and headed off, leaving Lucas to ponder his addled thoughts.

'We're leaving soon. Might want to get your luggage over to the cargo hold.'

Lucas turned towards the new voice, a passing incestuous Sydneysider. Having no recollection of his name and no real interest in re-learning it, he merely nodded. Lucas did, however, have an interest in whether or not the young in-breeder would be packing a phone.

'Hey, man,' Lucas said, 'you don't have a mobile phone on you by any chance?'

'Sure, bud. Here you go.'

Lucas was suddenly annoyed that his had been confiscated while others still clearly held theirs. 'Thanks. I just need to send a quick text.'

'Good plan. I doubt we'll be getting reception where we're going.'

'True, that.' Lucas began tapping away at the screen, stoked he'd somehow managed to memorise Marianne's number. He honestly didn't call her that often … honestly.

'Lucas, what are you doing?'

Seriously? Was someone always hiding in the shadows just waiting to pounce?

Lucas ignored Malcolm and the Sydneysider's attempt to intervene as he quickly hunted through the phone's icons to finish his text. Unfortunately, autocorrect was being a real bitch.

I'm in the Anthill, please come bet on me before my balls are freezing and decimal points fall off.

Malcolm snatched the mobile from his grasp, eyeballing the screen, message unsent. A single brow rose, though not surprising given the absurdity of his message. 'What were you doing?'

'None of your business.'

'Who were you trying to contact?'

'Does it really matter? You've taken the phone off me. Crisis averted.'

Malcolm addressed the Sydneysider, whose half-assed attempts at reclaiming his phone were probably more out of confusion given Malcolm's seniority and distress at Lucas's usage of the device. 'Did he say anything to you?'

'He just asked to borrow my phone. What's the big deal?'

'This is *Lucas Manory*,' Malcolm said, handing back the phone. 'You tell me?'

'*The* Lucas Manory? Sorry, man, I didn't realise.' The Sydneysider pocketed his phone and took off to re-join the group.

Lucas frowned. Apparently he was a celebrity. What the hell was going on?

'Come on, Malcolm, you gotta tell me what that weirdness was about.'

'Do I?' Malcolm's raised brow and crossed arms begged to differ.

Lucas tried a new approach. 'I'm sorry I was rude before, but you have to understand, people are whispering about me and everyone's looking over my shoulder. I have absolutely no idea what's going on or what I did wrong.'

Malcolm's hard gaze softened. 'You haven't done anything wrong, Lucas. It's just that you're special and we protect and covet the unique.'

That explanation did nothing to alleviate confusion. 'Like Elena? Is that what you mean?'

'No, Lucas, I mean *you*. You must understand that your current growth and unparalleled skills as a maturing Protector are odd. You've advanced to new levels that need to be researched, and as you know, our research is top secret.' Malcolm squeezed Lucas's throbbing scar. Intentional? Lucas would never know. 'You should get your luggage over to the hold now. We'll be boarding soon.'

'I don't want to go,' Lucas blurted. Uncertainty and an irrational sense of menace welled inside of him. The mystery of The Protector's true agenda was worrying. 'I think I need to be somewhere else.'

Malcolm captured Lucas's chin between deft fingers, squeezing painfully tight. 'The world isn't a safe place anymore, Lucas. The IMI's protection is paramount and so is your role in our survival. Besides, don't you want to see Elena?'

Hesitation ate away at Lucas like maggots devouring the rotting flesh of a cadaver. 'I'm clearly missing something. Why aren't we safe anymore?'

'There's a war brewing, Lucas.'

'Since when?'

'The alliance is no more.'

'What? Who drew first blood?'

'The Vampires attacked headquarters, hence our new posting. How long do you think it will be before they attack the rest of our divisions?'

None of this sounded right.

'But to dissolve the alliance over one incident, isn't that extreme? They aren't all bad. Look at Elena, she ...' The mere mention of his sister's name in conjunction with talk of the alliance and headquarters' invasion stirred hazy memories.

Malcolm tightened his grip on Lucas's chin. 'It's not extreme when they invade our safe zones! The building was destroyed, the upper levels flooded and the walls smeared with blood.'

Lucas tried to shake free, certain of nothing else other than this information seemed wrong.

'Vampires have seduced your mind, Lucas,' Malcolm continued. 'In fact, I'd bet that you were trying to contact them just now.'

'Marianne, Thomas and William are friends of our faction, not puppeteers.'

'Are you sure?'

Lucas slapped Malcolm's hand away. 'Of course I'm sure. If they were planning attacks why not make a move sooner? Why bother to help us eradicate the London pack of Vânǎtors? Why have alliances at all if it's that easy to manipulate us?'

'Because the alliance has thus far protected us against Vânǎtor attacks.'

Malcolm must have thought Lucas was an idiot. 'I think this is a drastic and hasty decision based on an overly potent, irrational fear.'

Malcolm's brow crinkled like tissue paper. 'Whose side are you on, Lucas?'

'Why do I have to choose?'

'Careful,' Malcolm murmured, stubbing a piece of chipped concrete with the toe of his boot. 'You wouldn't want to find yourself alone and outnumbered.'

Lucas didn't want to know the specifics of that thinly veiled threat.

'But don't worry, Lucas,' Malcolm gave Lucas's cheek a quick pat with a clammy palm. 'Those who are with us will be well compensated.'

'So this is all about money?'

'Who said compensation was about wealth?'

The serum.

It echoed in his head with alarming clarity. The serum was significant but couldn't exactly remember what he knew about it. Clearly his vampire buddies were onto something when they said his memory had been wiped.

Lucas took a punt on Malcolm elaborating further. 'So compensation relates to the serum?'

Malcolm looked taken aback. 'I beg your pardon?'

Unconscious knowledge spewed from lips moving of their own volition. 'The IMI has created a biological weapon to aid in the destruction of all our enemies, right? Without an alliance, was the IMI hoping the Vampires and Vânǎtors would destroy themselves?'

Several seconds passed before Malcolm schooled his features and spoke again. It was just as well. Lucas was busy rearranging his muddled thoughts and wondering how his tongue had planned the hostile takeover.

'How do you know about this?' Malcolm asked.

'Am I right?'

'Close.'

'Bloody hell.'

'And what are you going to do with that information?' Malcolm asked.

'Nothing.' What could Lucas do? He was about to sail the seven seas on a rusted piece of crap. He'd probably be attacked by orcas and eaten by sharks before the day was through.

'You'd better stick around then, find out what role it is that you play in all of this.'

'Do I want to know?'

Malcolm grinned, a little too wide to be of comfort.

'I swear to God, if I don't get off this boat soon I'm going to scream!'

Lucas glanced at one of the younger, more vocal Melbourne girls. She was rugged up like the rest of them — woollen coats, waterproof parkas, gloves, beanies and heavy boots. Her nose was pink from the biting cold and her skin was chapped. Ten days trapped on a boat sailing through frigid winds and icy water was certainly reason enough to scream.

Lucas considered broadcasting an outburst of his own. Memories trickled through the sieve of recollection, filling his head with unsavoury thoughts — the most recent that he'd been brutally played.

He was a victim of the *Defenacus* spell and now knew that Elena would *not* be waiting for him in Antarctica. She was with Roshan, trapped and alone.

'What do you think?' George said, gesturing to the monochromatic landscape.

Lucas started at his father's sudden appearance — the last person he wanted to see. A few noxious ideas about pushing him overboard saw Lucas quickly tuck his gloved hands inside his coat pockets. He concentrated on the icy water churning beneath the boat instead.

George chuckled, entrapment a great big joke. 'I see you're still ignoring me.'

Hint, hint.

Lucas's lack of chatter inspired George to fill in the blanks. 'Did you know that the IMI was first initiated in nineteen twenty-three as the governing body for all Protectors?'

Still no response.

'Well, during those initial years, some of the wealthier constituents of our collective clans set up various businesses to fund our development. The Grand Hotel in Bucharest was established as the main research centre. A major sports stadium in Berlin was built to house a fallout shelter, and in Malaysia, we got involved in banking.'

Lucas's face spoke volumes about his level of interest.

'We found that Antarctica was an untapped resource. Our movements weren't regulated by governing bodies and in a state of emergency we would be isolated from our enemies.'

Lucas had no idea how that was possible. Even in the

twenties he suspected someone would have demanded excavation or research permits.

George was apparently reading his mind, or simply in the mood to hear the sound of his own voice. 'Our Antarctic establishment is, of course, legit. Our research facility investigates climatic changes and global warming, predictions of environmental disasters and desalination. We pass this information onto the appropriate government bodies and occasionally let visiting scientists spend time doing further research. Naturally they are unaware that travelling another fifty kilometres inland will take you to the real research facility.'

Lucas swallowed the icy lump forming in his throat. It was becoming abundantly clear that he was in way over his head.

'Please talk to me, Lucas,' George said, nudging his shoulder. 'Tell me what you're thinking?'

'I'm thinking that I have no control over anything.'

'You have control over your actions and choices.'

'Do I? The sarcasm was spread extra thick.

'Of course.'

'Then why did you use the *Defenacus* spell to get me here?'

George faltered. 'How ... I mean, it's not possible. Lucas, I—'

'Save it. I remember everything and there's nothing you can say. The only thing I want to know is what my role is in all of this. Why were you so desperate for me to come?'

George started to scratch his chin. He kept itching like fleas had set up camp. Paired with the nervous expression on his face, Lucas knew he'd hit a nerve. 'What do you mean?'

'Please. My body — my magic? You really don't think

that total dedication to training inspired me to be able to do this ...'

George was suddenly hovering several feet above the deck. Lucas had only to massage the throbbing centre of his mind to achieve this result. Spell words had long been redundant.

'Lucas, put me down!' George spluttered.

In the water?

Tempting though it was, Lucas set his father back onto the deck and into the waiting arms of a few curious observers from the Melbourne clan.

'Why did you do that?' George growled.

'I think the more important question is how did I do that without using magic?'

George brushed away the steadying hands of the other Protectors, grabbing Lucas's upper arm and hauling him into a private corner. The Melbournians followed regardless, perhaps just as curious about the answer. 'You didn't use any magic?'

'I haven't been for a while.'

George lowered his voice to a whisper, turning his back on the others. 'You've always been more advanced than other Protectors your age, Lucas. Karina and Lisa can probably wield one spell accurately between them. It takes years to master the craft, years to use it as expertly as you do.'

'That didn't explain anything.'

'I'm not sure what more you want me to say.'

'The truth. You know I've read the letters between you and Chester, so just tell me what the IMI have done to me.'

'This isn't the time or the place.'

Lucas clenched his fists, warm and cosy in his pockets, both of them eager to come out swinging. 'Well, when is the right time or place?'

'Later.'

'Later when?'

'Soon.' George held up his hand to prevent further argument. 'I can assure you, Lucas, that the IMI has never, or will never, do anything to intentionally harm you.'

'But you admit that something has been done?'

For several uncomfortable moments all that could be heard was the ship's bow as it crashed through the ice and the thrum of the engines underfoot. Either George wouldn't or couldn't answer but he also made no attempt to try. He just stood there, dumfounded.

Lucas was disappointed. Should he really have expected a different outcome? Had he truly believed public confrontation would force some semblance of truth from his father's lips?

He really needed to stop setting himself up for a fall.

CHAPTER SIX
Cellmate

Staring incessantly at the back of the rusted steel door did little to dispel unpleasant feelings playing havoc with my insides. I was overwhelmed by Roshan's resourcefulness and terrified by the thought of his next move. Was I just a toy? Had he truly discovered how to heal the Vânătors?

I blinked, milking my lids for moisture until I could see straight again.

Stop staring at the door.

What's coming?

Does it matter? You can't escape.

I rolled onto my side and clutched my stomach. Another cramp attempted to squeeze the lingering vestiges of my sanity. The thirst was fast becoming an unbearable torment and I was moaning loudly by the time Roshan re-entered the basement.

I didn't move, merely gritted my teeth to stifle my weakness. I couldn't endure another feeding so soon. He would surely kill me this time.

The rabid wolves of the den growled, barked, howled and snapped their snouts in unrehearsed unison. They were frenzied and suddenly everywhere, sniffing at my extremities, clawing at the concrete around me and then just as suddenly … gone.

The grating sound of metal on concrete and the snap of deadlocks indicated the door had been closed and locked, but where had the pack gone? Where was Roshan? Something wasn't right.

What is that?

I was now looking at shredded denim, covered in blood. An invitation? I didn't care. My mouth watered and I hungered for a taste of the smooth skin peeking from behind the gaping fabric. This had to be 'dessert' and I was planning on eating.

My canines ruptured the throbbing flesh of my gums, the sweet smell of those sugary veins, pulsing, inviting. I was already on my knees, eyes locked on the blood that dripped with promise. Common sense played no part. I cared not for whoever stood before me. I cared only for gratification.

I lunged at the legs, arms outstretched, fingers clawed and begging. I met with air and crashed into the concrete floor. My seemingly easy prey had disappeared. Was I hallucinating?

No.

The room was dark, but the figure loomed, bobbed from side to side, light on its feet and ready for flight. I could still smell its blood, a scent that was …

I inhaled again; the flavour rolled across my tongue and caressed it with sweet familiarity. Temptation never ebbed, but uncertainty rose.

'Elena?'

That voice. God, I had to be dreaming. Only in this prison would I be taunted by the achingly familiar.

'Elena, is that you?' He crept closer. It was no more than

I felt to be near him again. Surely he was an apparition, a ghost of my past sent to remind me of my failings.

'William?'

'Yeah, it's me.'

I studied his ripped clothing, dirty skin and tousled hair. What the hell had happened to him and what was he doing in Roshan's den?

It didn't matter anymore when William reached for me. I brimmed with newfound hope and launched myself into his arms. I guess he didn't mind, perhaps as eager as I was to see a friendly face.

'I'm so glad you're alright, Elena,' he said, holding me close.

Relief faded. Memories I'd recently decided to bury burst through my subconscious and soured the reunion. We hadn't exactly parted on the best of terms and I could hardly forget the disregard he'd shown me then.

'I've missed you so much,' he murmured, his fingers trailing the length of my spine while his lips brushed my cheek.

I allowed only seconds to revel in the memory of his touch before I pushed William away. I could no longer afford to place this Vampire on a pedestal. He'd made the ultimate mistake — betrayed my trust and left me defenceless when I'd needed him most.

'Elena?' I could hear the confusion is his voice. 'You know I won't hurt you.'

I scoffed. 'Are you sure about that?'

His emerald eyes narrowed as he watched me creep backwards. The filthy mattress now divided us but I'd opened more than the chasm of space between us. I was picking at old wounds, knowing they would bleed but helpless to heal them without closure.

William shook his head. 'I knew you would hate me for

leaving you at the IMI, but I can't and won't apologise for doing what I thought was right.'

'Leaving me in the hands of the enemy?'

'No,' he argued. 'You know that when I tasted your blood I lost control. I wanted more but the only way to stop myself was to put distance between us.' He blurred across the mattress, grabbed my shoulders and shook me as if I were in a trance. 'I told you when we met that your blood called to me, told you that if I ever tasted you, I wouldn't be able to stop.'

'But you did.'

William let go of me, growling. 'Barely.'

'If you'd stayed, just waited to talk to me, maybe things would be different. So much has happened.' I stopped myself before bitterness leeched into every word leaving my mouth.

'Elena you know that—'

'I read your letter,' I said. 'That lame-ass apology circled my head for weeks. I know you think you were being noble and protecting me, but you still abandoned me. We exchanged blood, I was forever changed, and I'll say it again, you *abandoned* me to the whims of mad scientists.'

'Elena, I might have killed you if I stayed. Your blood is—'

'I know what my blood is!' I snapped.

William sighed, a sound I sorely longed to smack right out of him. 'Look, the only reason I stopped was because you—'

'But you did stop.' I was all for interrupting sorry excuses. 'You even had time to write me a bullshit apology letter.'

'Elena, you know it's more complicated than that.'

'Did you ever really care about me?' I immediately regretted the words. I was lashing out, driven by months of speculation and bitterness.

I gasped as William dragged me against his chest and squeezed inhumanly tight. 'You have no idea what you mean to me, do you? I could tell you I love you but you would still doubt my sincerity. Yes, I've made mistakes but all I've ever tried to do is protect you … from everyone.'

I wanted nothing more than to forgive and forget, but the months apart had left me deconstructing William's intentions. Meeting had probably been a coincidence, but had keeping me from Lucius been purposeful? William was a former member of the Roman Guard, the enforcing group of Vampires from centuries past. William knew Lucius and, I suspect, had kept me from meeting him. There were too many coincidences to ignore.

'I don't think you realise what you've done, the mess you left behind.' I placed even more space between us, hurriedly climbing to my feet. I wiped an unexpected trail of tears from my cheeks and began to pace.

'Tell me.'

'You really want to hear that John's assault was nothing compared to what The Protectors put me through? You want to know that I was experimented on, starved and left to fend for myself after they just let Roshan in? My God, William, the things he would've done to me if—'

William was suddenly there again, strong arms enveloping me, his soft lips caressing the skin of my temples. 'Elena, I'm so sorry. I didn't realise. I thought you would be safe at the IMI.'

I couldn't breathe. I couldn't think. 'Stop touching me,' I cried, untangling his arms, tears now falling unbidden.

'Elena …'

'I just can't, William. I'm not the same girl you met back in Cairns and I won't be ever again.' I tried to ward him off as he advanced. I didn't need or want his pity.

'Please, Elena, talk to me. Tell me what happened.'

'Details won't change anything.'

'I know that,' he said gently, giving up the chase to sit back down on the edge of the mattress. 'I just need to know. I never imagined that I'd somehow endangered you.'

My wounded gaze softened. It wasn't his fault that Chester was a monster. It wasn't his fault that Vânǎtors wanted to sink their claws into me and it wasn't his fault that I was stuck here with Roshan now. The only thing William was actually guilty of was caring a little too much. Oh, and the niggling doubt that he'd kept my family's identity a secret.

As if I needed more shit on my plate, a ripper of a cramp twisted my insides with renewed vigour. Moaning didn't even begin to make me feel better, not even curling up on the floor into a ball. It was William's blood that still called to me, a promise of gratification I would hopefully abstain.

'What's wrong?' William said. His whole body twitched. Was he debating the pros and cons of consoling me? My face must have said it all. He stayed where he was, the outstretched hand recoiling.

I licked my parched lips, grateful he'd kept his distance. 'I'm thirsty.'

William was quiet for the longest time. 'This is because we exchanged blood, isn't it?'

I nodded. 'Like I said, I'm not the same girl you once knew, William.'

'Do you think that changes how I feel about you?'

'I think it should.'

'Well it doesn't. Months may have passed but it's still only your face I see.'

I cradled my stomach and concentrated on ignoring the scent of his blood … and confessions of love. 'But you don't know who I am anymore.'

William once again disregarded my personal space,

appeared before me, and tilted my chin until our eyes met. 'What are you really trying to say, Elena?'

'The obvious truth. You hate being a Vampire where I embrace it. You left because your conscience hit you hard and now I can't trust you.'

William's grip tightened to the point of pain. 'So, what you're telling me is that I'm disposable?'

'No, what I'm saying is that there's no trust. You decided what was best for both of us and didn't care what I thought.'

William let go of my chin, collapsing on the floor beside me. 'Do you want me to feel guiltier than I already am?'

'It's not about guilt. It's about the choices you've robbed me of.'

'Look,' William snapped, 'I'm sorry that my choices that have led you to this point. Just thinking about the possibility of that Alpha touching you …' William balled his hands into fists until the knuckles were white with tension. 'Has he touched you?'

'He wants me to be his mate.'

'Your body …' he whispered, eyes haunted as they scanned the length of me. 'Is it still yours? Or have you succumbed to his will?'

That was irrelevant and frankly too painful to discuss. 'Why are you even here?' I retorted, needing answers of my own.

'Just answer the question, Elena.'

'It doesn't matter. What matters to me now is …'

I stopped protesting. William's clenched fists and rigidly set shoulders illustrated just how wound up he was about my predicament. Perhaps guilt fed his anger and curiosity. The stubborn set of his chin and the tightness of his lips certainly emphasised his ire and pressed for explanation.

I sighed. Elaborating was sure to be a mistake. 'Roshan enjoys my blood.'

William took a while to answer, the tendons in his neck pulsing. Yep. His brain was heading into nightmarish overdrive. 'He feeds off you?'

'Yes.'

'In exchange for what?'

'My dignity.'

William leapt to his feet and ran for the steel door, curving his broad shoulders at the last moment and ploughing the immovable surface. When that didn't work, he pounded those clenched fists against the steel and cursed our captor. Didn't he think I might have tried that already?

'I've done more harm than good,' I heard him mutter. 'Now, because of me, you've been taken and fight constantly for your survival.'

'William, just stop it, okay? It hasn't been all bad since you left, only the last two weeks and this,' I said, gesturing to the basement, 'was my fault.'

He gave up on peppering the door with pointless punches and turned to face me. I could see the wheels turning, a million thoughts racing through his head again. 'Only two weeks?'

I rolled into a sitting position, still clutching my stomach. I nodded relieved I'd been given momentary reprieve from the pain.

'And before that?' William asked, now pacing as if his legs depended on the continual movement. 'Were you with the IMI?'

'Not for long.'

'So you escaped?'

'I had help.'

That seemed to bother him more. In fact, I was certain he was wearing the enamel on his teeth down as he gnashed them together. 'He … right … along.' William spoke under his breath, barely audible. 'He said ... months he's been ... I never should have left.'

'What? I can't really hear you, William.'

'Greedy, self-indulgent, murderous Vampires!' he shouted. William pounded away at the door again. Clearly he had his own ideas about how I escaped. I suspected we might finally be operating on the same wavelength.

'You do know,' I whispered, 'back at the IMI, you claimed to be protecting me from other vampires but failed to mention their significance. You knew all along they would come for me.'

'Don't say it,' he muttered. 'Please don't say it.'

'You should have told me about my father, William.'

He recoiled as if I'd slapped him. He looked like he wanted to defend his actions but in the end he knew he'd cheated me and there was nothing he could say to fix what was broken — although, he definitely tried. 'No one should have a father that cruel,' he said.

At least it wasn't another lame-ass apology but I was still hopping mad. Keeping me from my father because of William's personal history was brutal and probably unforgiveable. 'How could you, William? You knew I wanted to meet my father, knew that my relationship with Susan and George wasn't peachy. You had so many opportunities to tell me about Lucius and yet you didn't!'

'I was protecting you.' That statement had become his subscription to bullshit and I was sick of hearing it.

'Enough!'

'But, Elena, you don't understand ...'

I was on my feet pretty fast considering the debilitating cramps that plagued me. I stumbled, clutched my riotous stomach, and finally launched at William. My palm soon smarted, the fingers throbbing where I'd slapped him ... hard.

William reeled, a trickle of blood escaping his nose. He looked horrified as he touched his face, confirming the sting of my retribution. I couldn't believe I'd actually hit him.

'I did it for you, Elena. You don't know Lucius the way that I do. He's done things that would make your skin crawl.'

I was still gazing at my hand like it was a foreign object. 'You had no right,' I answered absently.

William attempted to hold me, and I almost let him, before I snapped out of my trance and darted away. He sighed, grabbing at air. 'Try to understand how much I love you and what lengths I'd go to in order to see you safe.'

'You keep saying that like it's your place to make decisions for me and it's not.'

'I know that.'

'Well obviously you don't!' I yelled, my anger peaking. 'Lucius is kind and decent, devoted to me in a way that George never was. Despite what you personally think, he's my father and you've stuffed up.'

I lunged and slapped him again, the hard angles of his jaw searing heat across my flesh. 'I *hate* you for keeping us apart.' I was honestly surprised by the amount of venom in my voice, and even more surprised that it just kept on coming. 'If it weren't for you, I would have met Lucius months ago. I never would have met John, never encountered Roshan and never have been hurt by the IMI and your desertion.'

Gee, I guess I *was* blaming him for everything.

I lunged and slapped him repeatedly, the hard angles of his jaw searing heat across my palm. William imprisoned me in his embrace and dragged me back to the mattress. I shrieked at the unexpected contact and fought for him to release me. He did let go of my hands, but by then I was wrapped in his arms, trapped against his chest.

'Let me go!' I screamed, snapping canines inches from his face.

William didn't respond, not even as I tried pounding his chest and cursing him with every profanity that came to mind. Excessive? Probably. But in that moment his feelings were irrelevant. I'd been tortured, now it was his turn.

I don't know how long I struggled in his arms or how long I cursed his name, but weariness finally took hold. I sagged in his arms, milked by anger and defeated by futility. 'I hate you,' I spluttered, tears once again falling unbidden.

'And I *love* you,' William murmured, stroking my hair in a vain attempt to smooth away the betrayal.

Damn him. My damp cheeks were suddenly flooded with a barrage of fresh tears. I tried to make it stop, annoyed I had no control. I cried for the family I'd thought once loved me. I cried for Lucas's absence and the events following William's betrayal. I cried for the time lost with my father and for what could have been in so many ways.

'I hate you,' I repeated as I tried to convince myself of that half-truth.

William's arms tightened around me, his lips gentle against my flushed skin. 'I know.'

He wasn't supposed to love me. It was frankly unwanted and too much to handle for an emotional cripple like me. I was angry and wanted to stay that way. He certainly wasn't supposed to accept my current loathing with calm tolerance. 'I'll never forgive you for this.'

'I know, Elena.'

'I hate you.' I really needed to make that clear but he just wasn't biting. I wanted him to lash out, to fight me, scream at me — anything. I wanted a justifiable reason to keep hurting him the way he'd hurt me.

But all he said was, 'Of course.' Calm acceptance in the

face of my burning hatred. I think I detested him more and more, or perhaps that was me. The line between the wrong and right of our past and current actions was blurring.

After that, words became a distant thought. William continued to hold me while I cried against his cool, unyielding chest. There were a million reasons to embrace this never ending resentment, but a part of me hoped the indignation would pass and I would finally see clearly again.

I had no idea how much time had passed when I next woke up, but it was almost a pleasant surprise to find William's emerald eyes watching me rather than Roshan's amber ones — almost.

I blinked, rubbed at my swollen and undoubtedly blood-shot eyes and tried to pay no attention to my pressing hunger or cramping stomach. I gave myself maybe half an hour before I was whinging about it again.

'How are you feeling?' William asked. His sweet breath blowing cool against the heated flesh of my face bugged me. I mean, surely his question was rhetorical?

'How do you think I feel?' I muttered, probably frowning. I wasn't sure anymore. William's arrival and last night's conversation had almost certainly etched a permanent scowl upon my face.

'I see.'

'I trusted you and you betrayed me.' I had a feeling we were about to start pulling punches for round two.

'I make no apologies for loving you and protecting you in the best way that I know how. I just assumed Lucius would disregard you as easily as he disregarded human life in the past.'

'He's obviously not the same person that you once knew, William. Time changes everyone.'

He looked unconvinced but at least he didn't argue. I really wasn't in the mood to keep flogging a dead horse. A change of subject was in order, one I'd wanted to address last night.

'So are you ready to tell me why you're here?'

William's fingers played through his hair in an attempt to tidy the mussed strands. He failed miserably. 'I was captured.'

'Care to elaborate, Captain Obvious?' I probably deserved the glare he shot me.

'I've been hunting this pack for weeks,' William continued, voice gruff. 'When I last saw you in Bucharest, it was apparent Roshan wouldn't stop hunting you, so I decided to focus my energy into locating his den and hopefully destroy it.'

'How's that working out for you?' I said, rolling onto my back. Susan used to say that sarcasm was the lowest form of wit. Lucky she wasn't present to hear me now.

William wasn't overly impressed by my tone either. 'Yes, Elena, I'm aware that I've been captured by the enemy.'

'And to think you probably wouldn't have been captured if you'd made different choices.'

I could feel his narrowed eyes upon me. 'Oh yes? And since we've known each other, how many times have you been imprisoned against your will, Elena?'

My nostrils flared. It was three, okay, three, and a sore topic since I was still raw about his involvement. 'Well, if it weren't for your idiotic hoarding of need-to-know information, all of the imprisonments you're referring to could've been prevented!'

'Of course,' William grunted, 'I knew this would all be my fault.'

I turned to rake him with a vicious glare. He was being such a douche. 'Look, we need to stop baiting each other. What's done is done and I don't regret my choices and clearly you don't regret yours.' *Even though you should.* 'I just wish there was something I could do about this predicament we're in.' I gestured to the basement at large. 'Getting out of here is hopeless.'

'That's a defeatist attitude,' William mocked. 'The Elena I know and love would never lie down and take abuse.'

I rolled my eyes. 'Stop presuming to know me. Do you honestly think I've been sitting here twiddling my thumbs? Many times I've tried to escape but it's not that simple.' I pointed towards the door. 'That's steel, ergo impenetrable. The walls and floor are made of solid concrete, and last time I checked, I couldn't dig my way out. Then, in the basement beyond this one, is a full pack of ravenous wolves hungry for blood and flesh.'

'I get it, Elena.'

I shook my head. 'No, I don't think you do. Now the Alpha, who you've met, has complete control over me. His compulsion literally kicks my ass into submission, thus making it impossible, I repeat, impossible for me to escape.'

'And?' William probed. 'I'm sure you have something else you'd like to add. You always do.'

Grrr. What a smartass. 'No. I'm just sitting tight until Lucius comes for me.'

William erupted with mocking laughter. 'I wish you the very best of luck with that.'

'Really? You're going there again?' I rolled onto my side and propped myself up on one elbow. The action brought us close, our faces only inches apart. I suppose I shouldn't have been surprised when my heart skipped wildly in my chest or that the sight of him stole my breath. Why wasn't being annoyed at him enough to crush the attraction I felt?

He probably knew it, too, the smug bastard. Those lush, smiling lips begged to be tasted, and those thick, dark lashes framing his ever-distracting eyes instilled lust. If I'd been asleep, I'd have disregarded our grievances by now, torn off my clothes and taken him. Lucky I was awake and perhaps slightly saner.

William's mind appeared to be running on a similar tangent. Five seconds ago we'd been taunting and scowling at one another. Now we couldn't seem to take our eyes off each other, the memories of our previous trysts coming to the fore.

I forced myself to look away, focusing on the concrete wall behind him instead.

I hate him. Try to remember that.

'I think we need to try and figure out a way to get out of here as soon as possible,' William said, now picking at the tattered fabric of the mattress with his fingers. 'I can sense your bloodlust rising and I don't think either of us wants to be around when it takes over.'

'I will control my urges, William.'

All urges.

He was quiet for a moment. 'If we can't get out of this soon, Elena, we'll need to think of options.'

'Such as?'

'You're not going to like it.'

'I haven't liked most of the things you've said in the last few hours.'

William's pained expression and the deep breath that preceded his 'bright' idea made me shelve my sarcasm. 'I want you to feed from me before you lose all control.' He placed his fingers over my lips before I could protest. 'Elena,

I won't be able to reason with you if full bloodlust kicks in. Remember when I first arrived? You didn't care who or what I was, you were going in for the kill regardless.'

I peeled his fingers from my lips, determined to have my say. 'And what happens when you get thirsty?'

'I'll be fine for a couple of days.'

Laughter exploded from my mouth as I collapsed back against the mattress. I couldn't wrap my head around his logic or the hypocrisy. 'You do realise that you're suggesting the very thing that got us into trouble in the first place?'

His frown was swift in its appearance. 'I won't take your blood ever again, Elena. That's a promise.'

Oh my, God. The urge to dish out sarcasm like Sunday night dinner was almost impossible to resist. 'That's never going to work. Eventually you'll get hungry, too, and if you're refusing to take my blood, what exactly is it that you'll take from me this time? Because honestly, I've got nothing left to give, William.'

He regarded me in stony silence, knifed again by one of my caustic remarks. At least, that's what I thought until his eyes settled on my mouth again. He licked his lips; the supple, pink surface now glistened with his essence. I knew what was coming and yet I did nothing to stop it.

My smile faded and William was suddenly there, curling his arm around my waist and pulling me against him. I was held captive by his emerald gaze, pinned by the emotion I saw there, compelled to remember what we once were. 'William I—'

'Hush,' he said, his lips grazing mine. 'You asked me what I want. Now I'm going to show you.'

Yeah. That should have been the moment I screamed out, *Stop, this is a really bad idea!*, but I didn't. I let William's fingers hunt through the ringlets at my neck, press his lips to mine and entangle our limbs. I was a victim of my own desire, wanton lust I'd stupidly believed extinguished after his betrayal.

Apparently not.

The possession was slow and sweet, but I ached for more. So soft were his lips and gentle were his hands. I longed to be ravaged, taken with the fierce need that urged my moans and pressed my pelvis against his swollen desire. I was on fire and wanting, but just as quickly, I was subdued by thoughts of Sebastian. Did I feel guilty for this indulgence?

William soon made me forget, rolling until he was nestled between my legs. His tongue delved deep, stroking, teasing and intent on making my toes curl.

My response was all animal. I clawed at his back and wrapped my legs around him. The need I suddenly felt was so intense that I lost control. My canines erupted and the taste of blood flooded my thoughts, trampling hormonal whims and common sense.

William, equally affected, thankfully came up for air. Ebony eyes and matching fangs looked back at me. We were a disaster waiting to happen.

He'd captured the hand I'd tried ramming between us. My intent was to push him away before all hell broke loose. Honestly, he looked like a juicy steak sandwich right now and the last thing I needed was continued contact.

'Don't fight what's between us,' William said, stroking my lower lip with his thumb. 'I know that I've hurt you, but I can't stand the thought of never being with you, never touching you again.'

What was he on about? Couldn't he see that I was doing my upmost not to rip out his jugular?

I attempted to roll away. It was easier to remove myself from the situation than it was to pretend I wasn't dangerous.

Unfortunately, William had other ideas. 'Did you hear me, Elena?'

I gave up trying to budge the slab of concrete nestled between my legs. Instead, I closed my eyes and imagined William's blood tasting like cow shit covered in maggots. That seemed to do the trick.

'Elena!'

I opened my eyes again only to find William glowering at me.

'Look,' I started, taking a few calming breaths. 'I'm sorry I just let that happen between us. I didn't mean to lead you on but you must know that I can't be with you, William, not now, not after everything.'

'Your actions beg to differ.'

Right. I'm a wanton hussy. Got it.

'William, there's no denying I'm attracted to you.' That weird, creeping tendril of guilt made a quick reappearance, twisting my insides as an image of Sebastian's face clouded my thoughts. Gah. I didn't need this right now. 'The bottom line is that you hurt me and I can't trust you anymore.'

'But what we had …'

'Was great,' I confirmed, watching his face crumple. 'I never said we weren't compatible, but I did make it clear when we met that it was just for fun and that I don't feel things the same way you do. I don't think I'm built for the great love found in romance novels.'

'That's ridiculous.'

Maybe, but I'd yet to feel what others described as an earth-shattering connection that stops the heart and transforms the soul. A part of me relished the safety in rejection. The idea of loving someone so completely that it caused physical pain to be separated? That was a weakness I simply couldn't partake.

When I tried to roll away again, William allowed it. I could only imagine what he was thinking, what my brush off must have felt like. 'I'm sorry, William,' I whispered, guilt gnawing at my insides. What else could I say?

'I understand,' he muttered, rolling onto his back. It didn't sound like it. 'I guess it just surprises me how quickly you moved on.'

'What do you mean?'

He cradled his hands behind his head, staring up at the ceiling. 'Well, there has to be someone else. Anger and betrayal aside, why else would you bench me if you didn't already have another player on the field?'

'Now just hang on a minute,' I chided, raising an indignant finger. 'You're jumping to some rather rash conclusions.'

'I know he must have gotten inside your head.'

'Who?'

'Tall, dark and handsome ...'

Great, so he was referring to half the population. 'Now *you're* being ridiculous.'

'Fighting for you is not ridiculous to me.'

Cue unbearable pain ...

I was suddenly taken down by a home-grown enemy, blindsided by the burning assault of renewed hunger. I bit down on my fist to stop myself from crying out, but fire tore through my insides like a wild beast and I was wailing for mercy in no time.

'It's okay,' William cooed as he wrapped me in his arms. 'Feed from me, Elena. You have to.'

'Please shut up,' I gasped, closing my eyes. 'I need to think.'

'Don't think about it, just drink. You'll feel better once you do.'

'I don't want to. I can't weaken us both.'

William tucked the greasy strands of my hair behind my ears. 'You can't hold out like this. You're making yourself sick.'

'I know that but we can't feed off each other. You'll end up turning me completely … or killing me.'

He nodded, perhaps finally conceding my point. William remained quiet as he rocked me in his arms. He pulled me close when I started to shake uncontrollably. 'Stay with me,' he murmured, calmer than I would've been under the circumstances.

'I'm here. Keep talking to me.'

'Okay.' He licked his lips. 'Have you thought about why the Alpha has put us together? He must know we have some sort of relationship.'

There was that innuendo again. 'Isn't it obvious?'

'What?'

'It's my punishment for not becoming pack. He knows that I'm starving and will eventually fall victim to my bloodlust.'

William snorted; the faint trace of humour now marked his lips. 'I'm always going to be a little stronger than you, Elena. I wouldn't be an easy kill.'

'I could take you,' I joked, elated to feel the cramping pass and levity between us return.

He looked doubtful. 'Perhaps.'

The lock on the steel door turned and William's hand stilled in my hair. I shoved him away, praying that he didn't opt to do anything rash. 'Stay behind me,' I ordered, certain he was rolling his eyes at my back.

Roshan and his wolves slipped into the room like shadows in the afternoon sun. They quickly covered the perimeter, fanged sentinels blocking our escape. As if we'd even try when the odds were clearly not in our favour.

'Come to me, Elena,' Roshan beckoned, hand out-stretched.

William snapped vice-like fingers around my wrist, holding me back. 'Don't do it.'

I shook him off, knowing that now was not the time to wage war. 'Just be quiet and stay still,' I urged.

Roshan smirked. 'You better listen to what she says, Vampire, or trust me, I'll make sure *you* regret it.'

My reaction was immediate and necessary. I knew that William would throw a fit and try to take on Roshan, so I blocked him telekinetically. He wasn't happy about ploughing face first into the shimmery surface. Only William was ballsy enough to launch an attack in a room filled with Vânători.

Stupid Vampire.

'That's my girl,' Roshan said as he swept me into his embrace.

'I'm not your girl and I'm definitely not doing it for your benefit,' I scolded, watching William as he studied us from behind my barrier.

Roshan laughed. 'You'll be mine when you realise what you are and give yourself over to the darker nature within.'

I scoffed, disgusted. 'I'm never going to be your *anything.*'

'Shall the puppeteer start pulling on your strings?' I could already feel his essence suffusing the air between us. 'Should I make you do something really dark to prove my dominance?'

'I won't do it,' I whispered, staying perfectly still. Roshan touched his tongue to the soft flesh behind my ear. 'I would rather starve than kill him.'

'Oh, I think you will kill him,' he murmured, tilting my head back, 'because you're going to be very, very thirsty after this.'

I cried out as Roshan sank his fangs into the exposed flesh of my neck, sucking greedily at the vital fluids that seeped from the ragged, gaping wound.

The wolves collectively howled, sent into frenzy by the smell of my blood. They circled the shrinking barrier like hungry vultures, knowing that William would soon be defenceless. The others scratched and barked at Roshan's feet, perhaps hoping for a piece of his leftovers — a piece of me.

I started to convulse. My tongue was thick and heavy in my mouth. I couldn't swallow and I could barely breathe. My eyes drooped and I had precious moments before I lost all consciousness — my barrier collapsing. I just prayed that William was smart enough to know when he was severely outnumbered.

My heartbeat slowed, the once fitful pounding now sluggish and uneven. Roshan was literally sucking the life right out of me and there was nothing I could do about it.

Anger pulsed within like a steadily beating drum, building momentum and somehow nullifying all other thoughts and feelings. It soon became an emotion so thick with purpose that all I could see was red. My objective? Killing Roshan and any other obstacle to freedom.

I hung onto that. Anger and vengeance were better focuses than pain. It didn't matter that my knees gave way and my legs folded underneath me. It didn't matter that Roshan continued to suck life from my flesh to coat his gluttonous lips. I would not be a victim any more.

I could smell fear, mine or others I didn't know. Howls of torment rented the air and suddenly it was a symphony of my aggressor's pain. Anger surged in waves and the certainty of my mind wavered. The barrier may have fallen, and William may have rushed to my defence but I didn't care either way.

Blood ran in thick rivulets, tangible on a tongue that was as dry as a desert's crust. Pain had a new sound, the succinct gurgle of a wolf drowning in its own fluids. Fangs raked flesh and talons tore limb from limb. The fantasy was almost complete, my Vânător half teased with desires of the dark side and rewarded by the cries of inflicted agony.

Contentment seemed to brush aside the blazing hatred. All riotous emotion was quietened with thoughts of fulfilment and embracing my Vânător nature. In this waking dream I didn't care for logic, only revenge.

Perhaps I was a killer after all? Dream or not, I was completely okay with being the sole survivor in the aftermath of chaos.

CHAPTER SEVEN
Bloodlust

Thick, coarse fur matted with dried blood clung to my sticky fingers. As I raked the tactile surface, catching hardened globules beneath my nails, I knew that something wasn't right. There was no movement beneath my touch; no breath, no twitching muscles, no flutter of life.

I reluctantly opened my eyes. Blood covered every inch of me.

I drew my legs up to my chest and wrapped my arms around my knees, surveying the bodies around me … massacred.

What happened? Why am I naked?

It seemed surreal, the aftermath of a terrifying dream, one that I had no conscious memory of. But despite being naked, alone and covered in blood, I was also strangely sated — no more pain, no more thirst and an abundance of energy.

The last thing I could recall was Roshan's touch, his fingers on my skin and his body pressed against mine. I remembered his fangs, too, buried in my neck.

Howling still echoed in my ears but it was joined by the sounds of struggle and gasping breath. To a certain degree I remembered William attempting to defend my honour, or some such bullshit, but I couldn't recall the rest.

I began to shake. Even the inside of my mouth was teaming with the aftertaste of arterial spray. Had I fed? When?

Why can't I remember?

I eyed the dead wolves around me. There were at least thirty, piled up like dirty dishes. Beside me was one covered in the gore of its own lacerated jugular, its black eyes wide and forever frozen in fear. The rest? Much the same, thick, meaty tongues lolling to the side, their furred bodies ripped apart and discarded like stinking piles of waste.

Blood.

I couldn't wash my eyes clean of the sight. It was everywhere, the room painted with its vibrancy. Red rivulets coated the walls and splattered the ceiling. A horror movie it surely should have been. How could the killer have not seen me? Why did they leave me unscathed if they had?

Oh my God, William …

I scanned the debris of fur and flesh but couldn't see him, uncertain if that was a good or a bad sign. Fear kept me rooted to the spot while my guilt fed slowly on the possibility of his demise. Some of my last words were that I hated him and now I didn't know if I'd ever get the chance to take it back.

Oh, God. If something has happened to him …

A choked sob escaped my lips and echoed around the lifeless room. Hesitantly, I called out his name.

No answer.

I started sniffing instead, desperately hoping that William's rich scent would call to me, but the sweet tang of blood and the oppressive stench of death were all I found.

I rose on unsteady feet, clawing at the walls for support. My knees could barely hold me as sickness roiled within. All I could see was the slaughtered wolves, executed by a creature that had taken great pleasure in raining terror.

Swallowing back bile, I took a moment to calm myself and gather my thoughts. I was relieved to be alive, but at what cost? I was already touching my stomach, waiting with baited breath for signs of movement, terrified I'd been violated.

Several silent minutes passed. If Roshan had impregnated me, there was an excellent chance I would already feel growth. It took less than three days to birth a Vânător pup and God only knew how long I'd already been out.

Nothing.

The sweet relief was like a swift punch to the abdomen. I bent over and sucked in air, three seconds away from a full-blown panic attack. I'd come so close so many times and yet I'd escaped that grisly fate yet again. How? Why?

'William?'

Silence. Still silence.

I forced myself to move, trekking slowly through puddles of blood. Warmth oozed between my toes and spilled over the tops of my feet. It sucked and squelched with every step, so loud in the eerie silence surrounding me.

I crept towards the steel door, easy enough to slip through now that it was ajar.

Outside, more wolves crowded the corridor, heads torn from their shoulders and discarded in separate piles. There were some in human form, too, though equally brutalised and perhaps more confronting to see.

I followed the corridor and headed up the stairs, pressing my back against the cold concrete wall, inching towards what I hoped was freedom. In the upper level basement the view remained unchanging — piles of bodies and copious amounts of blood. There was no life here at all — no sign of William.

Please let him be okay.

The January air wracked my body, cold and uncompromising in its icy touch but I had to ignore it. 'William?'

Still no answer.

In the corner, I spied another small set of stairs winding up and probably out, so I darted in that direction. At the top was yet another steel door, half open with blood smeared across the handle. I slipped through the gap and into the teasing fresh air beyond.

An old factory greeted me, deserted and decidedly creepy. Sheets of rusted steel lined the walls and redundant machinery sat collecting dust on large workbenches. Wrought-iron fretwork crowded the floor and hung from the ceiling and under my feet metal filings clung to blood like a second skin.

Shivering profusely, I wrapped my arms around myself and looked for something to abate the bone-deep chill. I spied a tattered, filthy sheet hanging limply over equipment in the corner of the workshop. I was in no position to debate sanitation, so I stumbled towards it and snatched it up, coughing and spluttering as dust billowed and clung to my sticky flesh.

Gasping, I moved away from the attacking dust motes, certain they were following me, desperate to reclaim their home amongst the rotting fibres of the sheet.

I was suddenly screaming as an icy palm clamped upon my shoulder. Thankfully my feet were already in action, running for the exit, desperate to avoid becoming a victim to the bloodied massacre behind me.

'Elena, it's me!' William shouted, appearing in front of me.

I barrelled into him at breakneck speed, snapping back in a painful rebound and landing on my ass.

'Wow, are you okay?'

I lunged for the sheet and pulled it hastily up to my chin,

modesty clearly my first thought. I didn't even see his blood-slicked body kneel in front of me or comprehend why I was screaming when he touched me again.

'Don't be afraid. It's me, Elena.'

I stopped and reassessed. It was definitely William, though not the dreamy version. His clothes were torn; his T-shirt clung in scraps and his jeans barely hung onto his slender hips. And blood. There was so much blood on him.

'Elena? Can you hear me? It's William. I won't hurt you.'

I patted the hand that grasped my shoulder, reassured that he really was okay. 'I can hear you,' I rasped. 'I thought you were dead.'

'No. Not dead.'

'What happened? I woke up to bodies and blood everywhere.'

William's hand slipped from my shoulder to cradle my chin. He tilted my face from side to side, examining me. It wasn't concern I saw in his shifting eyes; it was caution.

'William, what's going on?' I said, slapping his hand away.

'It's you,' he whispered, seemingly relieved. He leant forward and kissed the top of my head. 'I can't believe what just happened.'

'Tell me,' I pressed, clutching the sheet tighter around me, the cold provoking yet another shudder.

'Let me take you away from here first.'

'Are we in any immediate danger?'

He was looking at me with that wary expression again. 'I don't believe so.'

'Then I want to know why there are dead Vânătors everywhere and why I'm naked and covered in blood.'

'It might be hard to explain, or rather, hard to hear.'

'I can take it.' It was true. I was a tough bitch, a tough bitch with hot tears threatening to spill down her cheeks. 'I need to know, William. The worst part was waking up and thinking that you were dead, too.'

William laced his sticky fingers through mine. The blood squelched as our palms united. 'Do you remember anything at all?'

'Up until a point. I think Roshan took too much blood, I must have passed out.'

William was pensive, opening his mouth several times to speak but failing at the point of delivery. Could it really be that bad?

'W–what is it?'

'I'm sorry.'

'Okay ...'

'Elena, I'm sorry if my past actions have fuelled such a blinding rage inside of you.' He spat those words out like they burned his lips. I had absolutely no idea what he was talking about now.

'You killed them,' he elaborated, voice rising. 'You killed every last wolf in that den tonight.' He released my hand to wrap the sheet more tightly around my shoulders and abate the punishing assault of the frosty air. I was also at a loss for words.

What he'd suggested was madness. I *was* probably angry, but not freaking suicidal.

William responded to my head shaking with a simple, 'Yes.'

I didn't think there was anything simple about it. I knew exactly what carnage lay beyond the steel door and I knew I wasn't even remotely capable. 'H–how?' I stuttered, trying work out the logistics and failing.

William started to rub his hands up and down the sides of my arms, a pointless attempt at keeping me warm. It was about five degrees out and he was the walking dead. I needed a heater, not his stony embrace. 'We have to get you somewhere warm.'

'No. I n–need to understand w–what happened.'

William's eyes narrowed and he sighed. 'There's no easy way to say it.'

'So just s–say it.'

'Elena, I think—'

'Say it!'

'You turned into a Vânător,' he blurted. Just like that it was out his mouth like fire belched from a dragon. He couldn't take it back and I couldn't pretend I didn't hear it. I supposed that was why he kept tapping his fingers against his lips, all nerves, waiting for me to respond or flip out and kill some more people. I had no words. How could this have happened?

'I've never seen anything like it,' he continued, releasing his lips to brush a dirty hand through his matted hair. 'One minute you were in his arms, limp and lifeless, and in the next, you opened your eyes.'

I would have thought that was a good thing considering my apparent status as 'limp and lifeless', but judging by his dour expression it wasn't.

'Your eyes were pitch black,' William recounted. 'Like a Vampire or Vânător, it was clear something had shifted within you but no one really grasped the severity of that change until it was too late.'

'Why c–can't I r–remember any of this?'

He shrugged. 'I don't know, Elena.'

'What happened n–next?'

'You turned,' he answered, his eyes haunted. 'It was like you flipped a switch. In one breath it was you I saw, and in the next, you'd become this black wolf, big enough to rival Roshan. I've never seen a transition so smooth, so perfect, so ... deadly.'

Right. So that happened. Once again I was floored by the unexpected qualities of my mixed heritage. I knew eventually that my eyes would change, I'd grow fangs, sprout claws and possibly howl at the moon, but this? I'd actually turned into a full-blown werewolf, one that mutilated every living creature in the basement below.

'Elena? Are you okay?' William asked.

'No, I'm not okay. I'm cold, naked and s–suffering from memory l–loss.'

William's features softened, though wariness still rode the narrowed edges of his eyes. When he cupped my face it was tentative, his rough, dirty fingers shakily stroking my jaw. 'You had to have known that this was a possibility once you turned.'

'Honestly, I thought that p–perhaps the Vânător gene w–would make me a raging s–sex addict, not canine.'

'I suppose that would have been preferable,' William said, trying not to smile. 'Obviously our previous exchange awakened more than expected.'

'You think?' My sarcasm helped no one, but at least my burning self-loathing helped to abate that persistent chill in the air. 'Have you seen the m–mess down there? I'm like Jack the freaking dog-ripper. I p–piled bodies up like Lego and had no qualms about s–spilling their insides all over the floor.'

I closed my eyes in an effort to dispel thoughts of severed heads and torn flesh. It was a small blessing that I didn't recall the specifics of the blackout. What worried me now was the safety of others because I had no idea what triggered the change in the first place.

'You were angry and consumed by bloodlust,' William reminded me. 'Who could really blame you for doing what you did?'

I opened my eyes only to find a pity party staring back at me. 'Don't look at me like that. I know w–what I am and probably why I did it, I just n–never expected this manic level of d–destruction.'

'How could you possibly expect this?'

I was solemn while reflecting on the reason behind the blank spots during tonight's events and my deadly thoughts before I'd unravelled 'What really worries me is my apparent capacity to hate.'

'What do you mean?' William murmured, thrown by the deviation in topic. His forehead looked like my laundry pile — wrinkled.

I shrugged, uncertain if I could explain the fear and simultaneous rush of power that my urge to violence had produced. My morality had crumbled when faced with fierce opposition and I'd spiralled into a murderous rage. Continued resentment and burning hatred for Roshan couldn't be a healthy habit to maintain.

William didn't push for a response but he was definitely out of his depth. 'Look,' he finally said, 'I can see that you're shaken but your actions were based on a side you've never explored. Try not to be so hard on yourself for traits probably enmeshed in your DNA.'

I appreciated the sentiment but scoffed at the hypocrisy of it. 'This c–coming from the Vampire who ran away after tasting my blood? You c–can't even wrap your own stubborn head around your nature, let alone tell me to accept *this* m–massacre as a learning curve.'

William remained silent. Truth was often the harshest reality and the most difficult to accept. I think I'd made my point, though I had no intention of rubbing it in. His slumped shoulders and droopy lips made me feel guilty enough for calling him out.

'At least tell me I killed Roshan.'

'He's gone,' William murmured, still staring absently at the floor.

My sigh of relief sent a ripple of pleasure through my entire body. I definitely huffed and puffed and blew that bastard's house down. 'Well at least something went right tonight.'

'He's not dead, Elena.'

Of course not. That would be too simple. 'Then where is he?

William lifted his sombre gaze from the floor, fixing emerald eyes upon me. 'He ran the moment he realised his Alpha call was useless against your wolf.'

'That figures,' I sulked. 'He rules my human body but can't touch me when I finally do become his stupid pack mate.' It took me a moment to realise I'd missed something vital. 'What about you? You never did say how you got out.'

A wistful smile touched his lips. 'Oh, I ran like hell, too.' He continued to smile as he attempted to wipe the excess blood from my lips and eyes. Perhaps he needed to stay busy, keep his mind off other things. 'If it makes you feel better, you certainly roughed him up.'

'Did I hurt you?' I asked, fingering the shredded remains of his shirt.

'Just some broken bones and a lacerated abdomen.' He made it sound like he was ordering a salad, not listing his injuries.

The gaping hole in the centre of my face urged him to continue.

'I'm a born Vampire. I heal. Everything is okay now.'

Horseshit. I closed the distance between us and flung my arms around his neck, squeezing tight. Even after all the nasty words that had passed my lips, I'd never want to see

William hurt. 'I'm so sorry!' I sobbed against what remained of his collar. 'I would never consciously hurt you. I hope you know that. God, I'm so sorry, William, so very sorry.'

'That makes two of us,' he affirmed. 'I didn't mean to hurt you any more than you hurt me.' William made sure I could see his earnest expression and the intensity in his eyes.

I understood. We were even. He'd lied and abandoned me and I'd practically gutted him. How could we possibly hurt each other now?

'You d–didn't see where Roshan went, did you?'

'I wish I had but he disappeared right after you shredded his arm with your teeth and then I was otherwise … preoccupied.'

Fighting for your life, you mean?

I shivered, the winter chill really on a mission to break me down. Looking at the bluish hue of my goose-pimpled flesh, I also became aware that I still clung to William, naked, with only the sheet to protect my modesty.

I guess he must have realised it too because he cleared his throat and said, 'You must be freezing.' He averted his gaze, bundled me closer and wrapped the dirty sheet more securely around me. I felt like a sausage roll. 'Please let me take you away from here so you can get cleaned up and warm.'

'Deal.'

William rose, lifting me into his arms and against his chest. I wasn't about to argue that I could stand on my own two feet. I was shaking like Grandma Manory after too much bourbon and hot sauce.

'You know, you n–never did tell me why I'm n–naked,' I said, looking pointedly at the sheet.

William gave me the once-over as he headed for the factory exit. His cheeks hollowed, his teeth undoubtedly gnawing the tender flesh to avoid smirking. 'I think they might have been shredded during your shift.'

'I don't even have k–knickers,' I mumbled, stating the obvious. It bothered me that I could feel a draft. And, as I worked on crossing my legs in William's arms, inside the sheet burrito, I found it quite the challenge.

Meanwhile, William's face looked as if he'd sucked on a lemon. Containing his amusement was not working out quite so well. 'Is it really so bad?'

'You're kidding me, right? If I don't get warm soon there'll be frostbite on my nipples.'

Yes. Regrettably, I said that.

An uncontrollable burst of laughter sent William swooping down to my lips for a tender kiss. I responded out of habit myself, and allowed the gentle caress and taste of carelessness that followed.

'No,' William breathed against my lips, focusing back on getting us the hell out of there, 'it's definitely no hardship to see you naked.'

I'll bet.

'Don't worry, it won't happen again,' I said. Actually, I couldn't guarantee that.

I felt William's chest rumble with responsive laughter. 'Now *that* would be a terrible shame.'

Funny. He sounded just like Sebastian.

The enormous sable wolf launched through the wasted pile of the bloodied and dismembered pack. Long, saliva coated fangs gleamed in the darkness, quickly closing around Roshan's rapidly shifting arm as he tried to flee. Flesh tore and blood poured from the gaping wound as he attempted to shake her loose.

Panicked, Elena was quickly mobbed by the remanets of the pack and Roshan exploded from the scene like the coward he was, bursting through the exit and smearing blood all over the frigid, steel handle. Never in a million years could he have predicted this: the fall of his den and the rise of an Alpha female.

He clutched his ravaged arm against his chest and ran as quickly as he could, across the factory floor, and into the awaiting night. He needed to get as far away from this place as possible, regroup and figure out what his next move would be.

Roshan growled at the inconvenience of the injury. Shifting would only add to the pain, tearing ligaments and stressing bone. He needed shelter and time to think about how he could turn this situation to his advantage.

He pressed his battered frame against the disfigured walls of an old red-brick home, looked around and gauged the risk and potential for exposure. Roshan searched for hiding places as the pack's safe house was still in the next street over, being spotted the immediate issue.

His eyes drifted to windows absent of light and internal activity. It was late and most people slept soundly but the streetlights remained his enemy, unforgiving in their quest to reveal him.

Roshan ducked and weaved the persecuting ambience and waded through the hedges lining the footpath. He hadn't gone far before an unexpected scent gave him pause.

Sampling the heady aroma further, Roshan relaxed. It was another of his kin — not a member of his pack, but rather, an Alpha of equal standing.

Roshan's pace quickened. He shook off the foliage and

darted across the street. He rounded a corner, zipped across someone's front lawn and then leapt over the three foot gate marking the property.

Elias stepped free of the deeper porch shadows, his grim expression matching the gruff sound of his address. 'Roshan, what the hell is going on?'

Elias currently posed as a man in his late forties — greying hair, dull brown eyes and a body constructed of limp muscle and a plump mid-section. It baffled Roshan why the other Alphas chose to swap and change their human forms, especially when faced with such an unappealing specimen.

Roshan elbowed Elias out of the way, ignoring the question, eager to open the front door and get inside. The longer they stood idle, the more chance of exposure.

'The blood on you is Vânător, some of it your own,' Elias pressed as he crossed the threshold, watching wide-eyed as Roshan locked and bolted the door behind them.

'We were attacked,' Roshan finally answered, holding up his shredded arm for inspection. 'My den has been destroyed and I barely made it out with my life.'

Elias stumbled, clearly taken aback. The recent decimation of John's London pack was still fresh in all Alpha's thoughts and undoubtedly made hearing the news of another pack's demise less than comforting.

'Who?' Elias mouthed, his words chewed and swallowed down by shock, choked by an intermittent whisper. 'Who has done this to you?'

Roshan considered his options and chose his enemy based on impending plans and alliances. Mentioning Elena was not on the agenda, a secret prize he would keep to himself for now. 'Vampires.'

'Vampires?' Elias echoed, perhaps testing the idea on his

tongue. 'How did they locate your den? Have you not been covering your tracks?'

Despite Elias's urgent pleas for explanation, Roshan headed for the sparse kitchen, his bloodied arm prompting him to tend his wounds. The icy water from the rusted faucet stung like hell but was necessary to avoid infection. He hoped getting his hands on the serum would eventually negate the need for medical dressings and sickness — yet another secret he would keep hidden from his brethren for now.

Elias was hot on his heels. 'Roshan? I'd appreciate an answer.'

Cringing, Roshan turned off the tap and proceeded to wrap his still bleeding arm in a bandage he'd found in the cutlery drawer. 'I'm a little busy here, Elias, and yes, we do cover our tracks.'

'How many Vampires were there?'

'Too many to count.'

Elias trailed Roshan back to the run-down living room and settled down in one of the tatty, overstuffed chairs across from him. He tapped his chipped fingernails against the stubble of his chin.

'Look, all I know,' Roshan said, choosing his words carefully, 'is that we must continue with our earlier plans. Tonight's events only prove the necessity of them.'

'That's actually why I came to Paris. We've considered your suggestion of war and would ordinarily avoid such risky exposure but John's death has shaken many of us. He was hunted for three years by Vampires and finally defeated as you have been tonight. We cannot let them hunt us down one by one and destroy everything we have worked for.'

Roshan understood. Alphas were the only dependable breeders for the Vânător race, as pack mate efforts only bred stillborn cubs.

'Some of the other packs are already on the move,' Elias continued. 'Asia and the South Pacific have already abandoned their posts. The rest of us are moving in as we speak.'

'Good,' Roshan replied, surprised that his deception had wielded such quick results. 'Now more than ever we need to finish this. John was my friend. We shared a pack for many years.'

Elias stopped tapping his chin and twisted the nervous digits in front of him instead. God only knew the scattered thoughts that ran through his head.

It was almost as if Roshan could read that doubt twisting Elias's insides and felt it prudent to explain himself, in any lie possible. 'Besides wanting to claim retribution for the death of my entire pack, Vampires stop us from hunting freely and threaten the stability of our immortality via these attacks.'

That sounded good, didn't it?

'What about The Protectors? Since learning our weakness, we've been hunted more vigorously than ever.'

'The Protectors are the least of our concerns right now.'

'If you are that naive to think that they—'

'Elias,' Roshan interrupted, 'trust me when I say that The Protectors are not an issue at present.' He cradled his arm against his chest and snuggled back into the lumpy cushioning. It had been such a long, tiresome night.

Elias's eyes narrowed, his thin lips pursing. That confusion and suspicion he'd tried to dispel had begun to fight for equal rights upon his face. 'And why is that?'

Roshan took a deep, shuddering breath and ordered his heart rate to end its exuberant dance. There were some aspects of his plans that needed to be revealed in order to maintain trust and deflect true intent. 'The Protectors are not an issue because I have entered into an alliance with them on behalf of all our packs.'

Snarling, Elias now exposed decayed, human teeth and rapidly erupting fangs. Those nervous fingers had left his lap and sought the arms of his chair, chipped nails digging into the fibres and spewing stuffing all over the floor 'You had no right to do that, Roshan!'

'Agreed, but if you'll let me explain the results of such an accord, I'm sure you will agree that the positives far outweigh the negatives.'

Elias reluctantly lowered his pencil-thin lips over the infected gums and rotting teeth. His canines withdrew and his biting fingers relaxed their death-grip on the dust-ridden chair. His expression remained unchanging, his dull brown eyes shifting anxiously over Roshan's face. 'Explain.'

Another deep breath was drawn upon before the hastily constructed charade Roshan was selling spilled from his mouth in a jet of seemingly plausible lies. 'The deal I've made with The Protectors serves the needs of all our packs. At present, we are under constant attack from the Vampires, John's death and tonight's attack on my den irrefutable proof. Yes, I did ask for the pack's help in starting this war based on personal revenge but now it's also largely in aid of The Protectors' help.'

'What?' The outrage collected and congealed behind Elias's ruddy cheeks. Roshan could see hurried thoughts crossing Elias's wild features, perhaps itemising every decision and coming up empty-handed.

Roshan waved off the building animosity, certain an explanation would cool the heels of his wolf brother. 'I am under no illusion that The Protectors see us as equal or anything other than an enemy. But right now they are in a position of great power and they have something we need. They only ask for what our own packs seek as compensation: the death of all Vampires.'

Before Elias could speak, Roshan continued. 'You're wondering what we have to gain from this arrangement, what The Protectors have that we seek. Believe me when I say that the serum they offer has the ability to convert any being into that of a Vampire.'

Elias looked positively outraged, growling so vigorously that the folds of fat under his chin vibrated. Roshan could see that Elias was nowhere near convinced that negotiating such an elusive prize justified alignment with an enemy.

'This serum,' Roshan pressed, trying to persuade Elias of the positives, 'will match us in strength and stamina with the Vampires and above all else, complete our immortality. I'm talking about healing from any and all injuries, Elias. Not to mention that our offspring may actually have the opportunity to breed effectively, rather than leaving the repopulation of our species entirely on our shoulders.'

Elias sat silent and stiff for several minutes, his ragged breath hitching his shoulders heavenward. He remained unconvinced but certainly curious, mostly due to Roshan's infectious excitement. 'So,' he started to say, his voice still coarse with anger, 'what you're telling me is that this … serum … could be a cure for our weaknesses?'

Roshan nodded vigorously. 'And I have secured a way to get our hands on it, which is why it's important we follow through with our plans.'

'It all seems circumstantial,' Elias muttered, shaking his head. 'To believe in invincibility is an impossible dream we shouldn't place willingly in The Protectors' hands.'

'But since our goals our currently matched, what harm does playing along do? We always intended to destroy the Vampires. Now we have the incentive to hasten our bolt to the finish line.'

Elias didn't look convinced. 'I feel you've been rash and

a little naive, Roshan. Do you truly believe that all they ask in return for this serum is Vampire extinction?' Cynicism dripped from every word spoken.

Roshan licked his lips at the mere thought of sweet Vampire blood coating his tongue. 'I believe in nothing but the result of our own motivation. I will enjoy the hunt of all Vampires, but should The Protector's uphold their end of the arrangement, then I shall enjoy those benefits too.'

'And if The Protectors don't uphold their end of the bargain?'

'Do you take me for a fool, Elias? The Protectors have been perfecting ways to hunt and kill us for three hundred years. I am more than aware that they will not uphold their end of the arrangement. I suspect that they are merely using us to do their dirty work.'

Elias's pessimism tipped to a new level of uncertainty. 'Then why did you agree to the alliance?'

'I want the serum, and an alliance at least offers a temporary cease fire. Dealing with the Vampires will be trying enough.'

'How do you even know that the serum works?'

'I saw the results for myself.'

Silence gathered in the space between them, Elias taking what looked to be an uncomfortable gulp. He rocked forward in the chair, elbows now balanced on the edges of his knees. He craned his neck as if trying to hear better, his dark eyes alight with curiosity. 'What was it like? How did they prove the serum's worth?'

Roshan flexed his fingers and stretched until he winced, the pain in his arm radiating through every nerve bundle. 'A test subject known as "Beryx" aptly demonstrated the results.'

'Meaning?'

'He was fast, strong and his scent was strangely undetectable. I didn't see fangs, but I suppose that doesn't mean anything.'

'And healing?'

'A self-inflicted cut on his palm healed within seconds.' Roshan absently drew the design of the injury on his own palm.

'So, it works?' Elias probed, leaning so far forward that there was more of him out of the armchair than in it.

'It appears that way.'

'So, the test subject was human?'

Roshan shook his head. 'No. Protector.'

'Does he still maintain his magical abilities?'

'Yes.'

Elias broke into a smile, perhaps not convinced but certainly enticed by the possibilities of this genetic enhancement. 'Will it still be possible for us to stay Vânător after taking the serum?'

'I cannot say for sure.'

Elias bounded from the chair, folding his hands behind his back as he paced. 'I'm not sure what to say, Roshan.'

'Understandably.'

'I'm annoyed that you left us in the dark, but can't deny that your misguided efforts may prove invaluable. For now, I suggest we work on a way to get you safely out of the city where we can then reconvene with the other Alphas to discuss this matter in more detail.'

Roshan's thoughts shifted to Elena. Injured, he'd left distinct trails that she could easily follow, and if still in wolf form, still blinded by rage, then she might be tempted. Yes, leaving Paris was an excellent idea despite the designs he had on her.

'Can you shift?' Elias asked, gesturing to Roshan's injured

arm. He continued to pace, soon to wear a tidy trail in the sisal rug beneath his feet.

'It'll hurt like hell, I've been trying to avoid it, but I'm sure I could manage it if necessary.'

Elias nodded and urged Roshan to get on with it, already heading for the front door and opening the mouldy fixture to aid in their departure.

Although time was of the essence, Roshan dropped to his knees, taking a deep breath and easing into the shift despite the incessant throbbing radiating from his injured limb. Strangled barks and humanoid groans punctuated the crack of bone and wet sounds of reshaping muscle.

With Elias now in the grip of his own shift, Roshan could do little more than endure, his final, guttural howl a signal to the neighbourhood that something wasn't quite right in suburbia. Lights erupted in neighbouring windows and sounds of distress ensued.

They both left the building and Paris as quickly as their paws would carry them.

CHAPTER EIGHT
Brothers

'So, where are we again?' I said, nudging William with my elbow as I studied the front door of the small, rather quaint cottage in front of me. It was ripe with the smell of fresh paint and recently oiled timber; I was relieved to be free of the cloying scent of damp fur, freshly spilt blood and death. But as my gaze lingered on vines clinging artfully on trellises and the colourful flowers blooming inside the pretty white window boxes, I wondered why William would take me anywhere other than directly back to Lucius.

'It's a safe house,' William murmured as he stooped to retrieve a key hidden beneath one of the many flowerpots crowding the porch.

'Says who?'

The front door creaked as it swung open. 'Don't look so suspicious,' he said, slipping the key back in place. William gestured for me to enter. When I baulked, he rolled his eyes and took the lead, switching lights on as he went.

'Why didn't you take me to Lucius? I gave you the name of the hotel I'm almost positive they're staying at.' Thanks to the vision thing I'd had with Sebastian.

'I was concerned about getting you warm.' He gestured to my dishevelled appearance as if that explained everything.

It didn't, and honestly, I was getting a little tired of the men in my life thinking they knew what was best for me.

'You broke into the IMI, traversed buildings and funnelled through air conditioning ducts undetected, but you can't sneak me into a hotel?' I crossed the threshold and did a quick study of the sparse interior. 'I smell bullshit, Granville.'

'I knew you'd be safe and warm here.'

I had a brilliant retort sitting on the end of my tongue but decided it wasn't worth the drama to expel it. 'Whatever. I'm going to look for a phone.'

'Elena?'

'What?'

'Trying the phone is pointless.'

'I'm not staying here, William!' I yelled over my shoulder as I prowled the corridor looking for said 'pointless' device. 'I need to get home right away.'

Home. It was strange to draw parallels between that concept and Lucius. His embrace was still so new and unexpected, as was the bond between father and daughter. But the thought of clean sheets, Maria's cooking and my father's relieved smile felt both foreign and right to crave.

I claimed the receiver I'd been searching for and sandwiched it between my cheek and neck. It was a challenge holding the dirty sheet with one hand and dialling directory assistance with the other, though I questioned my telephonic aptitude when silence lingered and the dial tone failed to appear.

'William, the phone's not working.'

He was beside me in an instant, his fingers circling mine and simultaneously guiding my hand to place the phone back on the cradle. 'I know.'

'What do you mean, *you know*?'

'I had it disconnected a few years ago.'

I was already courting a fresh frown. 'So, this is your house? You knew the phone wasn't working, but you let me go looking for it anyway.'

'I did mention it was pointless.'

'What game are you playing? William, I really need to get in contact with Lucius and this isn't funny.'

'What you really need right now is to focus on getting cleaned up and getting warm. I'm surprised you haven't gone into shock yet.'

'I'll keep. Calling Lucius is priority number one.'

'Shower first.'

'William.'

'No,' he warned, features stern and uncompromising. 'One night to take care of yourself is not going to hurt him or you.'

'You're being completely unreasonable, not to mention stupid.'

'It's just one night.'

'William, I've been missing for two and a half weeks!' I chided, uncertain why he was being such an ass about this. 'There are people looking for me, people who are worried. I just want to go home.'

William flinched, perhaps taken aback by my defiance, one hand on hip, right foot impatiently tapping the floor. He sighed. 'Fine. If Lucius is in Paris looking for you as you say, then he'll probably turn up sometime before dawn. I undoubtedly left scent trails.'

'Was that such a good idea if Roshan got away?'

'I doubt tracking you is his biggest priority right now. Plus you have me to protect you.'

'My hero,' I gushed with the appropriate injection of sarcasm. 'Tell me where I can get cleaned up then.'

'First door on the left,' he murmured, jerking his head in that general direction.

I headed for the bathroom, knowing that once I was clean, I'd be looking for another way to contact Lucius, even if I had to spray paint SOS on the rooftop.

'Elena?' William called. His voice suddenly sounded so unnaturally quiet and reserved that I had to stop to hear him, the rustle of the sheet around my ankles scrunching like crepe paper at a kids' party. 'Do you think that for the rest of tonight that you and I could—?'

'No.'

'Elena, you don't even know what I was going to say.'

'You're right,' I agreed, knowing it was rude to interrupt. 'I don't know *exactly* what you were going to say, but I suspect it was to rehash personal shit. You need to know that my only priority right now is getting back to reality, finding out what's happened since I left and to let Lucas know I'm alive and safe.'

When William didn't immediately answer, I continued down the passage, unsure if adding anything else was helpful, pointless or just plain mean.

I stopped outside a bedroom door and assessed the gloominess. Sparse like the rest of this tidy cottage, I was pleased to see an ensuite bathroom. The thought of being truly clean again almost overshadowed all thought.

Almost.

William was right behind me now, his body only inches from mine. His cool breath fanned my neck and the scent of his skin was suddenly all I could think about. The tips of his fingers brushed the side of my arms and raised goose pimples all over my flesh.

I didn't move. I couldn't. I knew that if that if he turned me around, pulled me to his lips and kissed me, I would be gone. It was only the war that still raged inside my heart and the emotional baggage of his betrayal that stopped my surrender. I'd cried, kissed, and yelled at him in the space of twenty-four hours. What I really needed now was a shower, a phone and a vomit bag. I'd reached too many limits.

I willed myself to move but was stopped by a possessive grip. 'William,' I said, struggling to catch my breath, 'please don't. I can't do this with you right now.'

'We have to talk sometime, Elena, figure out what went wrong.' William's sure hands loosened their stronghold. He didn't let go, but slid his palms down my arms and lower until my hips were in range. Grinding himself against me and imparting soft, dewy kisses on the back of my neck would not weaken my resolve.

'Talking about it over and over again just seems pointless.'

'Elena ...'

Like a coward I bolted out of his arms and slammed the bedroom door in his face. I was flushed, confused and fully expectant that he would sense my hormonal shift and bust the door down, but he didn't. William's footsteps retreated down the hallway and my exhalation of relief was quickly followed by bitter disappointment.

A shower. I really needed a cold shower.

I couldn't put it off any longer. I was clean, feeling more like my usual self, but entirely apprehensive about exiting the solitude of the bedroom. I'd been straddling the threshold for several minutes. I was being an idiot.

I shook my head and eased into the hall and then ambled back towards the living room where I imagined William would be. He was sitting on the sofa, legs stretched out on the coffee table before him. He looked relaxed since he'd had his own shower, but I suspected he might have been as tightly wound as I was.

'Thanks for the clothes,' I said, burying my hands in the borrowed pockets of my new jeans. I was short on conversation and thought it best to remark on how resourceful he was. He'd laid out decent threads in just the right size by the end of the bed. He'd even procured a bra and clean underwear. I supposed that the *hows* and *whys* were irrelevant.

'No problem.' His tone was clipped, though not unexpected after my brush-off.

I sat in an armchair positioned next to the crackling flames of a fire William had started in my absence. The upholstery was warm and comfortable and safe distance from his touch.

William cleared his throat and threaded his fingers across his lap, settling deeper into the soft folds of the well-worn sofa. 'Are you avoiding me?'

'Of course not,' I lied, concentrating profusely on the task of analysing my damp hair for split ends. 'You know what I want, William.'

'I thought I knew what you wanted,' he said, 'but clearly I was projecting. I can't believe it's come to this.'

I continued to avoid eye contact where possible. Split ends were serious business and I was a pussy. I could handle bloodthirsty Vânâtors and unruly Vampires, but I couldn't handle emotional drama.

'After all the nights we spent kissing and talking into the early hours of the morning, I thought we could at least communicate now, but you can barely say a word to me. You can't even look at me.'

'I can look at you,' I muttered, giving him a quick once over.

Coward.

'That's not what I'm talking about and you know it.'

I worried my bottom lip, nibbling at the corner until it started to ache. 'Honestly, I just don't want to talk about where it all went wrong anymore. It doesn't change anything.'

'So, because you're done with our relationship, that's it? I don't get a say?'

Obviously my verbal and physical appreciation of him had been seriously misconstrued. 'What relationship? William, you knew it was always just a bit of fun, a fact I've made abundantly clear on many occasions.'

'Not to me.'

Really? I shouldn't have been surprised. He'd slung the 'L' word around like I needed the reminder I was emotionally retarded, but I'd never felt guilty about my lack of return until I saw the pain now welling in the emerald depths of his eyes. 'Look,' I said, giving him my full attention, 'I've never been anything but honest with you, William. You knew right from the start that I wasn't interested in pursuing something complicated.'

'Then you were lying to yourself.'

I fought the urge to lean across the coffee table, wrap my fingers around his throat and then toss his trying ass into the fireplace. Why did I even bother trying to explain?

I took a calming breath, climbed to my feet and headed for the front door.

'Where are you going?' William shouted. He cornered me by the threshold, my back now pressed against the wall and his arms an inescapable prison.

'William, please. Get out of my way.'

'No,' he murmured, his breath a sweet essence easily devoured when tied to compulsion. 'Elena, I want you to be strong enough, brave enough to tell me how you really feel, to tell me that you love me.'

'Oh, God,' I moaned, too tired and stressed to resolve a matter William clearly refused to drop. 'You know I can't do that, William. I care about you a lot — I always have — but I won't lie to you about something so important.'

Pain radiated like glowing embers behind his eyes and the tension contorting his usually sensuous, smiling lips twisted my insides. 'Why can't you love me, Elena?'

That quiet desperation robbed me of breath. 'I–I don't know.'

'Don't turn this into a joke, Elena.'

'That's the last thing I want to do. I just don't know how to answer your question.'

'Try,' William rasped, barely containing an outburst. His fingernails raked vicious divots in the wood-panelled wall at my back, stripping paint and revealing the soft pine beneath.

'Um ...' *Great start, Elena.* 'It's not that I don't want to love you, William. You're great. Actually, you're better than great, I just—'

'Love someone else,' he finished for me.

'What? No. How absurd.' I started to laugh somewhat hysterically, thrown by the implication and mocked by the possibility of its truth. There was no way, with everything going on, that I would have left myself open and vulnerable. William was wrong, wrong about everything. He had to be.

'Is it absurd?'

'Of course it is!'

William's head dipped to a point where his dark hair tickled the end of my nose, the floor at our feet perhaps more inviting than the expression on my face. 'Elena, it could be so easy if you'd just let me in.'

'I don't let anyone in,' I whispered, saddened by the truth

of that statement but certain of its necessity. I may have been achingly lonely but it was far better than feeling what William apparently felt now — rejection and heartbreak.

I didn't doubt that I could *learn* to love William. He was wonderful, but something stood in my path, something I couldn't grasp or control. 'I'm so sorry, Sebastian. I'm sorry I can't be what you need.'

I flinched and quickly turned my face to avoid a broken nose as William's head jerked up. His eyes were wild and features untamed as they yielded to the heat of his simmering anger.

Was it something I said?

Wait …

Oh.

'My name is *William,*' he seethed, voice eerily quiet.

I was too afraid to speak, too afraid I'd add insult to injury.

'I should've known,' William muttered. 'It's not like I wasn't warned. I just didn't want to listen. You'll never love me with *him* around.' He reared back and punched the panelling beside my head.

I shrieked and ducked for cover, surprised by the uncharacteristic violence and the raining destruction one little slip of the tongue could inspire.

William dragged me back to my feet, clutching my elbow. Grimacing, I was simply too stunned to object to the manhandling. 'Come on, I'll take you to make that phone call now.'

'William?'

He didn't even look at me. 'Do you want to call Lucius, or not?'

'Yes, but—'

'Just let it go, Elena.'

'Wait,' I said, pressing a hand firmly against his chest. He flinched at my touch. 'I'm so sorry, William. What I said … This is the last thing either of us need right now. It's been a shit night — teeth, blood … a disembowelment.'

William choked the door handle with intent, his teeth gnashing together as I spoke. It took several minutes of silence and for me to remove my hand from his chest before he finally calmed down enough to speak. 'I used to be so sure of you, of us. I used to think I knew your heart, but now I'm not sure of anything. It's almost as if you don't see me anymore.'

I unhooked his bruising fingers from my elbow and moved to catch his melancholic gaze. My back was now pressed against the front door and we were far too close not to call intimate. I was bound to stuff everything up with words but William needed to know that he was important to me — cherished.

With trembling hands, I took his face between my palms and cursed my naivety in the face of a 444-year-old Vampire. 'I've always seen you, William. I think it's me that you don't see clearly.' I put a finger to his lips as words of protest attempted to bubble forth. 'You see, I think you have this picture in your head about who I really am, who you want me to be, but deep down you already know that this shouldn't be so hard if it was meant to be. It's why you fight so hard to make it so.'

The lines on William's face creased in a veritable roadmap of possibilities. Negative thoughts were highlighted across his brow and the corners of his narrowed eyes. Then it was the soft words of his denial that came pouring forth, not the inevitable conclusion of our relationship I'd been expecting. 'All I know is that I want you no matter who tells me I can't have you.'

Who? That begged questioning and I probably would have pursued it if it weren't for William's hands suddenly on my hips and his body pinning me to the back of the door. 'I want you, Elena,' William said against my lips. 'I can't be your friend after everything we've endured, not when my body craves you this way, not when my mind constantly seeks to envision you.'

I sucked in much needed air in the hopes it would calm my racing heart and erase the wanton thoughts now flooding my head. But as familiar heat pooled between my legs and William pressed his desire against me, I was robbed of sensible decision. I should have pushed him away and denied my own need, but time and circumstance hadn't altered my bodies' desire to be explored by William's touch.

And then, as his lips made the frighteningly quick journey to mine and complicated the situation twofold, I allowed the delicate caress and even added to the gesture by wrapping my arms around his neck and pressing myself against him. I was an idiot — a stupid, selfish, wolf-driven idiot.

William's response was to drive me harder into the back of the front door, his lips punishing me with pleasurable torment. His fingers dug into the flesh of my hips, holding tight as I explored his neck and shoulders and fed from the frenzied desire our intertwined bodies emitted.

'Is this what you want?' he breathed against my quivering lips.

'I–I don't know,' I stammered, suddenly unsure. Every part of me throbbed with aching need but my head was a riotous mess of conflicting emotions.

'I can't do it, Elena,' William said, focusing on my throat now, his lips smooth as silk against my heated flesh. 'I can't be with you like this and then let you go. If you want me then you need to accept that I can't give up on us, that I have to fight for your love.'

Oh boy.

'I want you, but, William … you're going to get hurt. I'm going to get hurt. Pursuing this is a really bad idea.'

William cut my protest short by reclaiming my lips and exploring every contour with an expert tongue. I melted against him, completely overwhelmed by the primal urge to tear our clothes off and claim him in the most basic way as he cupped my backside and ground his hardened length against me. Devouring William completely and relinquishing my innocence to his eager touch was a sobering thought I chose to cling to.

Almost immediately, I pushed William away. 'Stop now.'

He reached for me again, eyes dark and canines brushing lips that were parted and slick with the promise of more delight. 'I don't want to.'

'I don't either,' I admitted.

William inched forward, his hands already encircling my waist again.

'William … I …' *Damn I want him!* 'Just stop, okay? I need to think.'

Annoyed, William took a step back and raked a hand through his hair, bunching his fist in the silken mass. 'Elena, I can't pretend I don't want you. I can't—'

'I know.'

'So, where does that leave us?'

I shook my head and slumped against the door, feeling empty and seriously unsatisfied. What the hell was wrong with me? I was only making this situation that much more complicated to resolve.

'Just forget about him, Elena. Forget about him and come away with me.'

'I can't do that.'

'Fight fate, Elena. Don't let them tell you who to love.'

William silenced any burning questions with another almost violent kiss, his mouth desperate in exploration and his tongue delighting in the taste of me. I was willing, despite all doubts and inner warnings, and moaned against his lips as he lifted me off the ground.

By the time we broke, we were panting and my whole body ached with fierce need. William's vampiric nature was ultimately the chaperone we needed on our path to irreversible damage. His black eyes and sharp, pointed canines, clawed fingernails and mounting hunger were our warning to stop.

'I missed you,' William murmured, pressing his forehead against mine. 'I missed the taste of you, the feel of you, the way you look after I—'

'I missed you too.' It was an honest answer. William had always made me weak at the knees, especially now with the hardened length of him still pressed against me. But there were definitely a few 'buts' that needed to be added to the end of that statement.

'I meant what I said before, Elena. I want you, and thus I will pursue you even to the detriment of my own sanity.'

'That's a really bad idea.'

William shrugged, offering a chaste kiss before he set me back on my feet. I was unsteady and so tightly wound inside I was afraid I would break if he continued to touch me. 'I can't help how I feel any more than you can. Why don't we leave it at that?'

Brow wrinkling, my fingers worked to smooth the confusion as I concentrated on digesting his words. 'You want to leave this completely unresolved? That sounds like something I would say, not you.'

'Well, until you decide who you want to be with ...'

I folded my arms across my chest, maintaining the steady frown I simply couldn't erase. 'What are you talking about?' I wasn't sure if my earlier slip of the tongue had been somehow poignant, or if he was referring to me living and maintaining a relationship with my father.

William didn't seem inclined to respond either way, his features resigned. 'Do you want to call Lucius now or what?'

Surely I was right to be suspicious? 'Why the change of heart?'

'Another argument I can't win.'

Are we keeping score?

I squeezed his hand and chose not to antagonise. 'Thank you. Lucius will be ecstatic to hear from me. He's had it rough, you know. The prospect of losing another child would be hard on him.'

'I don't care.'

For several shocked seconds I had no idea what to say, surprised at his callousness. 'How can you say that? What happened between the two of you?'

William's face hardened, all lines and jutting angles. 'I'm not discussing it.'

I was amazed how quickly my mood had spiralled from amorous to provoked. 'Okay, fine.'

'Really?'

I shook my head. 'No. Tell me what happened to make you hate Lucius so much.'

William dropped my hand and reached for the doorknob. Making a run for it undoubtedly crossed his mind; divulging information from his past was a conversation he often avoided. 'Why?'

'What do you mean *why*? You keep slagging him off in front of me and you kept us apart for months. If you want me to understand your point of view, you have to explain it to me.'

'It's not that simple. You don't know Lucius and his men as I do, Elena.' The doorknob began to squeak under the assault of his fingertips. I pried them away, one by one, certain he was overreacting.

'I never said I was an expert but people do change, William. Well, Marcus has probably always been a little bit of a fruit but Lucius has done some great things in the last few years alone.'

'Is that so?' William's dour expression suggested he would remain unconvinced.

'Synth blood and the opening of all Neutral bars are just to name a few.'

William's still dark eyes darted back and forth across my face, his disbelief evident. His lips moved to speak but foolish pride and his stubborn view of Lucius's past exploits robbed him of speech.

I thought I'd better clear up a few ill-conceived misconceptions. 'Lucius is the founder of Synth Corp, William. He's the reason we all have synthetic blood and safe places in which to buy and consume it. He even thought to manufacture synthetic animal blood for Vampires such as yourself that refuse human blood.'

'I am aware.'

'Then how can you be so—'

'Don't tell me how to feel!' he scolded, reclaiming the handle and yanking the front door open. He left me standing in the shadow of his wake, disappearing into the front garden, muttering something about my pushiness.

I sighed, closed the front door behind us and quickly followed after him. He hadn't gone far. William paced the tiny cobblestone path from front gate to porch and back again, his hands balled into tight fists. I waited calmly, leaning against a jasmine covered pillar, knowing he would eventually spill.

On the seventh trip back to the porch, William finally stopped. He kept his eyes lowered but extended a shaky palm out to me — an invitation?

I remained silent as I slipped my hand into his and followed him back down the path to the front gate. William didn't speak as he ushered me past the creaking pales and out onto the decidedly eerie, tree-lined street beyond.

'Do you really want to know?' He spoke so softly that I could barely hear him above my shoe scuffing. I wasn't used to the ballet flats he'd procured. They were a half size too big and definitely not crafted for stealth.

'Of course I want to know. It's why I keep pestering you.'

William squeezed my hand and managed to drag his eyes away from the road long enough to actually smile at me. His face was still pinched with tension, but he'd dusted off the cobwebs of indecision. 'Conflict arose the day after the alliance was wagered between Protector and Vampire,' William began. 'Lucius asked me and a few other members of the Roman Guard to search all the surrounding villages at the centre of the Vânător attacks and flush out the Alphas who had gotten away. Some villages were decimated, the dead littering the ground like rubbish and others already impregnated. We cleaned up the mess, burned the bodies and destroyed the unborn pups, but every new village we encountered was much the same. The Alpha's thirst was uncontrollable, unlike anything we'd ever seen.'

I didn't interrupt, but William went silent as he helped me down a steep embankment, taking a short cut through a neighbouring property until we hit a wider, well-used bitumen road. In the near distance I saw the glowing phone booth with its graffiti-covered glass and shredded number directory.

'The last village we crossed seemed unaffected by the Vânătors,' William continued. 'So we scoured surrounding outbuildings and ventured further into the forests of the Carpathian Mountains looking for tracks or clues as to the wolves' whereabouts.'

'So, they evaded you?'

William nodded. 'Back then we didn't know the full extent of their abilities. We didn't know they could shape-shift into the body of anyone they had fed from and merely presumed their minds were wild, not capable of conscious thought.'

'We've all been fooled by that,' I remarked, suddenly flooded with a tidal wave of my own bitter memories.

William squeezed my hand to bring me back to the present. 'Should I go on?'

I squared my shoulders and shook it off. 'Definitely. Sorry.'

'We begun to retrace our steps, certain we'd missed something vital.' William paused to see if I was listening; satisfied, he continued. 'The women had become pregnant in our absence and all of the men had been slaughtered. The children were uncompromised but particularly wary of us, hiding in their hovels and refusing to come out. I didn't hesitate to order the immediate death of the impregnated women — humane compared to the suffering they would endure. As for the children …'

William clenched his fingers, remiss of the fact that he was about to crush my bones in his grip. I cried out and managed to shake him loose but he barely noticed. 'I sent two of the Guard back to Lucius, petitioning that reinforcements be sent to protect what was left of the village — the children.'

'And did he?' I asked, massaging my sore hand.

Bitterness twisted William's face until he was snarling, his words clipped and filled with venom. 'Key members of the coven arrived with a swiftness that was unsettling. I was relieved of my duties, told I was incompetent and that they'd been sent to finish what I *would* not and *could* not do.'

'And what was that exactly?'

'Murdering every last child I tried so hard to protect.'

Now bathed in the ambient glow of the phone booth, we stood together in tense silence. William seemed reluctant to continue, but I needed to understand. I couldn't imagine my father killing any child for sport.

I elbowed William in the ribs. 'What happened next?'

William sighed, his shoulders slumping as he hugged himself, chin tucked tightly against his arms. He looked suddenly frail and emotionally damaged, a small child lost in the memories of his past. 'I went back to Rome, intent on raping blood from Lucius the way blood had poured from his victims, but since he is the master Vampire and cannot die, I gained no ground. I was beaten as an example and told never to question his motives or challenge his authority again.'

I kicked a lump of dried earth by my foot, unsure what to say. There had to be more sides to this story, despite the fact that William's version was filled with pain and unending bitterness that begged further explanation. 'I should probably make that phone call now.'

William dropped his arms, regarding me with surprise. 'I was hoping my story might have changed your mind.'

I tried to analyse why the tale hadn't dimmed my affections towards Lucius and honestly came up empty. 'I guess it's because he's my father.'

William snarled and shoved me out of the way. Admonishment was on the tip of my tongue until I noticed his nostrils flaring and eyes growing black. He wasn't focused on me at all, the flash of fang entirely for another as he hurriedly positioned himself in front of me. When I tried to move, he slammed me into the side of the phone booth, his protective instincts just a little on the rough side.

'Was that necessary?' I snapped, slapping the back of his head. 'You just about dislocated my shoulder!'

'Stay back,' he hissed, ignoring my tirade.

'What is it?' I whispered, hunting for a way to peek at the desolate street from underneath his arm. 'Is it a Vânător? Is it Roshan?'

He shook his head. 'No. This is ten times worse.'

I squinted to see form in the darkness, the sporadically placed streetlights providing next to no illumination. I sniffed the air and sorted through the various aromas tickling my nose — dog, grass, bitumen. A midnight snack being reheated somewhere close by was forgotten the moment four figures broke through the darkness, heading right for us. Their gait was purposeful, controlled, the dark warrior at the front of the pack adopting a recognisable swagger.

A smile erupted across my face, relief virtually tangible. 'Sebastian!' I shouted as I darted out from behind William and ran full pelt into Sebastian's waiting arms.

He dragged me against him in a crushing embrace, one hand holding my head against his chest while the other one touched me everywhere, perhaps doing inventory. 'Elena,' he purred in that sexy Italian lilt of his. 'You're safe now.'

'What took you so long?' I teased, punching him playfully on a rock-hard pectoral. 'I've been with the wolves, you know.'

'Trust me, Elena,' a voice I recognised all too well said from behind, 'he's been tracking you as fast as he possibly can.'

I peeked over Sebastian's shoulder to smile at Caleb. With blond, pink-tipped hair, black nail polish, studded accessories and Goth clothing, he certainly painted a picture. 'I'm sure he did,' I murmured, my gaze travelling back to the Vampire that held me tighter than any friendly embrace should reflect.

'It wasn't fast enough,' Sebastian chastised, his supple lips planting a chaste kiss on my forehead, nose and finally the crook of my neck.

Two of Sebastian's oldest friends, Nicholas and Eric had also joined the party. They'd originally helped rescue me from the IMI, before Roshan's abduction. They greeted me warmly now. 'It's good to see you in one piece, Elena,' Nicholas said, his blond hair tickling the end of his chin. His fingers worked incessantly at trying to tuck the strands permanently behind his left ear. He was failing. 'After we saw the mess at the steel factory, we thought you might have been dead.'

'Thanks for the vote of confidence,' I drawled, happy to remain in Sebastian's arms as a thread of violent images plundered my thoughts.

Silence stretched uncomfortable fingers upon our lips and it was a long time before anyone spoke, or at least that's how it felt as I recalled pools of blood, decimated flesh and unresolved anger.

A not so subtle cough reminded me of William's lingering presence. I tried to extricate myself Sebastian's arms, but he refused to let go and gripped me tighter. 'Don't even think about it,' he said. 'I let you walk into the arms of our enemy once. You're crazy if you think I'll ever let you do that again.'

'William isn't the enemy.' I knew the two men in my life had some kind of unspoken history, but surely Sebastian realised that my safety tonight was a product of William's attentiveness.

'I would never hurt her,' William confirmed, now standing close enough to touch me, close enough that I could hear the snarl in his throat.

'That's not how I see it,' Sebastian answered, tension seeping into the strong limbs that held me rigidly in place.

My curiosity piqued as contemptuous glares passed back and forth. 'I know that you both know each other, but can someone tell me what all the animosity is about?'

'It's nothing.'

'It's obviously not *nothing*,' I persisted.

'Let it go, Elena.'

I was getting whiplash from glancing between them. 'I've already established you were both part of the Italian coven and or Roman Guard, so spill.'

They both sighed as if dealing with a particularly trying child. Was it really my fault that I sought answers when endlessly left in the dark?

'Well?' I demanded, tapping my foot.

'He's my brother,' Sebastian answered, William only a heartbeat behind.

'Brother?' Well, shit. I couldn't have been more shocked if I'd shoved a butter knife in the toaster.

CHAPTER NINE
Altercations

I stood open-mouthed and wide-eyed for what felt like the longest time. I'd butchered the subject to death, repeating the word 'brother' like I'd somehow misheard. Not drawing a connection sooner made me feel like a total tool.

'Why have you never told me?' I spluttered to no one in particular.

'You didn't ask,' Sebastian answered.

My fist should have been knuckle deep in his face right about then if not for my burning urge to hear William's equally lame excuse for collusion. 'Why didn't *you* tell me?'

'It never came up.'

'Horse shit.'

I should have known they were related. Dark hair, same height, a similar, muscular build and the same angular facial planes — strong jaw and high cheekbones. The only difference was their eyes, emerald green versus the same brilliance with twisting tendrils of silvered grey. They even shared the same annoying, habitual tendency to circumvent the truth.

'We may be related but we aren't brothers,' William argued. 'And we haven't been for a very long time.'

I figured this intense animosity for Sebastian pertained

to recently revealed stories of the past. 'Does this have to do with—'

'Some,' William acknowledged. I had to wonder what part Sebastian played in William's believed betrayal and the ties that bound that hatred still.

'Look, William, I appreciate all you've done to keep Elena safe this night, but you can go now,' Sebastian said as he wrapped a possessive arm around my shoulder. He pulled us close enough that we touched from hip to knee; his eyes flashed with an intense hostility.

I didn't appreciate being used as a prop in their battle of wills and quickly unhooked his arm. 'Hey now,' I said, 'William doesn't have to go anywhere.'

'Perhaps I should,' William agreed. 'Unless of course you're willing to choose now?'

I snorted. 'Choose what? Between you and Sebastian? Don't be ridiculous. There's no competition.'

William read his own inference into that sentence, curled his lip in disgust and walked away.

'He's not very friendly, is he?' Caleb remarked, picking at his painted fingernails.

I chased after William before Sebastian could attempt restraint. Sure, he could have caught me, threw me over his shoulder and taken me back to the cave, but Sebastian knew he'd see the sharp end of my tongue if he interfered, a weapon he often sought to avoid.

I caught up to William in record time, but he wasn't stopping for anyone. I had to jog to keep pace, and in the end, stand right in his path and wrap my hands around his waist to make him stop. 'Why didn't you tell me you had a brother?'

He unlatched my arms and took a mighty step back. He couldn't even look at me. 'What difference would it have made?'

'A big one.'

'You mean, if you had known Sebastian was my brother, you might have avoided developing feelings for him?'

I felt my cheeks go pink. 'No, but you must have drawn the connection, known that Sebastian was with me … ah … that we were together, I mean … shit! I'm not saying this right.'

William's ever-darkening face made my insides twist uncomfortably.

'I just meant that keeping it a secret, like you did with my father's identity is another reason to distrust you, William.'

He toed a small divot in the bitumen, quickly forming a pothole that could have swallowed a minibus. 'So, you *are* going to keep reminding me of my mistakes.'

'No, but you make it hard, William.'

He nodded, turned on his heels and walked away again.

'Wait, William, don't leave. This isn't about Sebastian.'

'It's always about Sebastian,' he muttered, casting a dark look over his shoulder. 'I need to go, get away from here and leave you exactly where you belong. It's what I was supposed to do from the very beginning.'

'*Supposed to do*?' I echoed, hurrying in vain to catch up. William had alluded to outside interference before, the reasoning behind his cryptic words and nonsensical conclusion.

'Elena, I'm giving you an out, an opportunity for you to be with whoever you want.'

'I kinda thought that was my choice, regardless.'

He pressed on, mumbling something undoubtedly ludicrous beneath his breath.

'William, will you please just stop walking for a second? If you want to go, then go, but don't leave because you think you have to or because you think Sebastian's won this imaginary competition you've concocted.'

That stopped him in his tracks. 'Elena, you have no idea of the forces at work here. I've certainly been kidding myself and now I see your naivety in thinking you're not already a victim of fate's touch.'

'What are you talking about? And for once just give me a straight answer.'

William's angst-ridden eyes snapped to mine, a tightness forming around his lips. He was about to answer when Sebastian interrupted, sneaking up on us from behind. 'Let him go, Elena. William knows the score.'

I was cursing the timing but William was already on another tangent, snarling with teeth unbidden and heading directly for Sebastian.

The childish teenager within was fist pumping the air shouting *fight, fight, fight*. The mature part of my psyche shook her head, appalled and annoyed that once again questions were rebuked and the truth was left discarded like old rubbish.

William launched headfirst into the impending battle with reckless abandon. Their bodies collided with a thunderous crack and bitumen sprayed like out of control irrigation, leaving a giant crater in the centre of the road. All I could see were brief flashes of colour and hear the needless punches of aggravated assault. Bones crunched, grunts sounded, but neither yielded to common sense.

'Don't even think about it,' Eric reprimanded, capturing my wrist. I was surprised to look down and find my feet shuffling forward. What had I planned to do? Dive in the centre of their dispute and pull them apart?

Idiot.

'They're hurting each other.'

Nicholas appeared on my right and snorted derisively. 'It's hardly permanent, and besides, they've been fighting for over three hundred years, it's about time they settled it.'

Caleb was just as suddenly behind me, sniffing at my hair and creeping me out to the nth degree. Swatting him like a fly proved useless as he ducked and weaved around my pulse points instead.

'Get away,' I snapped, finally clipping one of his ears.

'Ouch. I thought we were friends.'

I rolled my eyes. 'We can be if you stop trying to eat me all the time.'

Eric let go of my other wrist, all the better to defend myself with. 'We won't let that happen,' he assured me, his features, as always, impassive as he eyeballed Caleb over my shoulder.

A change of subject was in order. 'Can anyone hear what's going on?'

'William just kicked Sebastian in the balls and called him a—'

'Caleb, watch your mouth,' Eric hissed.

'What? What did he call him? What's happening?'

Caleb pushed his luck and rested his chin on my shoulder, turning to smile at me like the Cheshire cat. 'They're too slap happy for consistent, coherent verbal communication, but someone by the name of "Araqiel" does keep coming up.'

'I've heard William mention that name before, but he never elaborated.' I squinted, trying to recall which lost conversations had been pertinent. 'I gather they're not a member of the coven?'

'No one I've ever heard of,' Eric remarked. Nicholas seemed to agree, his blonde tresses blinding him as he shook his head. His fingers busied themselves almost immediately on rectifying the untidy arrangement.

Eric pressed closer, dwarfing me with his six foot plus

magnificence. His aloofness had melted into curiosity and his already sloping eyes disappeared behind thinned slits. 'Are either of you making sense of this?'

'Making sense of what?'

'Did he just say what I think he said?' Nicholas mused. 'Soul mates?'

Everyone had their ear to the ground except me. 'What?' I barked, desperate for answers. 'Who said that?'

Eric hesitated; his narrowed, ebony eyes bounced between the scuffle and my wide-eyed gaze. His ruby coloured lips were poised to speak, but then just as quickly pressed firmly shut.

'Is anyone going to tell me what's going on?'

'You really don't understand how he feels about you at all, do you?' Caleb said, his pointed chin digging into my shoulder as he spoke.

'I—'

'She's Lucius's daughter and he's charged with protecting her,' Nicholas explained, talking over me as if I wasn't right beside him. 'There's a certain sense of devotion that he has to commit.'

Caleb snorted, unconvinced. 'Then you haven't seen the way he looks at her.'

'Um, hello. I'm right here.'

'He has to look at her to protect her,' Eric added, determined to slather a platonic layer upon mine and Sebastian's history-to-date.

'And Hell is just a sauna,' Caleb mused, nipping quickly at my ear lobe before darting away. He was an inch from feeling the claws of my wrath in his retreating behind.

'Regardless,' Nicholas continued, ignoring the erect middle finger and nasty expletive I issued Caleb, 'they both seem interested in obtaining Elena's affections. I personally have never heard Sebastian talking like this. Perhaps he's—'

'In love with her,' Caleb finished, daring me to argue.

'Alright, everyone just please shut up now.'

'Excuse me?'

'Seriously, just shut up about it.' Was that my voice that was laced with a dash of panic? I knew Sebastian was attracted to me and even insistent we pursue a more physical relationship, but this? Nah. Not possible. I refused to believe it.

Caleb coughed but it was somewhere between a strangled laugh and a good old fashioned throat clearing. And now he looked me up and down, smirking as if I were the butt of some perverse joke. 'Someone's in denial.'

'Someone must really want a fist to the face,' I mocked with a syrupy sweet smile. There was no way I would go on talking about this, and yet, Caleb remained undaunted by my threat, shaking his head at me as if I were missing the punch line.

I focused my attention back on Eric's narrowed gaze as he continued to study the fight with interest. I could tell Caleb was gearing up for round two, but there were more important matters to consult. 'What else has been going on in my absence?'

A pregnant pause was punctuated by the slapping sounds of flesh being abused and Caleb's exaggerated sigh. All were ignored as Eric met my eyes, perhaps sensing my urgency to be done with matters of the heart. 'Enough that it will take time to repeat,' he answered, 'and I'm not sure if I'm the best person to explain it all to you.'

'Come on, Eric. I've been stuck underground for weeks. At least tell me what's going on with The Protectors.' I pointed at the blurred mass before us. 'They're going to be a while by the looks of it.'

'The Protectors?' He suddenly seemed agitated, clenching and unclenching his fists. 'It's hard to say. Clearly a new agenda is in motion. Our recent requests for support in attacking converging Vânători within our borders have fallen on deaf ears. Most of our usual contacts at the IMI are missing and others we feel might have been compelled.'

'Compelled by vampires?'

Eric shook his head. 'No, this is magic based.'

'That's obviously the *Defenacus* spell in action, but why are The Protectors compelling their own?' I also wondered if the recent desertion of headquarters was coincidental or merely part one of whatever nefarious plan they're undoubtedly working.

'We're not sure,' Nicholas interjected, tracing the outline of the blade stashed unsafely in the front pocket of his jeans. 'But Sebastian briefed us on your re-entry into Bucharest and the IMI's desertion. Pair that with talk of a serum, the Vânător's bizarre new movements on our coven, and of course, the Alpha Roshan's extremely well-timed appearance at headquarters and you have to wonder about motive.'

I tapped a finger against my chin, thoughtful. 'Before I was taken, I did tell Sebastian that I believed that there could be ties between Protector and Vânător, but still ...'

'It sounds absurd,' Eric finished.

'Exactly,' Nicholas mused. 'But what could cause the end of a three hundred year alliance?'

'The opportunity for Vampiric demise,' I guessed. 'Both species have been spreading word of its temperance for centuries.'

'Even if that's true, how and what do the Vânători have to do with all this?' Nicholas probed. 'And if The Protectors do have something to do with this table-turning event, what could they possibly have to bargain?'

All good questions that I had no doubt begun and ended with the serum, a weapon I was yet to fully understand but smart enough to fear, knowing it had been produced from my blood.

'Okay, wait. What are the Vânătors doing, exactly? Eric, you said they're amassing on the borders?'

Agitated fingers were cracked in synchronicity. 'Sources say their packs are also expanding to the point of notoriety.'

'What do you mean?'

'Ludicrous sums of missing person reports have been filed and numerous deaths across Switzerland, France, Slovenia, Croatia and Greece have been reported in the human media. We've been monitoring the situation for about three weeks now.'

'Three weeks? So Lucius was suspicious of unfolding events even before Roshan took me?'

Caleb remained quiet, but both Nicholas and Eric nodded their heads. 'At first he believed Julius was responsible for the recent murders in Paris and surrounding cities,' Eric continued. 'But with so much death and the Vânătors seemingly structured approach to impending attack in these areas, he ruled it a coincidence that Julius has once again resurfaced, though he doesn't discount his threat.'

'So what's the plan?'

'We're working on it, Elena, but we don't have all our facts straight as of yet.'

'Are you still looking for Julius?' I fought the urge to shudder and failed miserably. Julius scared the absolute bejesus out of me. It probably had something to do with the fact that he was a deranged psychopath intent on reaping revenge on my body.

'He's as elusive as the wind,' Nicholas started. 'One

minute we think we have him and then the next he slips right through our fingers.'

'Slippery little sucker,' Caleb snorted, pleased by the vampiric pun and my reluctant smile. He looked as if he were about to add something undoubtedly inappropriate but stilled, his overly animated face suddenly slack.

'What is it?' I whispered, a sense of urgency creeping across my skin.

'The fight just got serious,' Caleb answered. 'Sebastian broke William's arm and blood has been spilled by both. They will heal but—'

'Caleb,' Eric warned.

The absolute lunacy of the situation made me groan. Enough was enough. Fighting for belief was one thing, but to fight for ego was shameful, particularly given the current agenda of all our enemies.

Caleb snagged my wrist in a death grip as I headed for the battle once more. With brutal force he pulled me against him and wrapped those inescapable arms around me. 'Stay where you are. They're both very volatile at the moment, especially William.' His cold breath tickled my earlobe and his soft lips drifted to my neck, suggesting nefarious intent should I follow my foolish errand to its end.

'Let me go,' I warned, struggling in his grasp. 'You really don't want to see me when I get angry, Caleb.'

I expected a fight, a war of witty banter, but all argument was suspended as the blur of bodies exploded into two, heavily wounded Vampires gasping for breath. William was a prisoner of Sebastian's overly tight headlock, his right arm twisted at an angle incongruent with the rest of his body. Claw marks ripped his face and blood coursed from an open neck wound. Sebastian fared no better. His chest and lower stomach had been ravaged, his hair mussed and his face streaked with dirt and blood.

I tried to go to them, but Caleb held me tight.

'Get your hands off me!' William roared. He kicked off the ground, taking them several metres into the air before they befriended gravity and fell. Grunts erupted as bitumen and pockets of packed earth sprayed around them as a result of their brutal landing.

'Stop struggling and trying to hit me and I'll let you go!' Sebastian hollered.

'Both of you stop it!' I yelled, still struggling vainly to disentangle myself from Caleb's hold. 'You're supposed to be adults.'

I bit down in the general vicinity of Caleb's nipple, taking advantage of his surprise to slip free of his grasp. I ducked Nicholas's outstretched hand and did a base slide towards my feuding Vampires. 'We don't have time for this, guys.'

'She does have a point,' Nicholas mused.

Sebastian and William growled in unison. Wow, they really were related.

'Seriously, you both have to stop now. Attempted murder will solve nothing.'

Like wayward children, they shot me defiant gazes and Sebastian's hold seemed to conspicuously tighten around William's neck.

'Don't make me count to three,' I mocked, resigned to punch them both in the nuts if they didn't stop this shit soon.

William, perhaps the bigger man, finally tapped out. 'Let me go,' he demanded, concentrating on the dangling, slightly deformed limb by his side.

Sebastian released him and then rose slowly, making a show of flexing every lean muscle in his exposed abdomen and biceps. He knew I watched him, though I pretended to study his already healing wounds.

He was smiling by the time he'd retrieved his discarded shirt, prolonging the viewing experience with a painfully slow redress. William was snarling; no way near as appreciative of the sight before us or indeed my reaction to it.

'William,' Sebastian taunted, finally tearing his teasing gaze from mine. 'Stop getting so upset. You knew the score from the very beginning and yet you still tried to interfere.'

William's snarling intensified as words spewed forth in an angry tirade. 'I interfered because you should not be the one who gets to decide!'

'Ultimately I don't decide. She does,' Sebastian said shoving a finger in my direction. 'And it's been the ultimate gift I've had the privilege to receive for thousands of years!'

'I will fight it, just as I told *him* I would fight for her.'

All eyes were suddenly fixed on me. This was one moment in time where I didn't fancy being the centre of attention at all.

'You're being naïve as always, little brother.'

'I'm not your brother,' William hollered.

The admission would have cut me deep, but Sebastian remained unfazed. 'Don't deny your family, William. In this life we are brothers and you can't change that. I'm sorry you feel justified but you are trying to take what has always been mine, a fact I cannot abide.'

'Sebastian,' I begged, 'please don't start another fight.'

'You don't understand what we're fighting for.'

'We have a pretty good idea,' Caleb whispered through thinned lips, his innuendo not lost on the tense group gathered. My more, denial-driven thought process believed there had to be a deeper, more definitive, underlying issue that didn't revolve around me.

So I deflected like a true champion for the emotionally crippled and said, 'Actually, William gave me the particulars before you arrived.'

Sebastian's face darkened, a white hot look of lividness poured in William's direction. 'Why would you tell her what you don't understand yourself?'

'What are you talking about?' William grunted as he forced his broken arm back into place.

'I have waited far too long for you to screw this up with casual words!'

'Calm down!' I yelled, now perplexed. 'Surely William's extrication from the Roman Guard isn't a secret?'

It was Sebastian's turn to flirt with confusion. 'What?'

'I'm talking about Lucius ordering the destruction of a village that William was trying to protect from Vânǎtors. Why? What the hell are you talking about?' Boy. Did I really want to know?

Sebastian was at a temporary loss and William shook his head, seemingly annoyed that I'd raised the subject. 'Right. Well,' Sebastian started, 'did William tell you his version of events, or the truth?'

'Is there such a thing as the truth when it comes to the two of you?' It was a fair enough comment given that half-truths and deviations in story are what had led us to this uncomfortable stand-off.

Sebastian, undaunted, stepped close enough that I could feel the unnatural heat that emanated from his skin, feel his smooth fingers as they grazed my arms, tangled with the hair at my neck and finally held me close. With only a touch and the power of his swirling eyes, I was captivated.

'The truth changes everything, Elena,' he quietly reminded me.

'All I've ever asked for was the truth.' Was I ... breathless?

'Don't touch her!' William scolded. He yanked me backwards until I was stumbling into his arms and cursing his name. 'You're not good for her!' he shouted over the top of me.

'And I suppose you think you are? How much of her pain could have been prevented if you'd just done as you were asked?'

'Now look—'

'This is way above my pay grade,' Caleb interrupted, earning him a death stare from me. 'Although I do find you all thoroughly entertaining, I'm thirsty and thus, I must regretfully exit.'

Eric and Nicholas seemed inclined to agree, perhaps grateful to have a reason to depart. 'We'll leave you to figure this out,' Eric murmured. 'We'll send word to Lucius that Elena is safe.' They disappeared faster than a fart in a fan factory.

'You two have to stop this,' I muttered as I attempted to pry loose William's arms. 'Please. Sort your shit out now before I walk in the opposite direction and give up on the both of you.'

'We're never going to make peace over this, Elena,' William said, refusing to relinquish his hold on me.

'You are a fool,' Sebastian spat, annoyed enough that pacing was the only way to vent further frustration. 'You know no more what's best for Elena now than you did all those years ago when you confronted Lucius.'

'People died, Sebastian, and it wasn't the first time Lucius had made a call like that.'

'Perhaps not,' Sebastian reluctantly agreed, 'but in this instance, the children you fought to protect were already dead. Everyone knew they were Vânătors but you. You wouldn't listen.'

William's arms fell from my waist; the slight hitch in his breath the sound of disbelief. 'I don't believe you. I would have known.'

'You were young and inexperienced, and thought the world was against you. You never stopped to smell what was right in front of you.'

'That can't be true.'

'I'm sorry, but it is. Lucius had to make an example of you, William. He couldn't show tolerance just because Tiberius is our father. You were being a damn fool then and you still are now.'

'Stop talking,' William begged, his voice hoarse. His head bowed and shoulders slumped, doubt now resting in place of his self-righteous indignation.

Sebastian was relentless. 'Now you've failed Elena because of your personal quest for justice. You kept the one person who you profess to love from knowing her father because of your bitterness towards us — me.'

'Sebastian, seriously, you need to stop.' I wasn't impressed as I watched the colour leech from William's face. Guilt already consumed him, a wound so deep that Sebastian's attempt at a salt rub would only see it needlessly fester.

He continued regardless. 'The moment you met Elena, you would have known her ties to Lucius, you would have known what that meant to all of us. Why, William? Why would you forsake her happiness for your own?'

'Okay, that's enough,' I pressed, slapping a firm hand over Sebastian's forearm. 'No more.'

I focused back on William, my plan to comfort him during this time of doubt and revelation. He looked so lost, so defeated. So it was only fractionally surprising when he turned heel and headed in the opposite direction, committed to leaving both the past and present behind.

I ran after William. It took me longer than I'd have liked.

'I guess this means you're leaving again,' I said, drawing in a deep breath. I wiped beads of sweat from my upper lip and forehead, waiting for him to speak.

'It's for the best.'

'If you think so.'

'I do.'

William took my hand; his long, slim fingers brushed over my knuckles in soothing motions. I was suddenly gripped by sadness so oppressive that I found myself fighting all instinct to cry. A few hours ago I'd hated him, now I … Well I didn't know, but I certainly didn't want him to go. 'Will I ever see you again?'

'I don't know.'

'I bet you wish you'd never met me.'

William growled and yanked on my hand until I was in his arms, forced to meet with the melancholic depths of his emerald eyes. 'That's not true.'

'It might have been easier.'

'For who?'

'Both of us, I guess.'

There was a momentary pause. 'Do you regret us?'

'No,' I answered honestly.

'Then don't say things like that.'

I nodded and pressed my face against his chest a final time. I inhaled the sweet scent of him and then quickly retreated to the furthermost point of his embrace. My knees shook and my heart was heavy, but there was no point in delaying the inevitable. 'Well, you know where I'll be when you want to see me again.'

I turned for a hasty retreat as the tears threatened to spill, but found I was soon gasping for breath, crushed in William's life-stealing embrace. He pressed his lips against mine and took me with an urgency that bordered on desperation. I tasted blood, pain and misery. There was nothing sweet about it.

'Come with me,' he breathed.

I coughed, gasping to draw in oxygen. 'I can't, William.'

'Why not?'

'You know why. I've been missing for almost three weeks. A lot has happened and I need to get to Lucas.'

'But, Elena—'

'Why don't you come with me? It will give you a chance to smooth things over with Lucius and your father.'

William shook his head. 'No, I don't think I'm quite ready for that yet.'

'You have a lot to think about, I suppose.'

He nodded, angling to kiss me again. I wasn't sure I could handle it. His misery had almost suffocated me the first time round. 'I guess we'll always have Paris.'

Laughter felt decidedly unnatural given the circumstances of our parting, but I couldn't help but be amused by his cliché. I wrapped my arms around his neck, hugging him close. 'I don't have good memories of Paris.'

William smiled and clicked his tongue, perhaps now just realising his *faux pas*. 'Sorry, I just went with it.'

'It's okay.'

He kissed me again, quickly, chastely and then pulled back, smoothing his thumb across my lower lip. 'I will see you soon.'

'You will?'

'I doubt I could ever stay away from you for long, Elena.' He winked and once again spun on his heels.

I watched him leave, his shoulders slightly hunched, hands now buried in his pockets. I was smirking, my own hands finding comfort on the slightness of my hips. 'You know that's what you said last time, right? You're a walking contradiction, William Granville.'

'Next time I won't let you down.'

'Yeah, yeah — promises, promises!' I shouted after him.

Laughter rented the air, a touch of the old William I would always cherish even if a broken promise was a truth I inevitably foresaw in our future.

CHAPTER TEN

Conclusions

I folded my legs beneath me and tucked my ridiculously cold feet into the soft cushioning of the plush armchair, angling the rest of my body towards the still burning fire. It was nice to be back indoors, even if the house was not mine and William was gone.

Comfort was found in the sound of the crackling flames and the slowly warming fingers I pressed towards the heat. Embers glowed at the bottom of the hearth, filling the room with ambient light and the rather pleasant smell of smoke.

Sebastian sat on the sofa across from me, feet propped on the wooden coffee table, an eerie reminder of William's earlier movements. He talked quietly with Lucius on his cell phone, hashing out details regarding my continued safety. I'd already suffered the inquisition but was still nevertheless, looking forward to seeing him again, too.

'Lucius is pleased that you are unharmed,' Sebastian said as he snapped his phone shut. I watched with amused interest as he attempted to re-pocket the device in a seemingly non-existent space at the back of his too-tight jeans.

'I hope you're not in trouble because of me?'

'I was, but not anymore.'

My lips twitched. 'I'm sorry.'

'Are you?' Sebastian teased. I marvelled at the way I was drawn to the upward pull of his lips and the slight blush in his cheeks. I wondered if I would ever tire of gazing into his swirling eyes or doing my upmost to impart happiness upon his features.

Ugh, mushy much?

Sebastian's smile faded as quickly as it had appeared, his eyes knowing the truth of my digression. My appreciation of Sebastian's fine form still confused the hell out of me, and I could only assume that my growing scowl had broken his mirth. 'What's wrong, Elena?'

'Where do I even start?'

'Try the beginning.'

I smoothed the ever thickening lines between my brows, massaging the skin into submission. Start at the beginning? We'd be here forever. 'Can you just explain why you and William were having it out over me tonight?'

Sebastian's tongue left a moist trail across his lips, a reflexive action I couldn't tear my gaze from. 'Why?'

'Because I want to know the truth about the soul mate thing.'

He brushed his thumb over that glistening path, nibbled on his cuticle for a bit and then finally folded his arms across his chest. The sigh he emitted said he still wasn't done fidgeting. 'You heard that?'

'I did, so spill.'

Sebastian's fingers now dug into the flesh near his elbows. 'Elena, you asked me once about your dreams and why I was in them, even before we'd met. The answer is right in front of you, in the very concept you question.'

Soul mates? Yeah, so not ready to wrap my head around that.

'Shouldn't I remember you?'

'We're in a different life now, one in which we've only just met.'

I stopped massaging my brow. 'Sebastian, are you seriously suggesting that my dreaming about you is some sort of past life regression?'

He shrugged.

'Suppose for a second that I humour you about our past. How does that make us ...?' I paused, my tongue thick and heavy, rolled like an overstuffed enchilada with too much hot sauce. My lips were parted, but my voice was choked. I seriously hoped the implication of soul mates was absolute bullshit. I wasn't ready to digest an emotional enema today.

Sebastian did a terrible job of hiding his rising smile, if he even tried at all. 'Elena, what exactly do you think a soul mate is?'

It was my turn to shrug, indifference a coat I thought I could easily wear. 'I don't know. Someone you carve your initials into tree trunks with and run hand in hand through wildflower meadows?'

His derisive snort did little to ease my apprehension.

'Look, this isn't my thing, Sebastian. I wouldn't have asked if I knew the answer.'

'It will come to you.'

'Why do you always do that? Why don't you just tell me? It would save so much time.' And heartache.

'The rules,' he quietly reminded me.

The rules. Jesus. He'd mentioned them back in Budapest. I'd craved explanation then and he'd shut me down with vague referencing to these 'rules' he supposedly had to follow. I was starting to think he was an escapee from the funny farm or ex CIA. It was easier than believing Sebastian and I were intrinsically tied for all eternity.

Sebastian's smile faded, his expression turning serious as

he sat up straight, clasped his hands in his lap and twisted his fingers in knots until the knuckles turned white. 'Elena, you know that I want to be with you. Isn't that enough?'

It was more of an admission than I felt compelled to face. I was already stamping down the stereotypical blush of rose that crept up on my cheeks. 'Maybe for you, but I want all the answers.'

'Answers I can't give you,' he said flatly. 'Unless …' The look he suddenly gave me would have melted steel.

I surely hadn't forgotten. Sebastian had once proclaimed a kiss between us would open doors and answer riddles, but deep down I knew that would complicate everything more. My body was a traitor and my head was a confused pile of questions. Locking lips with the enigma would be like tossing me down the rabbit hole.

I shook my head with such vigour that pain flared behind my eyes.

'So, tell me what it was really like then,' Sebastian murmured, sighing as he hunched forward, elbows on knees and fingers still subject to the strange contortion he wreaked upon them.

'Huh?' I'd heard the words, but I couldn't make sense of them.

'Tell me about Roshan and what he put you through.'

'What? Why?' I looked left and then right, certain avoidance was the key to continued sanity. 'You don't need the details, Sebastian.'

'You told your father you were unharmed, but we both know there's more to this. The carnage at the factory raises a few questions alone.'

'I don't really want to rehash.' I began to pick at the loose threads on my jeans.

'I need to know if he raped you, Elena, a very serious

question we cannot skip over or pretend I should not ask for a second longer.'

My lips parted and all breath was caught in a metaphorical catcher's mitt lodged in my throat. I always knew he'd ask; I just hoped he wouldn't. 'I thought he was going to,' I stammered, unsure of the weakness I could hear whispered in my voice, 'but he didn't.'

'Were you intimate at all?'

'Sebastian ...'

'Did you ... enjoy it?' he pressed, the mere suggestion like a bad taste in his mouth. I almost didn't respond. It was the storm clouds gathering in his eyes and the welling of blood — Vampire tears — that stopped my cruel retort.

'I'm half Vânător, Sebastian. You can't ever forget what that means.'

The flash of silver, a tumultuous, iridescent spark that raced across his corneas shaped my arms to hug myself in comfort.

'Why didn't he rape you?' Sebastian muttered under his breath, an apparent mystery he thought he could solve with continued reflection. It really wasn't a puzzle.

'He liked my blood more than my body.'

Sebastian grunted and folded himself back against the cushioning, ill at ease. 'I'm so sorry, Elena.'

'It's not your fault, Sebastian. It's mine.'

'Elena—'

'Let's just drop it now, okay?'

I could tell he wanted to argue with me, but blissful silence ensued and we stared at the fire until the cooling embers began to dim and my eyes grew heavy.

'What are you thinking about?' Sebastian asked.

I stifled a yawn as I looked across at him, hitched my knees up to my chest and wrapped my arms around them tightly, heels balancing on the edge of the armchair. 'Nothing … everything … you?'

'I was actually wondering how you and William escaped Roshan's den.'

'Oh … that.'

'I saw the bodies, Elena. I saw the blood and the rage of the attack. Although I have faith in William's abilities and yours,' he quickly added. 'Two of you against the sixty or seventy wolves I saw disembowelled seem like impossible odds.'

'I know.'

'How did you survive? And why was William even there?'

'I'm not sure you'll believe me.'

'Try me,' Sebastian tested. A lock of dark hair tickled his cheek and attempted to cloud his vision before Sebastian absently swiped it behind his ear. He grew agitated when the stubborn kink claimed freedom and fell in front of his eye once more.

What will he think of me when he knows what I've done?

I took a steadying breath, cracked my neck and then just blurted the extraordinary without any real degree of finesse. 'I turned Vânător.'

Several seconds passed without breath or reply. Had I actually gathered the courage to admit it?

'Say that again?' Sebastian finally answered, eyes wide. 'I'm not sure I heard you right.'

I took another deep breath before I spoke, surprised I'd been holding it for so long. 'You heard me, Sebastian. A big, black, hairy wolf attacked Roshan's den, and that big, black wolf was me.'

'This isn't a joke, Elena.'

'Do you see me laughing, Sebastian?'

He studied the seriousness of my expression with

narrowed eyes. Whatever he saw written there must have made him believe. 'The massacre was *your* doing?'

'Apparently.'

'Apparently? What does that even mean?'

'W–well, I don't really remember it happening,' I stuttered. 'One minute Roshan was draining me of blood and then the next, I was naked, waking up amongst a pile of dead bodies.'

'Was William witness to this?' He didn't wait for my response before shaking his head, mouth forming a grim line. 'Why was he even there?'

I shrugged, just as perplexed. 'He said he was hunting Roshan but he got caught.'

'And what happened to Roshan?'

'He got away.'

'And what was William doing during your shift?'

'Kissing his ass goodbye. I almost killed him, Sebastian!'

'And you don't remember anything?'

I shivered violently, certain the creeping fingers of winter had nothing to do with the chill that caressed my spine. 'Maybe I don't want to remember.'

'We have to tell Lucius about this.'

I was horrified. 'Why?'

'Because he is the master Vampire and your father.'

'So? He has no experience with this. I'm the first of my kind and I just know he's going to overreact.'

Sebastian smirked, climbed quickly to his feet and headed for the window. He fingered the drapery and peered into the darkness beyond. 'It's going to be daylight soon. You should get some sleep and then we'll head back to Rome.'

'Is that safe?'

'Going back to Rome?'

'Yes.'

He frowned, lowering the curtain. 'What did the others tell you?'

'That the Vânǎtors are present at every border around Italy.'

'They shouldn't have worried you with that.'

I waved off his needless concern with an eye roll. 'I told the others that it could be a coincidence.'

'Vânǎtors don't uproot from their dens without just cause.'

I rested my chin on my knees, but sleep faded quickly from my thoughts. 'What would be considered *just cause*?'

'You're asking me to interpret the minds of animals.'

Fair call. 'Nicholas also mentioned that a lot of Protectors are absent, perhaps under the duress of the *Defenacus* charm? I'll bet my left arm on it being about the serum.'

'Is the *Defenacus* spell permanent?'

'As far as I know.'

Sebastian stood pensive while I plunged forward, more questions unanswered. 'Has Lucius investigated the reasons for Bucharest headquarters closing yet?'

'Elena, we were busy searching for you.'

I cringed, grateful but alarmed that details had been dismissed in lieu of my rescue. 'Now I feel like a massive hindrance.' I rubbed at my sleepy eyes and tried to think where best to start. 'I'll have to get in contact with Lucas ASAP, pray that he knows something that could be useful. I guess I just don't understand why they would dissolve the alliance now. I mean, I have ideas, sweeping notions, but nothing factual.'

'No alliance equals opportunity.'

'The serum could still just be a cure. We could be wrong about everything.'

Sebastian looked dubious. 'Elena, do you really think The Protectors are innocent? Look at how they treated you.'

'So, what are we doing about it?'

Sebastian leant against the wall and watched me intently from across the room. I felt vulnerable under that gaze, and yet compelled to surrender myself to the swirling irises and whatever suggestion they may hold.

'Lucius has called a multi-coven gathering set for the end of the month,' he started. 'There are roughly 200 of us in Italy, but if the Vânătors *are* gathering their numbers for an attack, we need to recruit and investigate with all covens. We can't be idle or second guess The Protectors, we need to be prepared.'

'Agreed.'

Sebastian was about to speak again when I interrupted, a fresh flow of thoughts running rampant. 'Wait. Focusing back on the wolves for a minute, why the Italian borders? What is it about the Italian coven that appeals?'

'I think we have something they want.'

'And that would be?'

He cocked his finger at me. 'You.'

I scoffed and unfolded my arms from around my knees, letting my feet drop back to the floor. The cool hardwood touched my soles and I instantly recoiled, pulling my feet back under me and curling back against the warm cushioning. 'No, I don't think this is about me. The Vânătors have been at this for a while and I've been in their possession for nearly three weeks.'

'What if Roshan kept you a secret from the other Alphas?'

I shook my head, unconvinced. 'That doesn't explain advancing on Italy. It has to be about Lucius, possibly another member of the coven, but most likely someone in a position of power.'

'No one has more power than Lucius.' He was making my point for me.

'Sebastian you've always said that Lucius isn't very popular.'

'But what do they have to gain? Lucius cannot die.'

'Yeah, but do the Vânătors know that? Hell, I didn't even
know that until a month ago. But, if I were fresh onto the
scene and out for blood, unaware of Lucius's Vampiric abilities, he'd be the one I took down first.'

'Why?'

I frowned at his curiosity, certain I couldn't be the only
one working the logic. 'Kill the leader and kill the threat.
It's like cutting off the head. The rest of the body becomes
useless. I mean, Vampires and Protectors now hunt the
Alphas because they know it will eventually end the repro-
ductive cycle. So, it only stands to reason that the Vânătors
are applying the same logic to Vampires.'

Sebastian gnawed on his lower lip. 'I still think you have
something to do with it. The Protectors founded the serum
on your blood. What's to say that the Vânătors haven't
established similar results since your capture?'

'Because it doesn't make sense. Roshan said—'

'Elena ...'

I held my hand up, trying to recall the details of a conversation I'd had with Roshan. 'Just give me a sec. I need to
figure something out.'

I tapped a finger against my chin, trying to recount
specifics. I'd previously messed around with thoughts of
Roshan striking deals with the IMI to gain access to the
serum, supposing the serum made Vampires and not cured
them. Had I been too quick to dismiss such an absurd idea?
Could the absence of some sections of the IMI relate to
the encroaching Vânătors? Was Sebastian right and did I
somehow play a part in this?

Huffing, I tried to establish why the Vânătors would

move now and how that related to Lucius. As far as I knew from John and Roshan, Vânător motivation consisted of killing, breeding, and if they could manage it, figuring out a way to become true immortals.

'Does Lucius know a way that the Vânators can self-heal?'

Sebastian had moved away from the wall and was now squatting in front of me, perhaps waiting for the great revelation I was hoping would come. 'Not as far as I know. The Protector's serum is the first attempt at changing Vampirism any of us have heard of.'

I willed myself to think harder. The answer had to be somewhere in the juicy folds of my brain matter, yet the information I had to date was all still speculative. 'It's strange that the two correlate don't you think, the knowledge of the serum and the Vânător's impending attacks?'

Sebastian looked taken aback, even grazing my fingers as he touched the arm of the chair to steady himself. It was most distracting. 'Are you suggesting that the IMI has struck some sort of deal with the Vânators?'

'Sebastian, I have no idea.'

He was the one to shake his head this time. 'The Protectors hate the Vânators even more than they hate Vampires.'

'That's true.' I couldn't deny his thought process. Something still ate at me. 'What if it's not about choosing sides? What if it's about pitting us against each other? The alliance has solved nothing, so why not nurture the hate between the beasts The Protectors wish to eradicate?'

'We aren't beasts.'

'I know that,' I murmured, glancing down at the fingers that now gently stroked the top of my knuckles. 'I'm just stating the obvious.'

Sebastian's swirling eyes played havoc with the pit of

my stomach as he gazed up at me. 'How could this have happened, Elena?'

It took a minute for me to catch my breath. 'C–Chester knows Roshan through idiotic endeavours to track and trap him. I thought Chester's minions might have perished in their efforts, but what if some were successful, found Roshan and kept tabs on him?'

'And what would that have achieved?'

'A possible new alliance — the serum in exchange for our deaths.'

Sebastian's fingers stilled upon mine. Just as well. My mouth was going dry and my lips were trembling. 'We don't even know what the serum does.'

'That's not really the point. The Protectors could have told the Vânǎtors what they wanted to hear in order to gain their help.' I reclaimed my hand but was unsure what to do with it, waving it around uselessly before placing it in my lap.

Sebastian smirked. 'I don't know, Elena. It's pretty to think we could figure this all out, but I'm not sure the two are related.'

I nodded, doing my upmost to focus on his scepticism rather than the chiselled jaw and upturned lips determined to upset my equilibrium. 'You said that The Protectors were just biding their time, waiting for the alliance to crumble. If I'm right and they are sitting in the background, pitching the rest of us against each other, then we are in serious trouble. We won't be able to beat them if the Vânǎtors whittle our numbers in war.'

'I'm hoping it won't come to that,' Sebastian said, climbing to his feet once more. He started to pace, moving around the room like a caged predator. 'It would seem all motives are a mystery for now.'

'I could call Lucas and get some answers. Here, give me

your phone.' I was already smiling and waggling my fingers at him. Just the thought of speaking to my brother after all this time killed my somewhat sombre mood.

Sebastian made no effort to retrieve his phone. Instead he stopped pacing and gazed into the barely glowing embers of the fireplace.

'Sebastian, please give me your phone.'

'It won't do you any good,' he murmured.

'That's ridiculous. Lucas is a Protector. Plus, we haven't spoken in weeks and he'll probably be worried about me.'

'I'm sorry, Elena. But we've lost contact with him.'

'What?' I said, staring at him blankly. I could hear his words, but they didn't make a lick of sense.

'I haven't been able to contact Lucas for over a week. Not since the new year, to be exact.'

'You've been talking to my brother?'

'I have been keeping him informed since Roshan took you.'

I smiled, touched. 'Thanks, Sebastian. That was really nice of you.'

He shrugged. 'If it was me, I'd want to know what was happening, too.'

'So, tell me what happened. Why did you lose contact?'

'I honestly don't know. His phone is switched off or unavailable and we aren't that well acquainted that I would know who else to call. He doesn't like me very much so our conversations are usually short and sweet.'

That didn't sound like Lucas. He could talk underwater with a mouth full of marbles. 'Why would you think he doesn't like you?'

'Because I let you leave with Roshan back in Bucharest.'

I chortled, loving the fact that my brother felt the need to overprotect, but I supposed the feeling was mutual. I'd call him, sort this out. He couldn't be completely out of reach. 'I'm sorry Lucas thinks this mess with Roshan is your fault, Sebastian. Just give me your phone and I'll smooth all this over. He has a few cell phone numbers I could try that you probably don't have.'

Sebastian continued to stare at the glowing embers, unmoving. 'I should never have taken you to Bucharest. It was a stupid idea but I did it anyway to keep you happy.'

My sigh was loud enough that he finally looked my way. 'Please stop blaming yourself for my decisions. It makes me look and feel like a helpless idiot.'

A reluctant smile touched his lips. 'We can't have that now, can we?'

'Hell, no.'

We took silent comfort in the swell of one another's smiles, warmed by the sincerity that reached each other's eyes. 'You're so brave, Elena.'

'Don't you mean stupid?' I cackled, certain it was what he was really thinking. 'I'm not brave. I just don't tell anyone when I'm scared.' I slapped my knees to bring the conversation back on point. 'Anyway, how many times have you tried contacting Lucas?'

'A couple of times a day.'

I signalled for the phone again. This time he handed it over without protest. I cycled through every number in my head that I knew and even tried calling Karina and Lisa, The Protector daughters of Martha and Malcolm, to no avail. All phones were disconnected, even the emergency line at the IMI. Something wasn't right.

'I have to find him,' I said, rising from the armchair, my intentions not yet fully realised despite my wayward feet making headway for the door.

Sebastian tracked my movements. 'What, now?'

I found myself nodding enthusiastically. 'Lucas is, and will always be, my number one priority, Sebastian. If anything has happened to him, I'll never forgive myself.'

'So, your plan is to what, fly to Cairns now?'

A millisecond of hesitation passed through me before I nodded again. I hadn't actually resolved a plan, but starting back at the beginning seemed like a pretty good idea.

Sebastian's eyes widened with disbelief. 'I'm sure there's an excellent reason why your brother has not answered his phone. Flying thousands of miles before we've researched all avenues seems a little hasty, don't you think?'

'True, but now that I think on it, there's no way he would have just stopped calling you for updates on my capture if something hadn't have happened.'

I watched a vexed Sebastian flirt with the idea of slapping me for my incessant, ultimately dangerous travel plans born via unfounded theories. 'Your father will strongly object to this idea.'

'If something has happened to Lucas, then I need to know.' I made my way to the front door, my attitude now as steely as my resolve. 'Are you coming?'

'Do I ever really have a choice?' Yep. He definitely wanted to thump me.

I grabbed the handle and twisted the door open. A flood of cold air breached the warmth of the room and sent a chill down my spine. I would not view it as an omen. 'I don't need you with me, so yeah, you do have a choice.'

Sebastian rolled his eyes, clearly of a differing opinion.

'Look,' I stated, knowing he'd validate my point sooner or later, 'the Vânătors haven't made their intentions clear, and we can't rely on The Protectors for answers. Lucas is ultimately the best lead we have, but I do realise that I may not find him in Cairns if things have soured, and thus, we can then explore any new leads we may find there, perhaps revealing the IMI's intentions.'

Sebastian looked positively unhinged. He was clearly opposed to everything I'd said, but the look of defeat in his swirling eyes spoke volumes. I was going to get my way again, even if he really, really didn't like it. 'I can't believe we're playing Sherlock Holmes again right after you escaped a hostage situation.'

I scowled. 'This isn't a game, Watson. This is my brother and *everyone's* future that we're talking about.'

'But why is it always you?'

'Excuse me?'

Sebastian's jaw worked overtime on a tick. He was seriously upset with me. 'Why are you always the one who has to save us all?'

'Because I look freaking awesome in tights.' I turned my back on him and surrendered myself to the frigid air of the porch. 'Are you coming, or not?'

Sebastian threw his hands into the air, not the least bit amused by the prospect of a new adventure. 'Your father is going to kill me this time for sure, Elena.'

'Sebastian, you're technically already a corpse.'

He slammed the front door behind us and mumbled something under his breath about staying dead this time.

'Don't be so dramatic. We'll be in and out of Cairns before you know it.'

Was it bad that his nostrils were flaring?

'You said that about Bucharest, too, and then you ended up spending two and a half weeks with a vicious pack of wolves.'

'What's your point?'

'I think it's safe to assume that your best laid plans don't necessarily work out.'

I was momentarily pensive, determined to lighten his mood. 'Well, I promise if the shit hits the fan again, I'll try and act surprised.'

Sebastian pinched the bridge of his nose, shaking his head. 'You're incorrigible.'

'Thank you.'

'It's not a compliment.'

'Oh.'

Sebastian lunged and scooped me up into his arms before another word was spoken. Despite limp legs now dangling over his left forearm and my head being wedged between his chest and the crook of his right arm, my mouth flew open, prepared to shriek at him to put me down.

'Don't,' Sebastian warned, silencing me with his death stare. 'If you insist on dragging me into yet another one of your stupid ideas then at least let me do it my way.'

'You don't have to come with me,' I pointed out.

'If only that were true.'

'It is true. You know I'm only going to get you into more trouble.'

Shifting me around in his ever tightening grip, Sebastian rushed forward to greet the early morning air. He growled, some virulent part of him incensed by my reasoning. 'You really don't get it, do you, Elena?'

'Get what?'

I was subjected to yet another nostril flare and pursing of lips. Any second he was going to dropkick me back to Cairns instead of taking us to the airport. But Sebastian surprised me by taking a deep breath, killing his irritated features in lieu of stoic calm and then muttered, 'You're killing me, Baby Vamp. You're really killing me.'

At least I was consistent.

CHAPTER ELEVEN

Cairns

I held the phone gingerly, away from my tender eardrums as I listened to every potent word my father felt necessary to expel. Hopping on a plane to Cairns so soon after my abduction struck a raw nerve. Perhaps giving me that platinum Visa card had been a mistake.

'Lucius, I just thought—'

The yelling persisted, so loud that even Sebastian cringed.

'Lucius, I think—'

I placed the phone at arm's length, surprised by the continuing tirade. Ten minutes had lapsed. Two of them revolved around my current geography. Eight minutes and counting had been allocated to verbal teardown and promises of punishment.

'Lucius, please just let me tell you what—'

'Elena, how could you do this? With everything going on and how worried we've all been, you just take off? Do you realise how irresponsible you're being?'

'Yes.'

'You don't need ... *What*?' That shut him up.

'Yeah, Lucius, I know this is shit timing and that you're worried about me, but I have to find Lucas and figure out what's going on. I can't just sit back and do nothing.'

'You've been in the hands of our enemies for over two weeks — two weeks, Elena!'

'I know, Lucius, but Lucas is my family, too, and now that I'm here I might as well find him and try to figure out what's going on with The Protectors.'

Regrettably he started again. This time I couldn't get a word in edgewise.

Sebastian, possibly bored by the exchange, motioned for the phone. I happily passed it on, wondering how he could improve a declining situation. 'Lucius, it's Sebastian.' He nodded a few times. 'Look, it was either come with her, or let her do something stupid.'

I scowled, but if I was being honest, I knew he was right.

'I know I let you down last time, but that won't happen again. She's currently safer here with me than she would be back in Rome.' Sebastian paused, listening. 'Yes, I'm sure that is her intention.' He listened again. 'Look, once we have any information, we'll return. Until then, I'll watch over her.' His shoulders slumped. 'Yes. Thank you for reminding me.'

Sebastian hung up the phone, sliding it back into the rear pocket of his insanely tight pants. I flirted with the idea of trading places with the phone and then wanted to slap myself for the errant thought. Yet as I shuffled behind Sebastian in the taxi cue, it became clear I wasn't the only one infatuated.

'Your father,' Sebastian said, seemingly oblivious to the attention he was drawing, 'is clearly overprotective of you because of his past. If he hadn't lost his wife and child, maybe he wouldn't be so hard on you now.'

'I know.'

Truthfully, I was too distracted to listen. My fascination with Sebastian's rear end was tempered by the other women gathered in the taxi cue. Seductive glances, a show of leg and the sudden releasing of shirt buttons had me concerned.

'I suspect it's no different to how you feel about Lucas,' Sebastian continued, trying to make a point that I was currently unavailable to acknowledge. 'Lucius has been trying to ease you into the bonds. He doesn't want to push himself upon you, but at the same time, you're his long lost daughter. It's hard to rein in the fear of losing you again. It's twice as hard now that everyone is after you, including Julius. I think that worries him the most.'

Hmm, the bond, our blood connection. With just a touch, Lucius could sift through my memories and thoughts like old photographs. I really freaking hated the invasion of privacy, intentional or not. I needed to figure out a way to block him from future, metaphysical break-ins.

'Are you even listening to me?' Sebastian joked. He flashed me that cocky, megawatt grin over his shoulder. My insides melted and my legs turned to jelly. Shit. That smile was like an all you can eat buffet for overeaters anonymous and he'd just invited everyone at the damn restaurant to eat.

The two teenage girls behind us started to giggle. When I looked back they flipped me off and then went back to ogling Sebastian. I wasn't surprised by the gesture. I'd once seen a wheelchair-bound grandmother bulldoze gathered admirers at an airport terminal and run over my foot just to get a single shot at him.

Jealous? Me?

Hell, yes.

Behind the two girls more women flocked — four senior citizens and their oblivious husbands and three no-fuss women dressed in business suits holding briefcases like weapons. Behind them was a travelling group of varied ages. One held a *Lonely Planet* guide and eyeballed me like she wanted to ram it down my throat. Another one whipped out a nail file like a prison inmate, the impossibly sharp points of her nails, and her weapon of choice, poised for an eye gauging.

Jesus.

Sebastian didn't notice, or if he did, he pretended he hadn't and if he was waiting for an answer to whatever question he'd asked me, then he'd be waiting a really long time.

My mouth parted as the teens hiked up their skirts to inappropriate lengths. A surprised exhalation followed when the senior citizens pulled out their dentures and made puckering noises with wrinkled lips. *Lonely Planet* lady started suggestively licking the spine of her book and the prison inmate used the nail file to snap the buttons on the front of her pants. As for the briefcases, you don't want to know what they collectively started to do.

I tugged nervously on Sebastian's arm. 'You're doing that thing again. You might want to ease up.'

'What thing?' Sebastian said, leaning down to brush an errant lock of hair from my cheek. 'We were talking about your father. Focus, Elena.'

'Ow!' I spun and glared at the snarling mob as I rubbed the back of my head. The projectile nail file now lay abandoned at my feet and I stooped to pick it up, clutching it tightly and fisting it at prison inmate. 'You're not getting this back!'

She flipped me off. What a bitch!

'Are you all right?' Sebastian asked.

'Shit!' I squealed, bending to pick up the *Lonely Planet* book that had just clipped me on the shoulder.

'What's going on?' Sebastian murmured, finally turning to eye the enthusiastic crowd behind us. 'Oh, I see.'

I made a point of distancing myself from Sebastian. As

far as I was concerned, he could fend off the army of oestrogen on his own. Been there, done that, got the damn T-shirt.

'Where are you going?'

I jerked a thumb over my shoulder. 'They're trying to kill me with their travel paraphernalia, so I'm going to stand over here, clear of the imminent stampede.'

Sebastian pointed to the grossly overweight, shirtless male tourist now in front of me. 'You're only safe if he doesn't back up.'

I snickered, amazed by the river of sweat pooling in the flesh folds of his lower back. Clearly not used to the hot and humid weather that Cairns summers dictated, I was equally repulsed by the glistening strands of hair that covered his shirtless back. Honestly, if he hadn't been wearing sweat-stained cargo pants and holding onto a backpack, I might have mistaken him for a wild animal, whipped out a tranquiliser gun and taken him down.

Yuck.

Squeals of delight drew my attention back to Sebastian. He'd done that smiling thing again, totally encouraging and completely irresponsible. The crowd surged and I was catapulted by an urgent shove. I hit the sweaty tourist, my hands glancing off the sides of his glistening skin a second before I face planted his hairy back folds.

Sebastian was a dead man.

I came up for air, steadied my feet and began maniacally wiping salty fluid from my face. Trying not to vomit was the hard part, but apologising for the bungle when I'd been the one to almost drown in sweaty flesh? Yep. That set my teeth on edge.

When the next available taxi arrived, I hauled ass into the back seat and yelled directions as I continued to scrub at my face. Sebastian climbed in beside me, giving the mob an indulgent wave. The women pouted and scrawled phone numbers in lipstick across the windows.

I swallowed back a mouthful of bile.

The taxi driver sang along with the radio as he pulled into the wave of exit traffic, while Sebastian sat beside me, eyes on my profile. I pretended not to notice and instead indulged in thoughts of finding antibacterial facial wipes.

The city of Cairns was a welcoming distraction as it sprung up around us. Hotels, bistros, minimarts and beer gardens were apparently ready for the influx of more tourists.

Locals were already prepping businesses for the long day ahead or fighting with the early morning traffic that filled both inbound and outbound lanes. Some were out jogging or walking their dogs. Others sat sipping coffee at one of the many, graffiti-covered bus stops. Strangely, I missed this place, missed the predictability of it.

'No matter what happens,' Sebastian said, 'whether Lucas is here or not, I promise we'll figure this thing out together.' They were decidedly heartfelt words when teamed with the warm fingers that suddenly encircled my hand and stroked me tenderly.

I looked down at our entwined fingers and nodded, uncertain how else to respond. Fortunately I didn't have to think about it too deeply as 'Cairns Fine Furniture and Accessories' approached us on the left.

I shrugged free of Sebastian's hold and leant forward to tap the driver on the shoulder. 'Excuse me? Would you stop in front of that store over there please? I need to make a pit stop.'

'A furniture shop?' Sebastian asked. The taxi driver obeyed without question and pulled to a stop by the curb.

'I used to work here.' I lowered my voice. 'It's owned by

a Protector called Martha. Her daughter Lisa and I studied together at the local branch of the IMI.' I turned back to the taxi driver, who was brazenly ogling me in the rear-view mirror. 'Please just keep the meter running. We shouldn't be too long.'

'Whatever you need, Miss.'

Great.

I opened the door and climbed out, Sebastian only a second behind. He followed without question, threading his fingers through mine as we navigated the long driveway to rear car park and docking area currently absent of vehicles.

The roller door was down, no doubt locked, but I didn't think it would be too difficult for us to break in. Yanking it upwards saw the locks busted within seconds.

'Nice,' Sebastian teased, eyeing my handiwork. 'I always thought you were a law abiding citizen. Apparently not.'

'I have a key to this place ... somewhere. I just don't have it with me right now.'

Sebastian looked pointedly at the mangled locks. 'I don't think it really matters. What are you looking for anyway?'

'Anything that may help us figure out what's going on.'

'And you expect to find it here, in a furniture shop?'

I shrugged, moving through to the back. There was a key for this door under the smoker's tin. Glen, the store manager, believed no one would ever look there. He was probably right. 'I honestly don't know what we'll find, but it doesn't hurt to check.'

With the door now unlocked, Sebastian wandered into the main showroom while I hung back and checked the staffroom and office. The staffroom created no need to loiter with just the usual — a sink, a fridge and last week's rubbish.

I headed for Martha's office and stopped in the doorway

to survey the space. Nothing had changed as far as I could tell. Papers were still scattered across the desk, open client files and fabric samples everywhere. She had never been very tidy.

'Um, Elena?' Sebastian urgently whispered from the front.

'Yeah?'

'You might want to come out here.'

I headed hastily down the short corridor to the front of the store. Glen had changed all of the displays since I'd been here, but that was no surprise. Months had passed. 'What's up?'

Sebastian was drawn to the front window, eyes chasing a car that now rounded the taxi's bumper and hooned down the side driveway.

'Shit.'

'I gather you know who it is?'

I looked at the clock on the wall behind the front counter. 'It's Kayla, but I would have thought it'd be too early for her to be here.'

Sebastian lifted his nose and sniffed. 'She's human.'

I nodded, wondering if we should hide or make a run for it. I didn't know if seeing her again was a good or a bad thing. She'd been my only friend outside of the IMI, but I hadn't kept in contact since leaving Cairns. There was an excellent chance she'd be pissed at me.

'What are we doing about this?' Sebastian pressed.

'I don't know.'

A car door slammed, the time left available to make a decision dwindling.

'What the—'

Kayla was already on the dock, undoubtedly surveying the broken roller door. I'd forgotten about that, so hiding was well and truly out of the question.

I ran down the corridor and burst through the back door, scaring the absolute bejesus out of her. She screamed and dropped her mobile phone, a rather fortuitous turn in events since I assumed she'd begun contacting the cops with it.

Kayla stumbled, fell on her ass and cried out once more when the phone smashed on the concrete dock. It was only as the adrenaline finally began to fade did her wide eyes recognise me. 'Elena?'

I rushed to her side, grabbed her arm and hauled her back to her feet. 'Jesus, Kayla. I'm so sorry to scare you like that.' I then bent down, scooped up the scraps of her phone and handed them back to her.

She studied the cracked LCD and exposed silicone with a scowl. 'What are you doing here?'

'Long story.'

'No, seriously, what are you doing here? I was just about to call the cops. I thought we'd been broken into again!'

I grimaced. 'I just came for a visit.'

Kayla tossed her long mane of platinum blonde hair over her shoulders and glared at me like I'd just run over her dog. 'Elena, I haven't heard from you in months and now you just show up and expect ...' She stopped speaking. Her narrowed eyes shifted and her furrowed brow smoothed out. Anger had been replaced with surprise, her dainty, scarlet-painted lips now moving, but absent of bitter words.

Curious by Kayla's rapid change in demeanour, I turned to see what she was staring at. I suppose I should have known better.

'Hi,' Sebastian said, coolly leaning against the doorframe and resting his head against his arm.

Oh pul-lease ...

Kayla giggled, batting her eyelashes, all anger forgotten. 'Hi.'

'I'm Sebastian.'

'I'm Kayla.'

'Nice to meet you, Kayla.'

My face darkened and my stomach twisted in knots. I couldn't help feeling slighted that my friend and ... Sebastian were maintaining any form of extended eye contact.

I stepped in front of Kayla, effectively blocking Sebastian from view. 'You're at work early,' I chided, annoyed that I couldn't disguise the bitterness in my voice.

Kayla craned her neck to see past me, her intent more than obvious and gut-wrenchingly infuriating. 'Yeah, I'm making up some hours. I took some time off last week.'

'It's good to see you, Kayla. I missed you, you know.'

'Yeah, missed you too,' she said, pushing me out of the way so she could offer Sebastian one of her teasing smiles.

Should tears have stung my eyes in that moment? I knew that Sebastian had this effect on women. Shouldn't I know better than to get upset over situations in which I had no control?

The answer was yes, but jealousy and my friend's current disregard for my presence stung the very centre of my core. 'Please, Sebastian,' I begged, 'I don't profess to understand why you are the way you are, or why you won't explain it to me, but please don't do it with this one.'

I couldn't look at Sebastian as he approached, worried that the roiling emotion within me would spill those ridiculous tears upon my cheeks. Why was I allowing myself to feel this way? I was solid, unmoveable and emotionally untouchable. Wasn't I?

Sebastian's warm breath caressed my cheek with unnerving persistence, his nearness and the scent of his charmed skin almost overwhelming for both Kayla and I. She practically vibrated with pleasure, incessantly licking her lips and cracking the fingers at her side.

He leant closer still, his lips brushing my lobe. I couldn't contain the shiver the rolled through me. 'I've told you before, Elena, I have no control over this effect I have on human women. And, despite what you may think, I would never intentionally hurt you by taking up with your friend, or for that matter, succumbing to the temptation of any other offers.'

Words evaded me. Our time apart had only strengthened the confusing affection I'd gathered for him since first meeting. Perhaps my tied-tongue was in fact for the best. I didn't want to say or feel anything that would break my focus and weaken my heart.

But then a gentle hand was on my chin, his probing gaze my undoing. Our eyes met and I was lost, consumed by the same spell that had Kayla bouncing up and down like an excited puppy at my feet. 'Elena, I have never touched another woman in my entire—'

'You can touch me!' Kayla shrieked, no longer able to contain her enthusiasm. She seeped lust like her pores could no longer suppress the urge. 'Please,' she moaned, 'I'll do anything if you just touch me like you're touching her!'

A sudden flurry of wind that ruffled our hair and dried my damp eyes came and went as quickly as the warmth of Sebastian's touch. He may have been gone but my unease still lingered.

Kayla blinked as if waking from a trance. She rubbed her sleepy eyes and smeared mascara across her face. I was still annoyed enough at her not to mention it. 'Elena? Oh my God, Elena. I'm sorry, I totally spaced. I'm so happy to see you.' She threw her arms around me, rubbing her cheek against mine. She smelled like designer perfume and talcum powder.

I relented and hugged her back, blaming her behaviour entirely on compulsion. 'I'm happy to see you, too.'

She pulled back, smiling excitedly. 'So, is Sebastian your new boyfriend?'

'No.'

'Really?' She groaned and punched my arm. 'Seriously, what's wrong with you? You keep meeting hot guys and nothing eventuates.'

'Hardly.'

She scoffed and rolled her eyes. 'Please. Who was the last one, William something or other? Anyway, if you don't want the latest serving of tall, dark and handsome ...' She wiggled her eyebrows at me and giggled when irritation spread across my features. 'Okay, okay. Hands off, I get it. Are you on holiday?'

I shook my head. 'This visit definitely wasn't planned.'

'How long are you staying?'

'I don't know. Not long.'

Kayla's rather upbeat mood suddenly somersaulted off a cliff, taking a nose-dive towards the fiery pits of the underworld. 'What happened to you, Elena? You never called.'

I knew this question would come, so I gathered both her hands in mine and squeezed. 'I'm so sorry, Kayla. I never meant to stop calling. It's been a rough couple of months. The places I've been have made contact virtually impossible.'

She toed the edge of the smoker's tin, averting her eyes. 'I left so many messages. It just felt like you didn't care anymore.' I didn't miss those chocolate brown eyes swimming with moisture. 'I thought we were friends, Elena. Friends don't stop calling no matter what.' She rubbed her eyes yet again, smearing even more mascara across her porcelain cheeks. She looked like she was going to war.

'I even called Lucas,' Kayla continued, her voice shaky, 'but he said you were in a remote area without service. I went and saw him three days ago to get more information, but now he's gone, too.'

'I see.'

'The house is up for rent. How come you don't know this?'

'That's an excellent question.'

'I don't understand.'

'You and me both,' I muttered.

'Do you need a place to stay?' Concern dripped from every word. It was obvious I was adrift in a sea of lies. I had no idea what had happened to my family and Kayla knew it, making it her duty to rescue me.

In effort to be brave, my voice came out choked and slightly raspy. 'No, I'm fine, thanks.'

'But if your family isn't—'

'I'm fine, Kayla.'

She grunted, pursed her lips, but didn't push the envelope with further comment.

'The trip wasn't entirely wasted, I got to see you again,' I said, forcing an air of levity back into the conversation. I hoped my smile wasn't as transparent as my disappointment.

Kayla wrapped an arm around my shoulder and returned my smile begrudgingly. 'Look, I'm glad you're here, Elena, but I'm still pissed at you for not calling.'

'I know and I really am sorry.'

She nodded, accepting. 'And I'm sorry about whatever weird shit is going down with your family right now.'

'Thanks.'

Kayla squeezed my upper arm and then pushed me away, her mood flipping like a pancake as she squawked excitedly, 'But now that you are here, there's a great party on this weekend and—'

'I can't stay for a party.'

Kayla rediscovered her pout. 'Can you at least stay until Glen and Martha get in? They'll be happy to see you and then maybe we can do lunch or dinner together tonight?'

I shook my head and wrestled Kayla into a bear hug before protestations could begin. 'I would love that, but I really do have to go. There's a taxi out the front with my name on it.'

Kayla returned my embrace with a fierceness I'd not expected. 'Please don't go yet. I've missed you, Elena.'

'I've missed you, too. I'm sorry this has been the shortest catch-up in history, but I really have to go now.'

She sniffed, rubbing at her ruined make up again. 'You had no idea your family bailed on you, did you?'

I wasn't quite sure what to say, so I changed the subject. 'Please don't tell anyone that I was here, especially Martha.'

'How am I supposed to explain the damaged locks on the roller door?'

'Kayla, please. It's important Martha doesn't know I'm in Cairns.'

Her confusion morphed into suspicion. 'Why?'

'Just because, okay?' It wasn't even close to being a decent explanation, but then again, I'd never been able to give Kayla the absolute truth about anything. 'Speaking of Martha, is she okay?'

'Seriously? Now you want details when you won't give me any?' She was understandably incredulous.

I grimaced, toeing a rough bit of concrete at my feet. 'I know I'm acting weird, but please humour me. Has she been acting like herself lately?'

'What do you mean exactly?'

'Spacey, uncertain …'

Kayla's lips twisted with disapproval. 'She's fine, more focused on work than ever.'

'What about her daughter Lisa?'

'A hormonal teenager who hates school. Seriously, Elena, what's with the twenty questions?'

'Wait, so Lisa's in school? No more home tutoring?'

Kayla was all but tapping her foot now. 'What's your point?'

I leaned in for a final hug, now so distracted by my thoughts that I barely noticed Kayla's stiff posture and lack of response. 'I'll call you soon. I gotta run.'

'Elena!'

I was already jumping the dock and running down the long driveway back towards the taxi. Being a shitty friend was the last thing on my mind as I was consumed by thoughts of Protectors mainstreaming. Why was Martha working full-time and Lisa now attending high school? Both sounded shackled to normality and I wondered if in doing so, they had also disbanded the use of magic?

Sebastian was already in the taxi when I returned, his head reclined, eyes closed.

'Where to now, Miss?' the driver asked. I gave him the address of the hardware store Susan and George owned. I needed answers and hoped the more stones I overturned the more chances of unearthing the truth there'd be.

Silence filled the cab for several uneasy minutes until Sebastian moved to touch my hand. 'I'm sorry,' he said, swirling eyes apologetic. 'I need you to know that I don't do what I do on purpose. I would never knowingly attract your friend and—'

'Don't sweat it,' I interrupted, consumed by more important matters than my jealousy or Sebastian's transcendent charisma.

'I'm serious, Elena. I don't want you to think of me like this. Who I am, the things I do, all of it is—'

'You have no idea what I'm thinking.'

'I know that you think I'm a player, preying on every girl I see.'

I reclaimed my hand and tucked it into the safety of my lap. 'I don't think about you at all, Sebastian.'

Liar. Liar. Liar.

Silence returned, bar the drone of the soft rock radio station now playing in the background. I dared not look at him, knowing those eyes were drilling holes in the side of my temple.

'Then I'm not doing something right,' Sebastian finally murmured. 'I guess I'm going to have to take matters into my own hands. This can't go on.'

'What can't go on?'

'Your inability to see the truth.'

'The truth according to you.'

'We're here, Miss,' the taxi driver interrupted. 'Do you want me to wait around again?' He was back to objectifying me in the rear-view mirror with a sleazy smile and puckered lips.

'Yes, please.'

Before Sebastian and I could enter into yet another pointless and circular conversation, I made a hasty exit, slamming the car door behind me and glancing up at the familiar store sign. Chain stores had stolen a bit of business in recent years, but the location was handy for tradesman and city dwellers, so we'd survived. Or should I say the new owners would survive. It was hard to miss the 'under new management' sign pasted over the metal banner above.

Through the window display I spotted Wesley — all six foot seven inches of him. Blond, blue-eyed and eerily resembling the rest of the Manory family, he'd been working alongside Susan and George since he was sixteen. It was good to see that some things didn't change, even if everything else did.

I waved and waltzed through the front door. 'Hey, Wesley.'

'Elena?' He put down the money he'd been counting out from the cash register. To say he was surprised to see me was an understatement. 'What are you doing here? I thought you moved overseas on an exchange, or something?'

'That what Susan and George told you?'

He nodded. 'Well, yeah.'

I smiled, happy to play along. 'I'm on a break.'

He started to nod again and then faltered, his brows furrowing. 'Can I help you with anything in particular?'

'No, I was driving by and saw the sign outside. I didn't realise we'd sold the shop.'

Wesley relaxed, the easy smile he wore back to coveting his features. 'It's been in the works for a while. The contracts went through about two weeks ago and I've been running the place ever since. I'm surprised Susan and George didn't tell you.'

'So, you're the new management?'

'I am.'

'Congratulations,' I offered, not really sure what else I could add.

'Thanks.'

We both turned as the bell announced Sebastian's arrival. He wandered past some shelves, pretending to study the merchandise.

'Can I help you?' Wesley called out, his eyes focused like a hawk on the possibility of a sale.

Sebastian shook his head. 'I'm just looking. I'll call you if I need anything.'

Wesley focused his attention back on me. 'Well, it's been

good to see you again, though I'm surprised you're back in Cairns when the Manorys just left. Is everything okay? Do you need a place to stay?'

Sebastian coughed, capturing Wesley's attention again before he stooped to study some garden hose on a lower rack.

Ignoring Sebastian's antics, I said, 'Nah, I'm good thanks, Wesley. I guess I was just hoping you might be able to tell me how long Susan and George are planning on staying away and if you have some way to contact them.'

Wesley put the remainder of the money he'd been counting in the cash register and closed the drawer. His blue eyes narrowed substantially, his fingers tapping the edge of the counter. 'You don't know where they are?'

'Um ...' I wasn't really sure how to answer that without bolstering his concern.

Wesley nibbled the corner of his lower lip and said, 'I'm worried about you, Elena. After the contracts were signed, I didn't need to keep tabs on Susan and George so I have no idea where they are. I feel like I should be calling child services, or something.'

'No, don't do that. I'm okay.'

'I don't think so.'

Uh oh.

I started heading for the front door, backing away like a frightened kitten. There was no more to learn from here and nothing to gain but an overnighter in a government building filled with do-gooders.

'Elena, wait, don't go.' Wesley's fingers were already poised above the phone, twitching and uncertain.

'Bye, Wesley.' I rushed through the door, presuming Sebastian would follow. As I slid into the taxi, buckled up and attempted to catch my breath, Sebastian finally sauntered out of the store, expression neutral.

'What took you so long?' I asked as he slipped in beside me.

He tapped the side of his temple and lowered his voice to little more than a whisper. 'I erased his memory of your appearance.'

'Oh, okay, yeah, good idea.'

The taxi glided away from the kerb, the driver taking fresh directions to the Manory residence. Even knowing Lucas wouldn't be there, I had to see it for myself.

Meanwhile, Sebastian made good use of the travel time by contacting Peter's martial arts academy, Kim and Vincent's law office, and Malcolm's language school to substantiate suspicions.

Peter now worked full-time, apparently setting up a lot of new classes he'd never had time for in the past due to his commitments as an IMI trainer.

Vincent now dabbled with unemployment. The practice informed Sebastian that Kim was now the sole owner of the law firm and that legal aid would be handled swiftly and professionally by any other member of staff. Naturally, they wouldn't divulge his reasons for leaving, or his current location, but reminded us of their capable and friendly staff.

'Friendly' wasn't exactly a word I'd use to describe Kim.

As for Malcolm, the language school was now short a Spanish teacher. He'd quit before the New Year and apparently left the country with his daughter Karina. It was a curiosity why some key members of our faction were now gone and others had stayed. The IMI had always been most influential in any Protector's life. Now the institution appeared to be taking a back seat to the prioritisation of making a buck.

'Do you think The Protectors still in this area have been be-spelled?' Sebastian asked.

It was a good question. 'I don't know. Unless I see them for myself and ask them questions, I wouldn't know.'

'I don't want you near any of them. It's too dangerous. I won't risk entrapment again.'

I nodded. 'That's fair, and I agree with you. If the others have been be-spelled, they won't know where the others went, anyway. It would defeat the purpose and put us both at unnecessary risk.'

'You're worried they still might recognise you.'

'Probably.' I glanced out the window, noting we were close to my old house. 'Just pull over here, please.'

'Another pit stop?' the driver asked, winking at me. Gross. The taxi rolled to a stop on the corner of my street, the meter ticking over to a questionable amount.

'Nope, we're getting out here.'

'That's a shame.' He turned and smiled, his teeth laced with calculus build-up and unappealing spots of decay. Should I mention his greasy moustache, fake tan, eighties perm job and the fact he was probably twenty years my senior?

I grappled with the doorhandle. 'Um, thanks.'

'It was certainly all my pleasure.'

Sebastian's nostrils flared. 'Turn around, little Italy. You've got no chance.'

The driver shrugged, his bloodshot eyes undressing me from head to toe. 'You can't blame a guy for trying.'

'You'd be surprised what I can do with an unmarked grave and five minutes of free time,' Sebastian muttered, throwing two hundred dollars at the driver before climbing out of the car.

'Did he just threaten me?' The driver didn't seem overly concerned as he set about pocketing the greenbacks. Still, he fixed me with a scowl and indicated with a jerk of his thumb to get on out of his musty old cab.

'Sorry my ... uh ... *brother* is a hot head.'

Yep. Total face-palm moment. Of all the relations I could have chosen — partner, cousin, super-secret agent — I went with the *Flowers in the Attic* variety of crazy connections.

Sebastian missed nothing. 'Brother?' he chided, slamming the taxi door behind him. He started to pace, shaking his head at me. Muffled Italian profanities followed, most of which I understood and wasn't entirely certain I deserved. At least he was smart enough to mess with the driver's memory too.

I scrambled out of the taxi, the driver coughing up an abundance of bilious exhaust fumes as he peeled away from the curb.

Sebastian still paced, clearly annoyed by my choice of words. Brother? Even I was questioning that phrasing and the urge I'd felt to explain myself to a sleazy stranger.

'Are you okay?'

'No, I'm not, okay,' Sebastian spat, turning to face me with a look of dark intent. 'Do you really look at me like I'm your brother?'

'Hardly.'

'Then why would you even suggest such a thing?'

I shrugged.

'Why did we even take a taxi? I'm a Vampire. I can run us anywhere, and in less time.'

'Really? You want to debate the cab ride?'

'Of course not.'

'So you're upset because ...'

Sebastian's hands were suddenly on my shoulders, fingers digging for bone, his face inches from mine. 'Let's get one thing straight. Under no circumstances are you *ever* to refer to me as your brother again.'

'Stepbrother?' I wrestled for freedom. 'Is this about William?'

'Elena!'

'What? I didn't mean to upset you. I don't even know why I said it.'

'I mean it, Elena, never again.'

I gnawed my lower lip, a little bewildered about the guilt I suddenly felt over a passing remark. 'Jeesh, I'm sorry, okay? Why are you so antsy about this? I mean, would it really be that bad to be my brother? Would being tied to a half breed like me really disgust you that much?'

Sebastian's eyes closed momentarily; his fingers tightened on my shoulders and a steadying breath followed. 'It has nothing to do with your genetics, Elena. It was not my intention to make you feel … inadequate.'

I huffed, perplexed as ever. 'Then why are we still having this stupid conversation?'

'Because brothers don't do this …' He finished the sentence by capturing my lips with his, our breath mingled and tongues collided.

Shock was fleeting; overwhelmed by the complexity of emotions Sebastian awakened. I fell into that kiss as easily as we argued and laughed about nothing, delighting in the taste and unexpected sense of promise.

As the kiss urged greater passion, I disregarded ramifications and acted on impulse, dragging him against me with burning need. I'd tasted him in my dreams, drunk from his lips, but never imagined it could feel like this. So incredible was the wanton pull of our touch that I surrendered doubt to the molten feel of his mouth and submerged myself in pleasure.

It was like magic. It was like …

Drowning.

Outside the kiss a storm was brewing. The raging wind of knowledge pelted my resolve, blowing my mind and sanity to unravel the mystery of a past long forgotten.

Sebastian had once told me that a kiss would change everything between us, and now I could see true desire, but was inept to interpret the complexities of my heart and soul.

So I broke away, gasping for breath, confused. I needed to think. I needed air. I needed to rewind the last few minutes and claim back my sanity. There was no way that what I'd just seen and felt in Sebastian's arms could be tangible.

I stumbled despite Sebastian's sure grip, overwhelmed by the tide of feelings unleashed with sudden and brutal force. I could barely see straight; my whole body tingled from his touch and my mind was adrift in a sea of memories I didn't understand.

My lips trembled and knees quaked, and when I found my voice, it was meek and breathless. 'Why didn't you tell me?'

Sebastian hesitated to speak but nevertheless reached for me, and when our fingers collided and warmth emanated from that gentle caress, I knew our relationship was forever changed. 'Would you have believed me if I had?'

'That's not the point.'

He studied our unified fingers, stroking the top of my hand with his thumb. 'I have rules I must follow, Elena.'

I scoffed. 'Your rules are stupid. You should never have kept this from me. This … this changes everything, Sebastian.'

'I hope so.'

'Don't jest. I'm confused and feel like I've lost all control. I hate it — hate knowing I have no real choice about us.'

Sebastian released my hands and moved to wrap his arms around my waist. Ten minutes ago I would have rejected the advance, now it felt like coming home. What the hell? 'Why don't we just concentrate on figuring out what the IMI are up to and once you've had a chance to breathe, we'll talk about this.'

'We're so wrong for each other,' I mumbled, my palms absently smoothing the hardened planes of his chest. 'Love makes you weak, stupid and vulnerable and honestly, Sebastian, you think monogamy is something furniture is crafted from. We're both messed up and emotionally retarded.'

He laughed, resting his chin on the top of my head while fidgeting with the curls at my nape. It felt good and wrong and … 'Elena, all you have is assumptions, not facts.'

'Do I? Can you honestly say you're not different from all the versions of you I saw in my head?'

'It's complicated, but basically I'm whoever you need me to be, Elena. It's how it's always been.'

'Complicated?' I repeated. '*Complicated* doesn't even begin to describe whatever this is, Sebastian.' I extricated myself from his soothing embrace, putting space between us. 'I can't believe this bullshit is conceivable.'

'Please don't swear,' Sebastian murmured, eyes darkening.

Challenging him I said, 'You dropped a bombshell on me with that kiss, Sebastian. So shut up and deal with the mood swing or walk away.'

He did, turning and heading in the opposite direction.

I stared after him, crestfallen. I'd expected a fight, some sort of resolution that wouldn't involve confronting my own emotional turmoil. Wait. Was it normal for my lips to still be buzzing from his kiss?

I touched the slightly swollen flesh and sighed. 'You don't even know where you're going!' I yelled after him, muttering more profanities as I reluctantly hurried to catch up.

Sebastian didn't wait. He ducked and weaved the morning sun, silent and eyes locked on the street ahead. I wondered if he was as affected by the kiss as I was.

The tune from early morning birds worked as a temporary distraction. Kookaburras hiding in willow trees or sitting high on the electrical wires burst forth with their contented laughter and made a mockery of my internal trepidation.

In the distance a cane train clattered along rusted tracks, compression brakes squealing as it rounded the corner. Teamed with the summer breeze that blew gently through palm fronds and I was still thinking about Sebastian ... and his mouth ... and other things.

'What's wrong?' Sebastian asked. He was now standing in the shade of our neighbour's carport.

'Nothing. I'm fine.'

'You don't look fine.'

'Gold star for you,' I mumbled. A real estate sign was pitched just over the fence, a glaring indicator that our property was indeed up for rent. The empty house and pile of cardboard boxes stacked high in the carport confirmed it.

'Elena?'

'I said I'm fine, Sebastian.'

'Perhaps we should not delay our talk. Perhaps what you need is answers.'

I started to laugh, bemused by the offer after weeks of evasion. I'd run out of fingers if I counted the number of times I'd made the same suggestion.

I must have been oozing sarcasm because he said, 'Elena, I will try to explain.'

'Unless they are breaking your rules ...'

'Of course.'

I snickered and shook my head. 'Why kiss me if you knew we would come back to this circular conversation?'

'I wanted to kiss you.'

My amusement faded. 'What about what I want?'

Sebastian squinted against the morning brightness, easing further back into the dark depths of the neighbour's carport. 'What do you want, Elena?'

The answer seemed simple enough. 'I want the truth.'

'The truth is complicated and changes everything.'

'And the kiss didn't?'

I could barely see him in the shadows but knew his eyes were upon me, a flash of silver in the darkness indicating his otherness. 'Okay,' he finally agreed. 'The kiss changed things, but nothing you didn't already know.'

'Certainly nothing I was prepared for,' I retorted.

'It was always all there in your dreams.'

'And that's all I thought they were until you opened Pandora's Box.'

Sebastian moved to the fore, shifting restlessly from foot to foot. His arms were folded in front of his chest and his brows furrowed. What could he possibly have to be annoyed about? I was the one constantly left in the dark. 'And now that you know about our past together, is denial really the answer?' he asked me.

'What are you talking about?'

'You deny your feelings, bury the truth inside the darkest part of you, and yet, in your mind it's okay for me to take all the risks, tell you secrets that could mean my ultimate demise but you don't have to put yourself out there for me.'

'Come on, ultimate demise? It's not the same thing.'

'It's exactly the same.'

'It's not. I'm asking for the truth and you're asking for my heart.'

Love. I was uncertain what the word even meant. But looking into Sebastian's eyes now, I had a feeling he'd willingly help me translate. I was just scared to put feeling into words and words into action without exposing myself to pain or vulnerability.

Great. I knew what this meant: more fun-filled, emotionally charged moments on the horizon, a fun and confusing year which I'd undoubtedly find a way to screw up.

Could I be any more out of my league?

CHAPTER TWELVE

Messages

Pushing aside the buzz from the kiss and emotions Sebastian had unearthed was easier said than done. My mind was a riot of thoughts and my knickers in knots, but I forced myself to think of only one thing — Lucas. At least I didn't have to remind Sebastian what we were here for. He was apparently much better at compartmentalising than I was.

'Stay behind me,' he murmured, taking the lead as we crept around the corner of the fence line.

I scowled. 'The house is empty. Why do I need to stay behind you?'

An impatient look greeted me. 'Caution is important, Elena. The Protectors have the gift of invisibility.'

'They aren't here.'

'Although I agree, their scent lingers and we should be sure before being arrogant.'

I scoffed, pushing past him. 'Come on.'

Sebastian grabbed my arm. 'Elena, be smart about this.'

The skin tingled where he touched me. 'We should go around the back, easier access.' I shook him off and headed through an opening in the fence and into the overgrown backyard. Sebastian followed, muttering negativity under his breath.

I moved through the jutting, dense foliage, traipsing the familiar path to the back door. I pressed my face against the smudged glass, seeing nothing inside but an empty room. No furniture, no rugs, no dining table, and certainly no signs of life.

'Are we going in?' Sebastian's breath was warm against my ear.

I shivered. 'This door makes too much noise. I'll show you another way inside.'

We were outside the laundry door a minute later. I removed the butterfly clips that held the flimsy window screen in place and then reached through the gap between the glass louvers to seek out the doorhandle. The lock disengaged and the door swung open.

'You're getting quite good at this whole breaking and entering thing,' Sebastian mused. 'I wonder what other felonies you've committed.'

'Wouldn't you like to know?'

Jesus. Was I flirting?

Sebastian, indifferent, shrugged as he walked past me and into the house. I felt robbed of the teasing retort I'd expected to pass his perfectly formed lips.

Deflated, I closed the laundry door behind us and followed Sebastian into the hall. The staircase on the right led to the two upstairs bedrooms and bathroom. Going left would reveal the front entry, kitchen, living areas and Susan and George's old bedroom. We started downstairs first, finding nothing.

I quickly headed for the stairs, taking the treads two at a time. My bedroom was the next stop, a room now filled with stench of mildew and coated in a fine layer of dust. Deep lacerations on the timber floorboards were evidence that furniture had once decorated the space. All other evidence of my previous habitation had been erased.

'Was this your room?' Sebastian asked, appearing at my back.

'My bed used to be here,' I answered, marking out the space. 'Over here was my desk and chair, and over here was my dresser and clothes.'

'It still smells like you in here.'

My nose wrinkled. 'That's reassuring considering it smells like decay.'

Sebastian left the room, obviously satisfied there was nothing more to gather from my sarcasm or the empty space.

I paused at the threshold just long enough to run my fingers over the rough surface of the recently replaced door. The old one had been knifed by William, an interesting moment on the path to familiarity — the day he'd discovered my dual nature and I'd believed he might kill me.

'Penny for your thoughts?'

I picked at a tiny splinter threatening to embed itself in the tip of one of my fingers. 'What? Oh,' I murmured, attempting to suck the rest of the wooded debris free, 'I was just thinking about the past.'

'Yes?'

'Well, I guess despite everything — namely the lies — I had a pretty good life here.'

Sebastian reached for my hand, picked free what remained of the pesky splinter and then knotted his fingers through mine. 'I'm glad,' he said. 'To know that you had a childhood where you were protected and sheltered is a relief.'

'Why would that matter to you?'

Sebastian's swirling gaze met mine, a whirlpool of emotion that battled for supremacy over an expression he kept tightly reined. 'I think you already know the answer to that.'

Because you love me.

I glanced away, afraid my own eyes would betray me. 'I just don't understand how two people who barely know each other can feel so ...' Words evaded me. Perhaps I was distracted by the thumb he kept stroking in soothing circles over mine.

'Connected?' Sebastian finished. 'And we barely know each other because you don't take the time to change that.'

'Not true.'

'You never actually talk to me, Elena, just judge and speculate.'

'Is that right?'

'What's my favourite colour?'

'Seriously? What does that have to do with anything?' I muttered.

'Everything. You're only interested in what's relevant to you, with no desire to get to know the real me unless it may satisfy some curiosity.'

'You make me sound like a heartless bitch.'

Sebastian shook his head. 'Your favourite colour is yellow.'

I rolled my eyes at his attempt to prove a point.

'You hate cucumbers and people who ask stupid questions.'

'Who wouldn't?'

'You listen to Annie Lennox when you think no one is around.'

'And I'll kill you if you ever tell anyone that.'

'See, Elena. I know you because I care enough about the details.'

'I care about the details!' I stammered, shifting from foot to foot. I was just better at ignoring them and what they represented — familiarity, intimacy.

'Do you? Do you really care about—'

'Your favourite colour is blue!' I yelled at him, pushing past his bulk to reach for Lucas's door. I'd had enough of the games. 'I know that because you said the Kawasaki Ninja you owned before your BMW was custom painted in your favourite shade of midnight blue. You even had your helmet spray painted to match.'

When Sebastian didn't respond with anything other than wordlessly flapping his guppy lips, I continued. 'You listen to heavy rock music, mostly bands from the late seventies and early eighties. You cringe at pop music, but have a major soft spot for the classics, a million scores written by composers like Beethoven and Chopin you admire enough to remember their music by heart. You read comic books about superheroes and you secretly watch *Project Runway* with Marcus when you think no one is around.'

'I …'

Ignoring him, I burst into Lucas's room. I didn't know what I'd hoped to find there, but the disappointment of yet more emptiness was crippling. I sank to the floor, unsettled by yet another dead end.

Sebastian slid down the wall and sat beside me. 'So you do see,' he mused. 'I'm not sure about the *Project Runway* thing, but—'

'Don't deny it,' I grumbled. Frankly my mind wasn't up to continuing this conversation. I was more concerned about Lucas's whereabouts and The Protector's motives.

Sebastian cottoned onto my angst, nudging me with his shoulder. 'I'm sorry he's not here, Elena.'

'Me too. I was really hoping there would be something — *anything* — that might tell me what happened to him.'

'Are you sure there isn't? If he were to leave you a message, where would he hide it?'

'I don't know.'

'Then you might have to accept that he is a Protector and possibly left willingly.'

I sighed, resentment barely repressed. I didn't like the implication that Lucas might have abandoned me. 'I don't think he would have.'

'How can you be sure?' Sebastian asked, lifting his arm to drape it across my shoulders. It felt good; too good to take up issue with the comforting gesture.

I concentrated back on the conversation. 'I know my brother, Sebastian.'

'Of course, but I'm sure he had his reasons.'

'Like?'

'Well this double life Lucas plays cannot be only to satisfy your curiosities regarding the IMI. He probably has his own reasons for delving deeper into the IMI's fold.'

'I assumed it was because of my treatment in Bucharest.'

'But now you're not so sure?'

I pinched the bridge of my nose, snuggling closer to Sebastian. Tears unexpectedly gathered in the corners of my tired eyes, threatening to spill and reveal my angst.

Sebastian captured my chin, examining my pained expression in detail. 'Elena?'

'I'm sorry,' I gushed, feeling stupid and vulnerable. 'I'm sorry I dragged you here knowing it was probably a dead end.'

With a tender caress, Sebastian erased the wet saltiness sliding down my slightly inflamed cheeks. 'It's okay.'

I sniffled, nodded but still felt ridiculous for tearing up all over again. Not knowing where Lucas was or if he was in trouble as I had recently been, set my teeth on edge and encouraged my stomach to roll with sickness.

'Please don't cry,' Sebastian said, now frantically wiping at my tears. 'I don't know how to fix this.'

Could we really fix what we didn't entirely understand? There had to be something that I was missing. Wasn't there?

'Are you sure Lucas didn't leave you some sign? It seems a waste to have come all this way and not be completely thorough in our search.' Bless him for trying to cheer me up.

'Agreed.' I glanced around the room, knowing Susan and George would have done a final sweep. I was betting they even found Lucas's secret stash of porn.

Wait. The porn pile. Why didn't I think of that sooner?

I left Sebastian's side and scrambled across the hardwood floor, running my fingers over the tongue and groove, and hunting for the knotted floorboard that gained access to the darkened cubby hole.

Sebastian watched as I ripped up the loose board and peered into the recess. He reached in uninvited, grabbing a few of the magazines, claiming the need to look for evidence.

What a crock of shit.

My lucky dip procured a mobile phone, though what I was supposed to do with it was a mystery. Perhaps somewhere on the device was a map with a cross stating, *The bad guys are here.*

'Sebastian,' I said, holding the phone up for his inspection, 'why do you think he left this?'

'Hmm?' he murmured, far too engrossed in one of the magazine's centrefolds to look up.

I wiped the dusty screen clear with the edge of my t-shirt. 'Sebastian, put that stupid magazine down and pay attention.'

He smiled, eyes finally drifting from the page to meet mine. 'Are you jealous?'

I scoffed, making the mistake of glancing down at the naked woman he was perusing. I might have thrown up in my mouth a little. 'That should be illegal.'

'The magazine or the manoeuvre?'

'Both.'

I attempted to turn on the phone, but clearly it was dead. Sebastian obviously believed he was tech support because he robbed me of the device, depressed the power button and then …

'What the …?' Sebastian's palm glowed like the noon day sun before the phone yielded life and the light disappeared as if it had never been. I couldn't explain what the hell had just happened and I doubted that Sebastian ever would — just like everything else.

'Here,' he said, handing back the phone like nothing had happened.

I dropped it like it burned and grabbed his hand, turning it over in my grasp to study his palm. 'What did you just do?'

'It was nothing.'

I shook my head. 'Nah uh, you just had an ET moment.'

Sebastian moved until he was reclined against the wall again, pulling one leg up to his chest where his wrist dangled precariously over his knee. He remained silent, disinterested in explanation. Stubborn bastard.

'Come on, Sebastian, talk to me.'

He took his time in answering, eyes raised to the blandness of the ceiling above. 'You're telekinetic, Elena. Can't I have a few tricks up my sleeve, too?'

Honestly? 'Sebastian, you can shoot fireballs from your ass if you want, but I still want to know how and why.'

Sebastian's response came in the form of distraction. He leant forward, yanked on the corner of my shirt and pulled me across the floor until I was parked next to him again. His lips were soon buried against the sensitive flesh below my ears, nibbling, tasting, and teasing. 'Just check the phone and see if there's anything on there from Lucas — messages, photos, videos …' He finished off with another kiss to the sweet spot, long and languorous.

'Stop it,' I meekly protested, attempting to swat him away. 'I want to know how … oh …'

Sebastian thrust the phone back in front of my face, his lips fervently insistent on my pulse points. I knew that studying the flashing cell screen I was supposed to be doing something important, but I couldn't remember much bar the feel of Sebastian so close, the smell of him deconstructing common sense.

Short of physically slapping myself, I refocused, trolling the cell phone with renewed vigour. Firstly, I studied the office management program directly linked to word documents and emails. Finding nothing, I scoured the media section, scrolling through several photos of me and Lucas goofing off at the IMI.

After briefly reminiscing, I located a recently saved folder. With the insignia of the IMI peeking at me from the corner of each photo, I knew I was onto something.

I squinted at the screen. Even enlarged they were difficult to read. I wondered what Lucas had hoped to achieve, unless he figured I'd have a vampire in tow.

Lucky.

'Read this for me?' I said, shoving the phone back under Sebastian's nose. Thankfully he was no longer glued to my neck, but equally interested in the contents of the superfine text.

'The date stamp says they're from a year and a half ago. Do you still want me to read it?'

'Definitely. These might be some of the documents Lucas said he found in George's desk late last year.'

'Why didn't he send these images directly to your mobile

rather than keeping them to himself and hiding them under the floorboards?'

I chewed on my lower lip, uncertain. The vampire had a valid point. 'I honestly don't know.'

Sebastian frowned, appearing more and more disgruntled by what he was reading. 'You're not going to like this, Elena. Some of the content could be the reason why Lucas never sent these images to you.'

'Then why leave it for me to find?'

'Evidence, and don't assume he left it for you.'

He really didn't know my brother at all. 'Then wouldn't he have taken it with him?'

'In case it was found by someone else — a member of the IMI.'

I rolled my eyes, knowing he was at least half right. 'Read it, anyway, I have to know.'

His long look of resignation spoke volumes, but he continued regardless, once again tucking me firmly under the crook of his arm.

Dear George.

Your progress with Elena greatly pleases us. For fifteen years of age she has adapted well to her circumstances and we are happy with the training she is receiving.

However, we do feel it would be prudent to test Elena in person. The blood samples sent to us monthly are not sufficient in quantity to begin formulating the serum. We have been testing ideas and formulating certain variations of her strengths and weaknesses from the sample sizes, but it's not enough. We need to gain more or she will have to be transported to headquarters.

Regards, Chester.

I swallowed the golf ball sized lump in my throat. It was still difficult to hear that I'd been considered nothing more than a science experiment to The Protectors and the parents who'd raised me. I was glad that Sebastian was preoccupied with the next message, never stopping to question the shaking hands in my lap.

'Okay, this one appears fairly recent. It's dated August last year.'

'Read it.'

'Are you sure?'

'Yes.'

Dear George.

We have tested the newest sample of Elena's blood, but cannot determine change from previous withdrawals. Despite her recent ingestion of Vânător blood — namely Alpha blood — and your suspicions of increased physical strength, her DNA remains unchanged.

Elena's extra chromosome, as is common with all Vampires, shows no significant, concerning changes. We still don't expect anything surmountable to occur until Elena's eighteenth birthday.

However, if she does begin to manifest any changes, please notify us immediately as we can adjust the schedule of her shipment from next year to as early as next week if necessary.

Please send my regards to Susan and arrange a progress report on Lucas's training and development. I would be very interested to see how he's adapting as Elena begins to mature.

Regards, Chester.

'Why would Chester need to know about Lucas and his connection to me?'

Sebastian grimaced. 'Perhaps they were concerned he might switch loyalties if you both grew too close? Or, perhaps Lucas had a clue, the very reason he kept these documents from you in the first place.'

I shook my head in an attempt to dispel doubt. 'Lucas wouldn't keep this from me.'

'Yet he didn't email or text you these documents,' Sebastian reminded me. 'There must be a reason for that.'

I was still shaking my head.

'Let's see what this letter says? It might explain more.'

'There's more?'

Dear George.

It is interesting to hear your suspicions about Elena socialising with Vampires. Do not interfere. Watch closely, see how she reacts to them and how they react to her genetic disposition.

Also, we are planning on shifting the schedule forward. We want to finish manipulating the quality of the serum as soon as possible and can't wait until her eighteenth birthday. We need vast quantities of her blood if we are to supply the Protector populace with our weapon.

I look forward to hearing from you.

Regards, Chester.

PS — How is Lucas's training going? Will he be ready in time? He must be at the IMI in early January. We cannot possibly predict what may happen to him on his birthday, hence precautions must be undertaken.

'What the hell!' I yelped, repossessing the phone. 'What have they done to my brother?'

Sebastian attempted to squeeze my arm reassuringly. 'I don't know, Elena, but somehow, I suspect it relates to the serum.'

'He'll be eighteen soon,' I remarked.

'So? How is that relevant for a Protector?'

'I don't know,' I muttered, teeth tightly clenched, 'but when I find out …'

'You don't suppose Lucas has been tampered with on a genetic level?'

'I don't know what to think! But I'm going to kick Lucas's ass for keeping this from me if I ever see him again!' I was breathing heavy and making shallow threats. It was a sure sign that I was seriously scared. I'd always known I was destined for a petri dish but not Lucas.

'You've said before that Lucas is capable of taking care of himself.'

Flabbergasted I said, 'But he's with people that did whatever this is to him and he couldn't or wouldn't even tell me about it. How can I help him when he's obviously conflicted about trusting me?'

Sebastian was pensive but a moment. 'Elena, it's true that we don't know what the IMI have done to Lucas or what they might intend to do, but whatever it is, we will find him and get him back so we can help him figure it out together.'

I sniffed, only marginally satisfied by his assurances. 'We don't have much time. It's the eighth of January now and with everything else that's going on — Julius, the Vânǎtors — it seems impossible. We don't even know where to start looking.'

'I am bound by certain obligations — the coven gathering, for instance. But if you want me to look for him, then I promise I will start the search as soon as these obligations are met.'

I tried on a calming breath for size but nothing could really ease my apprehension. 'It could be too late by then.'

Sebastian's fingers smoothed my heated cheek, the touch fleeting but nevertheless an attempt at comfort. 'Have faith, Elena.'

Faith? I almost blew a raspberry at him. 'You will include me in this search, right?'

'I would like that.'

'And you won't try to stop me?'

'It's Lucius you'll have to convince. Not me.'

I sighed, knowing the outcome of that conversation before it even began. 'Asking permission isn't really one of my fortes.'

The sudden, ultimately sensuous smile Sebastian returned was devastating. 'No it's not, but for your sake I'd try to be reasonable or he'll simply force the information right out of you.'

I grunted, scrubbing a hand through my semi-tangled locks. 'I hate that he can see into my thoughts and memories with just a touch — so embarrassing,' I mumbled.

'Then I suggest you work on shielding your mind if you so value your privacy.'

'How?'

'You figured out most of your telekinesis through trial and error, so follow your instincts.'

'But could you help me? This isn't something I can ask Lucius.'

'I can try.'

'And the Vânător thing too,' I added hesitantly.

Sebastian's amusement ebbed as suspicion narrowed his eyes. 'What do you mean, *the Vânător thing*?'

I shrugged, reaching for nonchalance and coming across shifty instead. 'Well, I can partially turn vampiric, but I don't understand how or why I shifted into a Vânător at this stage in my growth, or for that matter, why I don't remember the anomaly occurring.'

Hmm. It couldn't be good that his swirling eyes shifted into the murky grey depths of gluttonous storm clouds. 'I'll have to think about it and you'll have to consult Lucius. It could be dangerous.'

'Consult Lucius? Sebastian, really, do you think—'

He growled, like a proper vampire with full throat action and everything. It certainly cut off any additional excuse I may have wanted to add.

'Okay, dangerous,' I concurred, though mostly to appease. 'But it might be helpful in finding Lucas if I can control a shift.'

'You have my answer.'

'But if it happens again, I want to be prepared. I want to control it, not give into it and kill innocent people.'

'Elena …'

'All right,' I muttered, all but pouting. He wasn't giving an inch and I was too jet-lagged to continue the debate.

Sebastian motioned to the mobile phone still sandwiched between us. 'Do you want to see if there's anything else on there?'

Wow. I actually *was* pouting, but I pulled my game face back on and started to scroll through the remaining multimedia options. I finally found an audio file titled *Elena*, date stamped from several weeks ago, before Roshan had taken me.

'This could be something,' I said, clicking *play* and switching the phone to speaker.

'E, it's me,' Lucas's voice started, clipped with urgency. *'I don't know why I'm recording this message, but I guess I*

just thought it would be a good idea in case my role as James Bond blows up in my face and you're left wondering what the hell happened.

'*Look, I'm sorry I couldn't tell you everything I found in the IMI official documents. I didn't understand them and I still don't, but I didn't want to worry you. I'm your big brother which you sometimes conveniently forget. It's my turn to carry the burden for a while.*' There was a sudden intake of breath, shaky, before he settled and slid back into his speech.

'*I'm sorry that when we talked about the serum and about the changes I felt within myself that I never mentioned the tie between those coincidences and the letters from Chester. I guess I didn't want you to freak out. You were dealing with your own issues with the IMI and I didn't want to load you up with mine.*

'*All I can say now is that I was serious when I told you something was different. Whatever it is, it's not exactly bad. My spell casting is, shall we say, beyond normal expectations and my skills as a fighter have increased tenfold. I've grown taller and stronger, though I'm not entirely sure why, but whatever the cause, I'm not entirely convinced it's the worst thing that could have happened to me.*'

He paused again, taking another breath. '*It's strange, I almost thought for a while there, after reading the documents that I might have been turning based on references to my eighteenth birthday. But since I'm a Protector and human, I quickly ruled it out.*'

'*If you're even listening to this message then something went seriously wrong and if that's true, then I don't want you beating yourself up about not being able to stop whatever it is that the IMI have in store for me. I need you to focus on keeping safe. For once in your stubborn life, worry about yourself. Let me sort out my own issues.*'

He coughed and then said, *'I'm going to get soppy now. It doesn't happen often so just listen. I love you and I miss you, dickhead. There. I said it. Don't tell Thomas I broke out the big guns. He'll never let me live it down.*

'Anyway … I hope you never hear this, E. I hope by the time I see you again I'll have this all figured out and you won't have to worry about a thing. I'm sorry.'

The recording stopped.

I looked down at my hands. They were shaking again and tears fell anew. The mobile screen was a blur and my eyes burned. Hearing Lucas's voice again left me raw and a little defeated. 'I guess I now know why Lucas kept the documents from me.'

'He was protecting you,' Sebastian said. 'Nothing less than what you would have done for him, I'm sure.'

'That's true, I suppose.'

He patted my arm, opened his mouth to speak and then abruptly stopped. He made motions to comfort me again but appeared confused, opting to clear his throat instead.

'Just say it, Sebastian.'

'Without sounding callous, there are serious issues in Rome requiring our attention right now.'

I thought about slapping him. Hard. 'I'm aware.'

'Lucas will be okay,' Sebastian continued, though tentative in his delivery. 'But I cannot say the same for Vampires if the Vânătors are in fact planning an attack on our coven and if The Protectors have turned their backs on us. There's also the urgent matter of Julius, not to mention Roshan who's probably already tracking you again.'

'So, what you're really saying is that we're not looking for Lucas anytime soon.'

'We've been over this.'

Callous much?

I massaged my wet and tired eyes with the heels of my palms, wondering when the drama ever ended. I was beginning to think Lucius might have been right and that I was part of a massive game played by a bunch of bored, narcissistic, supernatural assholes.

'Can I ask you something?' Sebastian's breath was like feathery butterfly wings against my neck. I was compelled to run my fingers over the goose pimpled flesh, convinced his essence lingered like a gentle caress.

'Since when do you ask permission?'

'It's a personal question.'

I resisted the urge to groan and rolled my eyes instead. 'Go on.'

'What do you intend to do with your life once things return to normal?'

'Normal?' What a joke. 'I'll worry about it when it happens, I guess.'

Sebastian pressed on. 'Yes, but what is it that you want?'

'Besides a garage full of classic cars?' I thought about the question more carefully, especially since Sebastian was frowning at my glib response. 'As lame as it may sound, I just want to be happy. I want the people I love and care about to be happy too.'

'Happiness — a seemingly simple notion,' Sebastian murmured. He curled his fingers through the ends of my hair and tugged playfully. 'I once met a poet called James Oppenheim in New York at the turn of the century and he said, "The foolish person seeks happiness in the distance; the wise person grows it under his feet".'

'What's your point?' I'm sure he had one.

'Don't plan for happiness, just be happy.'

I snorted, pressed the mobile phone to my ear with the

pretence of taking a call before I offered it to my stupid vampire. 'Hey, Sebastian, the seventies just called, they want their rose-tinted glasses back.'

He merely smiled, ignored the jibe and raised the phone to his ear in jest. Perhaps the American poet was right. Perhaps I needed to stop seeing the negative in every situation and focus on the positives. The problem was, I really didn't' have a clue where to start.

CHAPTER THIRTEEN
Access

'Everybody gather around, please!' Annabel shouted, standing on her tippy toes. 'I have important information to impart before we see the rest of the facility.'

The small, mixed crowd of Protectors immediately gathered, both to hear her speak and to keep warm.

'I'm aware that you're all very tired after the last ten days at sea, but I must assign your sleeping quarters and establish the rules. As you can imagine, with over five hundred of us stationed here, there needs to be some semblance of order.'

Everyone nodded their heads in agreement.

'When you go through this door, the cargo hold follows.' Annabel jabbed a thumb in the direction of the rusted door's location. 'Supplies are stored here as well as the tractors, snowmobiles and other transport vehicles. Another door will precede this in which the coloured ID tags I'm about to present to you will allow access. It's essential that you keep your ID tag on you at all times because it's used everywhere, particularly for the rationing of food and other personal supplies that you may need during your stay.'

She took a breath. 'Once through security, the door opens to the corridors. All of them are well marked to indicate the mess hall, sleeping quarters, laboratories and research areas.

In regards to meals, your schedule for eating and/or serving is pinned in your bunk. Any questions?'

No one raised their hand. It was pretty straightforward stuff.

'Okay, to keep the parents happy, we also have a school-room for the younger children who have not yet finished their education.'

There were plenty of groans from some of the younger members of the group. Annabel obliged them with a smile before continuing. 'There are also four different training rooms, also working on a rotation-based system.'

She cleared her throat, eyes scanning the crowd. 'You will also do well to remember that the research laboratories are strictly off limits to anyone without appropriate security clearance. This also applies to the communication room and security office. In regards to the sleeping arrangements, couples will be placed together but individuals will be grouped with others of similar age and gender. Space is at a premium people!'

Annabel started to hand out the ID tags. Each was designed to hang around the neck, represented by photo ID, colour, number and a barcode required for security clearance within the facility.

'Lucas Manory?' Annabel yelled, eyes searching the small crowd.

Lucas pushed through some of the Sydney surfers to grab his card. It was a bad photo of him taken about a year ago, a representation of his shoulder length blond hair and blotchy face stubble. He couldn't believe how much he'd changed since then. He was now a skinhead with defined cheekbones and a strong chin. He would've likened him-self to Jason Statham if he was certain no one would die laughing.

'Twenty-four, blue,' Lucas murmured, draping the lanyard around his neck.

'Has everyone got their ID badges?'

There was a collective murmur of *yes's*.

'Right then,' Annabel said merrily. 'Follow me.'

The group ambled through the thick snow and poured though the security door, pushing and shoving their way into the cargo hold. Audible sighs of relief rent the air as warmth caressed wind-whipped faces and heated sodden layers of clothing. Beanies and gloves were immediately removed to celebrate, but many still rubbed their hands together and stamped their feet to generate extra warmth.

Lucas studied his new surrounds, having expected the facility to be big, just not this big. There was crate after crate of shrink-wrapped food supplies stacked as far as the eye could see. Numerous forklifts unearthed the goods and delivered them to God only knew where and recreational and transport vehicles inhabited the rest of the space.

'When we get to the security door,' Annabel shouted again, 'please have your ID cards ready. Once we've descended the stairs, I'll leave you to explore the facility on your own.'

'Great,' Lucas muttered, falling into step behind his parents. He couldn't wait.

One by one they all went through the security door, toting their luggage behind them. Strangers filled the preceding corridors, the noise incredible. Walkways zigzagged in every direction, lighted signs indicating training rooms, the mess hall or other areas in the near vicinity.

Curious, Lucas left his parents, branching off towards the heart of the facility, following the lighted signs indicating 'mess hall' and 'training rooms'. A dome-like space soon greeted him, the ceiling opening to allow for a mezzanine floor that covered most of the upper segment. Marked by balustrades of glass, the mezzanine provided additional seating if required. At ground level, food counters lined the perimeter, each station intended for a different task before more corridors prevailed, lit signs once again highlighting the way.

Lucas quickly left the mess hall to inspect the training rooms. They were floored with safety mats, the walls padded for protection. Some people were gathered inside and sparring, both physically and magically. The facility seemed settled, well used.

Continuing down the corridor, a sign indicated more training rooms to the right and a research lab to the left. Lucas went left.

'Can I help you?'

He started, turning to find a slender woman in her late thirties with short, blonde hair and gentle brown eyes. She sounded Southern American, but he couldn't be sure. 'No thanks. I'm just looking around the facility.'

'In the research area?' she said, raising an eyebrow. Yep, definitely American.

She studied the ID badge hanging around his neck. Surprise flirted briefly with her features but was just as quickly chased by something indeterminable. 'Your badge, Lucas Manory, states that you don't have clearance in this area.'

Lucas squinted at the ID badge around her own neck. 'Stephanie? Wait, are you from the Bucharest division?'

She paused before answering. 'Yes. Why?'

'Elena's mentioned you a few times.'

Stephanie tucked her slender hands inside the baggy pockets of her white lab coat, perhaps picking at lint with nervous fingers. 'I've heard a lot about you, too,' she finally answered.

'Hasn't everyone?'

She nodded and smiled despite his sarcastic undertone. 'There's never been a Protector like you before, Lucas. Your powers are exceptional for someone your age.'

'I wonder why that is?' Lucas added with an acerbic edge. Jaded was one way to describe how he felt about everyone having the inside scoop regarding his genetics.

Stephanie still persisted in smiling in spite of his hostile tone. 'Do you think it's a coincidence?'

Lucas screwed his face up. 'What? A coincidence I'm a freak? I don't think so.'

Stephanie eyed him thoughtfully once more, now rocking back and forth between heel and toe, her hands still buried in her pockets. 'Then maybe you could come to my lab sometime, allow me to draw blood so we can figure this thing out together?'

'And what is it that you think you'll find in my blood?'

'I don't know.'

'Ah huh.' Lucas wasn't buying it. 'I think you know more than you're letting on.'

'Perhaps.'

Several seconds passed where neither said anything, Stephanie still eyeing him speculatively, Lucas frowning. 'I'm going to go look for my room now.'

'I hope we can talk again soon,' Stephanie replied. 'There's so much you need to know. So much you should know.' Her voiced faded to a whisper, her eyes now unfocused and the corners of her lips in descent.

'Why would I be interested in anything *anyone* here has to say?'

Stephanie's expression was now pinched, her previous smile wiped from existence. She stopped rocking on her feet and withdrew her hands, folding them across her small chest. 'I couldn't help her, but maybe I could help you.'

'Her?' Lucas echoed. 'By *her*, do you mean El—?'

'Just think about it,' Stephanie interrupted. 'I don't offer this lightly.'

Lucas wasn't sure what the hell that meant exactly, but he couldn't afford to trust her or anyone else in this God-forsaken place either.

'And, Lucas?' she added as she turned to leave.

'Yeah?'

'Please remember that the research and lab areas are completely off limits to you.'

'Yeah, I got that,' Lucas muttered, flicking his ID tag.

Stephanie hesitated, taking only a few steps in the opposite direction before stopping again. 'There are some areas you can go, some more helpful than others.' She glanced up at one of the many wall-mounted security cameras lining the corridors, a fleeting look of indecision on her face. 'I've got to go.'

Lucas watched her retreat, still unsure of what to make of the scientist and her offer of help. So he decided to file the conversation away for later assessment, focusing instead on finding his room and settling in.

After a few wrong turns, Lucas arrived a sleeping warehouse filled with row after row of metal compartments marked by both number and colour. He swiped his ID tag in front of the sensor pad and waited for the automatic door to open and reveal the shoebox beyond.

Correction, toilet cubicle, Lucas thought as he stooped to step inside his compartment. On either side of the entry door were twin closets, only big enough to hang five or six items and store a few folded clothes. One had already been claimed as had the single bed closest to the door. Lucas guessed that left him the spare bed next to the bathroom.

Great.

Lucas dumped his suitcase on the bottom of the spare bed, collapsing next to it. Exhaustion was no longer just a thought.

He nabbed the singular, depressingly flat pillow provided and tucked it under his head. Groaning, he rolled over and closed his eyes, his long legs dangling over the top of his suitcase. His stomach growled, but was ignored. There were too many other things to consider; lying parents, the serum, nutcase researchers and continued entrapment — also all ignored. All he could muster the enthusiasm for right now was some much needed shut-eye.

Everything else would just have to wait.

Lucas sat bolt upright, dazed and a little disorientated. It took several seconds for his eyes to adjust to the dim light and to remember where he was — Yeti country.

He yawned, pawing at his sleep-crusted lids and the drool that smothered his chin like foamy stubble. The mattress springs continued to groan with each movement and the blankets wrapped around his thighs like cotton vines hampered his attempts to get up. What time was it?

'Good morning.'

Lucas screamed and clutched at his chest.

'Sorry!' the stranger quickly offered. 'I didn't mean to frighten you. I'm your bunkmate — Beryx.'

'Beryx?'

Lucas knew the name well, having heard Elena mention it on numerous occasions in the past. It shouldn't have surprised him that he was rooming with someone directly connected to Elena and the research and science division.

'It's good to meet you, Lucas. I've heard a lot of good things about you.'

Lucas grunted, relieved that his new bunkmate had refrained from mentioning or laughing about his soprano introduction. It also gave him pause to assess Beryx's freakishly shiny auburn hair, porcelain skin and coal black eyes. The guy was a looker and definitely built for combat, too.

'Anyway, I came to get you for breakfast,' Beryx continued, sitting cross-legged on the edge of the bed opposite Lucas. 'Since you only arrived yesterday, I figured you might need the heads up on our rotation.' He pointed to the schedule posted on the back of the door. 'The details are there for future reference.'

'Thanks,' Lucas said, patting his rather displeased stomach. 'I'm starving.' He made motions to grab a fresh change of clothes and head into the bathroom. 'How long have you been here now, Beryx?'

'About a month and a half.'

Shit. 'That makes me want to kill myself,' Lucas muttered under his breath.

Beryx blinked, his eyes glazing over. 'I'm sorry, what did you just say?'

Lucas shook his head. 'Nothing.'

On the walk to the mess hall, Beryx was silent. A couple of times it looked as though he was about to say something, but then promptly closed his mouth and frowned. Lucas didn't push either, being already late for the blue segment's breakfast rush.

'What's good to eat here?' Lucas asked, collecting a tray and handing one to Beryx.

'Everything except the eggs. They're powdered.'

Lucas held the ID tag up as instructed by the Protector behind the counter. The woman scanned his barcode and entered his food portions into a computer. She then waved him away so she could do the same for Beryx.

'So,' Lucas said as they finally settled in at a nearby table, 'what's the deal with this place?'

'The deal?'

Lucas waved his fork around. 'Why are we really here? And *don't* say reassignment.'

Beryx picked at his food, pushing it around his plate. 'I don't know.'

'Yeah, okay. Elena's mentioned you a few times, so I know you work alongside Chester.'

Beryx snapped to attention, his fork dropping to the plate. 'Elena? You spoke to Elena about me?'

'I speak to Elena about a lot of things.'

'When?' Beryx pressed, leaning forward like an eager child.

Lucas smiled, shovelling a fork full of bacon into his mouth. 'Wouldn't you like to know?'

'Yes, I would,' Beryx added enthusiastically. Obviously sarcasm was lost in translation.

'Ah, Lucas!' came a shout from across the room.

Both Beryx and Lucas turned, watching as a solid nerd with a lip duster and crazy big glasses waved at them from across the room. Judging by the hideous golfing pants, suspender belt, and flashy gold tooth, the nerd in question had to be Chester. Elena hadn't missed a thing in her description of him.

The only thing that stopped Lucas from jumping out of his seat and causing grievous bodily harm to the Protector who'd hurt Elena was the witness. And the fact that Lucas was all talk and limited action, otherwise known as a pussy.

Shit ...

Chester moved across the room with surprising grace, helping himself to a chair and some of Beryx's untouched bacon. 'Lucas,' he repeated, unhindered by the mouthful of masticated pig, 'I'm so glad that you're finally with us.'

'That makes one of us.'

'You've grown into quite The Protector, or so I've been told,' Chester continued, ignoring the barbed retort. 'We met once when you were a small boy. I don't suppose you remember me at all?'

Lucas shook his head, wishing he were more like Elena, taking out those that pissed him off like it was open day at the gun range.

'You were only four years old at the time. I suppose it would be a stretch for your memory.' Chester slapped Lucas's shoulder and then smiled devilishly as his fingers knowingly kneaded the sweet spot.

Ow! Ow! Ow! Lucas fought hard to suppress the pain that radiated through his scar.

'I see you've already befriended Beryx. I knew it would be a good pairing when I put you two together. I must say, I'm looking forward to seeing you both in action this morning.'

Lucas swallowed the lump in his throat and wiped at the perspiration beading on his forehead. 'Say what?' He looked to Beryx, but his dark eyes were watching the food he'd begun pushing around his plate again.

'I booked you both in for a training session.'

'Why would you do that?' Lucas asked.

'Because I want to see you paired against one another.'

'Is this some kind of experiment?'

'Yes.'

Right to the point.

Okay.

Lucas's appetite evaporated. 'Look, not to be rude, but

I don't even want to be here, so a training session is kinda low on my priority list right now.'

Chester laughed. 'Beryx won't injure you too badly. We don't want to see any permanent damage.'

'I don't think you're listening,' Lucas begun.

'Excellent,' Chester said, ignoring Lucas completely. He looked down at his watch and then rubbed his hands together in delight. 'I'll see you both in Training Room Three in about,' he looked at his watch again, 'ten minutes.'

Chester left before Lucas could even raise protest.

'I'm not sure what just happened,' Lucas said, gently kneading his sore shoulder.

Beryx shrugged, still disinterested. 'He has a new project now.'

'What?'

Beryx looked pointedly at him. 'You.'

On the way to the training rooms, Lucas tried to engage Beryx in further discussion, but clearly he wasn't a big talker.

'This is really stupid, you know.'

'Agreed,' Beryx replied.

'We should keep on walking, blow the training gig off.'

'Chester won't allow it.'

Lucas supposed that might have been true given what he knew of the scientist. With Elena's imprisonment coming instantly to mind, pushing the psychopath for the sake of being decidedly obstinate seemed like a fruitless venture. 'So, what's your skillset anyway?'

'Nothing special.'

'Um, sure,' Lucas drawled, eyeing the rippling muscles in Beryx's biceps and forearms. He seemed to unconsciously flex his bulging physique as he swiped his ID badge over the sensor panel of Training Room Three. Maybe the guy worked out?

The room they entered was large and already prepped for combat — or someone in a straightjacket, depending on how you looked at it. There were some weapons fixed to the padded walls, but Lucas knew this fight was set to determine physical supremacy.

By the time Lucas caught up to Beryx in the locker room, he was already shucking his clothes in favour of training apparel.

'There should be a pair of clean tracksuit pants in that locker to your left,' Beryx instructed with a nod.

Multiple pairs, roughly folded and in varying sizes, spilled into Lucas's awaiting arms. Smelling relatively clean, he plucked one out of the pile and shoved the rest back where he'd found them. He then proceeded to play 'shy-guy' as he stripped, knowing that Beryx was finished and now sizing *him* up.

'What are you looking at?' Lucas finally asked, tying the drawstring on his pants.

'Don't hold back.'

Lucas huffed, unnerved by the continuing scrutiny. 'I never do.'

'Good.'

Lucas chased his opponent's shadow out of the locker room and back into the training room. He was immediately taken aback by the amount of spectators now crowding the previously empty space. Where seats were taken, others filed in and stood against the wall, waiting expectantly.

On the far side of the room Chester sat rigidly with a notepad and pen, Lucas's mother and father next to him, deep in conversation. In the opposite corner was Stephanie, smiling and waving at Lucas like an adoring fan.

What the ...?

Beryx made his way to the centre of the training platform, stretching his arms above his head while pitching his torso from side to side. His neck cracked like bone china but that didn't seem to bother him as he went for round two.

'Good luck, Lucas!' he shouted. 'Remember, don't hold back!'

Hold back? As if he'd hold back with a Romanian tank coming right at him. In fact he was already trying to dodge the blurred fist stirring the air around him. Knuckles skimmed the side of his ear, turning it pink as it buzzed with warmth. Lucas's heart pounded a million miles an hour as he tried simple evasion manoeuvres to avoid the next punch.

'What the hell?' Lucas gasped, bobbing and weaving in an unsuccessful attempt to throw in a few punches of his own.

He's so fast!

Another blurred fist came from the right and Lucas moved, rolling forward and then springing back to his feet to kick Beryx in the abdomen. 'Shit!' Lucas cursed, his foot possibly connecting with concrete ribs.

'Don't hold back, Lucas!' Beryx shouted at him again.

Shut up! Lucas thought as he hopped backwards, favouring his uninjured foot. He was going to need some ice and fast. He didn't think the swollen appendage was broken, but it hurt like a mother. How the hell did his brawny bunkmate walk away from that kick seemingly unscathed?

Beryx was now building the *Light of Mellar* spell within his grasp. It was obvious and clumsy compared to the ease in which he dominated physically. To Lucas, magic was his proverbial muscle and neutralising the spell with merely a thought was reflexive. It allowed him time to operate a tactical second strike, otherwise known as *Kick Beryx's Ass.*

A quick shoulder drop and ram saw Lucas plough into his opponent. Despite Beryx's slight stumble and lost footing, Lucas once again copped the brunt of the impact and lost the fight with gravity. Before he'd even had a chance to roll to his feet, Beryx was on him, landing a punch to his solar plexus, ripping away any air left inside of him.

Is he trying to kill me?

A mercy call perhaps, but Beryx gave Lucas reprieve to catch his breath before attacking once more. It was more than most opponents would offer, but most opponents weren't built like brick shithouses, either. Was this guy pumping steroids?

'What are you doing, Lucas?' Beryx whispered as he helped yank Lucas back to his feet. 'Don't fight me with your fists. Use your magic.'

Lucas wheezed, uncertain whether or not he had broken a rib. 'I'm a good fighter … usually.'

'No matter how you come at me, you'll never be able to take me down without hurting yourself first.'

'What the hell does that mean?'

'I don't want to see you beaten and broken over one of Chester's experiments. It's not worth it.'

'You seem so sure you can beat me.' Bitterness crept easily into Lucas's voice, but since humiliation was coming a close second, he rolled with the negativity being thrown at him.

'In hand-to-hand combat, I can beat anyone,' Beryx boasted.

Love yourself much?

Lucas drew another hindered breath, pushed thoughts of pain aside and beckoned Beryx forward with a flick of his wrist. Beryx obliged, shaking his head in disapproval, confident that he would win the fist fight.

Lucas danced backwards, ignoring the throbbing pain emanating from his foot and the first onslaught of blows. He seemed determined to land punches mostly to his face, a blur of motion that was almost nearly successful on every occasion.

Lucas managed to block an uppercut by bobbing to the left, but was clipped from the opposite direction. It sent Lucas to the mats, a heavy thud drowned out by the roar of applause for his opponent.

Blood pooled in his mouth but thankfully all teeth seemed to be solid. Ringside, Lucas could hear his mother shouting, demanding an end to the match before serious injury ensued. Apparently that wasn't a concern for the scientists.

Lucas dodged another one of Beryx's mediocre spells, the blue bolt of power missing its mark by a wide margin.

Physically exhausted, Lucas knew it was time to play to his strengths.

Centring his mind, Lucas cast a shield of manipulated air particles that glistened under the harsh, fluorescent glow. There was a collective gasp followed by *oohs* and *ahhs*, Beryx's latest attempt at the *Hevannatara* spell exploding against the surface like ineffectual fireworks.

The roar of applause was distracting and Beryx was on him again like a fat kid on a cupcake, determined to rain blows upon his face and body. A sneaky blow to the upper cheekbone knocked Lucas off his feet. Pain lanced through his skull, only heightened as he collapsed against a folding chair. Despite bruised flesh and the pile of kindling now beneath him, everyone urged continuance.

Come on Lucas, you can do this. You can beat him.

Flexing his aching muscles, Lucas climbed unsteadily back to his feet, much to the delight of the cheering crowd. He hobbled back to the training mats, Beryx already a whirlwind of limbs bound for round three.

A fist grazed Lucas's right eye. A lucky evasion, he was surprised that he managed to spin, work with his opponent's forward momentum and land a kick to the centre of Beryx's back. Crowd surfing was unavoidable.

Everyone was suddenly on their feet or caught in the collective tangle of body parts. Beryx didn't stay down for long. He was back on his feet again in under a minute, studying Lucas like some kind of tormented, wild animal.

Like a panther, Beryx leapt with grace and accuracy, but was thwarted once again by Lucas's magical prowess. Blue shards of light emanated from Lucas's palms, blinding with brilliance and glowing with power. It was almost too easy.

Now incapacitated, Beryx dropped like a lead balloon, a rather quick and simple defeat at the hand of a consummate caster. Applause rang, but Lucas was physically defeated and uncertain of his victory to offer acknowledgement. Instead he fell in a heap by Beryx's frozen form, cradling his various injuries.

'Congratulations, Lucas!' Chester shouted above the din of spectators. 'I honestly thought Beryx had you there for a while, but your unusual magic appears to be incontestably a game changer.'

Lucas rolled his head to the side, studying Beryx's stiffened attack formation. Something wasn't quite right with his bunkmate. He'd known it since the moment they'd first met. 'Does Beryx take performance enhancers?'

A hush fell over the room, uncomfortable and full of question.

'Why do you ask?' Chester finally answered.

'He's strong and fast, more so than anyone *human* I've ever met before.'

Silence was punctuated by the abrupt burst of laughter that erupted from Chester's mouth. Thus was the extent of his amusement that he slapped his knees and wiped a tear from the corner of his eye. He never answered the question, merely continued the charade, signalling for support staff to carry Beryx away.

'Where are you taking him?' Lucas asked, wincing as he struggled to pull himself upright. Oh yeah, Beryx had done some damage.

'Come on!' Chester shouted. 'Show's over. It's time for everyone to go about their business.'

No answer yet again.

The room cleared out quicker than the effects of an enema. Even Chester was swept along with the crowd, disappearing from sight. Lucas looked for his parents. Gone. He supposed his mother wasn't so concerned about his welfare after all.

'He's like that, you know,' Stephanie said, suddenly appearing beside him. 'He never answers questions.'

Lucas didn't mean to jump, but the woman had somehow managed to surprise him.

'I wanted to congratulate you.'

'I don't think I actually beat him,' Lucas admitted, glancing around the now vacant room. 'Certainly not with my fists, anyway.'

Stephanie leant close enough that Lucas deliberated her intent, her warm breath tickling his cheek. A million thoughts fired across all synapses, but when she fingered the scar on his neck, he couldn't have been more surprised. 'Where did you get this?'

Lucas flinched, scowling at the bruising pressure she applied. 'Get your hands off me.'

'I'm sorry, I just thought—'

'Don't.'

Stephanie backed right off, placing several feet of space between them. 'Lucas, I didn't mean to offend. I just wanted to see it up close.'

Lucas gently massaged the small, mottled patch of skin. 'Do you know how it happened?'

'Do you?'

Lucas offered the pixie-faced scientist an eye roll. 'Really? We're going to play that game?'

The corner of Stephanie's lips tightened but her expression remained otherwise deadpan. 'Those are some nasty cuts you've got there, Lucas. If I were you, I'd head to the nurses' station and see what you can find.'

'Thanks for the stellar advice.'

'Believe it or not,' Stephanie murmured, 'I did just help you. It's up to you to figure out how.' She headed for the door while he mulled that over. 'And Lucas? You'll like nurse Alba. She's helpful, friendly and decidedly remiss about guarding patient records.'

'What? Oh. Shit. Wait!' Lucas yelled after her, but she'd already swiped her access card and disappeared into the corridor beyond. After that, Lucas didn't hesitate in passing out.

CHAPTER FOURTEEN
Records

Alba, the nurse, was a pleasant, unexpected surprise. For one, she wasn't a Protector, but the wife of one. She was tall, blonde and rocked Lucas's fantasy world with visions of naked flesh, stethoscopes and fishnet stockings.

'I've heard my husband talk about you, Lucas,' Alba said, turning to fix him with a kind smile. 'In fact, everyone's talking about you. At breakfast this morning I heard nothing but stories about your abilities.'

Lucas attempted to tuck lurid thoughts away as he pulled himself up onto the tiny cot, his legs dangling over the edge. 'It's not that big a deal,' he said, trying to act nonchalant.

Alba stooped to retrieve a small washbowl and towel, an action that saw Lucas's head at a sudden right angle. Jeesh. Was he really trying to ogle her panties?

What a dick.

She absently smoothed her skirt and stood tall again, filled the bowl with a little water from a nearby sink and then added antiseptic. When she was done, Alba strode back over to the cot, placed the bowl on the bed sheets next to Lucas, and rearranged the other medical paraphernalia within reach.

She giggled and patted Lucas's knee twice. 'You're so tall

for a seventeen year old,' she said, now preparing the wash-cloth for a soaking. 'You might have to jump down and sit on a chair for me so I can reach your wounds.'

Lucas obliged. He felt stupid with his legs dangling like a four year old anyway.

Once he'd resettled, Alba began wiping cuts clean, alternating between dabbing and applying ointment. 'I don't think you'll need stitches, but you're going to have a few nasty bruises.' She touched his cheek, gently turning his head from side to side. 'What happened to you, anyway?'

'Training.'

Alba pursed her lips, unconvinced. 'Who were you fighting? A polar bear?'

Aww. She made an Antarctica joke!

Lucas chuckled. 'It felt like it.'

'Let me have a look at the back of your head.'

Lucas moved forward to grant better access.

'Ooh, this is nasty,' she murmured. 'I might have to put a few stitches in this one. You should probably stay with me for a couple of hours so that I can keep an eye on you, too, make sure that you don't have a concussion.'

Alba grabbed a penlight from her pocket, immediately directing the obscenely bright beam into his eyes. Lucas looked down, hoping to get an eyeful of cleavage but then spotted Alba's unoccupied fingers hunting blindly for weapons of mass reconstruction.

His heart skipped a beat. A suture kit lay sprawled amongst the medical supplies, a shiny, sterile needle winking at him under the fluorescents. 'Whoa, you're serious about stitches?'

'Unfortunately.' She tore open the package, an apologetic look on her face. 'I'll be gentle, but I'm sorry, this will sting a bit.'

End game.

Lucas woke up to Alba fanning his face and dabbing his forehead with a cool washcloth, the stitches tight and stinging. 'What happened?'

'You passed out,' she said, resisting the urge to smirk. 'But don't worry. I stitched you up while you were out, so we don't need to rehash. Do you want to tell me where else it hurts now that you're conscious?'

Lucas fingered the back of his head for Alba's handiwork. Sure enough there was a small bandage covering the sore spot. He was in serious danger of becoming a total pussy if he continued to point out his 'owies'. Then again … 'Um, well, I kicked my foot pretty hard and I got punched in the chest.'

'Show me your chest first.'

Lucas obeyed, hoisting the double sweater combination over his head, careful not to knock the stitches. He moaned anyway. His whole body felt like it had been pushed through a meat grinder.

'Goodness,' Alba murmured, soft fingers gently grazing his skin. 'That's nasty. I don't think ice will help that.' She shifted her fingers around the area, exerting pressure in certain spots and not in others. 'Does it hurt anywhere in particular?'

'It hurts everywhere.'

'What about when you breathe?' she said, reaching down and touching each rib section in turn.

'No, it's okay.'

'Better to take an X-ray just in case.' She looked down at his swollen foot. 'We'll put some ice on that as well.'

'Cool.'

Alba moved to the sink to dispose of any waste material and to prepare the used instruments for sterilisation. Lucas nearly hit the deck again when he spied the blood-soaked gauze. 'If you could hop back up onto the cot for me and lie down I'll take that X-ray now. I might take one of your foot while we're at it, just to be on the safe side.'

Lucas swayed as he stood, clutching the back of the chair for support before doing as he was asked. Alba followed shortly after, adjusting the X-ray arm above his head and covering him in the appropriate safety paraphernalia. She then moved to a door at the back of the room, presumably where the operational equipment was stored.

'Okay, hold steady!' she shouted. There was a short pause before a beeping sound signalled lift-off. 'Good, Lucas. Now sit up so I can do your ankle, too.'

It took no more than five minutes to gather all the X-rays required.

'Okay, we're done. You can pop your clothes back on and get comfortable,' she said, now easing into the chair in front of her computer.

Lucas hurriedly redressed. He liked that Alba's eyes flicked in his direction, lingering on the flat planes of his lower abdominals before his shirt drew the final curtain.

'I'll just be a few minutes.'

'What are you doing?' Lucas asked.

'Entering the details of your visit with me today.'

'Into some sort of IMI database?'

Alba nibbled her lower lip, studying the screen in front of her with renewed vigour. 'Yes. The IMI keeps very accurate and up-to-date medical records on all Protectors.'

'Really?' He suspected as much.

She nodded, continuing to type. 'Your doctor's visits, inoculations, surgeries and any accidents you've had since you were born are all listed here.'

The key tapping ceased and Alba stood abruptly, pushing

back her chair and grabbing a coat off the hook by the door. 'I have to go and collect the X-rays from the research department and consult with one of the physicians regarding the results. Will you be all right while I'm gone?'

'Of course.' Lucas glanced at the computer with interest. 'I'm sure I'll find something to do.'

She suddenly seemed hesitant, her eyes tracing him with concern. Had he blown it? Had he roused suspicion with a simple, eager glance? 'Whatever you do, don't go to sleep.'

No.

Lucas nodded, going to all efforts to look comfortable on the cot with a magazine he'd just nabbed from a side bench.

'Okay, good,' Alba muttered nervously. 'I should be back in about ten minutes. Don't close your eyes!'

Lucas made a beeline for the computer as soon as Alba left the room. He sat down, assessed her notes and started searching through his medical history.

Clicking on the tab marked 'previous medical history', Lucas scanned through a list of visits to the Cairns general practitioner. Most notations substantiated common colds, bouts of tonsillitis and even the occurrence of chicken pox at age eleven — nothing specifically untoward; however, there were small auxiliary notations regarding a check-up at age four and a half. They weren't from any Cairns practitioner but inserted via Chester himself.

Curious, Lucas brought up the notes and read them quickly.

Lucas shows a marked improvement. Transfusion has proven successful pending future developments.

Lucas scoured the database further, backtracking through entries until he discovered the first notations made by Chester some thirteen years earlier. Chester had alluded to a previous meeting, but Lucas had no recollection. Would a transfusion be the cause and the explanation for everything they had done to him and Elena?

Lucas read on.

Symptoms: Lucas bitten by adopted sister Elena — developing half-breed (see related notes). Vampire and werewolf DNA detected in saliva, torn flesh and muscle damage. Severe blood loss, traumatic effects to system — heart stopped beating at 3.07 pm.

Treatment: Transfusion using Elena's type 'X' blood.

Results: Skin cold, vital signs non-existent. At 3.09 pm resuscitation was successful. At 4.10 pm, Lucas regained consciousness — transfusion continued. Lucas showed marked improvement and even mobility.

Notes: Watching for changes in the healing process above and beyond expectations of the human condition.

Lucas slumped low in the chair, absently touching his shoulder and reviewing memories of the past. It wasn't a secret that Elena had bitten him, but he didn't know that the experience had been near fatal. Was his current developing condition, whatever that may be, the reason for the overly watchful eyes of the IMI? Was it possible for Elena's bite to fundamentally alter his human DNA even though she was still technically human herself?

Lucas clicked the next entry, reading through and glancing back and forward between the screen and the door, praying that Alba didn't come back anytime soon.

Notes: Lucas in complete recovery. Bite wound still weeping, has been stitched. All vital signs normal, no displays of change pertaining to Elena's blood. (See notes on Elena Manory, case 10553).

Prognosis: Full human recovery expected. Will be watching for preternatural changes. Next blood test set for three months.

Lucas followed the prompt, typed in Elena's case number and waited for the notes to appear. Most entries pertained to the multiple blood tests ordered by Chester over the years, every withdrawal resulting in a full pathology work up; however, the most recent were signed off on by Stephanie herself.

Symptoms: Blood ingestion. Human tissue also ingested.

Treatment: Not necessary.

Results: Elena found attached to adopted sibling Lucas Manory, drinking blood, eating flesh (See notes on Lucas Manory, case 10552). No trauma or sickness. No fangs as first suspected, human teeth the cause. Eyes remain human. Shape shifting also not present. Snarling and growling present during attempted extraction. Strength was not an issue. Stance and quality of defence similar to her genetic counterpart — Vânător.

Notes: Currently monitoring for changes.

Lucas looked again to see if Alba was making her way back. It was still all clear, so he read on.

Notes: Blood taken from Elena excessively to supplement continued loss from Lucas (see notes on Lucas Manory, case 10552). Elena's type 'X' blood provides the perfect composition, making her a universal donor and a possible base to work with for future endeavours. Self-healing re-established blood supplies after loss of consciousness. Elena has shown no further desire to drink blood, yet she does not repel from it either.

Prognosis: Changes must be monitored, further tests to be undertaken. Be watchful of future blood consumption or interest.

Lucas's fingers practically shook as he scrolled through other entries. Most of the information he already knew — her extra chromosome and the Vânător DNA. What he didn't was its presence in his own body, her genetic oddities reviving him from death!

Lucas started perusing recent entries in his own history again. Today's was now saved and logged, pending X-ray results. What he really wanted were details from three months ago, right around the time Elena left for Bucharest and Lucas started noticing changes.

'What are you doing?' Alba chided, brow pinched as the metal door clicked closed behind her.

Lucas jumped, heart racing as he rushed to bring up earlier notations and a solitaire game as potential cover. He wasn't sure she'd buy it. 'I'm playing cards.'

Alba edged her way around the desk, scrutinising the screen. She frowned at him again. 'You shouldn't be on here.'

He offered a sheepish smile. 'I was feeling sleepy after you left. I did what you said. I tried to keep awake.'

'What did you do to my notes?'

'Nothing, I just minimised them, see?' Lucas held the mouse cursor over the taskbar and then continued to play solitaire. 'Did you need the computer back now?'

Her frown didn't fade as she nodded and shooed him out of her seat. 'I have the results of your X-rays back.' She shook the grey envelope he hadn't noticed was in her hand until now.

'What's the verdict?'

'You're going to be sore but fine. There's nothing broken.'

Lucas settled into the other chair. 'Well, that's a relief, I suppose.'

She lowered her head to concentrate, clacking away on the keyboard with scarlet painted fingernails. 'Who were you up against in the fight, anyway?'

'My bunkmate, Beryx.'

'I know him,' she said, continuing to type. 'I just saw him in the research centre. Not a scratch on him. He must have really creamed you, huh?'

'Actually, I beat him.'

'Really?' she said, eyebrows arched in surprise. 'How did you beat him?'

Lucas groaned. There was no missing the scepticism. 'With magic.'

So much for trying to seduce the nurse. What woman would cheat on her husband for a seventeen-year-old guy who got the crap kicked out of him by a lab tech?

None. That's how many.

By the time Lucas spoke with Beryx again, three days had passed. Such was his continuing absence that Lucas wondered if Beryx had taken up permanent residence within the lab and research areas.

'Hey,' Lucas said, surprised to see his bunkmate. Dark rings blotted the skin around his eyes and his hair looked stringy, his skin unhealthy and pale.

'Hey,' Beryx murmured, dropping onto his bed and slamming his eyes home.

'You look like shit, man.'

'I feel like it.'

'What have you been up to? I haven't seen you since the fight.'

Beryx scrubbed a hand through his greasy hair. His eyes remained closed, and lips sealed.

Lucas pursed his lips. 'Okay, don't answer me, but I'd love to know how you got the better of me on the mats. What the hell are you taking, anyway?'

Beryx cracked one eye open. 'Excuse me?'

'Aw, come on, I've never met anyone who can pack a punch quite like you — no one *human,* anyway.'

Beryx's lingering look of discomfort had Lucas's wheels of thought suddenly spinning into overdrive. What if he was right to assume Elena's bite and blood had somehow changed him? And if that were possible, could Beryx have been affected by some equally freaky experience and or experimentation?

'I'm tired. Can we talk tomorrow?' Beryx muttered, rolling onto his side and away from Lucas's probing stare.

'And you'll tell me what's really going on?'

'Humph.' Beryx's breathing evened out, his shoulders slumped and he quickly drifted off to sleep. Lucas supposed that was the end of it then.

Finding no reason to linger now that Beryx was unresponsive, Lucas decided to seek answers elsewhere.

Locating Stephanie's quarters didn't take long thanks to the direction of others, and after a fitful banging of fists, the heavyset door to her bunk slid open to reveal a frazzled lab tech. 'Lucas? Why are you here? What do you want?'

'Can I come in?'

She peered over his shoulder and into the corridor, per-haps eyeing off the security camera he'd noticed mounted at his back. 'You shouldn't have come here.'

'I need answers and I⊠' Lucas paused, stepping past Stephanie and into the bunk. In the single bed next to the door was a small girl with pale skin and no hair. She was buried under a mountain of blankets and attached to a small heart rate monitor and IV. She was fast asleep, but her ragged gasps and skeletal arms made it obvious that she was sick.

Stephanie moved from the closing door and swooped down to place a gentle hand across the little girl's forehead. Seeing Lucas's shocked reaction, Stephanie sighed, kissed the sleeping angel and said, 'She's my daughter, Lila.'

'What's wrong with her?'

'She has leukaemia.' She kissed Lila again, lips lingering, quivering against pale skin.

'Look, I'm sorry. I shouldn't have come,' Lucas mumbled like the unwanted intruder he was. 'I can see that you've got your own issues. Mine seem irrelevant in comparison.'

Stephanie glanced at her watch. 'Just say whatever it is that you came to say before security shows up.'

Incredulous, Lucas meekly cleared his throat and quickly began to explain what he'd learned from Alba's computer. He recapped the transfusion and his theories regarding Elena's connection.

'That's very good, Lucas.'

'So, it's true?'

'Well, I certainly don't believe that your recent growth spurt and extraordinary magical talent can be linked to any other event.'

'So, the things I can do now are permanent?'

'I believe so.'

'And what about my eighteenth birthday? There's been reference to this as an important date. Why?'

She shook her head, clearly about to hypothesise. 'I can only assume that your ability may intensify. You may even wield new abilities pertinent to Elena's vampirism.'

Lucas slumped, his back slamming against the cold, harsh metal of the bunk wall. 'So, I might not be entirely human or Protector anymore?'

'I don't know.'

'So, that's why I'm really here,' Lucas said, piecing it all together. 'The IMI are afraid of what I might become.'

'That's certainly part of it,' Stephanie agreed. 'But we're also curious how you could help other Protectors.'

'You mean like the development of the serum?'

She snapped to attention. 'How do you know about that?'

'I've seen letters between Chester and my father.'

'Oh.'

'Yes, *oh*,' Lucas mimicked. 'What's it for?'

'I shouldn't say.'

Lucas scoffed and folded his arms across his still-bruised chest. 'You used Elena, drained her of blood and tortured her. If I'm supposed to play a role in this serum's production, too, then I want some answers.'

Stephanie's look of outrage was plagued by the guilt that watered her eyes.

'You know you let it happen,' Lucas pressed. 'That makes you just as guilty as Chester.'

Stephanie's flared nostrils were a match for the biting fingernails digging into her rigidly held arms. 'You're lucky I'm giving you anything. I'll be reprimanded for this little impromptu visit.'

'Do you think a little verbal thrashing from the boss compares to Elena's pain?'

'And Lila's suffering?' Stephanie admonished, voice rising. 'She has been sick for years. She is more important to me than your half-breed sister!'

Lucas swallowed his retort in lieu of her obvious distress. He glanced between the frazzled scientist and the sick girl lying still beneath the covers. 'Oh I see,' he whispered, puzzle pieces finally matching up perfectly. 'You hoped Elena's blood would act as a cure, leukaemia first and then ...'

She shook her head, so angry now that her face was beetroot red. 'Leukaemia? I want Lila impermeable to *any* disease. The serum's purpose is to make us invulnerable like Elena — self-healers with immortality!'

Lucas thought he'd be shocked to hear the admission, but supposed he'd always known The Protectors' desire to have Elena close could never have been anything other than self-serving. 'So what you're telling me is that Elena's torture was a necessary means to a selfish end?'

Tears welled in Stephanie's narrowed eyes. 'Can you honestly say that you wouldn't have sacrificed one person for the sake of changing fate and saving the life of someone you just can't live without?'

'Holy crap,' Lucas exploded, disregarding Stephanie's attempts to excuse the IMI's behaviour. 'Beryx is your test subject!'

'Open up, Stephanie!' Insistent fists beat against the steel door making Stephanie shriek and Lucas jump.

'They're here,' she said, wiping frantically at her swollen lids. 'If Chester finds out that you know about the serum, he'll find a way to silence you and me, so please, Lucas, keep quiet about all this.'

As if he'd run down the halls screaming, *You dirty, rotten bastards! I know everything!* — tempting though it was.

'Stephanie! Open up now.'

The locking mechanism was disengaged and several security personnel spilled into the already confined space. 'What's going on in here?' the burliest one said, slitted eyes scanning the bunk with interest.

Stephanie stuttered, obviously nervous. 'N–nothing, Jim. We're just talking.'

'What about?'

'Interest rates and the coming apocalypse,' Lucas grumbled, trying to escape past security and failing miserably.

Jim cinched his arm, halting retreat. Dark eyes shifted over the clearance tag swinging from the lanyard around Lucas's neck. 'I suggest that you check that attitude, Mr Manory. Late night interludes between scientist and subject are concerning.' He violently shoved Lucas's arm. 'Expect things to change around here, Mr Manory, you're being watched.'

Lucas's quivering lips were eager to give the pudgy bastard what for, but a barely noticeable headshake from Stephanie and his inner pussy robbed him of breath.

'Chester wants to see you in the lab immediately,' Jim directed at Stephanie. 'You know this isn't the first time.'

Stephanie nodded, forcing a smile laced with tension. 'I will be there directly. I need to make sure Lila is all right before I leave.'

Jim approved, his hardened gaze once again focusing back on Lucas. 'You can go now, Mr Manory.'

Lucas wasted no time in his efforts to exit, unconcerned as he stumbled over the threshold and tripped into the corridor. He was apprehended by two other guards who helped set him straight and then promptly pushed him in the opposite direction. He was surprised he was allowed to leave given the supposed fraternisation.

Did they all know that he knew the truth? And if they knew, why was he allowed to roam freely?

Because there's no escape from here ...

It was time to start making decisions. Was he going to stay a Protector, knowing that playing God outweighed their collective conscience? Or was aligning himself with creatures he'd been raised to consider enemies the solution to a future possibly dominated by experiments and supressed freedom? Did Lucas truly believe that the IMI would use the serum in any other capacity other than amping up their own powers to dominate the human race as Vampires had once done?

Lucas didn't know. What he did know was how he felt — confused and shit scared. He wished he were more like Elena, brave and impulsive, absent of thoughts of crawling under his bed and kissing his old life goodbye. If Elena were here she'd tell him to man up, get his act together and stop being a dumbass.

But that was easier said than done.

CHAPTER FIFTEEN

Conjecture

watched the afternoon sun splay dappled light across the pale pink rendered walls of the villa. Vines clung to weakened mortar and wrapped gnarled branches around trellises and balconies, reaching for the fading light as it settled over the horizon. All windows and doors were thrown open to accept any invitation of warmth and perhaps the return of a missing daughter.

Lucius would know I was home. He'd have heard the approach of the car, and even now, the chilled breath that left my lips and the steady thrum of a heart longing for the safety this place provided.

'Showtime, Elena,' Sebastian murmured, nudging me towards the entry. He led by example, one foot in front of the other, only stopping when he realised I hadn't followed. 'What's wrong?'

'Nothing.'

'Then why aren't you heading in?'

'I'll catch up.' I guess I was overwhelmed to be back here, and somewhat guilty that I was safe and Lucas was still unaccounted for. It didn't feel right to celebrate being home again just yet.

Sebastian shrugged, turned and headed not for the house, but for the garage instead.

'Hey? Where are you going?'

'Out.'

'You're not coming inside?'

'No.'

Curious, I ran to catch up with him. It wasn't like Sebastian to miss a debriefing. Then again, his frosty attitude on the plane suggested that perhaps I'd said or done something to piss him off in the last few hours. 'Okay, 'fess up. What did I do?'

'Nothing, I just have urgent business to attend.'

'Such as?'

He grunted, stopping so suddenly that I ran into the back of him, rebounded and just about hit the deck before his lightning reflexes caught my wrist and hauled me back to steadier feet. I slammed against his solid chest instead, air exploding from my lungs and wheezing from my mouth. Sebastian barely noticed. 'I need to feed, Elena. It's been much longer than it should.'

He said a bunch of other stuff, too, but I was too busy trying to catch my breath to make sense of it. 'Why didn't you say something?' I eventually gasped, rubbing my chest. 'You know I would have let you feed from me.'

Sebastian grabbed my chin and turned my face in his direction. He shifted his fingers as our eyes met, pinching my lips between forefinger and thumb. 'Do you even realise how loud you are?'

Oops. I'd forgotten about the other vamps inside the villa. I would have apologised, but my lips were still in his vicelike grip.

'Besides,' he began to whisper, leaning into my ear, 'you're still technically human, so there's nothing you can do to help me.'

As he began to move away, I hastily grappled with his shirt collar, scrunching the fabric between my fingers and pulling him close again. I slipped my other arm around his neck and held him close, trying in vain to stop him from running away.

Sebastian, ever the opportunist, found my waist and walked us backwards until we slammed against the garage wall. 'This is unexpected,' he teased, fingers splaying against my lower back. His lips urgently sought the soft flesh of my jugular, tracing a moist path across my shoulder and back up the side of my neck on route to my mouth. 'I wonder if your father will catch us …'

'This isn't a come on,' I chided, smacking him roughly over the back of the head. 'I just remembered that you owe me an explanation from when we were back in Bucharest.'

He groaned, growing slack in my arms. 'Now? I really need to go, Elena.'

'If you've got time for nookie, then you've got time for this. Now, tell me why you fed on Caleb in Bucharest, why you can spill vampire blood but not mine?'

Sebastian raised his head, nostrils flaring, his hand slapped across my mouth again, grip firmer than before. 'Keep your voice down.'

'Please,' I muffled, rolling my eyes, 'as if I'm the only one who's paid attention to your feeding habits over the last 2000 years.'

'I don't think anyone would understand even if they had noticed.'

'Why?'

Sebastian's hand fell away from my lips, eyes haunted and skin sallow. He didn't respond, perhaps uncertain what to say. He looked tired. He looked … thirsty.

'Why vampire blood?' I pressed. 'I mean, I know why I like it, I'm half Vânător, but what makes you different from me, from other vampires?'

'It's too hard to explain.'

Sebastian left my embrace, kicking instead at the gravel by our feet. I put my hands on my hips, suitably impressed that he hadn't yet run or brought up the vague rules he so regularly referred to and that no one else understood. 'You promised you'd try.'

Sebastian continued to kick at the ground while running an agitated hand through his unruly hair. 'Vampire blood is …'

'Is what?' I had the urge to start tapping my foot to hurry him up.

'Tainted.'

'What do you mean?'

He shook his head, running his fingers through his hair yet again. 'I don't think I'm going to say this right, but it's tainted with intent, with the memory and or promise of future wrongdoing. Essentially Vampire blood is a source blood, a direct line for feeding off the evil in the world.'

I screwed my face up. 'You're feeding off a sentiment, not the blood itself?'

He seemed to struggle with finding the correct response. 'No, it's still blood, the essence of what we all need to survive. The difference is that it's filled with everything that is wrong — unholy, for lack of a better word. Every time I take vampiric blood into me, I swallow some of the world's darkness and leave more room for the light.'

'You're right,' I said, my expression unchanging. 'You're not explaining something right because I'm not following you at all.'

'It's too complicated,' he muttered. 'You never should have asked.'

'Pft, maybe. But at least I now know you're definitely not a normal freaking vampire.'

He reluctantly smiled as he turned heel and walked away. 'Neither are you.'

'Don't you think I have a right to know? We're apparently soul mates, remember?'

'Believe me, Elena, I never forget what we mean to each other.'

'That did not answer my question!' I yelled after him. *Stupid men. Always so obtuse.*

'Elena?'

The urge to stamp my foot finally overcame me but running after Sebastian was a fool's errand. Instead, I headed into the warmth of the villa and towards the sound of my father's irritation. He'd been counting the seconds of my return and I was ignoring that ongoing concern by wastefully chastising Sebastian.

'Don't you ever do this to me again! Do you hear me, Elena?' Lucius chided, appearing out of nowhere to wrap me in a crushing embrace. 'I've lost my entire family. I couldn't stand it if I lost you, too.'

I managed to find some breathing space within the confines of his suffocating affection. I had about a million things I wanted to say, mostly excuses, but in the end, I figured the rant was because he cared.

'I warned you that it was not safe outside these walls,' he growled, finally releasing me. 'The next time I ask you to stay put, at least give me the benefit of the doubt.'

'Um ...'

'Good.'

Lucius gestured to the courtyard and the Thralls taking in the afternoon sun from canvas deckchairs. They didn't even glance up, Marcus doing his utmost to avoid any eye contact, period.

Tiberius, with his long, wavy hair and emerald green eyes

was the first one pleasant enough to offer greeting. Marcus continued to study the ends of his sable locks, while Decimus and Maximus, always quiet and agreeable, sat together in companionable silence.

'It's good to see you safe, Elena,' Tiberius said warmly.

'Thanks, Tiberius.' I clasped his outstretched hand in mine and squeezed gently. He pressed my knuckles to his lips and then shifted his feet so I could perch on the end of his lounge chair.

'We are very glad that you are home.'

Marcus scoffed, returning to the study of his follicles. Obviously he was still pissed about the broken floor tiles, a mishap during some telekinetic training with Lucius and Sebastian before my abduction. The tiles were yet to be replaced.

Lucius growled and squeezed Marcus's slender shoulders in warning. 'Elena, I know you have only just returned to us, but given your recent abduction and unauthorized travel, we need to know everything about the Vânători and if you learnt anything about The Protectors.'

'I can only tell you my thoughts.'

'And what of the serum?'

'Well, Bucharest was a dead end as I'm sure you already know. I was hoping that when I went back to Cairns, I might have learnt something there, but it was also a hit and miss.'

'Did you encounter any Protectors?'

'No. The only thing we learned was that Lucas might be part of some covert IMI experimentation, too.'

'Did you at least figure out where these Protectors went?' Marcus asked, sounding bored. Did he even care that my brother may have become a victim?

'No,' I muttered. 'They didn't exactly leave me a map saying, "You can find us here".'

Marcus scoffed, gaze flicking to the fingers that still squeezed his shoulder. 'Nobody likes a smart ass, Elena.'

'And nobody likes⊠'

'What *do* you have, Elena?' Maximus interrupted in a timely fashion.

I took a breath, stamped down any brewing annoyance and said, 'Some information on a mobile that Lucas left for me to find. There are some letters from Chester, the head researcher at the IMI, but they only confirm what we already know about the serum. But there are some brief details on Lucas's exploits, too.' I handed Tiberius the mobile phone in question and let him scroll through the evidence.

'Any references to what the serum can or could do?' Tiberius asked as he perused the glowing screen.

'No, the classification of it being a weapon is still rather vague.'

'What are your instincts telling you it could be?'

'Why would you want to know?'

'Humour us,' Lucius said gently.

I shrugged, at a loss just like everyone else. 'I really don't know, but I suspect it might be about gaining power. Using my blood as the basis of its production could enhance the qualities The Protectors lack.'

'Putting themselves on a level playing field with us?' Marcus queried, snapping his fingers at Tiberius to gain access to the phone.

I nodded reluctantly. 'Of course I can't say for sure, but it makes sense.'

Lucius released Marcus, contemplative as he begun to pace the terracotta floor. 'But why disappear?' he mused. 'Why leave some members of the cause behind and take others?'

'I don't know — maybe for their skillset?'

'We don't know a lot,' Maximus agreed.

Lucius stopped pacing to commandeer the empty deck chair beside me. He fingered the chain and wedding band dangling from around his neck, his face a mask of neutrality. 'It's safe to assume that the alliance is no more,' he said quietly. 'If The Protectors were still concerned about human collateral, they would have come to our aid with the Vânătors.'

'Let me float you another theory,' I began, my fingers writhing with consternation within my lap. 'What if The Protectors made a deal with the Vânătors to eliminate us?'

A shot of nervous laughter erupted from Maximus. 'Please be serious. The Protectors would not have tossed aside the alliance and embraced the Vânătors.' He laughed again. 'They are savages compared to us.'

I didn't disagree on any particular point, though instinct told me something wasn't quite right. 'I know it sounds crazy, but I learnt something with Roshan. He didn't need me; he wanted me. It was about possession, not discovering ways to unlock more power within his pack.'

Lucius's knuckles flexed, flesh and protruding bone suddenly whiter than snow. 'You think that the Alphas have entered into some sort of arrangement with The Protectors to get their hands on the serum?'

'I think we have to at least consider the possibility.'

'Wait a minute,' Marcus said, rising inhumanly fast to his feet. He folded taut, muscled arms across a broad chest, eyebrows slanted over dark, almond-shaped eyes. 'Lucius, please tell me you're not considering this. It's far-fetched, better examined as the musings of a bored teenage girl.'

'Watch yourself, Marcus,' Lucius growled, towering over his Thrall. 'Elena is my daughter.'

Marcus cowered in the shadow of his maker, sneering as

though I needed reminding of his contempt. 'Forgive me,' Marcus hissed, teeth clenched. 'I forget my place.' He bowed and once again took his seat.

'Elena could be right,' Lucius snapped, all eyes back on the master Vampire. 'Italy hosts the largest coven. Killing us establishes control and promotes fear. I simply wonder why The Protectors did not try this tactic sooner.'

'They didn't have the serum,' Tiberius replied.

'But what will killing us prove?' This from Maximus.

'They don't need to prove anything,' I said. 'They hate us, and, if they have promised the Vânătors the serum in exchange for handling the heavy lifting, then the IMI need only to concentrate on annihilating the Alphas, knowing that by killing them, you kill them all.'

'That won't be easy,' Tiberius said. 'The Alphas are smarter than we assume.'

'Maybe that's another reason the IMI needed Elena,' Decimus added. 'Perhaps the IMI found a way to extrapolate Elena's Vânător DNA and establish some sort of chemical product to attract the Alphas for final decimation.'

The theory was entirely possible given Chester's overt curiosity regarding my physical connection to Roshan.

I watched the lines on Lucius's face crack his neutral mask; his topaz eyes shifted uneasily. He looked worn by life's unending call of attention. 'Everyone leave now.'

What? No one moved. Confusion was evident. While we'd all been consumed by our own thoughts, Lucius had already moved the next chess piece, rendering us all checked.

'I said, leave. Elena, I want you to stay.' A dismissive wave of his hand sent the others quickly packing. The man sure knew how to clear out a room.

'Now that we're alone,' Lucius said softly, 'I want you to tell me what really happened when you were with Roshan.'

I frowned. 'You broke up the powwow to quiz me about Roshan? Didn't we do this over the phone?'

'Then when were you planning on telling me about your shift into Vânător?'

Uh oh. 'Did Sebastian say something to—?'

'We'll talk about Sebastian in a minute,' he growled, previous softness evaporating. 'Right now you'll tell me about your shape-shifting.'

'How did you even ...?' I stopped, frowned; instantly annoyed as I recalled the crushing embrace on arrival. 'You plucked out my memories again, didn't you?' I was certain my face flushed as other details resurfaced — the kiss Sebastian and I had recently shared, and oh shit, the heated moments with William.

Oh that's just perfect.

'Hey look, if we're going to continue this relationship, there are going to have to be some boundaries, Lucius.'

'Tell me about shape-shifting,' he responded, deliberately ignoring my outrage.

'What's the point? You've already seen it.' I got up to leave, but he grabbed my wrist, forcibly pushing me back into the deck chair.

'Not all images are clear. So please, tell me what happened.' He released me, an angry imprint of his fingers fading from my flesh.

I shifted nervously, drawing creaks and groans from the springs. 'I don't actually remember anything.'

He wasn't buying it. 'The carnage is very vivid within your thoughts, Elena. I saw your actions, saw what you did to the pack. How can you not remember?'

'I only know it happened because William told me.'

Lucius was silent for several minutes, rubbing the stubble of his chin between thumb and forefinger. 'Perhaps you closed your mind to the violence. Is this something you struggle with?'

'I don't think so. The IMI trained me to handle most situations, but when I think about what I did ...' I shivered, running my hands up and down my arms. 'I'm not proud, but I do want to learn to control it.'

'Control it?' Lucius looked incredulous.

'Yes. I almost killed William and I would never intentionally hurt him.'

'This is an unknown ability among our kind, Elena. You are the first and ultimately unpredictable. Controlling the beast within may not be possible while you're still human.'

'So, I'm supposed to sit on my hands until I turn? What if it happens again and I kill everyone in this house? Lucius, you helped me with my telekinetic ability. Help me control the Vânător shift, too.'

'I have no comprehension of how Vânător shape-shifting works, Elena. I cannot guide you and to think that I could would be dangerous.'

'There are benefits to trying,' I pressed. 'William said that Roshan's Alpha scent didn't work on me in wolf form and that I was super strong and lightning fast.'

'Out of the question.'

'Lucius, be reasonable. I don't want to hurt those I care about.'

He waved a dismissive hand. 'Enough.'

I bit my tongue, stifling the urge to tell him to shove it ... among other things.

'I gather Roshan is still at large and hunting you?'

I shrugged, annoyed that he expected ongoing conversation paired with civility. I could barely stop my bottom lip from jutting out and my fingers from fixing him with a stiff one.

Lucius cared little as he moved to sit beside me, our shoulders now touching — perhaps it was just another excuse for him to read through my thoughts. 'He is not the only male hunting you right now, is he?'

That turned my attention. 'Huh?'

'Sebastian and William,' he said, looking at me expectantly. 'They are hunting you, too.'

What was I supposed to say to that? Going into sordid detail with my father about the implications of either relationship? Freaking gross.

Lucius laughed, probably reading my thoughts. It was interesting that my sideways glance captured renewed warmth and an understanding that immersed itself within the dark depths of his probing gaze. 'Why don't you tell me what's going on with you and those two boys?'

'Um, no.'

'I've seen what you've been getting up to, Elena.' He tapped a finger to his temple to prove truth and revive my anger. 'You might as well talk to me.'

'I don't think so.'

His lips stretched beyond capacity, his white teeth gleaming. Great, my love life was entertainment. Didn't we have other shit to worry about right now? 'Sebastian seems quite determined to gain your affections.'

'Sebastian's a lot of things.'

'Indeed,' Lucius acknowledged with a small tilt of his head. His smile dimmed, his eyes now unfocused. 'Elena. I'm sorry for what you've been through. If I could take away your pain as easily as I read your thoughts, I would.'

I licked my dry lips, unsettled by the constant reminders of the brain invasion. 'Thanks, I guess.'

He patted the top of my head awkwardly, still unsure

how we should interact as father and daughter. 'I'm very happy that you are home.'

Happy.

I was reminded of the conversation Sebastian and I had sitting on Lucas's bedroom floor, perceiving grand ideas of what happiness represented. I knew only too well what would make Lucius truly happy — an end to this existence, a chance to see his wife and son again. It made me wonder how being happy *now* could simply be sourced from the assurance of my safety. Didn't he want more than that? How could I be so important to him when we'd only known each other for such a short space of time?

I wiggled in my seat, a little uncomfortable. I'd never known Lucius or my mother, never known what it was like to be a daughter. I wondered if his happiness was conditional, something easily swayed if given the opportunity to alter the past.

'Just out of curiosity, if you had the power to change one thing in your life, what would it be?' I enquired.

'Why do you ask?'

'I guess I'm curious about your definition of happiness.'

And my place in your heart.

He tugged at his necklace, probably thinking about Selena and his lost son Lucius. Would he wish to go back and change the circumstances that led to their death and his imprisonment as a member of the damned?

'Nothing,' he finally answered, face impassive.

To say that I was shocked by the admission was an understatement. 'I don't understand.'

Lucius offered his hand, outstretched fingers seeking the warmth of my own. His were cool and calloused from years as a Legionnaire in the Roman Guard. 'Did I ever tell you that Selena was pregnant when she was murdered?'

'Yes, on the night we first met.'

'I had no idea until Lucifer told me,' Lucius began, his fingers squeezing mine. 'You see, it wasn't just Selena and Lucius's deaths I was avenging. It was the baby daughter I would never know.'

'It was going to be a girl?' I whispered, swallowing the lump in my throat.

'Yes.'

'So, why wouldn't you want to go back and change that night? At least then you would be able to know her, see your wife and watch *both* of your children grow up. Wouldn't that make you happy?'

He shook his head as if I were missing some greater point. 'Of course seeing them again would make me happy, but I wouldn't change anything, Elena.'

'But why?'

'Because changing the past would disrupt the present, and if I did that, I wouldn't have you now.'

I looked around for the sledgehammer that had just taken aim against my chest. 'So, you're telling me that you would rather have lived 2000 years mourning your lost family just so that you could have me in your present?'

Lucius released my hands and cupped my face. He gently kissed my forehead, his lips so soft against my skin. 'My family are gone,' he whispered against my flesh, moving back far enough to look into my weepy eyes. 'But I choose you, Elena, because you are family, too, the precious baby girl I never had. How can I ask to save one and not the other?'

I gnawed on my lower lip until I tasted blood, unsure what to say. I'd never known the definition of belonging until this very moment, never known what it was like for a parent to truly love and want their child.

Shit, I'm bloody crying.

I bit my lip harder since I'd already healed, concentrating on the pain rather than the tumultuous flood of emotions working unwanted moisture upon my cheeks. 'Thank you,' I mumbled, sniffing back a particularly unattractive bubble of snot. 'I'm so sorry.'

'Don't be,' Lucius argued, carefully wiping the tears from my cheeks. 'I'm not.'

A breath of relief, an exhalation I'd been holding since we'd first met escaped my trembling lips. I'd been waiting for the rejection, waiting for someone to tell me that I could never have what others so easily took for granted — unconditional love. 'Please don't tell anyone I cried.'

Lucius patted my cheek, a smile present once more. 'I won't.' He let me go, chuckling quietly to himself as I scrubbed my shirt across my dampened face. 'Just out of curiosity,' he murmured, watching me hastily erase my emotion, 'what would you change if you had the chance?'

'I don't think I'm as accepting of past events as you are.'

'I see.' His face darkened, that earlier mist of sadness setting in. 'You want to erase your pain, every tortuous aspect of your own past. I can understand the sentiment, Elena.'

I shook my head. 'No, I don't think that fixing my burdens will change anything fundamental.'

'Then what are you saying?'

'I'm saying that if I had the opportunity to change anything, I would go back to the very beginning and change *everything.*'

'Everything?'

'Well, if you're going to rewrite history, you might as well start at chapter one.'

CHAPTER SIXTEEN

Opportunity

yanked out my earphones and strained, listening. I thought I'd heard a knock at my bedroom door, but couldn't be sure. I'd been too busy busting my eardrums with music in an effort to drown out recently unearthed emotions. I was just about to shove the buds back in again when I heard that definitive knock. 'Who is it?'

It was Sebastian, wandering into my room like he owned the place.

Typical.

'You're back,' I breathed, reprocessing our earlier exchange. Stating he fed off evil had really stumped me. Was he part Incubus? Mutant emo vampire? Reading up on demons and their various counterparts had not improved my knowledge of Sebastian at all.

He closed the door behind him and wandered over to the bed. For several uncomfortable moments he just stood there watching me, lying against the pillows, earplugs poised halfway back to my ears. Was he going to say something, or just stare at me all day?

I broke eye contact and replaced the buds, knowing he was bound to interrupt me shortly.

Sure enough, the mattress dipped and Sebastian made

himself at home, stretching out beside me, stealing a pillow from under my head and curving himself around me like a wanton cat.

'You right there?' I chided, wrestling for my missing pillow and failing miserably.

'What are you listening to?' Sebastian asked. The closer he got, the quicker I realised his proximity would lead to me requiring a cold shower.

'Music.'

'Annie Lennox?'

I playfully punched him in the arm. 'No, angry girl music.'

Sebastian snatched an earphone and pressed it against his ear. A mocking smile touched his supple lips. 'Liar.'

He handed it back, still smirking. 'What did Lucius and the Thralls say about your theories on the Vânătors and the serum?'

I switched off Annie so I could hear him better. 'Not much. They agree with some of my ideas, well, except Marcus. He thinks I'm full of shit.'

'What did Lucius say?'

'You haven't spoken?'

'Not about this. He called and told me to get back to the villa to keep an eye on you.'

'What have I done now?'

The smirk exploded into a small chuckle. 'Nothing, for a change. Lucius received intel that Julius was spotted in Nice, and since he wasn't here when I got home, nor were the Thralls. I assume they left immediately.'

I propped myself up on one elbow, giving him my full attention. 'Why didn't he tell me? We were only talking a few hours ago. I could've helped.'

'Julius is a problem we want you to avoid, Elena.'

I shuddered, the memory of the note he'd left at the villa threatening my life all too vivid. 'How long will they be gone?'

'A few days, maybe longer. Lucius was only specific about keeping you safe.'

I grimaced, flopping onto my back again with an exaggerated sigh. 'So, you're my babysitter?'

Sebastian's stiff smile suggested he'd already reconciled that I was a total pain in the ass and he was stuck with me regardless.

'Did Lucius mention my shape-shifting?'

'Why?' Sebastian said, dropping the lock of my hair he'd been absently fondling. I could practically feel the suspicion oozing from his pores.

'No reason.'

'Orders are to keep you safe and ...' His voice faded, lips pursing in displeasure.

'And what?'

'And to keep my hands off you.'

I snickered. I couldn't help it. 'Does that count if we're practising?'

'Practising what?'

I could see his mind dipping to tantric possibilities, the gentle caress of his finger up and down the side of my arm a definite giveaway. 'I was actually hoping you'd help get my fighting skills back on track.' I tried to hide my sudden discomfort by grasping at indifference. 'I'd also like it if you could help me manipulate my ability to shape-shift.'

'And Lucius approves?'

'Sure.'

'Elena ...'

'Don't *Elena* me.'

Sebastian rolled his eyes, his explorative hand dropping

to the mattress. 'So, I'm going to assume from your defensive reaction that Lucius said no?'

'What he doesn't know won't hurt him.'

'And how are you planning on keeping this plan from the great and powerful Oz?' His eyes narrowed. 'Which, by the way, I have *not* agreed to.'

'I'm going to work on finding a way to shield my mind like you suggested. If I can do it for my body, or even someone else's, I should be able to block thoughts.'

'Elena, you're acting like I said yes.'

'Thanks, Sebastian.'

'Elena ...'

'What? You know you will anyway, so why bother putting up a fight?'

'I did not say *yes*.'

'You just did, *twice*.'

The next day I found myself sitting cross-legged in the garden, watching the sun set in a distant horizon mottled with oranges and dusky pinks. Gazing higher, stars already peeked through the hazy afternoon, rendering night an unstoppable certainty.

The garden lights had just switched on, highlighting tree trunks and the leaves of the shrubs surrounding the pond. Water trickled down the rock face, splashing into the natural catchment below. Ice cold to the touch, I felt sorry for the inhabitants.

'Elena, I don't think you're concentrating.'

I slammed my eyes shut, trying not to smile. I was so bored, contemplating the silliest of things. Would scales keep fish warm during the winter? Would they freeze to death, or forget their circumstance in the first place? I'd read somewhere once that goldfish have a memory span of about five seconds. I suspected we might have been related at some point.

I cracked one eye open, only to be greeted by Sebastian's glare. His seriousness was my undoing and I collapsed in a fit of giggles. 'I'm sorry,' I gasped, biting down on my lower lip in an attempt to sober my mirth.

'No, you're not.'

I was overcome once more, heartily slapping the damp, coarse blades of grass beside me. 'I am, but I just don't understand how meditation's going to help me shape-shift.'

Sebastian sighed, impatience clear in the rigid set of his shoulders and tightly clenched jaw. Meditation wasn't working out so great for him either. 'I'm trying to show you how to centre yourself so that you can create lasting barriers around your mind and body.'

I hiccupped, another bubble of laughter gaining momentum within my throat.

Sebastian snapped his fingers in front of my face, beyond annoyed. 'Concentrate.'

Shit.

I was suddenly flat on my back, laughing like a lunatic. Seeing Sebastian — Zen master extraordinaire — grumpily embracing the lotus position had me in a fit of stitches that would not cease the longer he disapproved.

'I'm so glad this amuses you,' he muttered, folding his arms in front of his chest.

When I finally caught my breath, I rolled back into a casual sitting position. 'Sorry, I'm not poking fun at you. I just assumed we'd be in combat training, not sitting around like garden gnomes, chanting at the wind.'

'Meditation has been used for centuries to quieten the mind and centre the body. It helps you find focus.'

'Focus on what … boredom?'

'Okay, that's it.' He untucked his legs from on top of his knees and pushed to his feet. 'If you don't want to learn, then I'm out of here.' He headed towards the garden path, stopping short when he ran headfirst into one of my telekinetic walls of energy.

I stifled a giggle as he stumbled backwards, growling and flashing slightly extended fangs at my antics. I was so not bored anymore. 'Don't go. I promise I'll try to be good.'

Sebastian attempted walking in another direction, but my shields encircled him, barring retreat. 'Elena, let me go!'

'Aw, but I'm just starting to have fun.'

A menacing snarl was followed by a roar of frustration that saw me release him almost instantly. I barely had time to wrap the shields around myself before he was on me like white on rice. He hit the shimmery surface, rebounded a few feet in the air and then landed in a crouch, his breathing and ill-tempered mood barely under control. 'Why are you being such a pain in the ass?!' he shouted.

I shrugged, cautiously optimistic that his mood was already shifting into warmer territory. 'I feel … I don't know … suppressed with all this chanting crap.'

'I thought you wanted to take this seriously?' Sebastian said, straightening up and retracting his fangs. He ran his fingers through his hair, fixing his gaping shirt and re-schooling his features.

'I am. Just not the meditation part.'

'Elena, this isn't a game to me. How are you going to control your Vânător side if you don't learn control yourself first?'

I huffed, dropping the telekinetic shield. 'You really know how to suck the fun out of everything, don't you?'

'When it comes to protecting you, I don't have a sense of humour.' He crossed the distance between us and dropped to his knees in front of me. He gathered my hands in his and squeezed them tight — too tight. 'When Roshan took you, I'd never felt more helpless. I know you won't sit on the sidelines despite the danger and because of that, I want you to be as prepared as possible. Your lack of concentration and blatant disregard of my time scares me.'

I swallowed the last of my levity, easing my fingers from his chokehold. 'I'm sorry. I was just trying to have a bit of fun. I didn't realise—'

'Yeah, well …' He quickly stood, turned and headed for the villa, leaving me sitting amongst the coming shadows of night.

'Hey, where are you going?'

He was gone.

The evening lights were already blazing when I returned to the courtyard. The mosaic-covered fountain at the entry was aglow with soft, ambient light and warmth enveloped me like a welcoming hug, but a quick scout for Sebastian left me cold when I realised I was alone.

I climbed the stairs to the second level, wandering the passage until I was standing outside Sebastian's bedroom door. I knocked, pausing only momentarily before I pushed the heavy timber aside and stuck my head inside. He was sitting on the edge of the heavyset, ebony bed with his back to the door, holding a mobile phone to his ear and talking quietly.

I let myself in, absorbing the polar opposite of my usual surrounds. Glossy, raven black walls and moulded ceilings were devoured by darkness. The terracotta floors underfoot provided only minor warmth in the otherwise desolate scheme. A vast collection of musical instruments and the recorded versions of their mastery dominated almost every spare centimetre of space.

'I'd appreciate it if you could,' Sebastian said, looking grim as I sat down next to him. He shook his head. 'Yeah, you'll get paid, but only if I get something worthwhile out of it.'

Sebastian turned away at the raising of my eyebrows. 'Two thousand is all I'm offering, Caleb.'

I rolled my eyes and flopped back onto the bed, resting my hands behind my head. Caleb was the only vampire I knew that Sebastian had to negotiate a payment contract to do anything. Friendship was a word he used lightly, perhaps fearful that the implication of a discount might arise.

'This won't interfere with your duties. Lucius does not require your services at present.'

There was a short pause and a string of hurried, indeterminable speech at the end of the line. I suspected Caleb was listing the possible reasons to include hazardous pay.

'Okay, three thousand, but that's it.' Sebastian snapped the phone shut and turned back to look at me, incredulous. 'He's going to send me broke.'

I highly doubted that. 'What are you negotiating?'

'Negotiating?' Sebastian snorted. 'You mean financial larceny?'

'Okay, what's he extorting you for?' I said, unsuccessfully hiding my rising amusement. Sebastian's irritation was pressing all of my funny buttons today.

He sighed, falling back onto the bed next to me, a whiff of his cologne tickling my nose as he settled in close … real close. 'I asked Caleb to go to Cairns.'

Intrigued, I rolled onto my side to study his expression.

'Why? We didn't learn anything from Cairns when we were there.'

'I know, but we didn't linger, either, or look for alternate solutions.'

Anger rose quickly within. 'That's because you said I had to wait until after the multi-coven gathering!'

'I know, I know,' Sebastian soothed. 'That's why I'm sending Caleb back. We have preparations to make, but he doesn't. While you keep Lucius happy and focus on improving your skills, Caleb can hunt down leads, hopefully unearthing something we might have missed.'

'Like what?'

Sebastian smiled as he rolled onto his side to face me. We were mere centimetres apart, too close for comfort and yet, strangely, so far away it made my whole body ache. 'For one, there must be travel records and paper trails somewhere. For three grand, I'm confident Caleb will find them.'

The relief was palpable and I was suddenly smiling so wide that my face hurt. 'I thought helping Lucas was on hold until we figured out what to do about the Vânǎtors. And here you are trying to track him down for me. I really appreciate this, Sebastian.'

'Finding Lucas will also lead us to The Protectors.'

'Look, I know you didn't do it specifically for me, but I appreciate it, anyway.'

'Who said I didn't do it for you?'

'You just said—'

'You should understand my motives by now …' He reached out and pulled me closer until our bodies melded and his arm held me captive, a reminder that Sebastian was a predator in every sense of the word.

'What are you doing?'

'You're in my room, remember?' He stroked my hips,

eyes darkening as they skimmed the length of my body, finally settling on my parted lips that silently yearned for his touch.

'So? You come into my room all the time and I don't try to molest you.' My rebuttal was shaky at best and full of holes.

Sebastian dipped to my neck, lips tentatively brushing the throbbing pulse that seemed to want to dance with his tongue whenever he was near. 'My room. My rules.'

'I could leave,' I murmured, enjoying the feel of his lips upon me. 'But I have a feeling you'd try to take advantage of me anywhere.'

Sebastian stilled, the silken caress of my heated flesh forgotten. He moved away, his eyes now concealed by the long lashes I envied. 'Do you honestly believe that, Elena?'

I've somehow put my foot in it, haven't I?

'Perhaps not sexually, but you *do* take advantage of me.'

I just did it again.

Sebastian's possessive arm slid away from my waist, his fingers now busying themselves with tracing the creases in the satin sheets beneath us. 'How do I take advantage of you?' His voice was stiff, leaning towards anger.

Be honest.

'Um, okay. Well honestly? I think you play on my attraction for you by using my emotional avoidance as a shield to keep the questions between us unanswered but the physical side of me interested. I'm constantly confused by the truth you determine and about what we really are.'

'That goes both ways,' Sebastian muttered as he continued to finger the thread count. 'I refuse to reveal all my secrets unless you're willing to explore your own feelings.' He looked at me then, his eyes a swirling mass of grey. 'I have much more to lose than you, Elena.'

'How can you know that? You have no idea what it would be like to let go of my heart only to have it thrown back in my face.'

Sebastian's eyes softened, emerald compassion seeping back in. 'That would never happen.'

'Then prove it. Show me that I can trust you.'

Sebastian's bottom lip trembled ever so slightly, a hint of fear marring the tumultuous depths of his beguiling eyes. Whatever it was that bound him to his secrets made him tremble with an uncertainty that rendered me speechless. 'There'll be consequences.'

'W–what sort of consequences?'

'I don't know yet.'

'I can't take the riddles anymore, Sebastian.'

He shocked me as he bounded to his feet and smashed his fist through the intricately carved bedpost, splintering wood and sending shards of debris flying across the room. 'What you're asking could ruin everything!'

I was quick to make a getaway, rolling off the bed and backing towards the door. 'Ruin what?' I shouted back, now emboldened by the distance between us. 'We can't start anything because I can't trust you!'

'Then ask me your questions!' he boomed.

'Not until you calm down.'

'I am calm!' he bellowed. 'What you're asking ...' He shook his head, squeezing what remained of the bedpost between his fingers until it groaned and disintegrated within his palm. 'Ask your questions, Elena. I will deal with whatever is coming ... *alone.*'

'You don't have to be alone in this, Sebastian, if you just—'

'Ask your questions!' he barked, enraged more than ever.

'Fine!' I snapped, scowling. 'How long have you known that I was your soul mate?'

'A little over 13,000 years,' was the immediate, brusque response.

'Bullshit. You're only a little over 2000 years old yourself.'

'What do you want me to say?'

'The truth. Lucius is the master Vampire, the first Vampire. How can you possibly be older if Tiberius is still your father and you're still a Vampire?'

He looked right at me, eyes a swirl with tangled variations of grey, a million secrets just swimming through those tendrils of ire.

I stumbled over a forgotten rug in my haste to exit, falling to my knees, trying to wrap my head around the logistics of Sebastian's implausible existence. I never saw him approach. I never saw him drop to the ground in front of me, or notice how he pulled me against his chest and whispered in my ear, 'I've only been a Vampire for 2000 years. I was many things before that.'

I shook my head, his burly chest impeding the movement. 'What you're saying is not possible.'

'It may seem that way.'

'But how? How do you know what no one else could possibly conceive? How could you know or even remember past lives?'

'I choose my existence as I chose to be a Vampire.'

'You were turned.'

'No. I chose to be a Vampire. I can be anything I want in any life.'

Dismayed, I found myself recoiling from his touch, uncertain of his power and the purpose of his interest in me. I was a mere speck in his seemingly unending existence, an existence I couldn't fathom. 'Then what the hell are you?'

'Anything you need me to be.'

'Cut the shit, Sebastian, you're freaking me out.'

He rocked back on his heels, uncertain, hands now a tangled mess within his lap as he summoned the courage to continue. 'I don't know how else to explain it to you. I just am whatever you need me to be.'

'How can you choose?'

'I'm not tied to any particular being or entity.'

'Um, like a ghost?'

He searched heavenward, lips moving in silent prayer. I saw him close his eyes; lids squeezed shut, the delicate skin creased in frustration. I sensed that his explanation for everything sat spectacularly out of reach even though probably poised on the tip of his tongue. If I could pluck it from his mouth I would, though knowing what to do with the knowledge was another matter entirely. 'There are some things I cannot reveal, Elena, no matter what.'

'Then at least tell me why you chose to be damned?'

'I knew that if I chose to remain human — mortal — then I would've grown old and died, never having a chance at rebirth.'

'Because Tiberius is your father and became a Thrall — immortal?'

'That's right,' Sebastian agreed. 'I claimed immortality as a Vampire and waited patiently for Lucius to father you into this immortal life, a life I'd otherwise have missed if I'd remained human.'

Breath and sanity itself seemed somehow lodged in my throat. 'You chose Vampirism for me, to be damned for all eternity on the off chance that Lucius might one day father another daughter, father me?'

Unexpected tears threatened to spill a trail of unstoppable wet saltiness, but I slammed my eyes shut, cinching the lids tight and forbidding release.

'I didn't do it for you, Elena,' Sebastian finally said,

caressing my cheek until my glistening eyes opened and looked back at him. 'I'm much too selfish for that.'

'Then why?'

'I did it for me.'

'Because you, um … oh …'

Because he loves me.

Nothing had ever been more obvious and I'd stubbornly ignored the signs, every touch, soft spoken word or burning gaze. But why me? Why choose a stubborn and emotionally retarded sixteen year old from Cairns? The world was a big place and I was just a drop in the ocean. I hardly seemed worth all the effort.

'What are you?' I whispered, awed and terrified of the entity before me.

His hand slipped from my cheek, listless in its return to his lap. 'I am a Vampire.'

I shook my head, now knowing the lie, the mask he wore to protect his true identity.

'Elena, I—'

A sudden flash of radiant light made me gasp and shield my throbbing eyes. Through the gaps in my fingers I searched the blinding ambience for explanation. A mass of downy plumes encompassed me, feathered limbs caressing my body with a softness that made me shudder. I could see only monochromatic layers of white and feel this exquisite brush of heaven against my skin.

So, I didn't expect the fist that connected with my face a second later, the knuckles that slammed against my temple with vicious intent.

I was falling, the floor rushing to greet me, terracotta suddenly under my cheek as I succumbed to unconsciousness. Darkness enveloped and pain flared behind my eyes in an explosion of indescribable torture.

'Araqiel! What are you doing?'

'She already knows too much.'

The two garbled voices faded and so did I, drifting and tormented by the knowledge that I'd been left in the dark in more ways than one.

Typical.

CHAPTER SEVENTEEN

Consequences

Sebastian lifted Elena carefully into his arms, carrying her to his bed and placing her gently in the centre of the mattress. He slid a pillow under her head, making sure she was comfortable before he turned and faced the invading angel.

'You had no right,' Sebastian muttered, pulling the sheet up to Elena's chin. 'She wanted to know.'

'It's not your secret to reveal. Not yet.'

'She would never tell anyone,' Sebastian growled, scowling at the pompous fiend in his perfectly pressed all-white suit and matching shoes.

Araqiel's silver-flecked eyes glowed with wisdom, his long, blond hair shining like Christmas baubles against the soft, feathered wings that denoted his makings. 'The darkness cannot know your true identity, Michael, and she is yet to choose her path.'

'In this life I am Sebastian Marcellus.'

'But you are still the Archangel Michael and you are currently hunted by Lucifer and his minions.' Araqiel shook his head, folding his arms across his chest. 'An idiotic move to reveal yourself to one of their players before knowing her position in the game, don't you think?'

'Elena is not evil and certainly not a player.'

Araqiel conceded with a nod. 'She is still a member of the damned and therefore a player. Her life and thoughts are monitored by the council and you know who sits on the council.'

'Samael and Mammon are unaware of my current whereabouts.'

'For now, but they do grow curious about your alter ego Sebastian and his connection with Elena.'

'And why is that?'

'There have been certain developments.'

Sebastian cocked an eyebrow. 'Developments?'

Araqiel's lips twitched ever so slightly, his eyes darting momentarily to the floor. 'I should not say.'

'Araqiel, you *will* tell me.'

The angel's eyes slanted, lips pressing together in a tight line. 'You are not in charge anymore, Michael. You cannot order me around like times past.'

Sebastian growled, his ire shaking the very foundations of the house. Plaster fell from cracks in the ceiling, raining onto the floor like snow that capped the mountains in winter. 'I *am* the Archangel Michael, Araqiel. Do not forget my power and do not test me. My words still have weight in Heaven despite my current standing.'

Araqiel unfolded his arms and fanned his wings for stability, his footing uncertain as he braced himself against the wall. Unease slipped across his skin. It seemed he'd forgotten the touch of Michael's limitless power and the embrace of his hostility when challenged. 'Forgive me,' he said, bowing ever so slightly. 'I still find it difficult to reconcile you putting *her* above your calling.'

Sebastian ceased the room's demise, the silver in his eyes fading to a dull grey. 'Elena *is* my calling now.'

'Which is why I fear I must remind you not to lose your

head. I know you have spent 13,000 years protecting her, Michael, but there are other factors to contend with now.'

'Such as?'

Araqiel looked uneasy. 'Elena is the key. She has the power to change everything.'

Sebastian's eyes narrowed considerably, the simmering fuel of his rage barely contained on the backburner. 'What are you talking about? What have you done?'

'I've been watching her,' Araqiel murmured, now pacing back and forth. 'She's the bond between the two dark species and has the power to rule both Vampire and Vânător but miraculously holds the potential for light.'

'Her mother,' Sebastian murmured.

'Yes. Uriel's possession of her mother during conception opened the possibility.'

'I'm aware of Elena's angelic bloodline, Araqiel, as undoubtedly everyone else is.'

Araqiel shook his head. 'No, not even the council members are aware of her divinity. Uriel acted on orders from above, a bigger plan obviously set in motion from the beginning.'

'I suspected as much from your lingering presence though I'm curious as to what it is that you hope to gain.'

'She has the ability to choose, Michael,' Araqiel answered.

Sebastian stood woodenly, studying the floor in earnest. 'I know she does.'

'She might not choose you this time and you know what that will mean.'

'Purgatory.'

'It would be for the best. Elena is the first embodiment in thousands of years to be able to wield the decision to change the past.'

Sebastian's head whipped up so fast that Araqiel actually

took a step backwards. 'You're talking about the Time Contract.'

Araqiel nodded, eyes fixed on the Archangel. 'I have bargained for it.'

'You did what?' Sebastian shouted, the room once again shaking. 'What have you done, Araqiel? What have you promised?'

'You have to understand,' Araqiel reasoned, wings unfurling of their own accord, 'this is my chance to correct past mistakes, for the light to triumph and for Lucifer to finally be enslaved to the dark without reprieve. Elena's will is strong and heart pure enough to turn from the petty needs of humanity. We need her.'

'You mean you need her!' Sebastian spat, knuckles clenched and white with fury. 'You can't get back into Heaven without her.'

Araqiel shrugged. 'That is true, but despite this, you know that the Time Contract in her hands can only change the past for the betterment of all involved.'

Deflated, Sebastian dropped onto the edge of his mattress, the springs groaning in protest. He was tired, so tired of hiding, fighting and lying, but a part of him knew that Araqiel was right. 'What are the terms?'

'Michael, I'm sorry.'

'What are the terms of your arrangement?' Sebastian repeated, numb.

'You, in exchange for the Time Contract.'

Sebastian slumped in final defeat. 'You've sentenced me to an eternity in Purgatory, Araqiel. Samael and Mammon will never stop pursuing me until I beg for a rematch with Lucifer in Hell.'

'Forgive me. It is the only way.'

'Is it?'

'She's the only one, Michael. I have never once interfered with your happiness before, but you know these orders came from the top. You know she had to have been chosen for a reason.'

Sebastian never questioned his maker's decisions, but he had to wonder why he'd been left out of the loop in this instance. 'When?'

'Not yet,' Araqiel murmured. 'The timing is off. Elena has a little more to learn before I am certain she will make the right choices.'

'And then you will come for me?'

Araqiel nodded, the soft waves of platinum hair framing perfect features. 'Death will eventually find you, Michael. It's the only way into Purgatory.'

'I cannot die, brother.'

'I'm afraid you can now.'

'What?'

'It is the consequences of breaking the rules. No one can know we are angels unless they draw their own conclusions.'

'She only saw my light and touched my wings ... I ...'
Protesting was pointless. He knew he was in the wrong.

'Michael, you need to know that if Elena dies in the mortal realm,' Araqiel continued, 'you will die, too, and follow her into Purgatory. Your punishment for revelation is such that if you should die alone, you will never be joined in another life with Elena again.'

Sebastian swallowed the bitter lump forming in his throat, his fingers clenched around the satin sheets beneath him. 'Who decided this?'

Araqiel looked up. 'You know who.'

Sebastian gritted his teeth and bowed his head in recognition. 'Then so it shall be done.'

Araqiel absently patted the Archangel's shoulder. 'I must go now.'

'Wait,' Sebastian said. 'I need you to promise me something.'

'What is it?'

'If something should happen to me before she is strong, powerful and knowledgeable, please protect her.'

Araqiel swept into a low bow. 'I would be happy to oblige, my brother. Take care, protect your identity and watch your back. Time is of the essence and this is your last chance at happiness, Michael, so don't blow it as the mortals sometimes say.'

Easier said than done.

CHAPTER EIGHTEEN
Revenge

awoke with a start, skin slicked with sweat and my head a jumbled mass of indecipherable images. I didn't remember going to sleep, just the memory of the fist that put me out. Sebastian was so going to get it the second I saw him.

What right did he have?

I mean, he did hit me, right?

I sat up slowly, cursing at the twisted sheets and woollen comforter tangled around my legs. Apparently I'd had a wild night beneath the covers of Sebastian's bed, breaking free the contorted limbs taking considerable effort.

The floor was frigid as I left the bed and crept across the tiles. I was at the door in seconds, gripping the handle and turning. The old hinges showed their age, groaning as I peeked into the corridor and then ran its length to my bedroom, slamming my own door closed behind me.

'Where's the fire?'

I stiffened, fingers digging into the timber at my back, my eyes scouting the room for the man that belonged to the lilting voice. He sat on the edge of my bed, dark, curly hair swept into a ponytail, blue eyes locked on my twitching form. Seeing Sebastian instead of this creeper suddenly didn't seem like such a bad idea.

'What are you doing here?'

Julius fanned his arms out wide, appearing to take in every aspect the room had to offer. 'This was once my home. Am I not welcome here?'

'What do you think?'

'I think you shouldn't act so surprised to see me. Did you not get my letter? I warned you I would stop in for a visit one of these days.'

I tried not to shudder and failed. This was a Vampire who wanted me dead, his letter detailing just how painful and drawn out he would make that experience. I had faced Alpha Vânătors and dealt with the IMI, but it was nothing compared to standing in the presence of a revenge driven, psychotic blood drainer.

Did I just crap in my pants? Hell, yes.

'Sebastian!' I screamed, knowing I was no match for this opponent.

'He can't hear you, little one.'

'What have you done to him?'

'I haven't done anything to him … yet.'

I screamed Sebastian's name again and again. If he were anywhere on the property he would have heard. Hell, the Pope should have heard me from Vatican City, so where the hell was he?

Julius looked disturbingly at home reclined on the end of my bed, leg hitched with his arm resting over the knee. In another time he might have been surrounded by bronze-skinned handmaidens feeding him grapes. Now only blood could appease him — my blood.

'Sebastian!'

'Please stop. You're embarrassing yourself,' Julius said, looking disinterestedly down at his fingernails.

'Where is he? What have you done to him?' I needed to

work on controlling the panic in my voice. I had the distinct impression that I was going to die a very slow and painful death today.

'He left about ten minutes ago, headed for Rome as far as I could tell.'

Keep him talking. As long as his mouth is moving, his teeth aren't ripping out my jugular.

'How would you know that?'

'I started a little fire at Synth Corp. With Lucius and the other Thralls out of the country, I knew that little Sebastian would be tasked with having to put it out.'

I made motions of reopening the door. I'd thought I'd been subtle but clearly not.

'I wouldn't,' he said, waving a finger and fixing me with a vicious glare. 'It's rude to leave guests unattended.'

'You weren't invited.'

'Hmm, I suppose that is true, but Sebastian lay down the welcome mat by leaving you alone ...' Julius leapt to his feet spectacularly fast and took one menacing step towards me. 'I merely made use of the invitation.'

'What do you want?'

Another measured step. 'Ah, straight to the point. I like that.' He clasped his hands behind his back, watching me from behind dark lashes. I was twitching like a Goddamn epileptic. 'What I want, little one, is to kill your father.'

I cleared my throat, determined to cut away the fear lodged in its centre. 'He's not here right now. Would you like to leave a message?'

Oh, that's just freaking brilliant, Elena. Why don't you just hand him a pen knife and get him to write it in your flesh?

Julius cackled, the cold, hard truth bearing witness to the fact that the local coroner and I were going to be fairly intimate in the near future. 'I'm quite aware that Lucius is not here, little one. I made sure of that by leaving him a few trails to follow in Nice.' He laughed again, a foreboding sound absent of warmth. 'Though I'm clearly not there, am I?' He moved until he was only a few metres away.

I grappled with the doorhandle again, but was thwarted by his indescribable speed and desire to pounce. Thankfully I'd erected shields before twisting the noisy handle.

Julius rebounded and staggered backwards, his surprise evident. It took him but seconds to connect the dots. 'I see that you are indeed your father's daughter, Elena.'

'Try to touch me again and you'll find out exactly what else I can do.'

It was reassuring to know that my tough girl facade was making a comeback despite my quaking knees and sweaty palms.

'Definitely a Valerius.'

'What do you really want?'

Besides me dead.

'I told you,' he said, skimming a finger across the shimmery surface. 'I want Lucius dead.'

'You have to know that's not possible. He's a true immortal.'

'A minor complication,' Julius assured me as he began to pace, still watching me with his intense blue gaze. I was kind of hoping he'd forgotten that killing me would be equally fun.

'Then why the vendetta if you know you won't be successful?'

'Who said I won't be?'

'You can't kill Lucius.'

'Then you are naive if you believe that the only way to kill a man is by destroying his body.'

Oh. 'So, do you really think that an eye for an eye will make you feel better?'

'He murdered my wife!' Julius raged, his façade crumbling as the burning darkness behind his eyes spoke volumes of his intent.

'And I'm sorry about that. I can't even begin to imagine what it must feel like to lose someone you … love … but she was no innocent. Entire villages were slaughtered as you both killed for mere pleasure.'

Julius sneered. 'You speak of things you do not understand.'

'I know what bloodlust feels like and I also know that if you both wanted to live an eternity together you could have learnt to control it.'

'We shouldn't have to!' Julius roared. 'We are Vampires! We were created to exact revenge and drink the blood of mortals. Why should we have been punished for living our lives as we were made?'

'Murder does not go unpunished whether you're damned or human. Wrongs must be righted. You can't use what you are as an excuse for acting immorally.'

'Then we agree on something,' he slurred as his fangs lengthened and pacing bordered on frenetic. 'Wrongs must be righted.'

Great. So, we were back to wanting to kill me again. The guy had a one track mind.

The plan now was to head for the French doors, recklessly jump to ground level, and then run like hell to the garage. I'd steal a motorbike, maintain my shields and then hopefully transfer them to Julius as I made my getaway.

Okay, so the plan wasn't solid. What else you got?

'Going somewhere?' Julius hissed.

I inched towards my exit strategy, very much aware that every step I took was tracked.

'You can't escape, little one. I may not be able to kill Lucius, but I can kill you.'

'And what will that prove?'

Julius threw his head back and roared with laughter. I took the opportunity to place more distance between us. 'I have nothing to prove. I merely want Lucius to spend the rest of eternity mourning *his* loved one as I have done for the last 2000 years!'

I ran into the armoire and stumbled. Julius compensated by testing my defences once again. Black-taloned nails scraped the shimmery surface in an effort to breach the layers.

'You had your chance to kill me last year when we first met at Synth Corp,' I said, trying to keep him talking. 'Why didn't you do it then? Why now?'

Julius's canines glistened with moisture and the promise of pain. 'I didn't know who you were until I tasted your blood. By the time I'd drawn conclusions, Lucius and Sebastian were already on the defensive. Retreat was my only option. I haven't stayed alive all these years by rushing into my plans.'

I was finally immersed in the halo of protective sunlight streaming through the balcony doors. Thralls were tolerant, but lengthy exposure still killed.

Julius tested the theory, hissing as the harmful rays of ultraviolet light splayed unrepentant fingers over his exposed flesh. The shadows offered reprieve while I gripped the railing behind me, slowly hoisting myself over the edge. 'Where are you going?' he barked, braving the sunshine to burden me with a stupid question.

'I'm going out.'

I dropped my shields, the particles wrapping around Julius like a cocoon. The unravelling pain from prolonged use was the only real indication that I needed to move more quickly.

Julius howled and beat his fists against the prison of my mind. I surrendered to smug glee, gripped the balcony rail, and swung over the edge. I rolled on impact to lessen the probability of broken limbs. Pain flared in my heels and ankles but I was otherwise uninjured.

Barefoot and half dressed, I swung my leg over one of Decimus's Ducatis and fired it up. I was tearing through the garage in seconds, speeding down the cobblestone driveway and roaring through the front gates before skidding out onto the back roads beyond.

In no time at all I was weaving through the bitumen back ways of Valle Santa, chasing the highway into Rome and making a mockery of the posted speed limits. I kept my eyes on the opposing lane of traffic, searching for a midnight blue BMW as I tried not to think about my wind-chafed skin, frozen feet and fingers, or the fact that my head was pounding. I needed Sebastian. The pressure of keeping Julius confined was taking its toll.

I cried out as my concentration eventually lapsed. The bike lurched violently beneath me, veering towards the side of the road and into oncoming traffic. The only consolation was the persistent pounding in my head had ceased, but the mounting fear in my chest was more tangible than ever.

Julius was free.

I avoided a potential collision by swerving dangerously, just clipping the back of a taxi's tail light which still made me wobble like an old lady's chin. Squealing brakes and burning rubber in the opposing lane caught my attention, Sebastian pulling all sorts of illegal moves to get to me. Smoke and tire fumes enriched the stench of the morning smog, but I welcomed that pungent smell of salvation.

I left a rather impressive rubber stamp on the highway as I screeched to a stop. I'd earned the horn blasts and choice words of opposition, Sebastian graciously accepting four one-finger salutes of his own. He ripped off his helmet, the sun already on a mission to punish his exposed flesh. 'What happened?' he said, frantically looking me over. Bits of smoke started to rise from his hair, blistering the skin around his ears.

'The fire at Synth Corp was a diversion. Julius found me at the house. I got away, but I couldn't hold him.' The panic in my voice was palpable. Psycho crazy Vampire was on the loose again.

Sebastian pulled me against him, our bikes clinking and limbs trapped between metal. We were oblivious to the traffic jam we'd caused and the sound of eager horn blasts urging us to move on. 'Are you all right?' he said, running gloved hands all over me.

'I'm fine. Just get me out of here. It's not safe at the villa anymore.' I grabbed his helmet and shoved it against his chest. 'And put your helmet back on. You're smoking.'

'Follow me.' He slammed the helmet back in place and kicked the bike back to life.

Tension eased from my shoulders as we ducked and weaved through the back streets of Rome, putting more and more distance between us and Julius. Within ten minutes we were in a parking garage and Sebastian was scooping me into his arms and rushing us into the building.

Up an internal stairwell, the echo of his footsteps on the treads was almost overwhelming loud. I never complained, never thought about protesting his over-protectiveness. In this situation it was warranted.

A gold key retrieved from a pocket on his leather jacket unlocked the door to apartment 6A. 'You'll be safe here,'

Sebastian said, switching on the lights and locking the door behind us. He set me down after initial safety checks were complete.

I looked around the mediocre space. Timber-lined floors, basic off-white walls and do-it-yourself furniture were the décor of choice. A couch, two armchairs and a television were set in the corner, positioned only to make use of the wiring. A shoebox-sized kitchen mirrored the lack of personality, followed by an insanely small bathroom off to the side of an equally bland bedroom.

'Where are we?'

'It's a safe house,' Sebastian answered, sitting gingerly on the creaking arm of one of the beige armchairs.

'Can Julius find us here?'

'I don't think so. The trail on the highway will be going cold and this apartment was bought long after he was part of the coven.'

'Are you going to call Lucius?'

'Of course. There's no point him being in France if Julius is here.'

'Maybe you should hunt Julius while you have the chance.'

Sebastian shook his head. 'No. I won't leave you unprotected again. It was stupid.'

'Don't beat yourself up about it. We all believed the villa to be safe.'

A myriad of conflicting emotions played across his face. 'Regardless, I shouldn't have left you alone, not after last night.'

I didn't want to talk about that right now. 'You do realise he has a very definite plan about killing me.'

'I know,' Sebastian muttered, slipping from the arm of the chair and sinking down onto the seat instead. 'We won't let that happen, Elena.'

'You can't always protect me.'

'I suspect you're about to suggest something ridiculously stupid.'

I frowned, annoyed that he always seemed to have a lead on my train of thought. 'Julius just made it abundantly clear that my combat training would not have helped me. The only way I can defend myself against any Vampire or Alpha of that calibre is to master shifting. I can only rely on tele-kinesis for so long …'

'Helping you realise your Vânător nature is not going to help anyone right now.'

'And leaving me completely defenceless against a Thrall is?' I was already exasperated by thoughts of uselessness.

'You aren't defenceless. I'm here with you.'

'But you weren't this morning, Sebastian. If I'd been able to shape-shift, I might have been able to kill him or even detain him.'

'How could you possibly know that?' Sebastian muttered. 'You have no idea what you would be capable of.'

'William said—'

'It really doesn't matter what he said.'

I glared at him. 'Regardless, you already agreed to help me with this. All I'm suggesting is that we step it up a notch.'

'It's too dangerous to do in the city, Elena, and we can't go back to the villa, at least not until Lucius gets back.'

'But if Lucius is here, he won't let me try at all. I know it.'

Sebastian shrugged, probably figuring it was a win-win situation.

I launched myself across the room, falling into his lap as I grappled for the phone he'd hunted in his jacket for. He held on with a vice-like grip, raising his arm well above our heads and out of reach. 'Sebastian, don't call Lucius,' I begged, attempting to climb up his body. He cinched my waist, pulling me down with an ease that really pissed me off.

'Lucius needs to know that his purpose in Nice is point-less.'

'I know that,' I said, attempting to reach for the phone again. 'But if you call him, he'll come back.'

'That is the point,' he reminded me.

'Please, I need this time. I need you to help me finish what we started.'

I was slowly gaining ground. His arm was lowering and I could see him weighing up the options. 'Elena, I don't know about this …'

Always the pessimist.

'I need you, Sebastian. Only you can help. I know it.'

The pouty plea, followed by a moment of stillness and it was easy to remember our positioning — his arm around my waist, my legs straddling his pelvis. The conversation soon seemed irrelevant.

Sebastian lowered his arm and I plucked the phone from his fingers, though my interest in obtaining the device was lost as he pulled me closer. 'If we do this, Elena, you must do absolutely everything I say, even the parts you think are pointless.'

'I will.'

'Will you?'

I nodded. 'I promise I will do everything you say.'

Sebastian's molten look was twisted by rising cynicism. 'I find that hard to believe.'

I had a snappy retort but forgot what it was, now lost to his gaze.

'I can already see this playing out,' he continued. 'You'll screw up somehow and Lucius really will kill me this time.'

I cleared my throat in the hopes of unearthing some

intelligent words. 'L–Lucius won't kill you. Besides, why would he if you help me to master my vulnerabilities?'

'Do I really need to answer that?'

Sebastian shifted, once again drawing attention to our intimate position. He licked his lips, hot breath escaping, shaky like the fingers I now glided hesitantly across his chest. They moved to his broad shoulders and slipped down his arm, stopping only when they found comfort in the curl of his own responsive fingers.

'Elena?' The question lingered in the space between us. Do we or don't we? My body may have been screaming yes, but I didn't trust the inferno that raged between us.

'Not yet,' I answered, hoping he would understand. 'As much as I want to …'

'You don't trust me.'

I grimaced. 'I don't trust how I feel. I don't trust my decisions after everything that happened with William, and last night,' I added, making a mental note to touch down on that subject matter again later, much later.

'I see,' Sebastian muttered, unimpressed.

'No you don't. I do care, Sebastian, and I promise I'll do whatever it takes to help in the coming war, to make my father proud and to protect you from the stupid decisions I know I constantly involve you.'

He sniffed, turning away. 'You care?'

'That goes without saying.'

He was quiet for but a moment, face expressionless. 'I'm impressed that you admitted that you constantly make a truckload of stupid decisions.'

'Sebastian, I don't think that's exactly what I said.'

He waved away my protest. 'Let's just get started, shall we?'

'Seriously? You're not going to fight me on this?'

Sebastian shrugged, fixing me with an unexpected smile. 'What would be the point? You always do exactly what you want anyway, Elena.'

'Um, sorry about that.'

'No you're not, so why don't you concentrate on shutting up, getting off me and getting into the lotus position.'

I groaned.

Sebastian growled.

I spent the next three hours on the floor, cross-legged with my feet balanced on my knees.

CHAPTER NINETEEN

Seriously

Training began almost immediately. We divided our time into portions, rest and nourishment versus meditation, hand-to-hand combat versus attempted shape-shifting. Part of the renewed deal included only one week of stupidity. After that, Lucius was getting a phone call.

Each day began and ended the same as the last: two hours of vigorous combat training followed by two hours for meditation (don't get me started). After lunch we visited tactics to release the wolf within, but then it was back to chanting again, which I was pretty sure was a complete waste of time.

As promised, I hadn't bitched and moaned. I'd done everything that Sebastian had asked, yet despite best efforts, I was no closer to achieving my goal. I was beginning to think that harnessing my Vânător nature was hopeless and the incident in Roshan's den was a fluke.

On a sidenote, I'd spent five days alone with Sebastian and hadn't abandoned all self-control. I hadn't killed him and I hadn't thrown my underwear at his head. I both relished and detested every minute, the lingering looks and harmless caresses versus the secrets deepening the ever-widening ravine between us.

Denial was turning into a very trying little game.

Meanwhile, as I now stared at Sebastian's ass, I remembered breakfast poised between my mouth and the bowl, milk from my cereal splashing all over my shirt and onto the bench top.

I quickly wiped my chin and mopped up the spilt milk with the sleeve of my shirt. I pretended not to notice Sebastian's curious gaze as he turned and caught me gawking, choosing instead to browse the Italian junk mail collecting on the counter.

'I think we should call Lucius today.'

'What? Why?'

Sebastian's expression remained cool, but it was clear he was agitated. 'I'm serious, Elena.'

I turned to wash the bowl in the sink, keeping my hands busy so I didn't try to throttle him. 'You promised you'd give me time. I have two more days, Sebastian.'

'Two more days wasted for the most prominent and needed members of our coven.'

'I know,' I agreed, guilt creeping over me like ladybugs in the long grass. 'I know I'm being selfish.'

I suspected Sebastian was nodding, displeased. 'Yes, you are.'

'Oh.' His honesty was a little brutal but not entirely unexpected.

'I do understand that you have good intentions, though.'

'You do?'

'Yes, which is why we're going to finish this day of training and then we'll be calling Lucius together. Enough is enough.'

I rehung the damp dishtowel over the handle on the oven door, finally turning to face him despite the allure of ignoring common sense. I supposed it was time to stop hiding and face all fears. 'I guess I understand.'

Sebastian slapped his hands together, frightening me with the suddenness of the gesture. 'Fine. Are you ready, then?'

'I'm ready if you are.'

'Good.' He spun on his heels and left me standing alone in the tiny kitchen.

'Hey, are you okay?' I asked, knowing it was a stupid question. Clearly he wasn't one hundred per cent.

Sebastian paused in the doorway, his back to me. 'Why?'

I picked at my cuticles, a big part of me bothered that he was disappointed in me yet driven to succeed with my plan. There was no way I would ever let Julius, Roshan or any enemy let me feel vulnerable or weak ever again. 'You've been a little quiet since we got here.'

'I have nothing to say.'

'Really?'

'Yes.'

'Are you angry with me?'

'No.'

One word answers — an excellent sign. 'Your round-house kick to the side of my head yesterday says otherwise.'

'That was an accident.'

'Ah huh ...'

Sebastian spun around, glaring like I'd just devoured an orphan. Was I really being that much of a selfish cow and putting him in that much of an awkward position?

Don't answer that.

'Did I not say sorry?'

I cleared my throat and pursed my lips, mirroring the hands he now rigidly had placed upon his hips. 'Saying sorry right before you kick me indicates premeditation.'

'I'll have to remember that.'

I gasped my outrage. 'I knew it.'

The ghost of a smile appeared on the edges of his lips. 'You could have kicked me back.'

'I was unconscious!'

'Semantics.'

I still gaped like a guppy, but truthfully, I was very happy to see him smiling again despite the reluctance to do so. 'Fine, let's just train. You haven't broken any ribs since we started, so maybe you can work on that angle today.'

My sarcasm inspired a head shake and low chuckle. I was rather pleased with myself, fighting the urge to smile back until Sebastian altered the game. He shucked his T-shirt, exposing the smoothest, most toned set of abdominals I'd ever seen. Pair that with low slung sweat pants, and my burning urge to smile soon morphed into ineffable surprise.

'I'm going to show you a few new things today,' he said, all traces of humour now erased from his features. He meant business, but how did he expect me to concentrate when he was walking around looking like a wet dream?

'Okay, this is the first move. When a Vampire comes at you like this …'

I stopped listening after that. I suspect he was demonstrating the ways in which a Vampire or Vânător might attack, chased by diffusion advice. Unfortunately I was distracted by his lean, chiselled muscles, smooth, touchable skin, satiny, dark hair and lips that …

I need a cold shower.

'Did you hear what I said, Elena?'

Not a thing. 'Yes.'

'Good. Now let's put it into practice.'

He came straight at me, his arms a blur and feet moving so fast I barely had time to dodge the first glance to my head. The follow up landed in my soft midsection with deadly accuracy.

I grunted, trying to capture breath and generally feeling pretty sorry for myself.

'Elena, what are you doing?'

'You didn't say go.'

Sebastian gave me a reproachful look. 'Seriously, Elena?'

Okay, okay. So it was a stupid thing to say.

'Pay close attention. No one else will say "go" if they're about to attack you.' He patted my shoulder and took a step back. 'Are you okay now?'

The pain faded and I nodded. I had absolutely no idea what I would do if I couldn't self-heal. Considering the company I kept, taking out health insurance probably would have been a great place to start.

Sebastian rushed for seconds. I'd only just digested the first course. His fists were coming straight for me, two meaty mallets intent on tenderising.

I fell backwards, trusting telekinetic energy to brace my back so I didn't collapse. It worked — *Matrix*-style action. Keanu would be jealous.

I rolled left and then kicked Sebastian as hard as I could in the lower back. The impact shot him forward but he turned with more speed than a salad spinner and caught the offending foot mid-air.

Anticipating that he would try and flip me and set me on my stomach, I jumped and rotated to land my free foot against the side of his head. The greedy bastard caught that one, too, flipped me and then kicked me hard in the stomach. It was a pretty sweet move.

I flew like I had wings, slamming into the wall with a force that rained plaster and left the perfect crime scene outline of my winded body. I soon dropped to the ground like a sack of potatoes. Sebastian discarded mercy, used the tattered wall to somersault off, and then body slammed my chest with the heel of his foot, expelling what little air remained.

Gasping, I clawed at his foot and tried to swing my legs up and catch him around his waist. Unsuccessful and close to vomiting, he dealt me a new blow, extended his talons and slashed at the exposed skin of my legs until I screamed. Blood dripped from my ankles and calves, painting the beige carpet red. 'What the hell are you doing?' I screamed.

'I just told you. Weren't you listening? Never get yourself in a position of exposure. Vampires will take advantage of it.'

He moved away, watching carefully as I healed.

'You could have just pretended!'

Sebastian frowned as if I were speaking a foreign language. 'I said that I wouldn't hold back today and you agreed.'

I glanced at my mostly healed legs. 'You weren't kidding.'

It went on like that for another hour — not the arguing, but the ass-whooping. Every time I thought I could get the better of him, he found a way to prove me wrong.

Zoning out was also a major issue. Usually so diligent in my goal to succeed, I was constantly distracted, watching the way his body moved or how his muscles rippled. Looking away proved impossible.

'Elena, you're not concentrating at all today,' Sebastian said as he scooped low and swept me off my feet for the fifth time in a row. I hit the deck, gasping as another breath was so easily stolen.

Okay. Enough's enough.

Telekinetic energy shamelessly cocooned Sebastian's fine form, holding him firmly in place. He tested the defences and then finally scowled, folding his arms across his bare chest in frustration. 'You're cheating.'

I climbed unsteadily back to my feet. I was totally beat.

'You're cheating, too,' I countered. 'Using vamp skills to kick my ass isn't fair.'

'Do you think a Vânător or Vampire will slow down to your human speed to make it easier?'

I fought the urge to stamp my foot. He had a point. 'No, but …' I had a myriad of excuses but no real reason to protest his methods other than the multiple blood patches decorating the carpet.

'But what?' Sebastian prompted, daring me to question his training.

'Nothing,' I growled.

'Do you want to try again?'

'Of course!' I snapped, fighting the urge to let my eyes shop for new fantasies. 'But you need to stop distracting me.'

'Me?'

'Yes, you!' I gestured to his naked torso. 'You need to put a shirt on.'

'Does my body bother you?' If he even thought about smiling, I was going to throw him out the bloody window.

'No, yes, no, well, okay in this instance when you and I—'

'What you wear, or don't wear,' he interrupted, clearly enjoying my discomfort, 'should not distract you from victory.'

I pursed my lips, annoyed by my own weakness and his seemingly unwavering ability to compartmentalise our ongoing battle of attraction. 'Is that so?'

He slowly nodded, perhaps not as certain of his resolve now that he could see the wheels of payback spinning through the narrowed slant of my eyes. 'You should be skilled enough to ignore any outside interruptions.'

My hands moved slowly and deliberately to my hips, thumbs hooking into the waistband of my sweatpants, the elastic drooping. 'And what if the shoe was on the other foot?'

'It wouldn't matter.'

'Are you sure?'

He swallowed, a lump seemingly caught in his throat. 'Of course.'

I walked to the sofa, removed my sweat-soaked T-shirt and draped it over the cushioned arm. Underneath, my firm-fitting and sweaty sports bra offered a full view of my toned abdomen and the swell of my breasts — a distraction to make him eat his words.

'Elena? What are you doing?'

Going the extra mile, I pushed the elastic on my sweat-pants lower, exposing more sweat-slicked stomach and untouched flesh. While I was at it, I tore away the bottom of the tattered sweats to mid-thigh, ruined anyway thanks to Sebastian's clawed attacks.

'Seriously, Elena, what is it that you think you're trying to accomplish?'

I finally faced him, the unease in his voice and inability to take his eyes off my chest somewhat gratifying. 'Ready?'

Sebastian's eyes dipped lower, finding my navel and travelling further south until he'd seen all the landmarks and made several return trips. He finally closed his eyes, clenched his teeth and moved to make some lower adjustments. Perhaps he thought he was being discreet, but there was nothing discreet about the bulge in his pants. 'Put your clothes back on.'

I shook my head. 'First we fight, settle this dispute.'

'This is stupid.'

'Oh, so it's stupid when your concentration is shot?'

Sebastian's eyes snapped open, his fangs now exposed and knuckles tightly clenched as he swung them at me. I was actually ready, sidestepping the attack and swinging back to slam my elbow into the back of his head. Sebastian grunted but had already moved into position to land a hefty punch to my exposed ribs before I could successfully duck the blow.

Bowing under the pressure of immense pain, I was unable to conjure defence as he wrapped an arm around my waist and took me back to the floor. I twisted my leg at the last second, caught his ankle in mine and rolled us until I was on top. I could barely catch my breath as pain seared what I suspected might have been cracked ribs, but I locked my fingers around his wrist as he twisted in the opposite direction. I tasted bile and heard the crunch of dislocated bones, his entire shoulder socket and arm suddenly slack within my grasp.

Sebastian hissed and opportunity for victory widened by moments of careless inattention. I mercilessly followed through with a lightning fast punch to his mid-section, chased by an uppercut that snapped his head back to the floor. He was done and now so was I.

I collapsed against Sebastian, groaning at the thought of ever having to move again. 'I win,' I panted, poking his chest.

There was an audible snap followed by a grunt as his shoulder popped back in the socket. 'Did you?'

'Yes.'

'Are you sure?' His fingers had snaked around the back of my neck, applying ever increasing pressure. I tried to squirm free, giggling as his other arm encircled my waist and the tickling began.

'Okay, I don't want to play anymore!' I shrieked, trying in vain to retreat.

Sebastian naturally ignored me, rolling us both until he was on top, his full weight against me, and my arms now pinned above my head. Thankfully the tickling had ceased, but I was faced with a terrifying, new agenda — intimacy.

'Get off me,' I admonished, bucking like a crazy bull. 'I won fair and square.'

'And you had to take all your clothes off to do it.'

I scoffed. 'Pu–lease. If I'd taken them all off you'd never have stood a chance. Besides, you started this.'

'Maybe I should finish it?'

I immediately stopped struggling against him. 'Um, say what?'

'You heard me.'

I was deathly still for approximately ten seconds, pondering his words and entranced by the long, branchlike arms of colour that radiated from the centre of his pupils, melting into the pool of emerald now focused specifically on my mouth. 'Um …'

Sebastian remained silent, watching, waiting for me to change everything between us with a finality I could no longer ignore.

Stuff it.

Before rationality kicked in, I lifted my head and pressed my lips against his. They were exactly as I remembered them — soft, warm and inviting, perfectly sculpted to trace my own with a tenderness and passion I'd always secretly longed for.

The building vigour forced my head back to the floor, his hands suddenly everywhere, caressing, holding. My arms quickly encircled his neck, pulling him close, my lips parting as he ground himself against me, but it wasn't enough. No matter how intimately we clung to each other, or the eagerness in which we devoured the other's lips, we couldn't get close enough, couldn't ease the throbbing ache within.

'We should stop,' Sebastian said. We were both panting, eyes glazed with a desire unfulfilled.

'Why?' Did I really just say that? I knew the reasons why,

I just couldn't seem to stop wanting him, needing to feel every part of him pressed against me.

'You know why.'

I took a deep breath, the air whistling my frustration.

Sebastian was equally chaffed by the pressing need to uphold my virginal state. At least he kissed me again, momentarily disregarding willpower in lieu of more exciting recreational activities.

'So why did you just kiss me?' he asked, backing off just before things got a little too out of hand again. He was smiling, almost gloating.

'Because I wanted to.' I turned my head, embarrassed and annoyed that heat flared under the paleness of my cheeks. 'What if I did it again?'

'Try me.'

He was setting a shocking example for this already impressionable teen. Tempting me further with whispered words of encouragement was only going to make us both sinners. Couple my already raucous hormones with the intensity of his heated gaze and I couldn't possibly be held responsible for my actions.

'Back to training?' Sebastian murmured a few breathless minutes later.

'Back to training,' I reluctantly agreed.

'What would you like to learn next?'

My eyebrow shot straight up in the air, the pull of my deviant thoughts cracking a smile upon my lips.

'Ah, I see,' Sebastian whispered, moving in for the kill once more.

We could have gone on like that for hours, tasting each other's lips and writhing around on the floor with reckless abandon, but naturally I found a way to ruin it. 'Do you kiss all the girls like that?'

Sebastian's eyes darkened, the swirling branches transforming into a torrential mass of silver-flecked grey. He rolled off me and bounded back to his feet, hastily turning his back as he began to pace. 'Why do you always do that?'

'Do what?' I said meekly, very much aware of the idiocy of my question.

'Bring up these *supposed* other women.'

I hauled myself back to my feet, a bundle of nerves. I just had to ask the question. I just had to know if I was special, different from the others. 'It's just a question.'

'A particularly stupid one.'

'Can you blame me?' I argued. 'I've heard the late night interludes coming from your end of the corridor.'

'You don't know anything,' he spat, his whole body now quivering with undiluted rage, a whiplash emotion after the rush of intimacy we'd just shared.

'So, enlighten me.'

Sebastian shook his head, searing me with another burning gaze. 'You've already judged me. What would be the point?'

I shrugged in an effort to appear nonchalant, the complete opposite of how I truly felt. What was I going to do? Have an outpouring of hearts and roses and confess that the thought of him with someone else made me want to barf?

Yeah. Not likely.

Sebastian cursed in Italian, mumbling something about a chicken and some bread. I really needed to learn the language. 'You know, Elena,' he started, clasping my upper arms and squeezing tight, 'I never stood a chance with you, did I? I know what you think of me … of the reputation I have.'

'Sebastian, you're hurting me.'

Surprised by his bruising grip, he immediately released

me and I stumbled backwards, colliding with the ravaged wall behind me. 'You don't know anything about me,' he continued. 'If only you knew just how faithful I've been, how faithful I've always been to you.'

I scoffed, concentrating on picking wall plaster out of my hair, so I didn't see Sebastian step in front of me or splay his palms on the wall either side of my head. His scowling face appearing mere centimetres from mine was also a surprise, but I endeavoured not to react, not reflect how little I trusted his—

'Elena, I have not made love in over 2000 years!'

What a thing to blurt, and what a way to render me speechless! Even after letting the words sink in and repeating them in my head over and over again did I not stop myself from bursting out in laughter. In fact, I laughed so hard that my stomach hurt and tears streamed down my cheeks.

'Yeah, okay, Sebastian.'

A few minutes of his complete silence and finally taking note of the hurt welling in Sebastian's eyes and the hilarity was rapidly stifled. I wiped the tears from my face and then dispensed with the smile, wanting to repent.

'Holy crap. You're serious, aren't you?'

He nodded his head slowly. 'Yes, I am.'

'Seriously?'

Sebastian took a steadying breath, momentarily closing his eyes, perhaps searching for calm. 'Yes, Elena. I have not had sex in over two millennia.'

Don't laugh. 'But all those women ... all that noise coming from your room at night.' My head shook with confusion. It didn't make sense and sounded ridiculous.

'I feed on Vampire blood, Elena. I have tried to explain this to you.'

'Well, sure, but what does that have to do with the Moaning Myrtles … unless they enjoy being the late night snack?'

Sebastian made no move to contradict me. 'There's something in my bite or saliva that can sometimes arouse the recipient, and in others … memory loss. I don't touch them, Elena. I don't kiss them and I don't sleep with them. I only feed from them because I must.'

'Jesus.'

'Please do not blaspheme.'

'Seriously?'

'I think we've covered this.'

'So, you've had no …?' I started melding my hands together, back and forth, imitating some sort of sexual collision. It would have been brilliant if we were playing charades.

'Sex?'

I dropped my hands, pleased he could translate and relieved I didn't have to say the word out loud. 'Yeah, that.'

'No sex, Elena.'

'How is that possible?'

'I've avoided temptation … until now.'

I covered a rising blush by looking down at the floor. 'I don't understand. You're a guy. Isn't that like … impossible? Doesn't something like, you know, fall off or turn blue?'

Sebastian's hearty chuckle lifted my gaze. 'No, Elena, I can assure you everything works just fine. I'm merely focused.'

'Focused?'

'Well, I knew eventually we'd …' He cut himself short, biting down on his lower lip and turning away as if embarrassed.

'We'd what?' I pressed.

'Meet again,' he murmured.

'That's—'

'Corny?'

'Yes.'

'Oh.'

'And a little scary.' I placed my palm against Sebastian's warm cheek, pressing gently until he turned back to face me. 'And a shit load of pressure. I'm just not sure what you want me to do with that info now that I have it.'

He shrugged. 'I didn't want you believing the worst of me. Contrary to popular opinion, I am not the vamped out version of Hugh Hefner.'

I snickered. 'No, you're the 2000-year-old virgin.'

He reeled from my touch. 'Please do not make light of my efforts.'

It was almost impossible to stifle my smile. 'It's just a little hard to believe, Sebastian, you're so—'

'Charming?'

'Sure.' I was quiet for just a moment before the wheels in my head started spinning again. 'There had to be at least one Vampire that got you all worked up.' I couldn't help but picture Graziella, the receptionist from Synth Corp I'd had secret fantasies about staking.

'No.'

'Seriously?'

'Seriously.'

'And the last time that you did have …' I started doing the graphic hand gestures again. He seemed to get the point because he rolled his eyes.

'It was with you, Elena.'

'Right. The past life thing.'

'Yes.'

'I must be pretty good, then.'

'I beg your pardon?'

I shrugged. 'Well, you keep coming back for more, so …'

Sebastian's head fell forward, the curtain of his hair hiding his current expression. For a minute I was worried my jesting had upset him, but then realised he was laughing, an infinitely more desirable result.

My own grin expanded, Sebastian abandoning the space between us until our bodies melded, legs interlocked and pelvises touched. His soft lips found my earlobe and he began to whisper. At first I strained to hear his words, but then my eyes widened, the intimate details of our last sexual encounter explained more thoroughly than expected.

'And then we did this …' he murmured, the picture in my mind expanding beyond my age rating. I was almost compelled to cover my ears, but a part of me remembered, and yes, apparently I was good.

'Seriously?'

Sebastian's lips insistent, graphic images were exposed with flourished detail. I was attentive but nevertheless virginally shy, uncertain, excited and terrified that my entire existence, in some way or another, had been spent in the arms of this Vampire. I could only wonder what the future would bring.

CHAPTER TWENTY

Shifting

I smiled shyly, watching Sebastian as he arranged the comforter from the bed onto the living room floor. We'd made a bit of a mess: blood, plaster, clothing — just the usual suspects of a training session. Neither of us was keen to clean up. Scrubbing the carpet and then meditating after. Not gonna happen.

Bleh. Meditating. I'd hoped he'd forgotten.

I pushed the rest of the ham and salad sandwich I was eating into my mouth, chewing quickly. Sebastian was already making himself comfortable on the floor, patiently awaiting my return. He seemed enthused, as always, to sit motionless for a couple of hours and ponder his thoughts. I was tempted to throw myself out the window. Concentrating after this morning's activities? Also not gonna happen.

Sighing dramatically, I took my place in front of Sebastian and sat cross-legged. The unsmiling face that greeted me suggested he was already back in teacher-student mode.

'Okay,' Sebastian said, closing his eyes and taking a deep breath in. 'I want you to empty your head of all thought, take a couple of deep breaths and then find your centre.'

I tried to do as he asked, but clearing my head was not so simple.

'Close your eyes.'

I would rather have stared at him all afternoon, a thought I intended to execute into actuality when I reopened my eyes just a few minutes later.

'Close your eyes, Elena,' he repeated, somehow aware of my activities. Vampiric hearing was a trip. Perhaps my eyelashes sounded like rusty hinges when they moved or fingernails on a chalkboard.

'They *are* closed,' I taunted, wondering if he would check.

Sebastian cracked open one eye, catching me in the act. 'Liar.'

I slammed both lids home, trying not to smile and failing miserably.

As I continued to sit in silence, both eyes now closed, knees incessantly bouncing and the *Ketchup* song running on loop through my head, I imagined countless weeks passing me by. Minutes were the currency, but I still imagined growing old in this singular spot and eventually dying from tedium.

'Elena, concentrate!'

I cracked open an eye only to find him glowering. 'My bad.'

'I thought you wanted this?'

'I want to turn Vânător.'

Yep. I just realised how that sounded, too. Five months ago I'd panicked at the thought of mutating into some sort of hairy-backed outcast. Now here I was, trying to figure out how to become the very creature I despised.

Ironic.

'Meditating is going to help achieve that goal, Elena.'

'Sorry. I know you're trying to help me and I know how crazy I sound asking you to help me become what we've both hunted, but—'

'You think this approach is stupid.'

'Well, yes.'

'You know, you don't have to deal with any of this. You don't have to become the enemy,' Sebastian said quietly.

I frowned. 'What do you mean?'

'Let us take care of the Vânătors and The Protectors. We can put you into hiding until you mature, until you're ready.'

'But what about Lucas? What about everything else going on right now?'

Sebastian squeezed my hand. 'It's not your problem. Let us take care of you. I hate that you think you need to do this so that you can fight with the rest of us. We can do it without you.'

I shook free of his supposed reassuring hold. 'I know you can do it without me. I'm not stupid. I just can't sit on the sidelines while everyone else defends our right to live.'

'Please, Elena, you don't understand. I would die if anything happened to you.'

Breathing suddenly seemed complicated. I had to concentrate on drawing in oxygen before I went blue. Was he serious? Wasn't that a little melodramatic?

'Forget I said anything,' he blurted, straightening his spine, closing his eyes and resting his palms back on top of his knees.

A subject change was in order. 'Do we have to keep doing this?'

'Meditating? Yes.'

'But we've tried everything. Even when I chant and sing *Kum-ba-ya* I still can't shift.'

'I doubt very much if colloquial campfire songs are going to help.'

'You know what I mean. How long do I have to sit in the lotus position and hum?'

'Fine,' he snapped, eyes springing open again. 'Let's approach this differently.'

'How?'

'Meditating is obviously not working. Not that you actually try.'

'Hey!'

'Look, the reality is that there aren't many options left.'

'If I'd known there were options I would have voted for the one that wasn't butt-numbingly boring.'

He frowned before unfolding his legs and stretching out more comfortably. 'Well, the only thing left to try is emotional connections.'

'Enlighten me.'

'Well, your Vampiric nature is heightened by moments of emotion. Your fangs grow during anger, arousal and even hunger. It's possible that the same applies to generating a shift. Do you remember how you felt before you turned Vânǎtor?'

I thought back to that night with some reluctance. 'I remember feeling protective.'

'How so?'

'I'd become accustomed to Roshan's cruel forms of torture, but I couldn't allow William to experience my thirst, my desperate helplessness and act on it. So I kept him telekinetically captive while Roshan fed from me.'

'And then what happened? How did you feel?'

'I was angry. William's life was not an idle game and Roshan was trying to make it one, teasing him and testing me.'

Sebastian nodded to keep the story moving forward.

'The weaker I became, the more volatile my thoughts. I remember being so angry that it practically consumed me.'

'And then?'

'You sound like a therapist.'

'Elena, be serious. I think we're onto something here.'

I sighed. 'Nothing happened. I blacked out. One minute I was imagining tearing out their throats and in the next ... nothing. I just woke up again and I was me.'

'Perhaps that's it.'

'What?'

He shrugged. 'Maybe aggression is the key.'

I made popping noises with my lips as I considered the suggestion. 'Do you think I should try it now?'

'Not a good idea,' Sebastian said, violently shaking his head. He bounded to his feet, slapping his palms together before pointing at me. 'I don't want you shape-shifting in this confined space when you're also due for a blood feed.'

I patted my stomach, admitting that he might have been onto something. 'So, when can we try?'

'Let me get you some supplies. Then we'll go somewhere out of the city where we can be alone.'

'Is that safe?'

'What? Being alone with me?'

'No, stupid, leaving the safe house when Julius might still be hunting me.'

'You'll be safe with me.' He briefly studied the wall-mounted clock. 'In the meantime, sit tight and don't move.'

I rolled my eyes at the absurd suggestion that I would even fart outside the apartment door without him. I may be stubborn sometimes, but I wasn't freaking suicidal. 'How long will you be gone?'

He disappeared, reappearing a moment later with his leather riding jacket and gloves in hand. 'No longer than an hour.'

'And if Julius found some way to track us and busts in on me while you're gone?'

'Run fast.'

Good to know we had a solid plan.

The preceding hours came and went. Julius was a no show and Sebastian returned, making me eat more food, drink a few tetra packs of blood and grab a few hours' sleep.

'Elena, wake up now.'

I reluctantly pried open bleary eyes, taking note of Sebastian's state of readiness. I must have looked a mess, drool covered chin and rat's nest hair. He looked perfect in his leather jacket and pants, V-neck polo and biker boots. No real surprise.

'It's getting dark,' Sebastian continued, moving towards the bedroom door. 'We should get going, so hurry up and put these on.'

I sat up slowly, rubbing at sleep-caked eyes while critically assessing the outfit he'd laid out on the end of the bed — a pair of jeans and the thickest, warmest turtleneck on offer. Not bad really. 'Can you turn around, please?'

'I can do you one better.' He left the room entirely.

I quickly changed out of my ragged sweats and ducked into the bathroom, supposing I probably had to set my hair on fire in order to bring it to some semblance of control. Surprisingly it looked okay. I'd been right about the drool, though. Embarrassing.

By the time I re-entered the living room, Sebastian was already at the front door, motioning for me to get a wriggle on. He didn't even ask permission before he scooped me up into his arms and took off like a bat out of hell.

Meatloaf would be proud.

No more than thirty minutes passed before the streaky

lights of Rome had well and truly faded and the scent of gravel, pine and damp moss clung to the air like a stain on the atmosphere. Dried leaves and pine needles crunched beneath Sebastian's boots, adding to the overly pungent aroma of nature.

I shrunk against Sebastian's chest, tightly gripping his jacket between my fingers as the mewling of a nearby wolf frayed my nerves.

'It's okay,' Sebastian murmured. 'It's just an ordinary wolf, not a Vânător.'

Is there such a thing anymore?

Sebastian finally set me down under a canopy of towering pines, firs and oaks. There was some open space, a clearing of sorts, but mostly we were surrounded by shrubs and wooded debris. 'This is as good a place as any and we're a fair distance from any walking tracks.'

I nodded, pleased to hear I wouldn't hunt down a hiker for a midnight snack. 'So, what should I do first?'

'Try getting angry again and then picture yourself as a Vânător.'

'I can't just make myself angry. There has to be a cause.'

'Okay,' Sebastian muttered, scratching at his chin. 'Those jeans you're wearing make you look fat.'

I rolled my eyes. 'That's just hurtful.'

'Okay, so tell me what to say to make you cranky.'

'Please, I spend most of my time pissed off at you about something.' I folded my arms across my chest, certain he'd come up with something fairly soon.

Sebastian rubbed his chin again. 'What about Lucas?'

'What about him?'

'Why don't you picture him at some facility the IMI have constructed? Imagine him held prisoner by Chester, every day a torment as they cut small pieces of flesh from him to feed to the Vânǎtors they keep as pets.'

'Sebastian!'

He looked genuinely perplexed. 'What? You told me to make you angry.'

'But that's just sick.'

'What if it's true? Look at what they did to you.'

I swallowed back bile. 'Sebastian, don't talk like that. The IMI are ruthless, but they would never compromise one of their own.'

'Lucas isn't one of their own. He's an experiment just like you were. From the minute he was born, they've been turning him into something unimaginable.'

I shot him a reproachful look, the first tremor of ire radiating from my body. 'Shut. Your. Mouth. You don't know what you're talking about.'

'Every second of your childhood was a lie,' he continued, voice coarse and absent of sympathy. 'While they were drawing blood from you and planning ways to turn what you are into a weapon, they used Lucas as a backup plan.'

'Sebastian, I'm serious. You're going too far with this.' My skin prickled with the heat of growing agitation. He was trying to rile me up, but this was too much. The images his words conjured were …

'Lucas was probably injected with a cocktail of chemicals, taken on nights when you were both sleeping peacefully, never aware.'

My hands fisted; my whole body shook. If he thought he was helping, he wasn't. My blood pressure was on a collision course for space and the mounting anger I felt had found a new target in him.

'Elena, you thought you were protecting him by moving to Romania, but what you really did was leave Lucas vulnerable, open to more experimentation. I bet when you left, the Cairns faction took advantage of your absence and finished what they started when Lucas was just a tiny, defenceless child.'

'I said shut up! Shut up!'

I sunk to the ground, my knees buckling underneath me. The anger was so debilitating I could barely see straight.

'Good, Elena, focus that anger. Use the techniques we practised during our meditative sessions to centre your emotions so you can control it.'

'Get away from me!' I hissed, my fangs extending, my muscles rippling painfully. He wouldn't move, so I shoved him, exerting more force than I thought possible, watching and relishing as Sebastian was thrown back into the trunk of a nearby oak tree. It fissured, groaned and then completely uprooted, plummeting into a nearby pine with a thunderous *crack*.

'Control your anger!' Sebastian shouted, shaking leaves from his hair as he pulled himself free from the wreckage.

'I can't!' I shouted back.

And I meant it.

I was soon horizontal, my arms and legs caught in the midst of various spasms. My limbs stretched and contorted, bones aching as they grew, snapped and then miraculously healed. Muscles shrank and expanded like rubber cords, wrapping around misshapen arms and legs that shook with uncontrollable tremors of fury. My spine was the final target, cracking and bowing upwards, eliciting a bloodcurdling scream.

Darkness found me, blanketing the pain and erasing memories as it went. The black depths of my mind were brutally efficient. The last thing I remembered: smooth skin replaced by sprouting, velvety fur.

Rage was tangible, a thick, choking cloud that hung above my head, saturating me with hate-laden moisture. I couldn't escape it. It consumed me, filling every pore and the emptiness within. All I wanted was to kill, to taste blood and tear flesh.

Sebastian.

My eyes snapped open and darkness retreated as if a burning torch had slain the very heart of its source. Every minute detail, texture, molecule captured my attention, an array of visual delights arrestingly confounding.

Next I lifted my nose to the sky and inhaled, the inner predator revelling in the various aromas of the forest — dirt, droppings, overturned leaves and carrion. But it was the scent of leather, freshly cut pine and the spring rain that teased my senses most, a reminder of what I needed in order to satisfy the inner beast.

I tried to get up and squealed in fright, or howled as the case may be, black, hairy paws with razor sharp talons were where my hands used to be. I was clearly a wolf. Mission accomplished in many respects, but to be bombarded with all of this loathing and continuing waves of murderous thoughts? Depressive. Sebastian would have to pay.

Every vein in my body throbbed for his blood, my newly developed teeth lengthening further at the prospect of shredding his flesh. I wondered what he would taste like, what his fear would taste like.

A growl ruptured my vocal chords, excitement palpable as leaves in the trees to the left rustled. A tiny bird fluttered in its nest, harmless and hardly worth the energy. I decided to ignore it.

I stalked on all fours, putting my snout to the ground and ears on alert. Underbrush grazed my fur and tickled my sides as I moved, the recently fallen tree saturated with Sebastian's scent but absent of his presence.

He was close. The wind caressed his hair and the faint scent of his shampoo ultimately nailed his position. I was going to delight in pulling him apart, limb from limb, savage him until there was nothing left but the aftertaste of blood and the remnants of bone in my fangs.

I stopped to crouch under a dense thicket of shrubs, my black fur but a smudge on the landscape and the perfect camouflage at night. I sat perfectly still, my newfound senses locating him instantly, perched on a tree branch, exactly fifty-two and three quarter metres from where I was positioned.

I reared back in preparation to pounce, but suddenly stilled. Through the all-encompassing darkness I saw his eyes, the swirling mixture of concern, a raw emotion of tenderness my Vânător half had trouble comprehending.

Did he regret the harsh words he'd spoken to me?

'Elena,' he whispered, his voice echoing like thunder in my overly sensitive ears.

I growled. How dare he use such a personal tone with me? We were enemies now!

'Elena, look at me.'

My tongue salivated at the thought of retribution, fairly vibrating with pleasure as I licked his scent from the air.

'Elena, control the predator and listen to the sound of my voice. Lift your eyes and see me.'

I didn't want to disregard my predatory nature. I wanted to embrace it, feed it and then become it. There would be no negotiating on this.

I revealed my fangs, drawing back the moist flesh and snapping my snout in rebuttal. I hated him. I wanted to kill Sebastian, eat his flesh and drink his blood. There was no need to deviate from my plan of attack.

I launched through the air, Sebastian making it all too

easy to bury my teeth in his arm and take him to the ground. He didn't fight back. Not even as my powerful hind legs dug into his thighs or my claws unsheathed to puncture skin and punish sinew.

'Don't do this, Elena. It's me, Sebastian.'

I know.

I discarded his arm, quickly clamping my razor sharp fangs around his throat. Just because he refused to fight back did not mean I was going to go easy on him.

'Elena, think about what you're doing. I won't hurt you. I won't even try to stop you. I want you to figure this out. I want you to understand that my life is in your—'

Sweet, molten blood poured into my mouth and trickled down my throat. Eagerness moved my tongue to even, lapping motions. I drew strength from his life force and revelled in the sweet symphony of his helpless moans of pain.

'Elena!' Sebastian choked, his windpipe inundated with fluid. 'Please don't do this. You don't *want* to do this!'

That's where you're wrong. It's all I want to do.

I sank serrated teeth in further, the crunch of his collarbone and the fresh sounds of panic delighting me. Garbled responses bubbled in his ravaged throat, but still he tried to persuade me.

'Elena, look at me.'

Blood dribbled from the corners of his lips and down the sides of his face, a beautiful canvas of arterial red, masterfully painted on the pasty white flesh of a Vampire I had every intention of killing.

Sebastian grabbed my head between his shaking hands, a move most unexpected given his current state of decline. 'Look at me!' he shouted, forcing every ounce of strength he had left into executing the command.

I involuntarily met his eyes, his steely grip ripping at

my fur and forcing me to obediently relinquish his throat. 'You're not in control, Elena. Find control.'

I growled at the nerve of him, snapping my fangs in response.

Sebastian cried out as he forced his legs apart and free of my hind claws, the sharp talons slipping from his thighs and slicing through the flesh until they made contact with the damp earth. He wasted no time in wrapping those bleeding limbs around my mid-section and interlocking his feet across my back, forcing me into submission.

I repeatedly barked and snapped my fangs at him, clawing at his shoulders and chest, tearing open the already jagged wound from my initial bite.

'Look at me, Baby Vamp,' he grunted, the nickname he used for me stirring something intimate and familiar within. 'Look at me and remember what we mean to each other.'

My wolf went crazy, confused by the memories of my human counterpart and the true affections laid bare upon Sebastian's features. I could see right inside the swirling depths and feel the strength of our 13,000 year connection. My whole head tingled with warmth, different to the hatred that had filled me since the shift. It numbed any desire to kill and made me yearn for something beyond Vânător reasoning.

Dear God, forgive me.

'It's all right,' Sebastian whispered as I collapsed against him, the ultimate submission being my guilt. 'You were not yourself.'

I stiffened, perplexed by the fresh wave of adrenaline-fuelled anger that began to swamp me once more. I automatically straightened, resuming earlier positioning, my weight pressed against his chest and claws gaining a foothold in his torn flesh.

What's happening?

'Control it,' Sebastian barked. 'Use the anger and the hatred you feel to fuel the beast, but not the mind. You are still you. Remember that!'

Could my beast give him a questioning look? I didn't know, but I tried, watching from within as if my wolf were on autopilot, my claws tearing a fresh path into Sebastian's open chest cavity. He was haemorrhaging so much blood that if I didn't stop soon, no amount of healing was going to help. Did I really want that? Did I really want him dead?

The pull towards malevolence was strong, but I resisted. I would not be a puppet to my own makings. I would reconcile the darker feelings and expel them, or at the very least, remember I was stronger than a splicing of unwanted DNA.

I promptly stopped clawing at Sebastian's mangled flesh. There was barely anything left, so much blood and exposed bone that I wondered how he could still be conscious, how I could ever look him in the eye again.

'That's it,' Sebastian murmured, running shaky fingers through my fur. 'I knew you could do it, Elena.'

I whimpered as Sebastian uncoiled his legs from around my back, wincing as he did so. He was already healing, but I immediately darted off his body, padding away from him and hiding behind a nearby shrub. I couldn't watch.

'Elena,' he said quietly. 'It's okay. I'll heal.'

It's far from okay. I nearly killed you.

'Elena, please. Come to me. It wasn't your fault.'

I can't be trusted.

'Please. I want you with me right now. It hurts.'

The pain in his eyes was undeniable. I didn't trust myself with him, but at the same time, I could hardly deny his request. So, I took a tentative step forward, then another and another until I was standing over him, surveying the aftermath.

Shit ....

He held out his hand, reaching for me like I was life itself. I bowed my head, abasing myself as I lowered my belly to the ground, waiting for his touch. His fingers skimmed the soft pelt on the top of my head and then shifted to my neck and chest. Through the pleasurable acceptance of his touch I could still feel the overwhelming violence inside of me, but I was controlling it, holding the reins and choking its persuasion.

I lowered my head on my front two paws and watched quietly as his body slowly began to recover. The polo he'd worn was completely shredded, the leather jacket marred with a few holes but not entirely unsalvageable. His pants were hanging off his thighs in strips and the blood that drenched the ground no longer seeped into the damp earth but pooled around Sebastian's still form.

I was relieved when he finally moved, rolling slowly to his side, wincing as the last of his wounds closed over. He propped his head onto his hand and smiled; the warmth that radiated down to the fingers that stroked my neck made me shudder in self-loathing. How could he smile at me after what I'd just done?

'You really are very beautiful as a wolf. Your fur is so soft and the colour is just like your hair.' He ran his hand across my back and down my rump. 'I can't stop touching you.'

I scoffed, turning away. I could barely look at him, let alone accept compliments. I'd almost killed him and I didn't think that was possible without silver, decapitation or sunlight. My crazy notion to become a Vânător had unnecessarily put his life at risk.

Sebastian captured my snout in his hand, holding firm. 'I'm proud of you, Elena. You've managed to control both your Vampire and Vânător halves. Now that you understand what to do, next time will be easier.'

Next time!

I growled, snuffling my disapproval. He had to be joking.

'What?' he prompted. 'You can defend yourself against Julius or any other Vampire who tries to hurt you now. Isn't that what you wanted?'

Not at the expense of your life.

Sebastian stared at me for the longest time, his fingers finally wiping moisture from the fur beneath my eyes. I hadn't even realised I'd been crying. 'It's okay, I'm fine. You won't have to live without me.' He started to smile, aiming for a joke of some kind, but my lacklustre response ate away at his mirth.

He straightened up, pulling my head into his lap, his fingers running up and down my back. 'You're really upset, aren't you?'

I barked once.

'Does this mean that you actually care what happens to me?'

I barked again.

He never did respond, his eyes losing focus as they stared into the brush somewhere behind me. I supposed talking was a pointless obligation neither of us needed to commit. He was lost to his thoughts and I was lost to mine. At least I now knew how I truly felt about Sebastian, tonight's events redefining a few emotional priorities. The problem was admitting them.

I mean, when was it okay to admit the truth? When was it okay to open myself up to vulnerability? Love may have been my own perceived weakness and an opportunity to break my heart, but surely knowing the extent of Sebastian's commitment was enough to thaw?

Perhaps I should stay a wolf.

CHAPTER TWENTY-ONE

Enough

'I can't believe I'm doing this,' Lucas muttered as he walked the corridors, heart heavy and filled with nerves. He was heading towards his parents' bunk, driven by the need for familiarity despite Stephanie's words. It was hard to admit that he couldn't handle any of this, the reality being that he needed his mum and dad.

George and Susan had been great parents until recently. Whether that was because life was simple, intrigue was at a minimum or Lucas wasn't big on asking questions, he didn't know. Now they appeared to be the driving force behind his experimentation and the co-signers of Elena's death warrant. Yet still he marched to their door. Still he sought their comfort because once Susan and George had been there, keeping the boogieman at bay and dispelling rumours of monsters in the closet.

For three months Lucas had hid his fears and bottled his emotions to gather information, but he just couldn't do it anymore. He needed to know where he stood. He wanted peace and for another to shoulder the burden for just a while.

'Lucas?' Susan frowned, opening the bunk door after a succession of fitful knocking on Lucas's behalf. 'Are you okay?'

He shifted from foot to foot, nervous. Why hadn't she invited him in yet? 'No, I'm not okay.'

Susan briefly surveyed him and finally did the mum thing, wrapping an arm around his shoulder and leading him inside.

'Who is it?!' George called from behind the closed bathroom door.

'It's Lucas!' she answered, making sure to close the heavy steel door behind them. She led him over to the edge of their double bed, sitting him down. 'What's wrong?' she asked, rubbing soothing circles across his back. 'Are you ill?'

'No. I just can't do this anymore.'

'Do what, Honey?'

'Pretend.'

George emerged from the bathroom, switching off the light and closing the door behind him. He smelt like soap and Old Spice. 'What's going on?' he said, folding his arms across his chest.

'I don't know,' Susan murmured. 'Something.'

George settled down on the other side of Lucas, arms still cradling his chest like he needed the support. 'What is it, son?'

Lucas shook his head and then buried his face in his hands. 'I can't do this anymore. I've had enough.'

'Explain,' his parents said in unison. Eerie actually.

'This,' he said, gesturing to the room around him. He supposed that explained everything and nothing all at once.

'Sweetheart,' Susan cooed, 'I know it's hard to adjust to a new home, but I promise it'll be worth it in the end.'

'Will it?' Lucas answered miserably. 'Nothing is worth this.'

Susan and George passed concerned looks between them. 'What are you talking about?' George asked. It was the gentlest Lucas had ever heard his father speak. He thought he could almost hear compassion in his father's tone.

'Is there an out, a way that a Protector can become an ordinary person?'

George's eyes narrowed, searching Susan's once more for support. 'Lucas, what's brought this on? Why would you want to leave the IMI?'

'Can you leave?' he repeated again.

'Yes, you can leave,' Susan answered frantically, flustered. 'But leaving also means that you become an enemy of the IMI. They won't protect you from Vampires or Vânǎtors and if you interfere with any plans they have or expose any of our secrets you're no longer aligned … you're hunted.'

'I can live with that.'

They were shaking their heads, exasperation touching their features. 'Why?'

'There are too many secrets and lies. The truth is an afterthought and my realisation of it started right after Elena left.'

'So, this is about your sister?' Susan expelled, looking more or less relieved. Lucas wondered if she was thinking that a few warm embraces and reassurances regarding Elena's absence would appease his sense of unease. Unfortunately he knew he'd never feel the same about being a Protector again. Elena's blood was inside of him; therefore he was an unknown … an enemy.

'I know what the IMI did to Elena,' Lucas started, voice raised. 'I know that Chester starved her, kept her locked in a steel chimney, drained her of blood and forced her into an experiment with an Alpha Vânǎtor.'

'So you *have* been keeping in contact with her,' George mused.

'What counts here is that she trusted you to keep her safe from harm and we've both been let down.'

His parents remained quiet, both hands now in laps, expressions unreadable.

'She was never really ours,' George murmured after a few minutes of quiet contemplation. 'Elena knew she didn't belong. She never called us Mum or Dad, she never sought affection and she never was one of us.'

'But she's a part of me,' Lucas retorted, fingering the scar on his shoulder. 'Her blood runs through my veins.' He dropped his hand, slumping forward until his elbows rested on his thighs and his head was cradled in his hands. 'I can't pretend that what the IMI have done to her and what you have condemned her to was right.'

'Hurting Elena was never our intention,' Susan said quietly. 'But she has what we need to make us all strong and capable in the fight against our enemies.'

Lucas pinched the bridge of his nose and closed his eyes. 'You keep calling them your enemies. Have you ever bothered to get to know a Vampire?'

'Lucas, you don't understand what you're saying. You can't leave The Protectors. You're one of us, not one of them and certainly not their friend.'

'Am I?' Lucas said, leaning back again to look right into his mother's pleading eyes. 'I haven't been a Protector since you pumped me full of Elena's blood.'

'Well, if you go out there, you won't be accepted either,' George grunted, pushing off the bed. He started to pace, irritable. 'At least here we can protect you, nurture your ability. Out there we can't.'

'You mean you can't manipulate me if I'm not here?' Lucas huffed. 'Don't pretend that you're protecting me. I know you only want me to stay because of the experiment. How I feel is clearly irrelevant.'

Susan snatched at his hand, crushing his fingers in her

palm and pulling it against her chest. 'We want you to stay because we want to protect you and because we love you. If you leave this facility, you will be banished. We won't be able to look out for you anymore.'

Lucas pried his captive hand free, resisting the urge to massage his bruised fingers. 'I think we both know that staying will only deepen the magnitude of deception. What happened with Elena and my part in it was no accident. I can't stay to see how this plays out, to always wonder if you'll let Chester turn against me as you allowed everyone to turn against Elena.'

Susan's lips were moving, but George's voice was the one that Lucas heard. 'That won't happen.'

'No? Then why are we really here?'

'To rise against our enemies and to⊠'

'Perfect the serum and equip The Protectors with unnatural means of retaliation?'

His parents were speechless, their ensuing facial features a photograph of indecision. He could see they inwardly fumbled whether to admit the truth or harbour more lies to protect the very organisation Lucas wanted out of.

'I–I don't know what to say,' Susan stuttered.

'How about the truth?'

'Lucas …' George murmured. 'You were never supposed to know any of this. You were never supposed to be burdened.'

'Well, I am burdened, so lighten the load by giving me an explanation.'

Susan and George shared looks wrought with tension and brimming with the fear of revelation. 'If Chester or any of the other heads of the IMI learn that we have told you everything, Lucas, we will be excommunicated and hunted ourselves.'

'You owe me this after everything you've put me and Elena through.'

Susan reluctantly nodded and asked George to stop pacing and sit back down. He wasn't impressed. 'You are right,' Susan began. 'We've kept a lot from you, mostly for your protection despite what you may think. Transfusing your blood with Elena's after the bite was the act of parents on the brink of panic. You died that day, Lucas, and we were willing to try anything to bring you back.'

'What were Chester's motives?'

'I'm sure you can guess given your current knowledge of the serum,' George interjected. 'It's always been about strengthening our own powers, giving us a leg up over our enemies.'

'So, I'm literally patient "X", the first in the experimentation to credit The Protectors with more power?'

George nodded. 'But since you've only recently started exhibiting symptoms—'

'Chester begun researching and actuating the serum in the event that the transfusion didn't eventuate into anything tangible.'

'Exactly.'

'Why am I only developing stronger abilities now?'

'We suspect it has to do with your approaching birthday, but we can't be certain.'

'What about the serum? Has Chester completed it?'

Susan appeared at a loss for words, so George carried the conversation with what Lucas perceived as reluctance. 'There are some side effects we didn't quite bargain for. The formulation is not quite right yet.'

'What sort of side effects?'

'I'm not privy to that sort of information, but so far it

would appear that the test subject is exhibiting greater agility, speed, strength and stamina.'

'Wait, *he*, as in, you're already testing the serum on ...' Lucas's voice faded, suddenly lost to wayward thoughts, consumed by the oddities of his apparently superhuman bunkmate. 'Jesus,' he breathed. 'You're talking about Beryx, aren't you?'

'Yes,' George answered.

'Has anyone else been taking it?'

'The formulation is still too unstable. We can't risk giving it to the rest of the populace until it's perfected, until we've explored all defects.'

'And Beryx volunteered?'

George scratched at the stubble on the bottom of his chin, appearing uncomfortable. 'Mostly.'

Mostly? Lucas shouldn't have been surprised. Disgusted by the ongoing antics of the IMI's scientific community, but not surprised.

'Lucas it's the only way,' Susan choked, clearing her throat to finish justifying bullshit excuses of injustice. 'Vampires are dangerous and will always crave human blood. It's our responsibility as Protectors to make sure that it doesn't happen in the future.'

Lucas was incredulous. 'And what about humans suffering now because we are hiding at the ass end of the planet while the Vânători go crazy?'

'The Vânători are not going crazy. Their intentions are focused.'

Lucas coughed, choking on a dry, humourless laugh. 'And how would you know that? Have you aligned yourself with the Vânători now, too? Did you promise them immunity in exchange for killing all the Vampires in our absence?'

When his parents failed to answer and he saw the truth

etched upon their traitorous faces, Lucas's bottom lip trembled. It was all just a little too much. 'No. I can't … I can't deal with this anymore. The truth only makes it all that much worse.'

Susan's hands were upon him once more, soothing and restraining, an uncomfortable combination of the two. 'Lucas, just take a minute to think about what you're saying. If you leave this facility, there's no coming back. The IMI will offer no assistance in getting back to the mainland and outside temperatures can kill you.'

Lucas looked to his father, pleading. 'I can't stay, Dad. I don't want what happened to Elena to happen to me. I'm not as brave as her. I need to just get out.'

'Lucas, you can't,' Susan murmured, redrawing his attention.

'But you said that I could!'

'You're our son. We can't send you outside to die.' She hastily wiped away the tears now steadily streaming down her face.

'Then come with me. We don't have to be pawns for the IMI.'

'Leave the IMI?' George huffed, eyeballing Lucas as if he was crazy. 'We can't.'

'Of course you can,' Lucas affirmed. 'Elena will make sure we're all safe, protected. You'll never have to do anything like this again.'

'The work of the IMI means everything to us, Lucas. Before either you or Elena came into our lives we spent a lot of our time liaising with headquarters and helping to set this facility up. We believe in what we are trying to achieve.'

'You mean you believe in trying to harness Elena's gifts as your own?'

'Lucas, can't you see it?' George said, pounding a fist into his hand. 'We would be as powerful as them. We could live forever, amass wealth and fear no one.'

'Aren't you forgetting something?'

'I don't think so.'

'What about the protection of mankind?'

George shrugged. 'Well, there is that, too.'

The nonchalance was the final straw. There was nothing redeemable to be found here. The serum wasn't for protection or advancement of the human populace. It was simply to attain power and conquer opposition.

Lucas rose, taking his mother's shaking hands. He pulled her to her feet and wrapped his arms around her tightly. 'I love you, Mum. I'm sorry that you can't see the right thing to do in all of this.'

Susan sobbed uncontrollably, heaving tears that left his shirt soaked through. 'Don't do this, Lucas, please don't leave!'

'You're making a grave mistake, Lucas,' George concurred, now standing beside them. 'Change your mind now before it's too late.'

Lucas shook his head, moving away. His mother collapsed on the bed in a fit of tears, choked with raw emotion. He too found it difficult but the numbness had begun to consume him, steal just a little of that aching pain within.

Holding out his hand, his father shook it, offering peace between them in these final few minutes. His grip was weak and tentative, the spell broken the second George let go to comfort his wife. It would probably be the last time he set eyes on either of them; uncertain if he'd make it back to the mainland but knowing he had to try, knowing there was nothing left for him here.

On that note, Lucas left.

He pressed the button next to the door and exited without a backward glance, his heart aching all the more.

Taking a left, Lucas traversed the walkways, considering immediate, necessary actions. He had to pack. He needed food. He needed to get out with his life. He needed to swallow his fear. Would it be easier to stay than taking a stand against something he didn't believe in?

'Lucas!' someone shouted behind him.

It was Karina. He hadn't given her much thought or seen her since arriving at the facility. He briefly wondered how she'd filled her days or why she'd want to talk to him now. He supposed he was about to find out.

'Lucas!' she called again. 'Wait for me!' When she finally caught up, her face was flushed pink from exertion and her green eyes bright and shiny. She looped her arm through his, effectively slowing him down.

'What do you want, Karina?'

'I just wanted to say that I thought you were great in training the other day.'

'You saw?'

She reached up, tentatively stroking the bruise still present on his cheek. 'He hit you pretty hard, didn't he?'

Lucas winced, jerking his head away from her cold fingers. 'It'll heal.'

'I know, but I'm still worried about you.'

Lucas frowned, confused as to her motives. 'Is there something you wanted?'

'I um …. I just …'

'You just what?'

She sniffed, smoothing glossy black hair away from her face. 'I was curious about whether you'd like to have dinner with me tonight.'

Lucas nearly choked on a laugh, somewhat dismayed. 'What? I mean why?'

Karina gnawed her lower lip, looking decidedly nervous. She tightened her hold on his arm. 'I … I like you, Lucas.'

Really?

Lucas shrugged free of her, unbuttoning his coat to pull the collar down and away from his ears. Surely he hadn't heard that right. 'Um, since when?'

'I don't know. I guess I've been thinking about it for a while, especially since you've begun to … um … grow into your looks.'

Arriving back at his bunk, he pressed the entry button and swiped his ID tag. He wasn't quite sure how to respond. Karina had rebuked his advances in the past and now the timing was really off.

'Are you going to say anything?' Karina muttered, following Lucas into the bunk, the steel door automatically closing and sealing them both inside. Lucas was suddenly preoccupied by Beryx's absence. Where was he? What did he do all day? Did he feel trapped and helpless, too?

He removed his coat completely, leaving Karina to glower after him as he wandered into the bathroom, distracted by the urge to start packing the essentials.

'Did you hear me?' Karina said, meeting him in the tiny bathroom. She'd removed her own jacket and lowered her voice, her movements uncertain as she stepped behind him and wrapped her arms around his waist. 'I said that I like you, Lucas.'

Lucas gulped. 'I heard you,' he croaked, clearing his throat and trying again. 'I just don't understand why.'

'We've always been friends.' She shrugged. 'Maybe we could be more?'

'It's not good timing, Karina. I'm leaving.'

'Leaving? Where? What are you talking about?'

'I'm leaving this facility, having a shot at life in the real world for a while.'

Her arms tightened around his waist, pulling him closer. 'Why would you want to do that?'

Gingerly, he slowly unwound her arms from around his waist, getting back to the task of scooping his toiletries into a bag. 'Because the IMI isn't the sort of place I thought it was. I need to get out on my own, think things through.'

Karina placed a delicate hand on his arm instead. 'Don't go. Whatever your reasons are, Lucas, don't leave this place. I really like you and if you go, we won't be able to … well, explore things further.'

Lucas stopped packing, glancing down at her touch, his chest tightening at the possibilities. She had the worst timing ever. 'Why now?' he asked, meeting her green eyes and wishing that he hadn't. God, she was all kinds of beautiful. 'Why now, after all these years have you suddenly decided that you like me? And why tonight of all nights when I decide to leave do you come to me and tell me?'

She moved her hand from his arm and curled it around his neck instead. They moved in unison until she was snuggled against him, her other hand pressed gently against his chest. 'You're not the same kid I grew up with, Lucas. You've grown into a man I would like to get to know.' The hand on his chest slid across his shirt until she touched the swell of muscle in his exposed arms, massaging the imbued strength. 'Plus, the way that you can wield magic now is incredibly sexy.'

Despite the tightening in his groin, Lucas was wary of where this was heading. Karina was coming on way too strong, a sure sign that something wasn't quite right. Was it possible his parents had something to do with this, hoping his raging hormones would convince him to stay? Was it possible for them to rally the troops and find someone like Karina to convince him not to leave within seconds of his confession?

Karina moved closer, undoubtedly aware that she'd pressed herself against his partially swollen crotch. Lucas resisted the urge to groan, torn between the interests of his body and the insurmountable wall of doubt.

The toiletries he'd been holding fell in the sink, his hands already moving of their own volition. The intent was to push her away, ignore the burning urgency in his pants and listen to the brain in his head. At least, that had been the plan until he felt the curve of her hips under his fingers, her smooth flesh and the feeling of her warm body pressed against his.

Ah, what the hell …

Lucas closed the gap between them and kissed her with the intense desperation he felt. Karina didn't seem to mind. In fact, her lips moved almost as urgently as his did, her hands roving across every inch of his upper body, her fingers tangling in the fabric of his shirt.

Her fitful moans spurred Lucas on, her lips parting to welcome the heat of his tongue. Exploration soon turned into frantic need, Karina's hands beginning a particularly unexpected journey south. Fingers trailed down the front of his taut chest, quickly securing the buckle on the top of his pants and releasing its grip.

Lucas didn't even pause, driven by his own desire and the throbbing torment demanding satiation. He supposed that given current liaisons, he could always leave the IMI in the morning, concern himself with the ramifications of this night then.

Karina yanked his belt free, hurriedly moving on to release the buttons on his jeans. The pads of her fingertips brushed against the sensitive flesh of his stomach, making him groan and eagerly press himself against her touch.

Karina was no exception, breaking the fevered kiss with a small gasp of pleasure as his own hands gently kneaded the small swell of her breasts and the roundness of her bottom. He dipped his lips to explore the curve of her neck, throwing his head back in surprise as Karina lowered his pants and ...

Shit!

Getting his privates fondled was definitely a plausible excuse for his lapse in judgement, his mind clearly fixated on the gentle exertion of pressure and stroking. It was no wonder entrapment came easily. Karina was focused, not just on providing pleasure but on the task of stabbing him in the arm with a syringe.

Women were such good multi taskers.

Lucas hissed, shoving Karina away, his eyes transfixed between the empty syringe in her hand and the pinprick in his upper arm.

Karina tripped in her efforts to get out of Lucas's way, slamming into the shower stall and cursing. 'Lucas, please don't hurt me,' she said, holding her hands up to shield her face.

He snatched the syringe from her hand and threw it angrily into the sink. 'What have you done to me, Karina?' he said, pulling her hands away from her face and pinning them to her sides.

'I did what I was told to do.'

'And kissing me, touching me? Was that all part of the plan?'

She looked like she was about to burst into tears. 'Yes and no.'

Lucas shoved her against the shower stall again, her head

hitting the glass a little harder than was necessary. 'What did you just inject me with?'

'I don't know,' she whimpered, tears now streaming down her face. 'Your dad told me to do it.'

'My father?' Lucas released her, taking a step back and re-buttoning his jeans. He should have known better. 'Get out of my room.'

Karina wasted no time in making her exit. 'I'm so sorry, Lucas. I had no choice.'

'We all have choices, Karina. You just made a stupid one.'

She made haste for the bunk door, repeatedly pressing the button for it to open. 'I didn't mean to hurt you.'

'Just get the hell out of here.'

Lucas suddenly felt a little unsteady on his legs; the few steps he'd taken to ensure Karina immediately left his bunk seemed to have worn him out. The door was getting further and further away. Karina was a distant figure in his vision, his footsteps now so heavy he could barely walk.

Lucas fell to his knees at the end of his bed, the sheets slipping between his fingers as he tried to find anything to hold onto, anything to keep him upright. He failed, his palms hitting the ground with jarring impact, the only thing stopping him from crashing head first into the floor.

The bunk door opened, but Lucas could only see at ground level, his cheek now pressed against the bitingly cold steel floor. He was virtually paralysed; paired with blurring vision and dimming consciousness, Lucas struggled to identify the intruders.

'He'll be out in a minute,' a long, heavy voice said.

'How much did you give him?' another asked. Lucas wasn't certain, but he suspected that muffled voice could have belonged to his father.

'The whole syringe.'

'Why did you do this?' the first voice asked.

'He was going to leave.'

'And you involved her?'

'Lucas has always been partial to Karina.'

'Well, he won't be leaving now.'

The room was suddenly dark and no matter how often Lucas blinked, the light never returned. He was in serious trouble. Whatever had been in that syringe was designed to stop him from leaving — mission accomplished, but to what end?

He was now permanently stuck on an icy continent, trapped by the weakness of his own body, trapped by the very people who had betrayed his sister. He finally understood what walking in Elena's shoes must feel like, a pair of size eights brimming with fear and the resignation that help would never come.

CHAPTER TWENTY-TWO
Clemency

woke with a start, heart beating frantically and icy breath forcing its way past lips that trembled with the cold. My limbs were rigid and sore, flecked with goose pimples, my teeth chattering loud enough to wake the dead.

'You're finally awake,' Sebastian murmured, laying a gentle kiss on my forehead. I snuggled into his strong arms, holding me so close to his chest as he ran. The winter wind tried to torment and Sebastian tried to combat by running faster than its touch.

I noted my trembling form covered only in his blood-smeared leather jacket. My stomach dropped and my face roiled with a heat that melted the chill wracking my limbs. I'd been down this path before. Hell, I even had the damn T-shirt. I just wished that I had it now to temper the unfortunate results of shape-shifting.

I blew out a resigned breath. 'I'm naked, aren't I?'

'Just a little bit,' Sebastian teased, humour pinching the skin around eyes he smartly kept fixed on the approaching horizon. At least his hands were nowhere inappropriate.

'I'm guessing you saw everything?'

'I've seen it all before.'

'Not in this body you haven't.'

The smile he'd been guarding broke free of all restraints. Now I knew he'd had a good look, possibly even whipping out his mobile phone and taking photos for posterity.

'How long did you look?'

'Is there really a right way to answer that question without you getting angry?'

'How long?'

'Long enough to cover you with my jacket.'

'Liar.'

'Okay, five minutes tops.'

'Sebastian!'

'See?' he argued. 'No right answer.'

I huffed, settling back into his arms. It wasn't his gawking that bothered me as such. It was knowing that my armpits currently resembled a national forest. I hadn't shaved for almost a week.

I groaned. I didn't even want to think about other currently untended areas. It was possible that you could probably braid my bikini line, too. 'Where are you taking me?'

'Subject change? Okay.' The relief was palpable. His shoulders sagged. 'I'm taking you back to the safe house. We're almost there.'

I looked down at my hands, the cold tips twisting together in knots. 'Sebastian,' I started to say, 'about last night—'

'Elena, don't,' Sebastian interrupted. 'You don't have to say it again.'

'I never did *say* it. I was a wolf at the time.'

Thoughts of me running around on all fours even hairier than I currently was made me realise something incredibly important, a significant turning point in my otherwise freshly modified shifting abilities.

'Regardless, please do not let us labour this point, Elena.'

'Wait, I was a wolf,' I said slowly, ignoring him. 'Sebastian, I was a wolf last night!' Perhaps all that humming and chanting had paid off after all.

'I know you were a wolf, Elena. I remember.'

'Yeah, but so do I!'

Sebastian nodded, finally understanding the significance. 'So, this time you can recall every detail?'

I nodded enthusiastically, though not exactly thrilled by the clarity of the recollection. 'I remember everything right down to how I felt, how I reacted ...' I looked up at Sebastian's chin, willing him to look down at me for even just a moment. He didn't. 'If I remember, I guess it could mean that I have control now. Well, at least enough control to let my head rule a shape-shift rather than the wolf inside me.' I swallowed, drawing a shaky breath. 'It also means that I really do owe you an apology. No, more than an apology. Sebastian, what I did to you, how I felt when I—'

'You don't need to say it.'

'Yes, I do. I'm so sorry, Sebastian. Words will never be able to express how sorry I really am. I have no idea how I lost control like that. I was angry with you for the things you said about Lucas even though I knew you were goading me into changing. I had no idea that I had the capacity for so much hate, that I could hurt you and that you would just let me.'

'I was not going to lay a finger on you.'

'Even to defend yourself? I could have gutted you, Sebastian. If that ever happens again, knock me out, kung fu my ass or anything involving both our lives being spared. If something happened to you, Sebastian, I couldn't ... I wouldn't know how—'

'Elena, stop. Everything is fine. I lived.'

'No thanks to me,' I mumbled. Just thinking of Sebastian absent from my life was a torment I wasn't willing to explore. He was under my skin, swimming through my insides and holding an iron fist around my heart. Maybe I should have killed him for that alone. Things were so much simpler when I didn't give a shit.

He looked down at me for the first time, his expression unreadable. 'So, how do you feel, anyway?'

I blinked. The question seemed a little leftfield considering we were currently supposed to be discussing *his* wellbeing. 'I feel fine. Why?'

'You drank a lot of my blood.'

'And?'

'And I don't know if that would matter,' he murmured. 'You know I'm not exactly cut from the same cloth as other Vampires.'

'An inescapable fact which you feel compelled to announce but never explain.'

'I can't, Elena, it's—'

'Complicated? Against the rules? Yadda, yadda, yadda. Bleh. I honestly don't care anymore. I'm just glad you're okay. But if I am going to sprout a pitchfork from my ass or blow toxic snot from my nose, you might want to explain why drinking your blood could be bad.'

Sebastian snorted, compelled to smile in spite of my sarcasm. 'I'm not sure if it would do anything at all. I was just curious and being cautious.'

'Well, I feel the same.' I took stock of his expression as it wandered into the field of concern. 'Look, if it makes you feel any better, my last changes only occurred after a bite and mutual blood exchange. You didn't even scratch me. You pulled my ears a little, but I don't think that counts.'

'That's reassuring, I guess.'

Sebastian started to slow, the buildings of Rome now discernible, the punishing wind no longer such a burden. Lights illuminated storefronts and apartments, traffic whizzed past, practically keeping pace. Late night pedestrians occasionally dotted my vision and I figured if I could see them then they could see me, too.

'Don't slow down!' I begged, sliding my arms between us until they popped out underneath and I could cup my bare backside. 'People will see me!'

'It's three o'clock in the morning.'

'And?'

'And ...' Sebastian shook his head, smiling. 'Never mind.'

He sped up again, the ground dipping quickly, the underground car park flashing by. The door to the stairwell slammed behind us, the stairs themselves rushing by in a blur. Before I knew it, Sebastian was unlocking the apartment door and pushing it closed behind us. Not one single spectator to block our path or gape at my fleshy bits. Hooray for the Vampire.

I moved my hands from my backside, pulling them back through Sebastian's hold so I could clutch his leather jacket close to me instead. There was no one else in the apartment to cop my brown-eye, so protecting the rest from another peep show was my only vested interest.

Sebastian's ongoing smile widened. 'Do you want me to close my eyes?'

'Would you?'

'No.'

I punched him playfully on the shoulder. 'Then why the hell did you ask? Just put me down over near the wall.'

Sebastian did as he was told, carefully lowering my feet to the floor but taking his sweet ass time about removing his arms and hands from my naked body.

'Now step away,' I instructed, putting a hand on his chest and giving him a little shove.

Sebastian's smile was endless, but at least he obeyed, backing up enough to find the armchair by the window and sit down in it.

I gripped the leather of his jacket, pressing it against myself like a second skin. I shimmied along the living room wall, my backside gliding along the painted surface until I found the bedroom jamb. I inched around the corner, Sebastian eyeing me like a sideshow at the amusement park. That was right about the time I slammed the door in his face, biting back my own laughter. I looked ridiculous and I had a splinter in my ass.

'You might want to hurry!' Sebastian yelled. 'Your father will be here soon!'

'What?'

I flung the door open again, the jacket still firmly in place, as was the splinter.

Sebastian's gaze took in my still nearly naked form. 'I *said*, your father will be here soon.'

'You called him?'

'You shape-shifted. That was the deal: make it happen, call Lucius.'

I leant my head against the doorframe. 'What did you tell him?'

Sebastian's eyes finally found my face again. 'I didn't mention our *activities* here, but I told him about Julius.'

'He's not angry?'

'Why would he be? He thinks it happened tonight, that I saved you and brought you to the safe house.'

I made a mental note of the white lie so as not to trip up later. 'Is he bringing the Thralls?'

'Decimus and Maximus will go back to the villa,

searching for lost trails, assuming normality. I think Marcus and my father will stay with us until the gathering. We can't risk taking you back to the villa until Julius is apprehended. It's something Lucius and I both agree upon.'

I sighed. 'This apartment has one bedroom and one bathroom. Sharing with you has been cosy, but your dad and Marcus?' I shuddered.

'We don't need to sleep, so we don't need the bedroom,' Sebastian reminded me. 'It won't be a problem. The bathroom we can share.'

'Why on Earth would Marcus volunteer for babysitting duties? He hates me.'

'He doesn't hate you, but I suspect Lucius is making him.' Sebastian rolled his eyes. 'Look, stop worrying. He'll live and so will you.'

'Well, we might both be dead soon if you don't shower and get out of those clothes, Sebastian. Unless you want to tell Lucius you played serious fisticuffs with Julius, you'd better clean up, or he's going to start asking questions.'

'That works both ways,' Sebastian murmured, gesturing to my appearance. 'If your father finds you naked, the first thing on his mind won't be my shredded outfit. It'll be your extracurricular activities.'

'Touché. I'll have a quick shower and get changed, then it's all yours.'

'Explain this to me again,' Lucius said, leaning back in the armchair. 'You've been here how long?'

'Only tonight.'

Sebastian gave me an appreciative look which I pretended

not to notice. He was leaning against the wall we'd been a little rough with yesterday, the fallen plaster still in a heap on the floor. He looked at ease, but his eyes said otherwise, particularly as Lucius kept looking at the blood splatter on the carpet, eyebrow raised questioningly.

'Right. So, the damage?'

'I was scared and angry after Julius tried to kill me. I threw some stuff around.'

Lucius's suspicious gaze swept across the room. 'What exactly did you throw around? Everything here looks intact.'

I bit back a smile. 'Sebastian.'

'Sebastian?'

Sebastian uncrossed his arms, mouth gaping like he wanted to object, defending his male ego undoubtedly the intent.

Marcus smirked and then snorted as if he could actually smell the bullshit.

'I only smell your blood, Elena,' Lucius observed, that singular brow now reaching for the heavens.

'I never said Sebastian didn't fight back.'

Sebastian threw his hands into the air, exasperated. He then folded them to rest on top of his head, walking around in circles as if he were controlling the urge to kill me.

'I told you to protect her, not bleed her!' Lucius shouted at Sebastian.

Sebastian concentrated on taking deep breaths. 'Lucius, if you'll just let me—'

'Seriously, Lucius. It was necessary,' I stumbled, trying to pull the conversation back on track. 'Julius could have killed me and Sebastian only showed me how to defend myself against a Vampire attack. I've never been trained by another Vampire in the past and thus I didn't really know how to fight him off other than turning to telekinesis.'

Sebastian relaxed, breathing a small sigh of relief as his shoulder slumped against the wall again.

'You're both lying to me, but I have too much on my plate right now to care why.' Lucius scrubbed a hand across his face, pulling at his skin until his features switched from baleful to downright exhaustion. 'Where is Julius now? Do either of you know?'

'Lucius, if I may,' Sebastian murmured, stepping forward. 'I'd like to head back to the villa, hopefully pick up the scent and start tracking him again. He's been very good at evading us, but clearly he wants Elena, so I figure he'll still be in Rome.'

'I want Elena guarded.'

'Agreed, but with the three of you here, she's currently safe. Having her hunter still at large is an issue. If I can track him down, bring him in, Elena can return to the villa.'

'Tiberius and I need to head into Synth Corp. Apparently there was a fire in our absence and if we are to keep up appearances, I must attend to business. Staying with Elena at present is not an option.'

'Elena will have Marcus.'

'What!' Marcus and I screeched in unison. 'I can't stay here alone with *her*,' Marcus argued, gesturing to the room and then finally at me. 'I am not a babysitter.'

'And I'm not a baby,' I muttered.

Marcus scoffed, tossing a lock of hair over his shoulder. 'Debatable.'

'Then it's settled,' Lucius said, rising from the armchair. 'Sebastian, get moving. You have until the gathering then I want you back here. Marcus, you will stay with Elena.'

'Lucius, I must insist—'

'You will stay with Elena.' The tone in Lucius's voice rejected all argument.

Lucius, Tiberius and Sebastian headed for the door. I suspected Sebastian avoided meeting my eyes on account of his urge to avoid bursting into laughter.

'You better not wet the bed,' Marcus grumbled in my ear.

Sebastian finally laughed, covering it with a cough as he slammed the door behind all three retreating men. Maybe I'd have to reconsider the notion of killing him after all.

'You're doing it all wrong,' Marcus complained, slapping my hand for the umpteenth time.

'What now?' I bitched, splattering paint all over the carpet.

For some reason, Marcus had the bright idea to makeover the safe house. A week had passed and so far we'd repainted all the kitchen cabinets, replaced the tiled splashback and screwed on new handles for all the doors. We'd scrubbed the bathroom from top to toe and replaced the broken plaster in the living room, patching and sanding until it was all brand new.

Marcus cussed, dropping to the floor to mop up yet another one of my spills. 'You need to apply even strokes, Elena. You're putting too much paint on the brush and it's splattering everywhere.'

That was a freaking understatement. Marcus's face looked like a paint palette. I had told him to stay out of the line of fire, but he wasn't real big on listening to me. 'You're lucky I'm even helping.'

He growled. 'What else were you going to do?'

'Read a book, watch television — anything but this.'

'Television? The pastime of idiots,' he mumbled.

'Fine.' I dropped the brush into the pot of paint at the bottom of the ladder. It went everywhere. I'd told Marcus about the benefits of drop sheets, but he was adamant we'd manage.

Bummer.

'Look what you've done now!' Marcus hissed, mopping up my newest spill. The sponge he held spread it across the carpet, pushing it into the fibres even more.

'Maybe if you were nicer to me, I'd try a little harder.'

'Be nicer to you?' Marcus echoed, still scrubbing away at the floor. 'I don't like children unless they're weaving me hand-knotted rugs from a sweat shop in Iran!'

All I could do was gape at him in shock as I stumbled down the ladder. I dropped into the closest chair, determined to think of some snappy retort while I cooled my heels.

'No!' Marcus screamed. 'You're spreading paint everywhere!'

I looked down at the handprint I'd left on the arm of the chair. 'My bad.' I pointed to the soapy bucket of water in front of him. 'Better mop it up before it dries.'

'Gah! How does Lucius stand you?!'

I shrugged. 'I'm pretty sure you're the only one who doesn't like me.'

'You're wilful and destructive. What's to like?'

'My sense of humour?'

Marcus snorted. 'Let me know when *that* kicks in.'

I frowned, snappy responses deserting me yet again. 'Look, Marcus. I'm sorry we've been stuck here together. I know you're not a fan, but come on. You're *so* mean to me. What have I ever done to you?'

Besides ruin the handmade, Turkish-tiled courtyard floor,

record over your Barbara Streisand concert video, reprogram Tivo and scratch your Lamborghini?

Crap. Okay.

He grunted some noncommittal reply I could barely hear. 'What?'

'I said you're—'

'I'm back!'

I jumped, the combination of the front door slamming shut and Sebastian appearing right in front of me. He wrapped his arms around my waist, yanked me to my feet before he dipped me backwards for a kiss. 'Did you miss me?'

I slipped a hand between our lips, conscious of Marcus's angry glare. 'Not really.'

Hell yes.

'Oh, don't stop on my account,' Marcus barked, resuming his floor scrubbing. He really was pissy at me today. 'It's obvious I'm no one's concern.'

'You've been busy,' Sebastian commented, easing his arms from around me. 'It looks—'

'*I've* been busy,' Marcus corrected. '*She's* been making a mess.'

I was apathetic about investing myself in yet another pointless argument, so I turned back to Sebastian instead. 'What's happening with Julius?'

'Nothing,' he finally answered. 'I tracked him within several metres of the Spanish Steps, but then the trail went cold.'

'What are we doing about it?'

'You're doing nothing.'

'Sebastian …'

He touched a finger to my lips and shook his head. 'The multi-coven gathering is set for sundown. Lucius ordered me back to protect you, so that's what I'll be doing.'

Marcus stopped scrubbing the floor. 'Does this mean I can go?'

Sebastian didn't even turn his head, eyes still focused entirely on me. 'Yes. I will stay with Elena now.'

'Of course you will,' Marcus muttered, climbing to his feet. He pointed at the assorted pots of paint and brushes. 'Someone needs to clean this up.'

'I will,' I muttered, falling back into the armchair again.

Marcus slapped a hand to his forehead, smearing paint all through his hair. 'You're a disaster! No amount of washing is going to get that paint out of that chair now.' He kicked the soapy bucket into our freshly painted wall. 'Now I'll have to hire someone to fix this! I'm going to miss Celine Dion in Vegas next month because I'll be here, directing a bunch of Neanderthals to fix your mess!'

'Calm down, Marcus. I said I'd clean it up.'

'Calm down?' Marcus whined. 'How am I supposed to calm down? I've been left for days with a monkey who can't paint to save her life and ...'

I stopped listening after that. I was too busy gazing at Sebastian's mouth and trying to ignore the blood pounding in my ears. I vaguely heard Marcus moving around the apartment, still complaining, but the front door soon slammed shut and silence reigned supreme.

I was on my feet and kissing Sebastian a moment later, the two of us drawn together like magnets. I drank from his lips like I was dying of thirst, one hand moved through my hair, fisting the silken strands while the other hand cupped my face, directing our lips.

'So you *did* miss me,' he said, finally pulling back. There was a smudge of paint on his chin now, another on his cheek where I'd touched him.

I laughed, attempting to wipe both away but somehow

smearing it more. 'I only missed you because Marcus is a dick.'

'He's not so bad.'

'Sebastian, this apartment was beige a few days ago.' I gestured to the pots of indigo paint on the floor and walls. 'This is what his idea of fun is.'

'Painting isn't so bad.'

I gave him a droll look. 'I'd rather poke my eyes out with a stick.'

'Decorating is a hobby for Marcus. It keeps him calm.'

I scoffed. 'He's a Versace-wearing drill sergeant. There was nothing calm about the last week. Do you know what we were going to do next?'

Sebastian humoured me by trying to pull on a serious face. 'No, what?'

'Embroidery.'

'What?'

'You heard me. He wanted to jazz up the scatter cushions.'

Sebastian gave up trying to be serious and started laughing again.

'It's not funny. I was seriously considering slamming my head in the bathroom door.'

Sebastian laughed harder, pulling me tighter against his body and smearing paint all over his designer jeans and T-shirt. Plenty more where they came from, I supposed. 'Fine. Then what's *your* idea of fun?' He wriggled his eyebrows, the image so similar to something Lucas would do that I had to take a breath and remind myself that we were coming for him soon. We just had to get through tonight. 'Elena? Tell me. What do you like to do for fun?'

'A loaded question if ever I heard one.'

'It doesn't have to be, but if your idea of fun correlates

with spending more alone time with me then I am happy to accommodate.'

'I'm sure you are.'

His face was only a few centimetres from mine now. 'Are you going to tell me?'

'No.'

'Do I have to force it out of you?'

'How about I show you?' I ducked out of Sebastian's embrace before he assumed I was seeking another lip-locking session. He was surprised by my tactics for all of two seconds, watching me as I backtracked to the ladder, slowly lowering to the floor, my hands scrambling for the abandoned paintbrush. I kept my eyes locked on his, knowing he'd eventually outmanoeuvre me with speed.

Before I'd even had a chance to dunk my brush, Sebastian was upending a pot of paint on my head, dropping it and darting off in the other direction. I screamed, declaring war as I scooped up the remaining paint and chased him around the apartment.

A good hour later it was safe to say that all the walls were in some way painted, but the carpet was cactus and Marcus was going to have a heart attack.

'Marcus is going to kill us,' Sebastian mused, sliding a slippery arm around my waist.

'Not us, *me*.' The carpet squelched underfoot, paint oozing between my toes. 'It's better than beige, though.'

'Yes, definitely better than beige.'

'What the—'

One by one the Thralls walked into the apartment, surveying the mess in front of them. Lucius was the last to enter, eyes circling the room once before they stopped on the two of us embracing, covered from head to toe in indigo paint.

Sebastian and I sprang apart, guilty and a little

embarrassed we'd taken such liberties with my father's property. Lucius looked none too pleased that Sebastian and I were even touching, Marcus positively fuming beside him. That was the only upside because I was about to get my ass kicked about everything else.

CHAPTER TWENTY-THREE

Gathering

fter Julius's attempted murder, a week locked up with Marcus and Sebastian's almost demise, any levity I'd felt quickly wore off under my father's current dictation.

I'd accepted that finding Lucas was on hold until I could gain Sebastian's support post multi-coven gathering, but now of course the rules had been changed. Lucius was sending Sebastian on a deathly hunt to locate the remaining nineteen Alphas including Roshan, and I was forbidden from attending the gathering, labelled 'a likely target' by Vampire and Vânător alike.

'It's not safe for you out there, Elena,' Lucius pleaded.

'According to you, it's not safe anywhere.'

'Roshan still hunts you, his packs and that of his brothers crowd our borders and press for a fight and Julius, though currently lost to the vastness of this city, undoubtedly still searches for ways to harm you. If you attend the gathering, there is an excellent chance that other Vampires will find your blood equally appealing. I'm sorry, Elena, but the answer is still no. You will stay in the apartment.'

'My brother's life may be in jeopardy. I've put finding him on hold for this gathering and if I'm leaving him without hope of rescue, particularly now that you're sending

Sebastian away, then I want to know why. I want to know what the Vânătors are up to.'

'And you will, *after* the gathering.'

'Lucius …'

'It's not open for discussion.'

'It should be!'

Lucius's look was so feral that I actually took several steps back, the wall suddenly pressed against my spine. I didn't believe he would hurt me, but clearly words of resistance were not appreciated.

'Elena …'

'Just go,' I murmured, chilled by his hostility.

Lucius hesitated, tentatively reaching out in apology. I was unmoved in every way. He knew how much finding Lucas ruled my agenda and yet all I could see was him sending Sebastian to his death and my so called *beloved* father holding me hostage.

Lucius dropped his outstretched hand, nudged by an impatient Marcus who was already rounding up the Thralls for exit. Tiberius lingered long enough to grasp Sebastian's shoulder, whisper something in his ear and then whirl on his feet and depart.

'I'm only trying to protect you,' Lucius affirmed.

My no reply and absent floor gazing set his feet in motion.

'Sebastian will stay with you for now. When the gathering is over, I'll come back for you.'

Whatever.

I peeled myself away from the wall and fell into the armchair by the window, gazing at the steady stream of traffic below, listening as the front door slammed closed and hope for Lucas's upcoming rescue faded.

'I suppose Tiberius was giving you a few extra tips on how to keep me confined to the apartment while Lucius is gone?' I asked Sebastian with an acrid touch of bitterness lingering upon my lips.

'Actually,' Sebastian said, clearing his throat, 'he was wishing me a safe journey, asking me to return to him in one piece after my hunt. He feels like he already lost William. He does not wish me to leave him, too.'

Oh. Didn't I feel like an ass? Here I was scowling at traffic, irritated by circumstance and protective restriction, and there was Sebastian, facing certain death. My wallowing was a selfish sentiment given the trials he undoubtedly faced.

I swivelled in the chair, tucking my legs up under me, determined to convey how apologetic I felt. 'I'm sorry, Sebastian. That was thoughtless. Do you know when Lucius will send you away?'

He shrugged. 'I'm assuming tonight. I'm only here to guard you during the gathering.'

'Oh.'

'Oh?'

'It's just that …' I twiddled my thumbs, tearing my eyes from his face to study the absent movements of my hands.

'Elena, what's wrong?' Sebastian urged, his voice drawing near.

I hesitated. Did I really need to remind him that what Lucius asked was tantamount to a suicide mission? 'Um, how exactly are you supposed to find nineteen Alphas and bring them and their packs down on your own?'

'I will have help.'

'You will?' I breathed a small sigh of relief. 'Who?'

Sebastian made squelching noises as he moved across the still wet carpet towards me. 'Friends.'

That was vague.

'Don't worry. Caleb is still searching for avenues for you to find Lucas. Not everyone has neglected your interests.'

'Thank you for not forgetting Lucas, but aside from that, I'm glad that you won't be alone when you go to find the Alphas.'

Sebastian nodded, perching on the arm of my chair. 'As am I.'

We sat in silence for several minutes, both of us lost to our own thoughts before I couldn't help but pester him about Lucas again. 'Has Caleb gathered anything useful yet?'

'No.'

'If you're gone, how will I know when he does find something?'

'I'll call you.' He moved to tuck a lock of hair behind one of my ears. 'Don't worry, we'll find him, Baby Vamp.'

I shook my head, accidentally freeing the restrained strand. 'I don't know, Sebastian. It seems like we're forever bogged down with the bullshit of bad luck. Between Julius, the Vânătors, the missing IMI members, the serum, Lucas, us …'

'Us?'

I rolled my eyes. 'Yes. Us. Being just friends was a little less confusing.'

'What are you getting at?'

'It doesn't matter.' I wasn't quite ready to admit that being *just friends* ensured that I could constantly lie to myself about the true depth of feeling that Sebastian invoked. I was quite comfortable in the land of deniability.

Sebastian suddenly looked taken aback, an emotion quickly chased by resignation. 'Look, Elena, I know you still have ties to William and that you shared an emotional connection which I'm probably never going to—'

'Oh, God no! That's not what I meant at all. William is …'

'William is what?'

'Let's just drop it, okay? Things are complicated, even

with you. Hell, you're a complete contradiction of Vampiric facts. You drink the blood of your own and you can charge mobile phone batteries with your hand. You're different yet somehow a permanent fixture in my past and present that I'm yet to obtain rational answers for.'

'Elena, I've explained my restrictions.'

'Blah, blah, blah,' I interrupted. 'I'll just settle for a favour for now.'

'A favour?' Sebastian quizzed, shaking his head in disbelief. 'Don't you think it's my turn to gain reward considering the amount of lying and *favours* I've executed for you lately?'

'I just want to go to the gathering.'

'That's not going to happen.'

'Sebastian, I need to know what's going on so I can assess —'

'Whether or not you have to stay and fight? Or whether the Vampire populace can handle it without you so you can slink away in the dead of night to find your brother?'

'I ... what?'

'Don't play me for a fool.'

'I'm not, Sebastian. Honest. I just want the specifics. My whole life I've been kept in the dark. I thought that changed when I came to the villa.'

Sebastian's expression softened as he attempted to re-tuck that stubborn lock of hair behind my ear. 'Things have changed, but none of us could foresee how much danger you would be in. You have to understand why we all protect you.'

I nodded. 'I do, I just—'

'Want to know what's happening.'

'Yes.'

Sebastian sighed, digging into his leather jacket, or rather, a new one that hadn't been shredded by my wolfy teeth and claws. 'Hold on for one moment.' He got up, pulled out his mobile phone, fingers whirring over the keypad. He held it to his ear for just a moment. 'Eric ...'

That was the only word I understood. After that, Sebastian reverted to his native tongue, speaking Italian. He talked no longer than a minute, pulling the phone away from his ear and pushing another button. The speaker phone was suddenly activated, a myriad of shouts and protest coming through the speakers.

'What's going on?' I said, looking up at Sebastian as he returned to balance on the arm of the chair.

'I'm giving you what you wanted.' *Like always* — the unspoken pause at the end of his sentence.

'There's mostly infighting at the moment,' Eric muttered, his voice loud and clear through the speaker. 'Lucius has already asked everyone to consider the prospect of war between the Vânătors. In fact, he opened with it.'

'That probably wasn't the best way to start,' I said.

'And what would you have done, Baby Vamp?'

'Started with the facts as they are. The Vânătors crowding the borders and the lack of IMI backup.'

'He's trying to do that now, but the crowd won't settle.'

All I could hear was a lot of static and cries of displeasure. 'Exactly how many Vampires are we talking about?'

'I'd say about 10–12,000,' Eric answered.

'Ten to twelve thousand Vampires all in one place! Shit, no wonder Lucius wanted me to stay behind. Where the hell are you?'

Sebastian immediately hindered the expected reply by momentarily disabling the speaker option and pulling the phone from earshot. 'Nice try, Baby Vamp, but we won't tell you despite underhanded attempts to elicit the information.'

I had to smile. I didn't think he'd catch me out on that one.

Sebastian cautioned my motives with a look, eventually reinstating me with the phone and the speaker back to volume. 'Play nice,' he warned. 'Or you can sit here and imagine what's happening. Deal?'

'Deal.'

'Well,' Eric interrupted via the phone, 'it looks as if Lucius is about to say something.'

I waited, the shouts persisting until an ear piercing whistle over the line made me cringe and fall back against the cushions. 'What the hell was that? Dial up internet?'

Sebastian shook his head at me, lips twitching as if they wanted to smile. 'My father just caught the attention of the crowd.'

'By gutting a pig?'

'Silence everyone!' Lucius bellowed. 'Let me explain my findings so that you might better understand the reasons behind this imminent war.'

'It is not a war until you draw first blood!' someone shouted in the background. There were a few shouts of agreement before the crowd simmered down again.

'That is true,' Lucius agreed. 'But the wolves have breached the borders, breeding into the tens of thousands, feeding off humans in the nearby towns.'

'Tens of thousands?' I murmured. 'They outnumber us.'

'They always have,' Sebastian answered. 'It is only now that we might actually come to fear them. It is only now that they have realised that their strength is in their numbers.'

'Milan, the largest city near the border, has already spotted wild dogs within the city limits,' Lucius continued. 'At present, the bulk of the pack extends into the national forest nearby, a lot still lingering just shy of the French borders. Soon their numbers will be so great that they'll have no choice but to move towards populated areas. They will need to feed and in doing so, expose what they are to the world at large.'

'Where is the proof that this is occurring?' another random shouted.

'I crossed the border into Nice only a week ago. I barely made it through undetected.'

'He's right,' an unknown female Vampire answered. 'I live in Croatia and slipping past the borders was near impossible. There were Vânători everywhere.'

'It's true,' another voice stated. 'I tried gaining access to Rome by foot, but the Vânători have multiplied — and very quickly.'

There was a lot of talk, the sound building to an incomprehensible amount of static on the line.

'So what?' someone finally shouted over the crowd. Everyone quietened. 'Who cares if the Vânători take Italy?'

'I care!' Lucius boomed. 'And you should all care, too. It's not just my coven that run the risk of injury or death. It's everyone who stands here tonight. Once the Vânători expose themselves—'

'Assuming they will,' another voice added.

'How can they not? Thousands of hungry wolves will not go unnoticed. There are already reports of people missing in various nearby towns.'

'But why must we be a secret? Perhaps the Vânători do us a favour by exposing what we are? You hide behind Synth Corp, dolling out synthetic blood for us to feed from but really, what you're asking us to do is to hide what we are, pretend that we're not really predators.'

'I ask you to remember your humanity,' Lucius answered. 'We may have been born or turned to this life, but it doesn't define who we are. Vampires do not have to be animals driven by bloodlust.'

A fresh new debate echoed through the crowd. Voices got louder and the din of indecipherable noise was back again.

'This isn't working out so well, is it?' I asked Sebastian.

'He needs to remind them of what they will lose if they allow the Vânătors to roam freely.'

'And what will they lose?'

'Freedom itself. They may hide in the shadows, but at least they aren't hunted. If the human race ever gains proof of our supernatural existence, they will hunt us all down until we are annihilated. Or worse still, subject us to experimentation that makes the IMI look like marshmallows.'

'You sound like you're speaking from experience.'

Sebastian's face darkened. 'Let's just say that I've seen a lot of terrible things over the centuries.'

'Humanity!' another voice shouted. 'We are Vampires! Humanity plays no part in our lives anymore!'

'It is not just your humanity you must strive to find,' Lucius answered. 'If these packs grow larger, attack Italy and expose us all, you will lose everything.'

'I will lose nothing.'

'You will lose your freedom.'

'There you go,' Sebastian murmured, a pleased look spreading across his face.

'Freedom?' a new voice shouted. 'What freedom is there being trapped to this life? We live in shadow and survive on tetra packs of blood. Perhaps others are right and life will be different for us if the Vânătors expose what we are?'

'Yes,' Lucius agreed, 'life will be very different. You will constantly be looking over your shoulder, not just for the next human that hunts you but for the Vânător that wants to feed off your flesh and blood. What kind of life is that, constantly living in fear? Is it not better the life that you now lead, free to come and go as you please?'

There were shouts of agreement from the crowd, the rumble of noise growing louder as various groups began debating the logistics. Lucius had a valid point and some of the Vampires had not missed it.

'Why are they converging on Italy?' someone finally asked.

'Campaigns from the past have taught me that to drive fear into the heart of your enemies is to seek out the strongest point, find the leader and annihilate the threat. We believe that the Vânător's response is similar. Their congregation at these borders and invasion of nearby towns and cities suggests that they are striking where it will be the most damaging.'

'And how would they know this?'

'I am old and I am known. It is not without purpose that the rumour of my existence might have found them.'

I looked at Sebastian, alarmed. 'Is he suggesting that someone informed the Vânătors of his whereabouts?'

Sebastian frowned. 'It would seem like it, but that would suggest a traitor among us.'

'So, he knows something we don't.'

'Possibly. He could also be surmising as you sometimes do.'

'You do not speak the full truth to us, Lucius,' another voice added.

'I speak what I know. My powers are known far and wide. The Vânătors are no exception to this — perhaps the very reason they avoided Italy in the past.'

'Why now?'

'Why not now?' Lucius answered.

'There must be just cause!' a new voice entered.

'Agreed,' Lucius responded. 'But to speculate is to waste time. Every day that passes is a day that the Vânătors grow in number. We must neutralise this threat if for no other reason than to protect the lives we have, to protect the anonymity we have worked so hard to establish among the humans.'

'I do not wish to be hunted again,' a new voice whispered.

'None of us do,' Eric quietly answered him.

'So we go to war, we fight the wolves and fight for our lives?'

'Yes, that is the plan.'

I squeezed Sebastian's arm, shocked to hear fear in a Vampire's voice. The ones I knew were strong and proud, unfamiliar with the concept of defeat.

'It's okay,' Sebastian cooed. 'They will all do what needs doing in the end. Fear may ride them, but their vampiric genes will dictate to the predator within and help them overcome hesitancy.'

'Some of these Vampires were turned, Sebastian. Some of them come from ordinary lives. Some were not in wars as you and Lucius and the rest of the Thralls once were. Some of them have to be scared about the prospect of dying. If they know what I know about where their immortal soul will go once true death finds them, it's no wonder they baulk at the favour Lucius asks.'

'We need them.'

'I know, but I can't help but think there should be a choice.'

'Choice?'

The crowd had started a group discussion, exploring possible ideas of why the Vânătors might be attacking the Vampires after so many years of neutrality. I blocked it out, focusing on Sebastian again. 'Yes, choice. Lucius gives them reasons to fight, to protect the lives they now lead, but he can't really offer them any solace for what will happen if they truly die.'

'There are no guarantees in life, Elena.'

'I know that, Sebastian, but think about how frightening it must be to some of them, especially those who are young and untrained and have never seen a war.'

Sebastian pried my stiff fingers from his arm and cocooned them within his hand instead. 'You can't speculate on the afterlife. You can only choose what you have the ability to control.'

'And how do you stop the fear from creeping in? How do you console someone who can lose everything they know in the blink of an eye?'

'What do you suggest, Elena?'

I shrugged. 'I don't know.'

Sebastian beckoned for me to give him the phone. He clicked it off loudspeaker and held it up to his ear.

'What are you doing?'

'Eric,' Sebastian said, ignoring me, 'can you get your phone to Lucius so that I may speak with him?' There was a pause. 'No, nothing has happened to Elena, but it is urgent.'

'Sebastian, tell me what you're doing?'

'Lucius,' Sebastian breathed. 'Apologies for interrupting, but I have an idea ...'

After that they converted to Italian. I picked out a few words here and there but nothing to help translation.

Sebastian let go of my hand and stood, urgently pacing the room, his lips moving a hundred miles an hour as he worked through his supposed proposition. His expression remained neutral, giving nothing away as I was left sitting forward on the chair, curious as to his idea and if Lucius would accept.

'Excellent. Yes, it was Elena that inspired it.' Sebastian winked at me, a smile deconstructing his previous stoicism.

After a few more bursts of conversation, Sebastian finally

handed the phone back to me, pressing the button to switch it to loudspeaker. 'Listen,' he said, resettling on the arm of the chair.

'What was all that about?'

Sebastian bobbed his head in the direction of the phone in my hand. 'Pay attention. You're about to find out.'

Someone shouted a question, but the phone wasn't picking up every detail with perfection. I mostly heard grunting and cries of agreement, the uncertainty forcing me to refocus despite wanting to know what Sebastian and Lucius had discussed.

'The Protectors are not dependable,' Lucius's now distant voice answered. 'The alliance has been severed and thus we can no longer count on their support.'

Fear and uncertainty increased in the tempo of the crowd's jumbled words. Without the alliance, the Vampires were on their own against the Vânători, something that they hadn't had to consider for over 300 years.

'Such outrage! When was this …?' I missed the rest of the sentence but thankfully caught another protest of, 'What have you done, Lucius? What have you done to make them turn from us?'

'We cannot hope to defeat them with our brute strength alone. We will be gutted!' This was from a new female voice, the fear evident.

The shouting match continued with insults slung from every angle. It was as if no one heard my father and no one respected his power, but soon those that doubted Lucius's supremacy shouted their dismay and shrieked their surprise. A thunderous crack silenced the crowd, the current actions of thousands of mute Vampires called into question.

'What happened, Eric?' Sebastian asked, leaning toward the phone.

'Lucius displaced the earth beneath our feet and slammed us all with a wall of his telekinetic energy. I feel it was a good reminder of how powerful our master Vampire can be.'

'Now, as I was saying,' Lucius continued, his voice now the only one to be heard, 'yes, The Protectors have severed the alliance, or so their absence seems to dictate. If we are to figure out what the Vânâtors want, drive them from this country and destroy their source, then we must work together.'

There was a lengthy pause. No one ventured to speak. Perhaps they now truly understood the magnitude of the situation if the master Vampire with all of his power was still asking for help from those not nearly as capable as he.

Sebastian elbowed me in the ribs, pointing to the phone. 'This is where you come in.'

'I am aware that not all of you are equipped to deal with this situation,' Lucius continued. 'Many of you are turned Vampires, forced to live in darkness and tainted with the very real possibility of death, self-healing not an option.'

There were very low murmurs of agreement from the crowd.

'Those of you that have never been faced with battle or unable to defend yourselves, I wish to train you, prepare you for what is to come. You will be linked with some of the best members of the Roman Guard, those who are qualified to help meld your bodies into tools for justice. We wish to instil you with the confidence to move forward with us, not linger on the sidelines consumed by your own fear.'

'And those of us that can already fight?'

'Romulus? Is that you, my old friend?'

'Who's Romulus?' I asked Sebastian.

'One of the original Thralls.'

'Oh.'

'Yes, it is I, Lucius. It has been many years.'

'It has, old friend. Do you stand with us?'

'I stand with you always, Lucius, for a united front is one that is victorious.'

'Agreed. So, in answer to your question, those of us experienced in combat shall seek out those who have already breached the borders, protect the towns and rid the human populace of Vânător presence. The rest will train, train until their confidence and skill is built and then we will strike in a second wave.'

'That could take months,' Romulus answered.

'We do not have months, my friend, but we will need some time.'

'The wolves will continue to keep breeding.'

'Yes, they will, which is why I have assembled my best tracker and a companion to hunt the Alphas while they are distracted by the war.'

'I fear to seek the Alphas amongst thousands of their brethren may be classified as a fool's errand.'

Sebastian rested a hand across my stiff shoulders, sensing my unease. I'd known it was going to be dangerous, but to hear his chances of return were slim made me want to throw up. 'Romulus underestimates me.'

'But he's right, isn't he?'

Sebastian took longer than I would have liked to answer. 'For other Vampires that may be true.'

'Sebastian ...'

'Shh, listen. This was your idea.'

'My tracker has unparalleled skills,' Lucius continued, attempting to put unease to rest. 'I have every confidence in his abilities and our trained forces to protect the borders. However, I do need all of you to help make our race strong, dependable and hopefully undefeatable during the second and final wave of attack.' Lucius took a deep, shuddering breath that silenced the start of any protests within the crowd. 'I have allowed the Vânǎtors to live for far too long and for that I am sorry. But now, we must fight to keep our freedom, fight to protect the very people who we were born to be. Do not forget your humanity. Remember that we were once fragile and unprotected against these supernatural odds. It is now our duty to rise above the calling in which we were marked by tainted blood, to fight back the evil that resides within all of us and recapture the essence of what makes us good and worthy to live amongst humans. Deny the fear refuged within yourself and rise against an enemy that shows no mercy.' Lucius paused, perhaps weighing the feel of the crowd before he said, 'Now who is with me, with us?'

I sank back into the armchair, on edge and counting the seconds of palpable silence before an uproar of applause echoed through the phone, raising a chill thick enough to elevate the hair on my arms and send goose pimples skittering down my spine. 'He makes a nice little speech,' I murmured, rubbing at my arms.

'The speech was excellent.' Sebastian seemed to search the ceiling, a strange smile lifting the downward pull of his lips. 'Perhaps there is hope for him yet.'

'Hope?'

'There is always hope, Elena, even for the likes of us.' The tips of Sebastian's fingers caressed my cheek, his warm smile a match for the uncoiling thread of concentrated silver within his ever swirling eyes.

'You truly believe that?'

'With everything I am.'

'And what is that exactly?'

Sebastian surrendered to laughter, throwing his head

back and filling the room with the honeyed sound of his amusement. 'You never give up, do you?'

I watched him laugh, determined to revel in the details that captured Sebastian's essence — supple lips, expressive eyes, a calming touch and magnetic personality. How would I be if anything happened to him? Would I be strong enough to do what needed to be done?

'No. I never give up.'

Just as well. The road ahead was bound to be rocky and giving up was not an option. Strength was a physical asset I needed my mind to possess, not just to maintain sanity but to support the burdens of others. I needed to dig deep and find the hope that Sebastian was so willing to believe in. I needed to hold it, accept it and imagine it as the rope that would keep us together despite the obstacles in our path.

Yes, the road ahead was assuredly rocky, but I had good shoes from Louboutin and people I finally trusted by my side. We could do this. Hell. The reality was I *had* to do this. Someone's life I loved and cared about was on the line.

Who you might ask?

I'll never tell.

EPILOGUE

Hope. It truly was a notion that Araqiel now clung to. While juggling sinister deals for the Time Contract, mapping out Elena's destiny and helping Michael to escape an eternity in Purgatory, Araqiel was in serious aid of it.

He watched now as Michael and Elena shared a final kiss, so much emotion flowing from them both that they unknowingly glowed with their unspoken love. Soon they would be separated, Araqiel having a hand in it, but knowing it was necessary. Elena would inevitably choose unselfishly, just as she had done in the past, a few helpful nudges from Araqiel the key to restoring balance.

In fact it was probably time for him to start intervening. Michael was forbidden to reveal his identity, but Araqiel was under no such obligations, having been cast out long ago. He'd recently aborted Michael's attempts at revelation as the Archangel being recalled to heaven on a technicality was not a part of Araqiel's agenda. Michael was instrumental in his trade for the Time Contract and reneging now was not an option.

Patience was Araqiel's virtue. He'd waited thousands of years for this time to come and he would continue to wait, masking his angelic signature from the immortals below and biding time until he had Elena to himself.

Michael was now gone, chartered with the difficult task to seek and destroy the Alphas. With the door to her room slamming home with finality, Elena was not taking the turn in events well, especially since learning that William Granville had been chosen as Michael's companion in the search.

Now alone, she collapsed on the edge of her bed, tears streaking her cheeks as she hugged herself tightly, fighting to contain the outpouring of emotion that so desperately begged release.

Araqiel took that as his cue and dipped his wings, following the will of air current until he glided onto her balcony, the terracotta cold underfoot but little bother. He slowly moved through the doors, shielding the room with power, intent to keep this rendezvous a secret from the rest of the undead household.

Elena stiffened, scrutinising every vantage point in the room as if sensing something amiss. Confusion warred with natural instincts, her crying a forgotten activity as she shielded herself telekinetically and quickly bounded from the bed, backing up against a wall.

'See,' Araqiel breathed into the air around them, a simple word with complexity of meaning designed to open the eyes of those blinded to what their minds couldn't traverse.

For a moment Elena just stood there, blinking as if a grain of sand caused an indistinguishable blur. But like all magic, once the trick is revealed, confusion fades and perspective is sought and though understanding is clearly within grasp, sometimes the shock of truth overwhelms everything else.

The truth was that Araqiel underestimated this baby Vampire. Although shock did widen her gaze and give her momentary pause, it was only seconds before she mobilised, dropping her shield long enough to pick up the bedside lamp and hurl it at him with incredible force.

'Who the hell are you!' she screamed, the lamp grazing his shoulder and smashing against the wall. 'And what the hell are you doing in my room!'

Araqiel arched a brow, kicking the broken shade aside and readjusting his suit. 'My name is Araqiel.'

Elena blinked, her stance faltering as she dropped her fists, expression unreadable; however, she quickly recovered, lifting her arms up in defence again, distributing her weight evenly between her legs. 'I know that name,' she murmured. 'I've heard you mentioned before.' She shook her head as if trying to dispel bad thoughts. 'Your voice sounds familiar to me, too.'

'We've conversed many times before.'

Elena shook her head, unwilling to consider any possibilities seemingly unlikely despite already knowing why his voice was so familiar. 'I'd remember meeting you and I don't.'

Araqiel tapped a finger gently against his temple. 'We've had many discussions inside *here*.'

Elena frowned, her eyes glazing over as she quickly sorted through the memories of a voiceover she often confused with insanity. 'So, you're telling me that you're really the voice inside my head?'

'Yes.'

Her stance remained unchanged, but her lips did thin into a hard line that matched the growing scowl upon her face. 'My own personal Jiminy Cricket? Did you know that I thought I was going crazy every time I heard you whispering in my head?' She rapped a knuckle against her own temple, seething anger thawing for a renewed surge of uncertainty. 'I'm not even one hundred per cent sure that this isn't one of those times.'

Araqiel shrugged, inching slowly across the floor. He dropped onto the cushioning of her chaise lounge, folding his wings carefully behind him. 'I am sorry if my intrusions have made you question your sanity.'

Elena gazed at the line of feathers that filtered the soft lighting from above and the graceful appendages that artfully disappeared once sheathed against his skin. 'You have wings.'

'An excellent observation,' he commented, no hint of sarcasm present.

She licked her already moistened lips, studying him more closely. 'You have wings and you're not trying to kill me.'

Araqiel was unsure of the new look dawning upon her striking features — not exactly bewildered but nevertheless interested. He momentarily wondered if she'd whip out a massive drawing pin and tack him to the wall like a specimen.

'You're an angel,' she blurted.

'Well spotted.'

'Um … thanks?'

'Is that all you have to say?'

Her nostrils flared, her look of intense interest fading under the assault of confusion and annoyance. 'Did you want a freaking *amen*?'

'Not exactly.'

'Then just give me a bloody minute to get my bearings. It's a lot to process, you know, and I'm still not entirely convinced.'

Araqiel fluttered his wings, once again drawing her attention to the softness of the down and the crisp whiteness of his purity. 'Do you think I got these at the costume shop?'

Unamused, Elena slinked forward, her eyes constantly fixed on him, watching for signs of movement. When she was close enough to reach out and touch him, she pulled her hands from behind her back, a small trail of blood winding a path back up her arm and into the incision on her palm.

'You're bleeding,' Araqiel said, gesturing to the healing wound.

'I wanted to check for a reaction.'

'I am not a Vampire.'

'I know that *now*,' Elena mocked, unabashedly reaching out to stroke the folded wings at his back. 'They're so soft,' she whispered.

'Ouch!' Araqiel complained as she pulled a feather from his plumage.

'And they're real.'

'Of course they're real,' Araqiel admonished, galled by her audacity.

Elena shuffled back until she found the edge of her bed and dropped down onto the mattress, still fingering the feather with open curiosity. 'So, you really are an angel.'

'Yes.'

'Why are you here?'

'I want to help you.'

'Help me?' she quizzed, a cynical look on her face. 'Why would an angel want to help me? I know what I am.' She rubbed shaky fingers across her eyes and then slapped her cheeks twice. 'Maybe this time I really have gone crazy. I used to just hear you in my head, but now I can see you, too.'

'Elena, you're not crazy. It's merely time for me to appear to you.'

'Why?'

'Because there are things that you need to know.'

Suddenly resolute, Elena squared her shoulders and sat up straight. 'Such as?'

'Your choices.'

'I'm listening.'

Araqiel smiled, finally understanding the sheer strength of will Michael had seen and was attracted to for so many thousands of years. 'The battle between the wolves and the Vampires is going to change the face of humanity.'

'Do you think the magnitude of what we face will expose us?'

'What do you think?'

Elena shrugged. 'I don't know, but it seems unlikely to keep what we are a secret forever.'

'Many people will die, Elena, deaths which you will not be able to prevent.'

'So, what can I possibly do?'

Araqiel shifted, crossing one leg over the other before leaning back in the chaise again, stretching his arm over the wooden back, seemingly at ease despite the subject of innocent death. 'Leave.'

'Leave?' Elena disparaged, slamming her palms against the mattress. 'I can't just abandon my family when they need me most.'

'Even when there are other family members that need you more?'

Elena's eyes were suddenly wide with fear, her breathing shallow. 'Has something happened to Lucas?'

Araqiel reluctantly nodded, his eyes a reflection of the true sorrow he felt. 'He remains currently unharmed, but as you know, his birthday approaches and changes are afoot.'

Elena took several moments to stifle her anger and regret, but the tears that rimmed her eyes were uncontainable. 'What have they done to him?'

'Nothing he cannot handle and hasn't already accepted as a part of himself.'

'Where is he? Where have they taken him?'

Araqiel bowed his head. 'I cannot say. The Protectors are still human and therefore under my protection.'

Elena clasped her hands together, a symbol of prayer. 'I promise I won't hurt anyone. All I care about is helping Lucas.'

'I can see that, Elena, but rules still bind me.'

'Rules! What is it with everyone and their stupid rules?' She pushed off the bed, anger congruent with the noisy slapping of pacing feet across the terracotta floor. 'You come and tell me my brother needs help yet you offer me no real avenue to do it and the one person that could have actually helped me get Lucas away from the IMI has been sent on a suicide mission!'

Araqiel stood as she continued to rant, crossing the room quickly to halt her relentless pacing. He gently grasped her shoulders; shaking her just enough to raise her stubborn-set chin to look him in the eye. 'Sebastian will be fine. Do not underestimate him.'

'Wait,' she said, pushing the angel away. 'You know Sebastian?'

Araqiel conceded yet another affirmative nod.

'He's never mentioned you, at least not that I can remember.'

'Why do you think Sebastian would know me?'

Elena contemplated the question long and hard before answering. 'Because he's "other".'

'What do you mean *other*?'

'Sebastian is different — special. While I'm mixed with two different types of evil, knowing you must mean that he's mixed with some sort of good.'

'You are not evil, Elena. Do you think I would bother whispering in your thoughts or visit you this night if I thought you were beyond saving?'

Her eyes narrowed. 'You mean it's possible to avoid eternity in Hell?'

'Of course it is. Have you never heard of redemption?'

'Aren't all Vampires and Vânători beyond that?'

Araqiel shook his head, taking a step back to fold his arms across his chest. 'No one is beyond forgiveness. You just have to ask for it, prove that you are worthy of it.'

'I'm not sure that I am.'

'You especially.'

'What about Lucius?'

Araqiel clucked his tongue, glancing away from the hopeful expression she wore as he attempted to choose his next words carefully. 'It would be possible if Lucius were able to die, but Lucifer has cursed him and consequently rendered him unable to qualify.'

Elena's bottom lip trembled, but she held her ground, refusing to allow any more tears to spring forth uninvited. 'That's not good enough.'

'I agree.'

Suspicion quickly masked her sorrow. 'You do?'

'Of course. I have watched Lucius for many years and believe he deserves to be forgiven, to find comfort in the arms of his wife and child again.'

'I do, too. I just don't know how to make it happen.'

'Everything is possible if you start to make the right choices.'

'By saving my brother ...'

Araqiel rocked back and forth between his heels and toes, delighted that she was finally beginning to understand, or at the very least, play her role. 'It's a good place to start.'

'And Sebastian?'

'Sebastian can take care of himself.'

'I'm not so sure about that. I don't doubt his abilities, I just—'

'Love him?'

Elena didn't answer, but the softened look of warmth on her face was enough to qualify his findings. She resumed her pacing, eyes averted and heart hardened with purpose. 'Can you at least tell me where to start looking for Lucas?'

'Trust in those who are already searching.'

'Who? Caleb?'

'I must go now.'

'What if he's found nothing?'

Araqiel vanished with the abruptness in which he'd appeared, leaving Elena glancing desperately around the room for answers. He prayed that she could muster the strength to do what needed to be done.

Getting Lucas back was just the beginning. She had a few more roadblocks to manoeuvre, Michael's inevitable death being one of them. Would she choose right? Would she follow him into Purgatory, follow her heart and then change the very fabric of time itself once the Time Contract landed in her hands?

Only time would tell, and luckily, Araqiel had front row seats to the impending show.

THE HUNTED

Elena Manory is by no means an ordinary teenage girl. Being born with the ability to heal herself from any injury, and with the knowledge that on her eighteenth birthday she will become a vampire, Elena is aware that she is more than a little different from other girls her age.

It isn't until she meets William Granville, an alluring and impossibly handsome vampire, that she begins to question her destiny and what secrets the Institute of Magical Intervention and her adopted family have withheld—secrets that could change the fates of not only her own life, but of the lives of all the immortals.

As events spiral out of control, William may be the only person Elena can place her trust in. He, and Elena's magical family, must fight to save her, joining forces to defeat a common, deadly foe. For William, it is his chance to save the girl that he has searched eternity to find.

The heroine in this highly-imaginative Aussie-based tale is a vampire—but she is something more. This is a fast-paced, intelligent and highly-entertaining novel ... The final chapters are climatic, desperate, chilling. For a first novel, Berridge ticks all the boxes. She has the makings of a career author. To attempt what is now a well-worn theme and produce something fresh, vital and entertaining is the mark of an enterprising and crafted writer.
—Wendy O'Hanlon, *Acres Australia*

This is a debut novel from a bright and bubbly young author. It is entertaining, quirky and has some wry touches of humour ... an adventurous lightly romantic read that will appeal to teenagers and other devotees of the vampire horror genre.
—John Morrow's *Pick of the Week*

THE DAMNED

Life for Elena Manory skipped past ordinary just over a month ago. Discovering she was born a practically invulnerable vampire-werewolf hybrid was shocking enough; but she's also become a target, hunted by an Alpha werewolf known as Roshan, who's fixated on the properties of her unique blood and the pleasurable possibilities of her flesh.

Moving to the Institute of Magical Intervention in Romania was supposed to provide her with protection and anonymity, but Elena soon realises her enemies are legion. No one is who they seem, no agenda truly without nefarious intentions.

A strange twist of fate and the actions of a vampire previously pressing for her affections lead Elena into the arms of another—one whose middle name spells trouble.

Himself a vampire, Sebastian is handsome, arrogant, and perplexingly familiar. He introduces Elena to a world she never thought possible, uncovers a past believed buried, and unearths a future she may not survive.

She is the real-deal Aussie vampire author who absolutely pulls no punches and has created such well-fleshed characters that the entire plot seems very plausible.
—Wendy O'Hanlon, *Acres Australia*

Kristy Berridge certainly knows how to draw you into her story within the first few pages, a rare gift for many writers.
—John Morrow

DIARY OF A TEENAGE ZOMBIE

DEAR DIARY. TODAY I ATE THE MAILMAN. MY BAD.

Being seventeen is hard — Katie Palmer has to deal with school, pimples, hormonal boys, and malicious cheerleaders. After the Zombie Apocalypse, though, she no longer sweats the usual teenage drama.

Athletics star by day and flesh-eater by night, Katie's done well to hide her transformation from friends and Zone-sanctioned security, but now someone or something's onto her secret and if she doesn't feed soon she'll start falling apart.

Dead bodies are piling up and all the evidence points to Katie's blood-stained hands. Will she end up killing the competition before security discovers she's rotten underneath?

www.ingramcontent.com/pod-product-compliance
Lightning Source LLC
Chambersburg PA
CBHW061509020726
47502CB00006B/1991